I AM SATAN

Tim Hawken

First published in Great Britain 2012 by Dangerous Little Books
This edition was published 2021 by Seahawk Press

Cover art by Menton3
Cover design by Xavier Davies

ISBN-13: 978-0-6482558-3-3

For those who came back…

1

I AM POWERLESS TO ACHIEVE MY AIMS, so I gather other strength. My love, my soul, my Charlotte lies in Purgatory, while I'm stuck in Hell. My torment is that she is trapped while he is free. It is the worst torture imaginable. I care not for myself, or my own wellbeing, only hers. I will free her, but I do not know how.

There must be a way…

2

Breathe.

Breathe.

THE HATRED BUBBLED just below my calm surface, like an undertow beneath the waves trying to rip my soul away from a sense of reason. I concentrated on my breath, lest I lose control of my eternal rage.

God is not what you have all been led to believe. He is not all good. He is black and white and all the shades of grey in between. He is more than human in the worst possible way: imperfect. His biggest sin is his pride; something that I will shatter before his eyes.

He had trapped me down in Hell by weaving a complex web of deceit. It was part of his wider plan to give me the power to rule the lost souls of the damned. My destiny, he said, was to reform the sinners of the universe and guide them back to Heaven. I wouldn't disappoint him in that. *I will lead all the demons in Hell to salvation,* I thought. *But their salvation will not be in the passing over to Heaven into his arms, it will be in his eternal destruction.*

I stood up. My fate to that point couldn't be altered, but my will to control the events of my future was resolute. For too long, I'd been dwelling on the events that had left me forsaken. It was time for action.

But where was I to begin? I was alone in that room, the firelight throwing ghostly shadows on the wall. I had been there for what felt like an eternity, thinking of my wife Charlotte, of Gideon, of Satan. Of God who is Satan and now calls himself Asmodeus. They are the same being. It was impossible, yet it was so. I had to accept it for truth before I could move on.

Walking over to the flickering fire that blazed in the hearth at the end of the room, I gathered the elements of water about my hand. I took each of the blue points of light from around me and melded them together into a flood in my palm. Thrusting a torrent of liquid into the flames I quenched them into a sodden stink of black ash. I watched as the smoke wisped up to the ceiling and spread away, like lost dreams. The smell of burnt wood made me think of my wife's last moments on earth. What was I waiting for?

With the greatest of efforts I opened the door of the room. Across the hall were the shimmering silver doors of an elevator I knew only too well. I pressed the button to ascend to the top of the infernal building. I wanted to view my new dominion.

The doors opened with a sharp bing. I stepped inside and pressed the button for floor 666. The number of the beast crept upwards on the counter as my stomach lurched into my shoes. The same music played from the speakers above that I had heard over a year before. The memories of my journey through Hell swept over me like a tide of nausea: mine and Charlotte's murder in the name of God, and my quest to get her back. I had journeyed through Hell to find out who I was, and found darkness. The blind prophet, Phineus, had led me to the powerful Perceptionist who had taught me to wield the powers of the elements. I was now a god in all but name: a human god. But in the end I'd failed. In my quest to save Charlotte I had damned myself to an eternity in Hell and her to an eternity in Limbo, sitting in Purgatory without any knowledge of what had become of her husband. I'd been beaten by Satan Asmodeus. Beaten by God. *He will pay*, I thought.

Bing. The doors of the elevator opened up to a lushly carpeted room with windows from floor to ceiling. The world of Hell was sprawled out below. It looked exactly the same: spidery webs of streets tangled around pillars of sin. Mount Belial still stood out like a sentinel of power against the bloody skyline. In the distance the lakes, The Three Eyes of Satan, still swirled with their twisted kaleidoscopic mists of sulphur. Before me, the gaudy streets of the suburb of Smoking Gun still shone with neon falsity. It all revolved around in chaos, the thundering skies streaked with lightning and hate. Clouds boiled, red and black above the city. I wondered if the souls down there had noticed that their master had been missing for more than a year.

"It's all the same," I said aloud to myself.

"No, it's changed," a deep voice growled from the corner.

I spun around in shock. I'd thought I was alone in the room. In the corner sat a raven-haired goddess. She was wearing a silky, black dress. Her hair, pulled back tight and wrapped in a bun, had a curved knife stabbed through as the lynch pin. Two rows of white, razor-point teeth framed by black gums smiled at me. The woman sat in a red, velvet chair.

"Clytemnestra," I said, recognising Satan's receptionist. "What are you doing up here?"

"I could ask you the same thing, Michael," she rasped. We stood there staring at each other in silence, each weighing the other up.

"The Lord Asmodeus is missing," she finally said. "I don't know where he is, or when he'll return. Of course this isn't the first time he's been gone for an extended period of time, but it is the first time he hasn't left someone in charge. I've been struggling to organize the new souls who are flooding down here like never before. There are already those taking matters into their own hands, inflicting what they call justice on each other, with no one to mediate. Some are beginning to question the leadership value of someone who doesn't appear to care. I need help."

For the first time I noticed the intense look of exhaustion on her face. Beneath her dangerous beauty, she looked like a weathered piece of leather, browned and cracked at the fringes.

"Asmodeus has gone for good," I replied firmly. "I am the new ruler here. This Hell is now mine. I will help you."

I thought for a moment. "Actually," I corrected myself, "you will help me."

"Gone for good?" she scoffed. "Where would he go? He can only survive on Earth for short periods of time before coming back down to Hell."

"He has gone to Heaven," I said flatly. "He won't be coming back."

A brief expression of distress twisted her features, quickly followed by a wry smile.

"Heaven, Michael?" she laughed. "Where is he? Is he hiding behind the doors? Or is that you, Asmodeus? Have you destroyed Michael and taken on his appearance for some reason?"

I shook my head slowly. Clytemnestra studied me through narrowed eyes which flitted up and down my form, looking for a sign of deception. I stood silent, holding her gaze. She approached carefully, as you would a wild animal. Finally, standing toe-to-toe with me, she reached out with sharp-nailed hands and pulled me close, pressing her body tight against mine. "It's okay, Asmodeus, you can confide in me. You share all your secrets with me."

I wasn't sure how to respond, so I simply stood still. She rubbed her hands over my chest, breathing heavily into my ear. She eased her hand down to rest on my groin. Her tongue flicked out from her luscious lips and wetly licked my neck. I shoved her away roughly.

"He obviously didn't share this secret," I snapped. "The one you know as Asmodeus, or Satan, is actually the being you hate the most. He is God."

Clytemnestra cackled a lunatic laugh as she looked me up and down. "Do you know how ridiculous that sounds, Michael?" she said. "He's worked tirelessly for thousands of years to destroy God and his work. Asmodeus embodies all that is desire. He is sex, He is murder, He is blood. Now you tell me he is the false light that shines in Heaven? It's, it's.... ludicrous."

"I don't expect you to believe me," I replied. "But why should I lie? What do I have to gain?"

"You're claiming the ruling power of Hell and you ask what you have to gain?" she laughed, smoothing her black hair and dress. "You wait until he returns. You'll be tortured for your insubordination. He'll feed you to Moloch," she spat. Walking over to the large glass windows, which overlooked the furnace of Hell city, she mumbled to herself:

"What am I going to do? How can I control this place on my own?"

"You won't have to," I said again firmly. "You can help by being my administrator and showing me the ins and outs of Hell, but I will do the controlling. I will keep the demons at bay."

I wondered exactly what it was I would do. The last thing I wanted was to bow to Asmodeus' wish and continue reforming these souls for him. But, without some kind of intervention, this Hell would tear itself apart. Then how would I be able to rescue Charlotte?

"The weakest of demons here could destroy you in an instant!" Clytemnestra interrupted. "You're but a baby to the afterlife. Even if you are the son of Asmodeus."

So she knew part of the truth, at least. I am the Devil's child. I am the Antichrist. I didn't say a word. I just turned from her to look out of the window, over Hell.

"Asmodeus would not leave me down here," she continued frantically, almost to herself. "He wouldn't leave you here either. He told me his plans. He said he wanted a general to help command his armies in the final battle, and that that leader would be you. But this was to be executed over a hundred years, with training and planning. We would stop turning people to the other side and build an army against God. I don't understand how this could have changed. He wanted to rule over the universe, sitting in Heaven with me at his side."

I looked to her. She appeared half insane, half scared. I felt pity for her. She had been lied to, just as I had.

"You're not the only one he has deceived," I said softly. "He's tricked us all. He hasn't revealed his true self to anyone until now. Asmodeus is the one you hate most; he is both Satan and God," I repeated. "I now know the truth because he revealed it me. At the beginning of time God split his single personality into two vessels: one good, one evil. He did it to test his powers. He tossed the evil side into this Hell, which He created to help cleanse souls of their sins before going to Heaven. Now, after thousands of years of being apart, your so-called Lord has reunited himself back into one body. That creature now rules in Paradise, while we left are here to fester and reform his tainted souls for him, so all can pass over to his loving arms. But He doesn't know love. He didn't create us from good will. We were created for entertainment. He will not get what he desires. He will not get his precious souls. He will get all the hatred he deserves and more. He is no longer even the one true God: He is Asmodeus. The evil side dominates his will. We must end him."

An idea had begun to form in my mind. We would continue his plan as Clytemnestra had said. We would stop turning people to the other side and slowly build an army. We would storm the gates of Heaven and kill Asmodeus. But my first desire was to save my love Charlotte from Limbo. She could then stand by my side in the final battle.

How can I control the demons in Hell long enough to do this? I asked myself.

I turned to look out to Mount Belial where Satan's home, Casa Diablo, stood. The mountain was a black, twisted crag of rock, covered in a forest of demented trees. It was the one place that every demon in Hell knew well, yet was forbidden to go to unless invited.

"Spread the word for all in Hell to come to the summit of the Mount in three days, where the Forest of Damned meets the ground of Casa Diablo," I said to Clytemnestra as I walked toward the windows, which stretched from floor to ceiling all the way around the room. "I will deliver a sermon to them. I will show them who the ruler of this place is. They will hear what I know. I will keep them at bay."

Clytemnestra started to say something behind me, but stopped as I raised my arms, and spread them wide above my head. I let the view of the elements seep over my vision. I could see all the colorful particles which make up the universe: fire, water, air, earth, spirit, emotion, intellect, desire. The infinity of colors shone in a collective mass. I could see it all; see its construction. And to see is to know. I could manipulate all to bow to my rule.

I focused my attention on the window in front of me. Rather than shatter it into a million pieces, I simply stepped through the weave of atoms, which made up its mass. As my feet touched the air beyond, I solidified an invisible path beneath me and began walking toward Casa Diablo.

Clytemnestra didn't see the elements. All she saw was me passing through a plate glass window and marching with purpose through the sky, toward Mount Belial. It would be enough to convince her I was worth listening to.

3

I STRODE THROUGH THE AIR towards Satan's old home, walking above the inferno of Hell. The heat pressed against me. It threatened to consume me. I could have cocooned myself in cool elements, but I let the oven bake me. I embraced the pain. Physical torment was nothing compared with my anguish at losing Charlotte to Purgatory.

I would gather a storm against Asmodeus. All the tainted souls in Hell would follow me. My plan was to give a magnificent show of power and recruit them to my cause. I would unite them under a banner of revenge and charge the gates of Hell, with a ferocity never before witnessed.

But how? Why would they follow me? I was just another one of them; another lost soul in the depths of Hell.

There was one other being wise enough and powerful enough to help me succeed: The Perceptionist. I looked toward Casa Diablo. The mountain would have to wait. I needed answers and I needed time. The Perceptionist had both.

Gathering the elemental air behind my back, I began to fly rather than walk. My course veered over the shimmering City of Hell, over the chief suburb of Smoking Gun towards its darkest corner, Satan's Demise. The furnace-wind buffeted my face as I soared. The red and black of damnation whipped past me at a blur. As the darkness of Satan's Demise descended around me, I slowed my flight, hovering for a moment above the evil suburb. It wouldn't be smart to barrel into The Perceptionist's home unannounced. I would need to approach with caution. Last time I was expected. That wasn't the case now.

As I floated softly to the ground, I looked around. Every building around me appeared identical. There was no pattern, just street after street of dilapidated structures lining the road. Shadows were shrouded within shadows. There were no markers or signs I could use to get a bearing. I had no idea where I was going. Mack the cab driver had brought me to the correct laneway last time. This time I was lost in a labyrinth of deserted streets.

Without a better plan I simply started to walk. The emptiness enveloped me in darkness. Foot over foot I moved through Satan's Demise. I didn't recognize anything. It seemed hopeless.

A faint scrape sounded behind me. I turned, but there was nothing there. I kept walking through the streets trying to find a building or a lamppost, anything that would help me figure out where to go. Another scrape sounded to my left, then right. It was a creeping noise, like claws being dragged on concrete. My first instinct was fear. I stopped and listened. Click, click, scrape. Click, click, scrape. The sound began to quicken, but wasn't coming from any particular direction, never even from the same direction. Remembering my elemental powers, I forced myself to stay calm. Creating a light around me I pushed it outward, trying to illuminate the assailant.

Then I saw it. Or rather, I saw them.

All around me sat hundreds of grotesque creatures. They were perched in windows, on buildings, and peering out from gutters. They were the size of big dogs, with small spikes protruding in random places about their canine bodies. Elongated muzzles snarled in a hideous chorus, scrunching back to bare horrid teeth. They had sharp, bird talons for feet, which scraped along the gravel beneath, creating the grating sound I'd heard. Slowly the creatures gathered in a pack around me.

One of the larger beasts barked a high-pitched noise, which sounded like an animal being slaughtered. As if it was a signal, they all crouched in unison, preparing to attack. I acted quickly. Using the elements, I shot a ball of flame at the one who had made the noise. Impossibly, the flame passed right through it.

The creature howled and all the demon dogs joined in. I shuddered at the noise. Fire had been like air to it. How was I supposed to defend myself? The first of the creatures leapt at me. Desperately I formed a wall of air about myself, expanding it quickly into a solid barrier. The dog smashed into it head first, snarling and snapping. It fell to the ground, but quickly scrambled back to its feet. The others rushed forward as well, barking. I pushed my cocoon outward, to give me some room. The diabolical things endlessly clawed and howled; some of them jumped onto the roof of my barrier, scraping, trying to find a way in. I was surrounded. All around and above me the dogs prowled. I tried to think quickly what I could do next. I couldn't sit there forever. I needed to get through and find The Perceptionist.

Despite my power, these wicked things terrified me. Any one of them looked as though it could rip me to pieces given the chance.

Tear me apart?

It was then that I remembered. It had been something I had tried to forget: the true murder of Gideon's soul in revenge for his part in Charlotte's death. In the end it had been impossible to block out. I could still see myself controlled by rage, ripping his being to shreds with my hatred, extinguishing his light. I'd literally torn apart the elements that made up his soul. I could do the same to these creatures. I looked at them, reluctant. Hideous as they were, it was still hard to kill something, knowing with certainty that there would be no second life for them. But what did that matter to me? They were just animals. *This is survival*, I reasoned.

I pulled anger around me. The black molecules of death surrounded my being. Looking at the closest dog, I unleashed malice upon it, trying to force myself within its life force. The torrent collided with its soul and exploded in a dazzling shower of sparks. I closed my eyes to shield them from the searing light.

Opening them again, I looked: the dog was still there. It was unmoved, still snarling at the barrier of air around me. This was unthinkable. Why had it not been destroyed?

The pack leader howled again, a long and putrid wail.

Abruptly, all of the dogs fell silent. The alpha male stalked around my circle, sniffing at the cocoon of air. It stopped in front of me and began scratching. Suddenly, one of its claws pricked through inside. I was aghast. I changed my perception to view the elements. The dog had moved them! It kept scratching frantically and the hole grew bigger. I threw more elements to replace it. The dog howled again and the pack joined in, hundreds of them scratching, above my head, all around. I rebuilt the holes as quickly as I could, but there were too many. They were breaking through!

One of the creatures snarled in triumph as its head wiggled inside my safety zone. It snapped at me, barely missing my arm. Their howls filled my ears. Was this how it would end: mauled to pieces by a pack of savage demons in the depths of Hell? Another head broke through, then another. The howls grew to a fever pitch.

I closed my eyes and prepared to be consumed bite by bite. No bite came. I opened my eyes to see the animals writhing on the ground and buildings around me, squealing in apparent agony. Then I saw it: the fires of guilt rumbling over the sky towards us. The maelstrom hit me like a wall.

4

"WHY DID YOU LEAVE ME? Why did you leave me to Satan?" Charlotte *implored with sadness in her eyes. Her glorious beauty was tempered by her suffering.*

"I tried to save you." I sobbed. "I'm sorry!"

The guilt of not being good enough to save my wife crushed me. I couldn't bear to exist. I was worthless.

"Yes, you are worthless," Charlotte hissed at me. Her loving blue eyes turned cold. "You love yourself more than me. You love your anger and your hate and your revenge too much to save me."

"No," I cried. How could my Lotte say those things? She was right though. I was nothing.

She turned and walked into burning flames.

Flames. Flames consumed me. Heat boiled and churned around me. Smoke filled my lungs. I was in Hell.

I was in Hell! I opened my eyes to behold the streets of Satan's Demise. The fires of a guilty sky churned, smothering everything. Satan had made me immune to The Guilt, which was visited upon the souls of Hell six times each day, to remind them what they had done to be damned. Now that he had left me, The Guilt was beginning to affect me again. I looked to the devil dogs scattered about me, yelping in pain. The Guilt hadn't taken as strong of a hold on me as it had these creatures, yet. I took my chance: I began to quickly pick my way through their squirming bodies, trying to get clear of the pack. There were so many of them. As I got closer to the edge of them I started to run. I could see the spell of the Guilty Fires beginning to wear off. I heard a bark behind me as one rolled onto its talon-feet, shaking its head. It looked up at me and howled. They all began to howl again. I was about to take to the air and leave Satan's Demise, when a black figure stepped out from the shadows in front of me.

11

"Get behind me," it commanded.

"Marlowe?" I yelled, skidding to a stop. I was confused, but relieved to see The Perceptionist's bodyguard.

"Get behind me, Michael!" Marlowe repeated as he walked backward down an alley, eyeing the grouping hellhounds.

I moved in behind my old friend and realized that we were in The Perceptionist's alley with the yellow door at the end. The dogs scraped towards us, but all stopped at the foot of the laneway we had entered.

"What are those things?" I asked.

"They're the evil animal souls of the world, which are now the scavengers of Hell. We call them Barghest."

"Evil animals?" I asked, confused. "How can animals be evil?"

"God deems them evil because they only follow their instincts and do not create good. That is their only crime. Some smart animals, like cats or dolphins, have the capacity for good and may sometimes go to Heaven. For the most part, though, only sheep are allowed in the hallowed place."

"Sheep?"

"They follow blindly." Marlowe smiled grimly. "They're like angels."

The Barghest at the head of the alleyway began to wail again. "How do you stop them?" I asked.

"Cold water," Marlowe said. "They hate it. But The Perceptionist prefers to leave them alone. Barghests are basically harmless, and they help keep away unwanted guests. Quick, let's go inside."

He opened the yellow door and stepped into The Perceptionist's antechamber. I tore my sight from the evil things which had almost destroyed me, and followed Marlowe inside.

It was time to see the most powerful being in existence, equal to Asmodeus. The Perceptionist would have the answers I needed.

5

MARLOWE LED ME INTO A GREY ROOM with a dining table and chairs set in the center. In the far right hand corner a man sat mumbling to himself. He rocked back and forth holding his knees to his chest.

"You remember Germaine?" Marlowe asked, indicating the man in the corner.

"I do." I recalled that this man was once an apprentice of The Perceptionist, but had lost his mind. He was a symbol. Power is nothing without control.

"Please, sit down." Marlowe smiled, pulling out one of the seats for me.

I sat down on the creaky chair.

"You'd think one of the most powerful beings in the universe could manifest himself some better furniture, wouldn't you?" I said, trying to break the tense mood which had followed us in from the street.

"Always the joker," Marlowe laughed, "even when you've come for serious reasons."

"Yes." I nodded. "People don't come seeking an audience here without good cause. I need to see him. I need to finish what we started."

"Your training." It wasn't a question. "I knew you'd be back at some point. I just thought it might be on better terms," Marlowe said.

"What is that supposed to mean?" I asked slowly.

I had told him nothing, but maybe The Perceptionist knew I was here to further my revenge.

"Have you looked at yourself in the mirror lately?" asked Marlowe, standing up. He walked over to a bench in the corner and picked up a small silver cooking pot. He handed it to me, indicating that I look at myself.

I peered into the grubby silver to behold my distorted reflection. Despite the curves throwing out all proportion, it was clear my face wasn't exactly as it used to be. My ears were growing into points. With my spare hand I reached up and touched them. Hair was growing from the fine end. I would have looked like an elf, except for the color. They were red. I bared my teeth. I was growing incisors like a wolf. How had I not felt this? Was I so wrapped up in my thoughts that this metamorphosis had escaped my notice?

"What's happening to me?" I asked, startled.

"You're becoming a demon. It's early stages, Michael, but it appears you're going to be a revenge demon. Is this quest of yours becoming an obsession? Is it consuming your every waking thought?"

Becoming an obsession? I asked myself. The answer was clear. It was all I wanted. All I needed.

"How long will it take?" I asked.

"It depends," Marlowe replied. "It's different for everyone. The ears and teeth go first. Then the hands, but it's still early. Are you thinking of revenge a lot?"

"Yes," I answered plainly.

"If that is your sole purpose the change could take just months."

"It's been a year already," I said, thinking of my time in the room of Satan's building, stewing on what I would do to my enemy when I met him next.

"Then it's not your sole thought. Not yet anyway. What's your reason for wanting revenge?"

"I want to kill the one who took my love from me," I answered.

"Ahhh." He nodded, looking me in the eyes. "So this is why you came last time. And you failed. That's why you haven't been consumed quickly. If you're still thinking of her, and it's the true reason for your hatred, then the love is counterbalancing. You are more about vengeance than plain revenge. You want justice, not selfish retribution. If love is the driver and you're trying to right a wrong, then you won't change quickly, if at all. It's only when the need to kill to even a score outweighs your thoughts of love for her that you'll truly be consumed. Where is she? When was the last time you saw her or thought of her?"

I sank my hands into my head. I couldn't bear to picture that pretty face and innocent soul. Charlotte was sitting in Purgatory, held there to spite me.

"She's in Limbo. I need to save her. That's my true goal. Revenge will be mine, but her salvation is still my greatest purpose."

"Better that she waits in the middle realms of Purgatory than suffering in Hell," Marlowe said sincerely. "Maybe I can help you."

A noise of chirping birds came from across the room. We both looked over to behold a being covered in eyes. Its head was thrown back in laughter. The sound of birds chirping was The Perceptionist's way of showing his joy. The tweeting cut short and a thousand eyes bored into me.

"You will not help him Marlowe," The Perceptionist said in a whisper that filled the room. "It is not our place to interfere. He wants a revenge that he cannot possibly attain. He wants to kill God."

Marlowe looked at me, bug-eyed, as if I'd fully transformed into a hideous demon right then and there.

"Have you lost your mind?" asked Marlowe, shocked. "Every demon down here toys with the idea of getting revenge against He who has forsaken us. But no one except Satan himself takes it seriously."

It was my turn to laugh, but there was no joy in it.

"So no one takes it seriously," I spat. "Unless God is thinking about suicide."

The Perceptionist tweeted again, obviously amused. Marlowe sat looking at me like I'd lost my mind.

"What does that mean?" he asked.

"I'll explain later," The Perceptionist cut in. "For now Michael and I need to discuss some more pressing matters." He waved his hand and a shimmering blue portal opened in front of him. "Come," he said in his rasping whisper, and disappeared into the swirling hole.

Nodding a goodbye for now at Marlowe, I stepped into the icy abyss which led to The Void.

6

I PUSHED THROUGH the freezing thickness of the gateway. The cold flowed over my body like liquid ice. Eyes closed tightly, I stumbled through the layer and then, without warning, emerged into nothingness. An unbearable lightness of being enveloped me. I was in The Void, a place The Perceptionist had created for reflection and learning. It was a true vacuum where nothing existed: no space, no time, just what The Perceptionist had brought here.

I opened my eyes and gazed around. Tiny swirling elements floated above my head and below my feet; thousands of lights twinkled their microscopic glow. When I had first come to this place I hadn't been able to see the elements, only the void that surrounded. The Perceptionist had taught me not only to see, but also to control these molecules of life.

"The Void is still the same." The Perceptionist's voice rang out. I could not see him anywhere. It was just me and the elements.

"But we have both changed, Michael," the whisper continued. "Your soul is transforming into that of a demon, obsessed with revenge. I have also undergone a transmutation."

Slowly, the points of lights started to take form in front of me and began to manifest into a solid body, arms and legs. The Perceptionist was bringing himself into view with will, knitting each atom together to make his corporeal shell.

I looked closely at The Perceptionist. At first the appeared the same as he always had, but then I began to notice slight differences. Rather than the five eyes he normally had on his face, arranged as you would see them on the side of a dice, he had eight eyes forming a perfect circle of blinking orbs. In the center of his face was his small slit for a mouth, but no nose, no ears, no hair. The rest of his body looked the same as before, covered in eyes every color of the rainbow. All of them moved, looking around at the

16

elements.

"You have three new eyes," I commented.

"Indeed," he replied. "I grew them on purpose to enhance my senses. They were my choice, just as your soul changing is your choice."

"I did not choose to become a demon!"

"All of life is choice," replied The Perceptionist calmly. "Your thoughts are slowly becoming dominated by the destruction of Asmodeus, instead of the recovery of your Charlotte. The love inside you was a redeemer before, but it is fading."

"My love for Charlotte has not changed! I love her with all of my heart. I would do anything for her."

The rage, which I barely kept in check at each waking moment, was hissing to the surface. I hoped I could maintain reason while in the presence of The Perceptionist. If I provoked him, he could easily snuff out my life.

"Yes, you would do anything for her," he continued. "But you start to think of her less and destroying Him more. If you let that loving part of you go, the demon inside will rule you. When I see your elements, they wrestle with each other. The dirty side is very slowly taking over the joyous side. Of course it's not too late, Michael, your love is still strong. You need to make the decision to focus on one instead of the other."

I quelled my fury, picturing my wife's innocent beauty in my mind's eye. It was always Charlotte who had been my motivation, ever since we met. There was no way I would forsake her over the murder of Asmodeus.

"We both know your first choice will be always Charlotte," The Perceptionist whispered softly. "The concern is what you do after you see her. If you're allowed to rescue her, will you still want to kill Asmodeus out of spite for past wrongs?"

He left the question hanging in the air, like the elements which floated between us.

"Until I kill him, we will have no freedom."

"That is an interesting thought, Michael. But do you mean freedom for all, or justice for yourselves? Even if killing Asmodeus and freeing the universe from his grip is the right thing to do, you pursue this aim for the wrong reasons. However, I'm talking a philosophy I do not believe in. It's not my place to interfere in things that do not concern me, and you are not here for a lecture. You are here for your training, for power."

I started to interrupt, but he held up an eye-covered palm and silenced me.

"Unfortunately we are not the only two things which have changed, Michael. I know that when we parted ways last, I promised that I would teach you the rest of the elemental gifts. I always keep my promises, and in time you will be as strong as me. However, since Asmodeus has reunited his soul and left for Heaven there has been a shift. It is no longer quite as simple to weave the elements of thought, emotion and intellect to create life. It appears he has built another barrier between the life-blocks and the rest of the elements. They are difficult to bond together." To illustrate his point The Perceptionist drew two of the more delicate molecules in the air towards himself. He pushed them together, but instead of sticking as they normally would they squashed flat then bounced outward, apart from each other. They sprang away, like two tiny rubber balls.

"It's genius really." The Perceptionist tweeted a laugh. "God has reaffirmed his monopoly on creation."

"But I just saw you bond your own body together a moment ago," I said.

"You are very observant, Michael," The Perceptionist replied. "But what you saw wasn't actual creation from scratch. It was a reconstruction from memory. There is a difference. Just as there is a difference between creating intelligent life and basic life. I can still create a being without intellect, as can you. However, you're not looking to create, Michael, you are wanting to destroy."

The Perceptionist took his left hand in his right, and pulled it free of his arm. I winced for him, but he appeared unperturbed. Letting the severed appendage float in the space in front of me, he quickly scattered its construction with a wave of his good hand.

"Fortunately for you, Michael, all of the elements are still just as easy to pull apart. You can decompose the universe however you desire."

I thought of what this meant for me. Yes, he was right. None of the plans in my head included the creation of anything accept an army. I could kill him, just as I had killed Gideon.

"Ah yes, Gideon." The Perceptionist interrupted my thoughts. "He was an anomaly, though, wasn't he? You could not destroy the Barghest outside, as simple as this should have been."

"I thought it was because they were special."

"More special than Asmodeus?" The Perceptionist asked. I remained silent, knowing the answer. "All beings are the same," he went on. "They are all made of a body and a soul. Of course some are more fortified than others, but they are still beings. The reason you were able to kill Gideon is because you used your soul's emotion. You wedged your malice within his being and ripped it asunder. This is impossible to do at will and can only happen with an intense hatred, an intense desire to destroy. It takes an unacceptable toll on your own energies which can never be maintained. If you try to wield the elements as you do now, you will always grow tired. It is much better to dissect with control than with blind madness. No?"

The Perceptionist's eyes twinkled.

"This I can teach you. This and much, much more."

7

A BEAD OF SWEAT RAN DOWN my forehead. I had all my energy channelled onto the small glowing orb in front of me. It was a concoction of life and body that did not contain intellect. A living being akin, perhaps, to a vegetable. I tried with my will to pull the molecules of its weave apart. It was impossible. It was too complex. The elements clung together in a thick atomic fabric.

"They are not too complex," The Perceptionist whispered from behind me. "They are much simpler than anything you wish to destroy. Think of it like untangling a knot of string. Pick out the key points and tease them apart. Work with your fingers if you must."

I reached out and touched the orb. It wobbled slightly and was slippery to touch. Taking it carefully in both hands, I pulled it toward my face, looking closely at how it was bound together. There were illuminated spirals winding around each other, in tighter and tighter circles toward the center of the sphere. Each strand was in the form of a double helix, the shape scientists on earth had discovered as that of DNA. I pinched the end of one between my fingers and twisted it clockwise. It began to unravel and separate. I took another strand and did the same. The ball of string began to loosen. I could see one strand in the middle which was joined to the rest. I took it in my fingers and turned it. It resisted. I twisted harder and the glow of the orb began to stutter like a strobe. With a wrenching effort I tore the string out from the center and scattered it to the void. The light of the orb went out.

I fell back onto my haunches and put my head between my knees. I felt like I'd just done battle with a monster. It was an exhausting effort to hold my concentration.

Birds chirped in my ear.

"Very good. Now let's try something more difficult."

"Please, can we rest?" I managed to say weakly.

"Rest?" The Perceptionist looked at me with hard eyes. "Is that what you would say to Asmodeus when you meet him? He will be harder to fight than a vegetable."

I dragged myself to my feet, swaying slightly. Closing my eyes I pictured Charlotte, pining in Purgatory, not knowing what had happened to me. It helped galvanize my energy.

"Good. You can use Charlotte's love to enrich your spirit."

"How can you read my thoughts?" I asked, still a touch wobbly. "How can you feel my emotion?"

"I do not feel." He said. "I do not read either. I see." He indicated the eyes on his face. "Each of these eyes corresponds to what you would call a sense. Hearing, smell, taste, touch and of course sight. These are the five basic senses, which you have. But I have also learnt to see the other three much more clearly: emotion, thought and time."

I remembered the prophet Phineus, and his promise to teach The Perceptionist to the see future in return for teaching me the elements.

"Yes, Phineus," he said. "The blind man who could see more than me. He showed me how to untangle the web of future paths. I could see the past before, but not decipher what was to come. It was then I realized my body was inadequate. I could even see some thoughts and some emotion before, but that was because my elemental eyes recognized their composition. These eyes," he said, motioning again to the circle on his face, "they see things not as an elemental whole, but as their component apart from their twins."

I was confused. I couldn't understand what The Perceptionist was trying to say.

"I will use an example, so you can understand," he said patiently. "Take emotion and thought. Mostly they do not exist apart, at least not in the human mind. Every thought you have is accompanied with its twin: emotion. Each gives the other context. You think: I want to kill, and the hatred behind that gives the reason why. You think: I must run, but that thought might be driven by an emotion, such as fear to run away, or desire to run toward. I used to be able to see it as complex strands. Now it is much clearer to see the two separately. I can decipher more easily this way. It is very similar to how you understand taste and smell; both are intertwined, and for most, one would not exist without the other."

I was beginning to understand.

"But what about time?" I asked. "Why is it that you could see the past but not the future? Is that because they are twins?"

"Yes and no. They are joined of course. You cannot have a future

21

without a past. But the distinction between the two is clear. I can see your past easily because it is one straight line which has been carved through space. Your present is the small circle, which surrounds your immediate space. The future branches outward in front, like pulsing veins. Some veins are thicker and pulse harder than other smaller ones. The key arteries are your likely futures. The smaller capillaries are your unlikely futures. However, they are all possible. The art of divining which path will actually occur is in looking at the forks. These are key events. Sometimes all of your veins culminate into one event and then fork out again into a thousand possibilities, or even end."

My mind was numb trying to keep pace.

"I'll show you," The Perceptionist said. He cleared a black space before us and drew a straight, white line starting at my feet, which arced into the distance.

"Follow me" he said and began to walk through the void, along the white line. The glow trailed behind us. "That is your past," he said, looking back at the line. "Clear, easy to see, simple to comprehend. You only have one past. It has happened and is unchangeable. Now this is your future." He shot a dazzling spark of lightning in front of us. Forks sizzled and streaked across the void, branching in front of us in every direction like a million shining tentacles. It was immense, so vast as to be almost incomprehensible.

"Think of it like a road map. There is one road behind and many in front. Every street or lane is a different possibility. You can take any one you desire. In the end you will only take one path, and it will destroy the other potential paths that were. Your single past will trail behind always. Until the end, there will always be these infinite potentials forward, awaiting your destiny."

I looked out into the void at the streaks of lightning in front of us. I could barely follow one line with my eyes without getting lost along the way and branching off into a dead end. My eyes started to ache as I stared, trying to see meaning in it.

"You can truly read this?"

"Yes. It is about formulating the probability of each fork in the road and taking the path of least resistance. If you know the possibilities it is easy to manipulate people's destiny. That is why Asmodeus has the advantage over you. He can see this as well as I."

I was disheartened. If someone could read my future and their own, then how could you ever succeed in besting them at anything?

"You have to remember this isn't foolproof," The Perceptionist told me. "Nothing is certain, nothing has happened until it has happened. This may change up until the last moment. Freewill continues to make the future impossible to determine with conviction. Your path collides with other souls at every moment, which complicates it even further."

"It is a major advantage though," I said, more to myself than to him.

"Yes."

"Can you teach me?" I asked.

"No," he answered. "You do not have the body for it."

I looked at him, once again confused. What did this have to do with body?

"Everything." The Perceptionist read my thoughts. "I had to grow these eyes to perceive the eight senses accurately. You do not possess the correct antennae for time."

"Could I change that?" I asked.

"You could," he conceded, "but you won't. Any major shift in your ability to perceive would mean a deformation of your body. Being able to detect Time, Emotion and Thought with honed accuracy would mean you would be unrecognizable to your beloved Charlotte. Would you like to grow more ears, mouths, noses and eyes?"

Of course I would not, but refused to give up so easily.

"You only have eyes. Could I grow more in places that aren't easily seen?"

"I grew only eyes because for me it was simpler to have one sense. By refining everything to sight, I am able to sort the data of the universe more easily. You are not built that way. Your brain, and the code you are used to, are separated into different organs. Your mind would not be able to fathom a change without going back and relearning everything you have ever perceived. It would be like a computer trying to read the wrong software. Each of your current senses is sorted into a different file. Tell me, what does green sound like?"

"What about Phineus?" I returned, dodging the question. "He can see the future, yet looks like a human."

"Yes, but you have seen his eyes? They are like a sky and clouds. They are not normal eyes. He also has a third eye, which helps detect the future. He sees the world in a completely different way. He is not human, although he appears so. Phineus is a seer. He has no ability to sense emotion or thought."

"Neither can I!" I said, exasperated.

"Yes you do." The Perceptionist's mouth turned upward in a wry grin. "You just haven't noticed it yet."

2

I WAS SHOCKED. I didn't know how to answer The Perceptionist's comment.

"I can sense thought and emotion?" I asked. "What do you mean?"

"What I mean is you have the receptors built into your body. They are far from perfect, like comparing your nose with a bloodhound's. However you do have the sense. It cannot separate thought and emotion, it only recognizes the twins as a whole, but it is there."

The Perceptionist drew a circle in the air and filled it to create a shimmering mirror. I stared into it, taking in my familiar form. Pointed chin, high cheekbones and green eyes. My ears had the red, pinched deformity which Marlowe had pointed out earlier. I splayed my fingers: they were thick and calloused. I touched my hair and felt the coarse black curls I was used to.

"Ahhh," The Perceptionist said. "You have found it."

"What?" I asked, puzzled. "My hair?"

"Of course. Have you not wondered why human women tend to be more sensitive to feelings? It is because most of them have a longer growth of hair that runs close to the sensors of their brain. Animals are similar, since they are mostly covered in hair. They can detect emotions like fear or aggression. Human men tend to be the least responsive of creatures to this sense, since their hair is generally short or pubic, which doesn't pick up the right vibrations."

I continued to stare into the mirror, twisting my curls around in my fingers. Could I change my hair so I could read thoughts?

"You will not be able to decipher thoughts accurately," continued The Perceptionist. "But if you extend your growth, your perception of emotion at least will be improved. Emotion is the more powerful of the twins, so it overrides nearly any thought you might sense. It will not be sharp, but if

24

you concentrate you'll be able to grasp a vague feeling of a person's intentions through the emotion they exude from their being. Would a growing of hair be too much for your Charlotte?" he asked. "Will your sense of beauty be offended by longer tendrils?"

I looked at my reflection again. It was interesting that even in the afterlife I was still anchored and restricted by my body. My conception of self-appearance limited my abilities. I knew this, yet was unwilling to change because I wanted my wife to still find me appealing.

"I'm sure a hair extension would be acceptable." I said slowly.

With a flick of his wrist, The Perceptionist threw a blend of elements toward me. I could feel a throbbing heat through my skull; hair sprouted quickly in curls from my head. It was an odd sensation, not painful but uncomfortable. As quickly as it began, the feeling stopped. I looked again at the mirror. Black ringlets flowed down my shoulders, before stopping at my hips. Now I appeared more like some kind of wizard than a fighter. I smiled.

"I think Charlotte may approve," I said.

"At the very least she will recognize you," The Perceptionist said. "That is all you require. It is a fine balance."

I reached out to see if I could sense any feeling from The Perceptionist. There was nothing, not even a whisper of love, or hate or, anything. I tried again, but the deadness of the connection between us remained the same. Maybe I didn't have the talent for this.

I shifted my vision to behold his elemental make up and studied him closely. Flowing around his brain was a pure golden light. There were no molecules of emotion to be seen. The light flowed down from his head in a line to the center of his chest, where there was a golden heart, pumping. I looked down at myself. My heart was a mess of colors. I could see every kind of emotion welling inside, but none of the golden light emanating from my teacher.

"You only have some of the same color inside your brain." The Perceptionist interrupted my concentration. I shifted back to regular sight and blinked.

"What is that light?" I asked.

"It is reason," he answered. "It is pure logical thought and knowledge. There is no shade or distinction because it is not mixed with emotion. That is why you can't feel anything through the strands on your head. I have done away with emotion. It has not proved useful to me in learning, so I discarded it."

No wonder I had felt nothing when reaching out to him. I tried to fathom what it would be like to exist without emotion, but could not. Love, hate, anger, joy; they were my driving forces. I could not function without them. To me, it felt like all intelligence was artificial. It is emotion that makes a human. The Perceptionist was nothing but a robot.

"Not a robot," he said. "I still have the ability to feel if I desire, but I do not. Maybe at some point, when my intellectual knowledge is complete I will introduce emotion again. If I want to achieve perfection, I must be systematic in gathering everything piece by piece. So far emotion has done nothing but get in the way, so I have eliminated it for now."

"What is perfection?" I wondered.

"I cannot tell you yet, for I do not know," he said. "This is what I am searching for. Once I find it, I will share it with all I can. What I can tell you is that perfection begins within, so that is where I am looking."

No emotion. It was unfathomable. Even the most powerful being in existence did not pretend to know what perfection was. I respected his honesty.

The Perceptionist took the mirror he had created earlier and ran his hands over its service. It shuddered and then began to bend into itself, forming the blue vortex, which I knew joined the void with Hell.

"It's time for an excursion," said The Perceptionist. "We need to try out some of your new talents in the real world."

"What?" I asked, startled at the unexpected announcement. "I thought we would be here longer, practicing."

"We could," he replied as he stepped an eye-covered leg into the portal. "However, the best practice is doing, not learning."

"But where are we going?"

"The Tenth Circle," he whispered as he disappeared into the blue whirlpool of light.

9

I STUMBLED OUT OF THE PORTAL to face Marlowe and The Perceptionist. Marlowe sat at the stark table, looking up at his master.

"Please get the car, Marlowe," The Perceptionist instructed. "We're going to Smoking Gun."

Without comment, the African nodded, got up and left the room.

"What is The Tenth Circle?" I asked again, still rattled at our hasty exit from the void.

The Perceptionist turned to look at me. He sat down in the chair which Marlowe had just vacated.

"Have you heard of the Nine Circles of Hell?" he asked.

I thought for a moment. I had heard of them somewhere, but had to drag the depths of my memory before I could recall it.

"It's just a story," I said, "The Nine Circles of Hell, from The Divine Comedy? Each circle is reserved for a different grade of evil, the first circle being for the mild sins, the ninth for the worst criminals in the underworld."

"Yes, a story. In reality it was more of a poem. And you are right, the nine circles do not exist, they are more of a concept than a place. It is now a grade scale the demons in Hell give for the potency of burden they feel when the Fires of Guilt rage through Hell each day. You may have noticed that the more evil a soul has committed, the worse they seem to suffer."

I did recall. When Satan had forced me to fight the demon Balthazaar in the Pit, it helped save me.

"If Demons experience a great deal of suffering during the burdens, they are said to have visited the ninth circle."

"So where are you taking me then? If these Nine Circles are just a myth, what is the Tenth Circle?" I repeated. "You said to Marlowe we were going to Smoking Gun."

"Poetry," The Perceptionist said.

"Excuse me?" I asked, confused.

"Poetry," he repeated. "The people who named the place thought it would be poetic. It is in reality a torture dungeon. It is where a group of self-appointed revenge demons reap what they call 'deserved justice' upon the most evil souls in Hell. Since Asmodeus left, this group has sprung up as an underground power. It is where the strongest fiends here try to destroy the strongest evils, through a baptism of pain. They call it the Tenth Circle, because it is reserved for elite evil, where souls are brought to a new level of suffering beyond that which even the fires of torment can achieve."

"And it's in Smoking Gun?"

"Yes, but it is hidden. The gateway is in Smoking Gun. The Circle itself is somewhere in a maze of catacombs beneath the streets."

"Why are we going there?" I asked.

"Better to show than to tell," The Perceptionist said. "During our journey you must remember to try to use your new gifts. Always reach out to sense feelings with your hair."

I sat, staring into space. This reminded me of my first ever day in Hell, when I was led through Damnation by Satan. It was a painful day; I hoped this time it wouldn't be so horrifying, yet I suspected it might be.

"What is Marlowe getting a car for?" I asked. "Why don't we just fly there?"

"The easiest way short term isn't always the most convenient in the long term," replied The Perceptionist. "In this instance, it's better for us to remain inconspicuous. I have looked into our futures and seen the best path to fulfill my desired intentions. It is also best for me to change."

I looked at him. He was an eye-covered humanoid. He had never worn clothes in the whole time I'd been in his presence. His lack of sexual organs made it seem superfluous in any respect.

"You misunderstand." The Perceptionist stood from his chair, letting it clatter to the ground behind him. He raised his hands above his head and, closing every eye on his body, began humming a low droning noise. His body began to shrink, morphing to take a size more akin to my own. As he did, each eye retracted back into his white skin, like molluscs returning to their shells. Bleach-blonde hair sprouted from the top of his head, and ears grew from the sides. His mouth slowly pushed down toward his chin, as a nose burgeoned in the middle of his face. Finally two green eyes formed out of sockets below two fully-formed, blonde eyebrows. It was incredible to watch the transformation. Within the space of half a minute, The Perceptionist had turned into what looked like an albino version of me. It

28

was disturbing. He'd even turned his ears into the same red points as mine.

The Perceptionist brushed his hands down his chest and a grey suit folded out of nothing to cover his nakedness. He clicked his fingers in my direction and my plain clothing was transformed into a crisp black suit, the same cut as his own.

"Now," he said, his voice the same audible whisper. "In this guise, we are brothers. You will call me Aldous while we're outside."

As he finished his sentence, Marlowe walked in.

"Hello Aldous," he said, smiling at The Perceptionist. "The car is ready." Marlowe turned to look at me. "Set to go, Michael?"

I simply stood there with my mouth open, looking from Marlowe to The Perceptionist, or Aldous as I was supposed to call him.

The pair turned without further comment and left the room. I had no choice but to follow. Exiting into the dark alley of Satan's Demise, I saw a black Jaguar parked to the left. Marlowe was holding the door open for me, waiting.

I was still dazed from the spectacle inside. I should have been used to such occurrences by now, but even a small irregularity like The Perceptionist changing his form was unsettling. I slid into the car and sat in the back next to my teacher. Everything was happening so quickly.

Marlowe pulled out into the shadowy streets of Satan's Demise. There was no sign of the Barghest; the streets were again eerily deserted. The car began to pick up speed.

"You must do exactly as I say, when we get to Smoking Gun," The Perceptionist said. "It will take precise timing to achieve what we wish. Do not question, just act."

I nodded.

"Good," he said. "No more questions for now. All will be unveiled shortly. Conserve your strength. You will be mostly just witnessing, but I may need to call on you to assist."

I remained silent and inhaled deeply. With trepidation, I waited as we drove onward.

The dark streets around us soon became a shade lighter. We turned onto a highway, full of roaring vehicles. As we merged into the constant stream of traffic, some cars screeched past, honking their horns. Marlowe sped up to match the relentless pace around us. There was no music on the radio, just the hum of the engine and the rumble of vehicles. Marlowe and The Perceptionist stared ahead, not talking. It did nothing to calm my nerves. My imagination was running wild with gruesome images of what The Tenth Circle would be like. Blood and gore filled my thoughts. Charlotte's horrid death came into my mind. I almost retched. I couldn't dwell on such things, or it would drive me insane. It was much better for me to focus on how I would rescue my love from Limbo, rather than recall why she was there. My path to becoming the leader of Hell and commanding an army still eluded me. I knew I needed to display my power to the demons of Hell to gain their support. I knew I needed to incite the same sense of purpose in them as I felt, to get revenge against Asmodeus. However, the finer details of how were just a blur of ideas in my head. Nothing seemed like a good plan. I'd thought that over the days and weeks of training in the void with The Perceptionist, we might have spoken about it, or a strategy would have crystallized in my mind. All I had found myself thinking about was killing Asmodeus when I found him.

Just the thought of him at that moment made my flesh crawl with anger and my heart rage with hate. I looked outside to distract myself. We were driving over a towering bridge, which spanned across a river of lava. The acrid stink of brimstone wafted up with the heat haze, which rose from the flow. I stared down and watched the glowing magma churn below. Across the bank to which we were headed, the shining buildings of Smoking Gun jutted out of the earth. The mesh of flickering neon lights sent a chill through my spine. This was the devil's playground. Casinos, brothels, bars, nightclubs and drug dens dominated the city. Nothing was illegal, nothing taboo. There was no such thing as too nasty, too sexual, too offensive. Hedonistic excess was central to the character of Smoking Gun, all set in a demonic backdrop of slick marketing. You could lose yourself in its savage delights if you wished. You paid only with your soul.

Our car slowed slightly as we came to the end of the bridge. Marlowe steered us rapidly to an exit and squeezed in behind a truck. We wound in a loop, down onto the main strip of Smoking Gun, slowing to a crawl as the traffic jammed along the street. I gazed out through tinted windows to behold the people and demons teeming along the sidewalk. A group of intoxicated, bullying demons pushed along the pavement near us, yelling abuse at weary onlookers and hooting into the air.

"Who are they?" I asked Marlowe.

He turned his head to watch the hulking monsters strut next to us.

"Football players," he replied.

I watched as one of the demons, who was covered in short purple hair, walked up to a small but beautiful looking woman and grabbed her around the waist. She shrieked, struggling to get away from him. The demon pushed his black tongue down her throat and threw her down onto the sidewalk, before roaring in laughter with his cheering comrades.

"They're pretty much the same wherever you go," Marlowe said, as he turned into a street on our right.

The buildings which soared above us on each side were made of black concrete and glass. There were no neon signs like there were on the strip, just dark, steel fire escapes clinging to the walls like metal spiders. We passed an overflowing dumpster, before entering a large open courtyard.

"Where are we?" I asked.

"We're nearly there," The Perceptionist cut me off.

I looked up ahead and could see a line of people snaking left to right through the courtyard. As we drew closer, I could see they were roped-in by a red barrier. At the end of the huge line, there was plain, white door. Above it was a small, red sign with white letters which read: Oresteia.

"This is a nightclub," I said.

"The most popular nightclub in town," The Perceptionist agreed in his deadpan whisper. "And the gateway to the Tenth Circle of Hell."

10

MY CHEST CONSTRICTED with anxiety as our car pulled to a stop in front of Oresteia nightclub. Not knowing what to expect when entering this Tenth Circle made me so nervous that I was shaking. It was as if being kept in the dark was worse than anything The Perceptionist could have told me. Sensing my fear, my master put his hand on my shoulder.

"No harm will come of us if you follow my instructions."

He clicked his fingers and Marlowe exited the vehicle. The tall African strode directly to the front of the snaking cue, which wound to the entry of Oresteia. Two security guards stood at the doorway. The first was a towering behemoth with the body of a gorilla and two ghastly heads – one a snapping hyena, the other almost human, except its skin was yellow and reptilian. This second face spoke to the patrons in the line as they entered the club; at this distance I couldn't hear what it was saying. The second doorman was short, around five foot high and slight in build. He looked like a black cat standing on its hind legs. He worked in fluid, feline movements, clipping and unclipping the rope barrier as he let patrons through. All the while he held a clipboard with a second set of red arms, which grew from his back. The limbs angled up and curved over the creature's shoulders, like two deformed wings ticking off names as people entered. It was this demon whom Marlowe approached. He whispered something in the creature's ear and indicated our car. The cat started shaking its head, but Marlowe pulled a brown paper bag from his pocket and handed it to him. Looking inside, his eyes grew wide before he looked back at Marlowe, nodding furiously.

Marlowe walked back to the car and opened the door on my side.

"You're the future ruler of Hell," The Perceptionist said as he motioned for me to get out. "Start acting like you are supposed to be treated with respect and you will be."

I exited the car with as much dignity as I could muster, smoothing out my black suit as I stood to my full height. All eyes in the queue watched as The Perceptionist got out behind me. He looked at them with indifference. I tried my best to mimic his attitude. Marlowe closed the door for us, and started to get back in the car.

"I'll be here when you return, Master Michael and Master Aldous," he said, loud enough for the crowd to hear.

Without a word, The Perceptionist, in the form of Aldous, hooked his arm around mine and guided me toward the entry of Oresteia. The cat bouncer opened the side V.I.P. rope for us to enter. There was a mutter from the crowd, but the hyena silenced them with a loud bark. I could feel a tremor of emotion seep through my hair, coming from the creatures standing in line. I concentrated a little harder and thought I could sense a feeling of collective indignity, but it was so faint as to be barely distinguishable. The security guard's second, reptile head looked at us as we passed through the ropes. He said in a smooth English accent.

"No killing inside. No fighting. No raping, or you'll be ejected," as if it were a matter-of-fact thing to say when entering a nightclub.

We walked down a long, black corridor which had tiny pinpricks of light coming from the ceiling, like small stars on a dark night sky. There was not a sound in the corridor expect that of echoing footsteps. There was a group of people in front of us, walking quickly toward the end of the corridor in silence. As we approached the other side of the corridor, I could see a glowing white waterfall cascading silently where there would normally be a door. The group in front of us walked through without breaking stride.

The Perceptionist turned to me as we neared the waterfall. "As we go through the entry," he said, "turn immediately to the left, go up the three stairs and walk to the back of the room. There will be two orange demons getting up from their table in the far corner. Sit down as they leave. Do not make eye contact with anyone, do not talk to anyone, do not stop to look at the club. We will have plenty of time to take in the scenery once we sit down. Is this clear?"

I nodded in reply. We were now at the white waterfall. It was eerie to watch the water tumble down into the floor in front of us without making a sound. Holding my elbow, The Perceptionist led me through. I expected fluid to soak us to the bone, but as we walked through the curtain of water it felt more like a warm breeze blowing down over us.

As we passed to the other side, my senses were assaulted with thumping music and flashing lights. I almost paused in shock, but felt the hand on my arm tighten and pull me softly to the left. With my head down

I followed my feet across ebony floorboards, over to a small set of steps. We leapt up the stairs and I lifted my gaze to the back of the room. The distance across the floor was only short, but it was packed with bodies. Demons, half demons and people were dressed in glittering dresses or formal suits. They all crushed together, bouncing to the beat. The music pumped all around us in deafening volume. So as not to make eye contact with anyone, I focused on the back wall. I spotted the set of orange demons The Perceptionist had described earlier. They were starting to gather their things. My companion increased the speed of his step and I followed. The group of demons stood and exited, leaving a free table in the crowded club. Just as we neared the table, two tall women and a short purple demon went in to sit down. The Perceptionist quickly slid in front of them and pulled me down into the softly padded corner. The short demon angrily shoved his face into The Perceptionist's and growled.

"This is our table, you peasant. Get up at once."

The Perceptionist calmly looked at him. "This is our table, friend," he replied in a whisper which was impossibly clear above the deafening music. The demon stepped back a pace.

"Allow me to get the three of you a drink for the confusion," The Perceptionist continued. He lifted his hand and the empty glasses each of the three were holding filled to the brim. "Now kindly leave us."

A look of fear spread across the demon's face at The Perceptionist's simple display of power. He turned and ushered his female friends away from us.

"That was easy." The Perceptionist looked at me. "I'm happy you followed my instructions. If we'd been a half second later, there would have been an unfortunate accident for him. Now we wait here. Don't get up until I say, but feel free to observe the domain."

I leaned back into the wall for support. It had taken all the concentration I could muster to focus on getting to the table without trying to take in my surroundings. Now I had some breathing time, I looked around. We were seated at the back of the room with our backs to the wall, slightly elevated above everyone else. I looked out to a whirling spread of color. The club itself was a gigantic circle. About ten feet in front of us there was a clear waterfall, which shimmered down from the roof, following the circle of the room all the way around. Behind it there was another curtain of water also ten feet in, then another, and another. Each waterfall formed a bigger circle around the next. It was hard to gauge how many waterfalls there were, since they all blended together and somehow enabled you to peer right through as long as you looked directly ahead. If I looked at an angle, the fountains split into a rainbow wall of color. I could see that the first

34

waterfall was red, the second was orange, the third yellow. After that it was a blur, but if I concentrated hard enough and focused my line of sight above the heads, I could see right through the center. There was a wide, circular dance-floor, jammed full of dancing revellers who surrounded a DJ playing inside a final black waterfall. It sparkled as he whirled around inside. The DJ had a full ring of turntables around him. He spun constantly, changing records and pushing buttons. Red, Orange, Yellow, Green, Blue, Indigo and Violet.

As I continued to look around, the layout of the club slowly became more obvious. There were seven waterfalls in all, each a color of the spectrum. I was able to see through if I looked dead ahead, because the colors would blend to create white light. The effect was wonderful, although confusing if you moved your line of vision too quickly. As I looked around I could see a distinct difference between the levels of disfigurements of the demons in each area. Where we now were, between the white waterfall entry and the first red waterfall, were mainly humans with the occasional demon. However, inside the first red curtain were all demons of similar deformity. Each was a different size and shape, and looked individual, but many traits were similar. They were hideous to behold, each had twisted crimson ears and jutting fangs, which stuck out of their mouths at odd angles. Their bodies were mottled shades of red all over. Some had an extra head, or arms, or legs, but the theme of their disfigurements was the same. Rather than dancing together, they were moshing instead, slamming into each other violently to the beat. I reached out with my mind to see if I could get a sense of feeling from them. At this distance it was incredibly difficult, but maybe because it was a group of people together I was able to feel it: anger. These were Wrath Demons! So this is what I would become if I let my quest for revenge consume me. I turned my head away, back to The Perceptionist, startled.

"Each colored waterfall corresponds to a certain sin," he whispered. "Seven colors of the rainbow; seven deadly sins. Each barrier creates a space where demons can congregate with those who enjoy the same sin. You are correct that wrath is red. Orange represents gluttony, yellow avarice, green envy, blue lust, indigo sloth and violet pride. The original white waterfall we entered through represents pure virtue, the black waterfall in the center, pure evil."

I looked back again peering over the crowd, which was indeed split into similar groups by their aquatic barriers. A revelation struck me. There were nine waterfalls, not seven! Nine circles within each other: The nine circles of Hell.

"Correct," The Perceptionist confirmed and pointed toward the middle of the room.

"So, the entry to the tenth is through the ninth, under the DJ's feet?" I guessed, looking across to where the black waterfall sat in the center of the club.

The Perceptionist nodded with a slight smile.

"But how are we supposed to get through there?"

Before The Perceptionist could answer, a red light started flashing above the DJ's head. He looked up and turned the music down. Everyone in the place stopped and looked to the middle of the room.

"Just watch," The Perceptionist whispered next to me. Leaning into a microphone in front of him, the DJ boomed. "One minute. One minute until The Guilt. Enjoy your suffering."

He then quickly walked over to a chair to the side of his turntables, sat down and pulled a seatbelt over his shoulders to secure him in place. Unbelievably, everyone else in the room did the same. Those who had a chair nearby took it. The rest flopped onto the floor where they were standing and remained silent.

I could feel the beginnings of the guilt start to probe my mind when I heard The Perceptionist's unmistakable voice inside my head.

"When I get up, follow me. We must run into the center of the room to the black waterfall. I will ensure The Guilt doesn't consume you. Sit next to the black waterfall and pretend to have the visions. You may keep your eyes open, but make it appear as if you're staring into space. I will answer your questions afterward."

Smoke began to billow in through the vents in the room. Everybody in the place started to convulse as the horrid fires burst into the club. The Perceptionist leapt up and nimbly began running toward the center of the room. I pursued him as quickly as possible. He disappeared through the first curtain of colored water. Each waterfall grew hotter and hotter as we passed through. When inside, only the two waterfalls on either side of us were visible. Bursting through the blue curtain I could see hundreds of lust demons thrashing about with guilt. Their engorged genitals were covered in matted black hair, and their skin was infested with weeping sores. I pressed on through the crowd and into the next circle. With solid blue to my back and dark indigo in front, I was assaulted by the smell of rotting flesh. Sloth demons. I could recognize them from my previous journey to Sloth's lounge. I rushed through the indigo curtain. As I emerged through the final violet waterfall, I almost tripped over a hulking body, which lurched on the ground in fits of despair. Its face was twisted in pain, a mirror clasped in its clawed fist. It was howling and tearing at its own body. Ghastly scars covered the demon's chest and neck, from what must have been other fits of forced self-loathing. So this was the punishment for the prideful.

"Quickly!" The Perceptionist's voice entered my mind.

I catapulted myself toward the black waterfall, staying close to him. Pretending to convulse on the ground, I imitated a fit like those of the other demons around us. I could feel the guilt trying to enter my body, but there was resistance. I shifted my perception to the elements. Looking down at my chest I could see a golden hand enclosed over my heart. Black and brown elements tried to hammer inside, but the hand repelled it. I knew this was the elemental hand of The Perceptionist. I could see it was made from molecules of pure rational thought, but couldn't understand how that was stopping my visions.

"Watch." The Perceptionist's internal voice whispered urgently.

I looked up, switching my vision back to normal perception. I was careful not to focus too clearly on one point, but remained looking into the distance. Just to the right of us a pack of figures slowly appeared from behind the violet waterfall. They were all deep red-colored demons of wrath, completely deformed by their sins. One after another came in a line. They marched silently across the floor, unperturbed by The Guilt, which wracked everyone else in the room. Each of the demons held a writhing body bag over their shoulder. They walked forward, through the crowd of bodies on the ground and stepped through the black waterfall to disappear from sight. In total there were twelve demons. As the last one walked past I shifted my perception to see the same golden barrier around his heart as mine. I then closed my eyes to avoid being caught looking, and kept convulsing on the ground.

"Ready. Now!" The Perceptionist whispered after a few moments. I opened my eyes to see him hurtling into the black waterfall. I got up and threw myself inside behind him. I tumbled downward, through scorching heat, falling down and down. As my body twisted in an uncontrolled fall, I struggled to slow myself. The flow of the water swept me along with it. Gradually my momentum eased and I was able to position my body feet down. Finally, I landed softly on my hands and knees on a cold metallic floor. The Perceptionist was right at my side. He held his finger to his lips, indicating silence.

I looked ahead. A slanted corridor ran off into the distance, where I could see the tail of a body bag being dragged around a corner. The Perceptionist quietly stood up. As I rose to stand, I felt a light rush of wind from beneath me. We both lifted slightly off the ground. I could see my master had formed a bed of elements to muffle our footsteps. He began to walk silently forward. I followed him, into the Tenth Circle of Hell.

11

THE CORRIDOR SPIRALLED DOWNWARD. Rusty metal walls curved away from us on one side and toward us on the other. Gradually, as we walked, the walls altered in their position. As one straightened toward us, the other fell away. It was a disorienting feeling which made me lose the sense of direction in which we were heading. At one point it felt we were circling down clockwise. The next it felt like we were headed counter-clockwise, even though we hadn't altered the course of the original circular pattern. The tilted arc of the walls seemed to bend matter and time without moving anything right in front of us.

Abruptly, The Perceptionist halted. I almost bumped into the back of him. He turned around and silently reached out with his finger, touching me on the nose. My stomach felt like it was being pulled out of my belly button. I looked down to see my body was turning invisible from the middle out. Looking to The Perceptionist I could see he was doing the same thing to himself. Eventually I could no longer see either of us.

"No noise," he said telepathically. "We will remain out of sight. The corridor ends around the next bend. We will walk into a room and move to the right, where we can sit on an empty row of seats and watch. Remember to reach out with your sense of feeling. Soak up the emotion and thought in the room."

Unwilling to answer or move, I simply stood silent where I was. I felt a light pressure on my shoulder willing me onward. Warily, I moved ahead. As we rounded the corner an orange light flooded my vision. My eyes adjusted to reveal what appeared to be a courtroom. There was a huge statue of blind Justice behind the empty judge's bench. The statue held scales in her left hand and a sword in her right. Either side of her head, sharp flames rose to the ceiling, creating the amber luminance which filled the room. A noise made me look to the left, where the group of demons we had seen earlier assembled in the jurors' dock. As each of them got inside, they threw their body bag soaring into the center of the room. Each bag landed with a terrible crunch. The sixth bag went scuttling across the floor near my feet. I moved with as much stealth as I could to the empty row of seats as The Perceptionist had instructed. As I slid along I could feel his presence next to me.

A door opened to the far left of the room and a figure entered.

"All rise for the honorable Judge Minos!" one of the demon jurors bellowed from his stall. I stayed seated.

As the figure moved out of the shadows and into the light of his bench, I could see he was horribly disfigured. His skin was puckered and blistered all over as if it had been seared to his bones. His ears were those of a donkey. A snake protruded at the base of his spine, like a hissing tail with fangs. It wrapped around his waist as he moved to sit down. Picking up his gavel, the Judge banged it down with three resounding smacks.

"I now declare the Court of The Tenth Circle into session. Who are the accused?" he asked, turning to the demon juror closest to him.

The juror stood and turned to Minos. He bowed before puffing out his chest and shouting loudly.

"I have called the Demon Screwtape to judgment. He has committed himself to a life of turning others to evil. For this he must pay." He sat back down and the demon next to him stood and repeated the same low bow to Minos.

"I have called the Demon Lilith to judgment," the next juror shouted with spit flying from his mouth. "She is a temptress and lust demon who has found a way to avoid the deformities of her sin. For this she must pay."

In the same manner, every juror in the line voiced similar charges to their assigned accused. As each revenge demon sat back down, a body bag slid along the floor as if by magic and stood up in a semi-circle in front of the judge. An orange flame sparked below each one, melting the covering to expose a howling figure inside. As each accused screamed, the noise in the room grew to deafening levels. The smell of bubbling flesh raped my nostrils. Although horrified, I refused to look away. As much as the ritual disgusted me, I knew I needed to see this. I channelled my senses toward the burning bodies. Pain and fear entered my head. I could feel what they were feeling only barely, but the intensity was unmistakable.

Judge Minos sat calmly, listening to each of the accusations. He nodded to each of the Jurors as they sat down and then cast his gaze over to the burning victims in the middle of the room. His eyes were dark and unforgiving.

The ceremony came to a head as the twelfth and final accused was stood in front of Minos. Their cries rang about the room, reaching a fever pitch; waves of empathetic terror poured into me from the accused souls. Their shrieks were almost deafening, but above the clamor Minos' voice rumbled in a fury. "I can see each of these demons' guilt," he boomed. "They are the inmates of Hell and abide here forever. They have lost their souls and their own innovations have caused their doom. The Guilt is not enough for these souls: they deserve pure pain that only we, the Court of The Tenth Circle, can deliver. It is time they tasted the retribution of Hell!"

The jurors roared in the dock, throwing their fists in the air in salute to the statue of Justice, who stood looking over the courtroom with veiled eyes.

Judge Minos hammered his gavel down and the scorching fires increased in their ferocity. The screams of utter dread sounded from the twelve burning demons. Minos stood from his seat and turned to take the Sword of Justice from the statue behind him. He swung its blade through the air. As he did, the stomach of each suffering demon split open. The smell was abominable. Intestines slopped onto the floor. I steeled my stomach. I wanted to stand up and stop it, but felt impotent to do anything but watch. Their throbbing anguish welled even stronger into me. Flames still licked the tortured bodies. Their faces were twisted messes of pain, their eyes rolling orbs of white terror.

With their bowels on the ground before them, all twelve victims unleashed a new cacophony of wails. The sense of pure despair and suffering seeping through my skull almost threw me into unconsciousness. If this was the intensity with which I could feel their plight, I could barely comprehend the immediate and direct misery within their own bodies. The jurors all moved out from their box to kneel before their chosen demon. They bowed in prayer and began to eat the entrails in front of them. The screams of pain grew louder still. Just below the wails I could hear the slurping and chewing of the demons. Each bite sent sympathetic jolts through my body. Finally, Minos swept his sword through the air again. Blood sprayed as twelve throats were cut in harmony. The screams fell to a muffled gurgling. Each juror, having eaten what was before him, moved forward and began to drink the blood from their quarry's throat. I wanted to retch onto the ground in front of me.

Minos turned around and placed a weight onto the scales behind him. They began ever so slowly to tip to the other side.

"The weight of justice is on our side," he declared, looking over to the twelve oozing victims on the courtroom floor being devoured by hungry demons. "As this scale turns over the next three days, you will be eaten alive. Once you have been fully ingested, you will then be reborn into a pile of vomit, to resurrect yourself over three more agonizing healing days. On the seventh day you will be taken to the feeding chambers below us, before you are devoured again. You are doomed to be consumed for your sins forever. You will still feel The Guilt of these sins as you are eaten, so you will always be reminded what you have done to deserve the Tenth Circle. This is the real punishment for your actions, eternal pain within eternal consciousness."

He slammed his gavel down one last time. "I now pronounce this court adjourned," he announced, turning to step off his podium.

"Stop!" The Perceptionist stirred beside me, his voice filling the room. "This court has only just begun."

12

MINOS STOPPED IN HIS TRACKS as The Perceptionist's pronouncement rang across the courtroom. He spun around to look up and around the room, still unable to see us.

"Who would dare interrupt the Court of the Tenth Circle?" Minos demanded, his voice shaking slightly. I could sense a very tiny amount of fear.

"It is your master, the true Satan, Michael and his servant," The Perceptionist said.

I felt a chill wash over me and knew that our invisibility had been lifted. I looked to my side, to see The Perceptionist in his true form. Each eye in his body blazed. A thousand fuming orbs of light were all directed at Minos. It made me tremble at what might follow.

Each of the twelve demons who were feasting on the accused looked up from their devilish communion to stare at us. Their faces were caked in the ghoulish blood of their victims, shining in the orange light. Growls began to sound in their throats, but were silenced as my hands rose involuntarily out before me, my palms facing the roof and my arms spread out toward them. I felt my mouth move, although I had not tried to speak.

"I have come to judge those who would presume authority they do not have," I said, knowing it was The Perceptionist pouring the words into me. "I am your Jesus, I am your Satan. I am your God. I am the final jury in this ethereal existence. You have no right to assume you speak for me or think for me. I have witnessed your disgusting acts of insubordination. I have felt the suffering of those on whom you prey. While they are most certainly evil, you are the greater scourge. It is time you were brought to witness for your own sins, your own evils. The light of life that shines within you is ugly, and it is time it is extinguished."

As the words left my mouth, The Perceptionist swept out from the bench toward Minos who opened his mouth to scream. Before any noise could escape his throat, The Perceptionist was upon him. There was no blood, or gall, just a thundering clap of noise as Minos exploded into a shower of elements and was gone. The enormity of what had just happened did not escape the twelve demon jurors. Complete bedlam broke loose. Three of the demons began running for the closest exit. Three surged at The Perceptionist and three at me. The others stayed where they were, shrieking in panic. Time seemed to slow as the scene unfolded before me. It was as if The Perceptionist and I were able to move at normal speed, while the others were immersed in water.

The closest demon to The Perceptionist burst into nothingness, while the others slowed and were held still in the air in front of him. The three jurors descending upon me were gaining ground, but their speed was hampered by something.

"Destroy them," I heard The Perceptionist say inside my head. "Dissect them as I have shown you. You have seen their evil, now act upon it."

Without thinking I changed my vision to view the elements. I saw the dirty light shining inside each of the beings in front of me. They were indeed ugly. Concentrating on the central molecules of life, I focused on the essential coil. I reached inside the first demon with a telekinetic hand and twisted the weave of his essence. As the atoms began to separate, I yanked with all of my will. The life force of the demon resisted. He was still gaining upon me as I fumbled within his soul. Sweat beaded on my forehead as I concentrated with all of my power. With a roaring cry, I tore the critical strand of elements out of his body. I felt a wave of fear wash over me before it faded into oblivion. He was gone; his existence at an end.

I looked over to the other two demons advancing toward me. I was exhausted, my energies severely depleted from the effort of tearing the first demon asunder. With a grunt, I threw each of my fists out before me. Pure light hammered into the demons, knocking each of them off their feet, shooting backward, skidding on the ground back to their cowering companions. I sucked in a breath to steady myself.

I looked over to The Perceptionist and his attackers. The thousand-eyed Elemental had completely destroyed what was left of the demons who had decided to advance upon him. He stood serenely, watching me.

"You should have pulled all of them apart," he whispered into my mind. "Now you have five ugly lights left to observe rather than the tranquility of emptiness."

His unemotional tone unnerved me. It didn't seem as though he even cared about what he'd just done. He had completely shattered four lives without a second thought. Rather than reply to him, I walked towards the five remaining devils who were quaking in the center of the room. I gathered the elements of air about them tightly. They began to wail, as their half-devoured victims had.

"Silence!" I yelled. This time my voice was my own. They ceased their cries, but continued to shake with fear.

"You think that revenge is your right, but it is not. You are covered in unjust blood. You are now my servants. Your existence from this point is beholden to me and only me. Flee from this Tenth Circle and tell all who will listen: Asmodeus has departed Hell and bequeathed the domain to his son, Michael. I am now Satan. Every soul in Damnation is to gather for a sermon at Mount Belial in two days hence, to hear my commandments. I am your Dark Shepherd. Seek out Clytemnestra. She is in the main building in the city center. Find her and she will lead the pilgrimage to the anointed place. Now go!"

I threw my hand out and let loose red elements from my fingertips. The firestorm shot out of the door from where we had entered the court. Without hesitation each of the demons ran, howling from the room.

Once they'd disappeared from the courtroom I fell to my knees. I braced myself with my hands, before wobbling to the floor and lapsing into unconsciousness.

13

I JOLTED AWAKE. A sharp, white light filled my vision. I blinked and shook my head clear. The Perceptionist's eye-covered form came into view. The room was a blur of orange. I struggled to stand, but felt a hand gently hold me down. I looked up again at The Perceptionist, who was silently pushing green, blue and yellow elements into my body. My sense of exhaustion dimmed, and was gradually replaced with a sense of energy. The Perceptionist stopped the torrent of atoms flooding into me and stepped back. I flexed my fingers. I was stiff all over, but otherwise felt strong. The memory of the events in the courtroom came back to me and I jumped to my feet, looking around. We were indeed in the same room, except the blood and bodily remains had been cleared away. It was just my teacher and me standing in the courtroom.

"It will not help you to melt into an unconscious state every time you end an existence," he said unemotionally. "You might have impressed upon those demons a sense of power, but if you are truly tested by someone great, you will fail."

Anger prickled into me.

"I don't want to be able to kill without a toll," I snapped. "Even if it is to end someone as wicked as those creatures, it's still wrong to take away their chance of redemption."

"Your humanity is a weakness," The Perceptionist responded. "How many chances do you want to give a soul to become what you think it should become?"

My head was swimming with questions. Was what I had done right? I had barely had a chance to contemplate. I had simply acted in the moment, caught up in the emotion of the events.

"That is your other weakness," said The Perceptionist. "Emotion."

I stopped and looked at him. He was a completely unemotional creature and that made him powerful. But did that make him happy? No, because happiness is an emotion, not a thought. No matter how weak it made me, I would never give up emotion. It was my reason for being, the love I felt for Charlotte. Without it, there was nothing.

The sudden thought of Charlotte made my lips tremble. I would go to any length to save her, to be with her. Was I losing my soul because of her? Or was she my soul to begin with? Yes, she was everything. My purpose was unmoved by what had just happened, in fact it was enhanced. I was now more powerful: a step closer toward being the ruler of Hell.

"We cannot stand in this room forever," The Perceptionist said. "I will learn nothing more from sitting here, and neither will you. It is time we left."

I looked to my elemental companion. This was an omnipotent being, but though he knew all, I wondered if he truly understood it. I shook my head and looked at the roof. A jumble of thoughts cluttered my brain. I had only two days until I had to deliver a sermon atop Mount Belial and I still had no real plan of what to do or say.

"Where should we go?" I asked.

"Forward." He turned to leave the room.

We trudged back along the metal corridor from which we had entered. Winding up along its elliptical path, ideas were racing through my head.

"Do you think what we did back there was just?" I asked.

"There is no such thing as justice," he answered. "Justice is a concept."

"Then do you think what we did was good?"

"The only good is knowledge; the only evil is ignorance," he said firmly. "All life is even. I do not judge, I observe. In this case what I witnessed, in terms of elemental activity, offended me. There was a set of brilliant lights being stifled by darker ones. There was no learning, nothing new; just selfish acts. I only wish to see beauty and that was not beautiful so I finished it."

He said it with no emotion, no passion. I didn't know what to say. What was next? I had acted upon impulse and sent demons into the world with a message. I had set a path and The Perceptionist had aided me, had even pushed me. Was this his plan all along?

"My only plan was to teach," he said. "I made a promise to you to teach you the elements and I have. I only interfered as much I as have to enhance your learning. This is all. I do not normally step into the world of beings, but I have for you. You should be grateful. A favorable path has been set in motion for you. Now there is a choice: to follow, or to resist. To follow is to save Charlotte. To resist is to lose her. For you there is no choice."

No choice. I was bound by my path. I was not disturbed by this, but rather comforted. At least I knew my aim. I had to charge toward it. The meaning made me feel confident, however, I was still unsure how to walk the right path.

"What is the difference between beauty and ugliness to you?" I asked The Perceptionist without thinking.

"Unity is beauty," he answered. "Selfishness is ugly. When I see someone acting with wholly selfish intentions, the energies of the elements are offensive to behold. Their light becomes muddy and hard to see. Their luminance is encased within the body, instead of shining and branching out and touching others. Selfless acts are more beautiful to watch because the energy spreads out. It sparkles. When it is truly great, a multitude of beings are connected by one spirit. There is a wonderful glow that surrounds it. When a group moves as one, but with selfish intentions, this glow does not exist; it is nothing but a crowd of sluggish lights moving in the same direction. This makes it easy for one of these bodies to break away when their motives change. They are not caught up in the light of unity. They simply want and so continue within themselves to commit acts that satisfy their own desires, their own greed. This does not bond anything, or teach anything. It spreads ignorance. It is ugly and I do not like to behold ugliness. Right now you are becoming ugly, Michael. The light that shone outward towards Charlotte is dimming. Your intentions are moving away from a loving, selfless action, towards a selfish and petty revenge. Your path to Charlotte is true unity of the souls in Hell behind you."

"But how do I do this?" I asked passionately. "Tell me."

"I cannot tell you," The Perceptionist said. "I have already interfered enough. My only promise was to teach you the elements, and that I have done. You have the power to rule. You are still weak, but you have enough to begin."

The shock of what he was saying made my heart skip a beat. He wasn't going to help me defeat Asmodeus. I had planned on his support. I stopped walking.

"But what am I supposed to do?" I asked.

"The true leader makes those decisions on his own," he said, turning back to me.

"But I need advice," I said, suddenly feeling very lost.

"In this you cannot have my help," The Perceptionist stated flatly. "I have nothing more to learn from this experience. I must return to my own contemplations. However, as my last act as your teacher, I will take you to where you can begin to be influenced by right the person."

"Who?"

"Your pilot friend, Smithy."

14

SMITHY. THE GERIATRIC PILOT who had flown me to Satan's castle during my first day in Hell. He was one of the kindest people I had ever met, and I still couldn't believe such a person deserved to be stuck in this place. My heart warmed as I pictured his smiling, wrinkly face.

Despite wanting to see him, I had no idea how or why Smithy would want to help me defeat Asmodeus.

"Focus on your goal, follow your instinct and the answers will come." The Perceptionist read my thoughts.

"Can I not persuade you to come with me?" I asked.

"No. But at another point in time our paths will cross once more. For now, I will take you where you need to go. Come."

The Perceptionist turned and continued to walk along the rusty path. He stopped at the space where the black waterfall flowed down before us. It ended in a murky pool at our feet, which did not grow with the water that ran into it from above. It simply rippled. The Perceptionist bent down and with his large, eye-covered hand drew a circle in the pool. He repeated the action ten times, and the flow of the waterfall began to reverse. He stepped inside the curtain of water and was raised off the ground toward the ceiling. I followed. The dark water drew me into its heat and pulled me up. I closed my eyes and was transported quickly to Oresteia. I expected music to greet us as my feet solidified onto the podium above; instead there was a deep cry. My eyes snapped open. All around, within the violet waterfall, demons of every kind were crowded. One of the juror demons who had fled the court was pointing at me from amongst the throng.

"There he is: the Soul Destroyer, Michael. He is our new lord!" He turned to the crowd and screamed, "Bow down to our new master, Satan, the one who owns our souls in this evil Hell!"

In silence, everyone in the room got to their knees and threw their arms in the air, bowing toward me.

I stood with my mouth agape, unsure what to do. I looked to The Perceptionist for support. He gazed out to the crowd with his all seeing eyes.

"This is what you wanted," he whispered. "Welcome your newest converts."

I drew air into my lungs. Pulling the correct elements around me, I turned my arms into flames and rippled the air in front of my mouth, to amplify my voice. With my arms extended in the form of a cross, the words boomed throughout the room.

"You are among the first chosen to bear witness to me. Yes, I am your new lord. However, I do not pretend to be divine. I am human like you all once were. I come bearing a hurtful truth. Go forth from this place and tell all who will listen. When the fires of guilt burn two days hence, Clytemnestra will lead you to the anointed place. I will then reveal this truth to you. Now make way!"

I stretched hands out before me and sent flames burning into the violet waterfall. It evaporated in a hiss of steam. As it disappeared, each waterfall behind it burst into a colorful mist, one by one. I could now see the thousands of demons gathered in the club, all looking at me in wonder. I felt powerful. Seizing the moment, I gathered air around me and floated above their heads toward the exit. They all began to bow and chant as I soared above them.

"Our lord, deliver us. Our lord, deliver us."

I reached the exit and walked out into Hell. The same security guards were still at the door, with a huge line stretching out into the street. They all seemed oblivious to what had just happened inside. I spotted Marlowe standing with the car and continued my stride towards him. He opened the door without saying a word. The Perceptionist got in behind me.

"You have a flare for the theatrical," he said, the sound of laughing birds tweeting around us, "Lord Michael."

I sat there staring ahead into space. What had I just done? I felt like a fraud, declaring myself their ruler. I was nobody. But it was what I had chosen to do and I was committed now. There was no turning back. I hoped I was right. I hoped I was working towards redemption with Charlotte and would not be overrun in the storm which I knew would follow. If The Perceptionist was correct, Smithy would help me somehow. Just one step at a time, I thought to myself.

If only I knew what that next step was.

The car pulled away from the curb and I continued to stare into space. I was numb with the uncertainty that surrounded me. I looked to my teacher. Our time together was running short. Was there anything that I could ask him while I had the chance? All I could do was run the events in the club over and over again in my mind. Had I said the right thing? Would they come? Yes, I thought. I had only performed parlor tricks for them, but they would come, at least to listen to what this false prophet had to say.

I looked outside, to the skyline where Mount Belial stood. I could make out the dark silhouette of Casa Diablo. Behind it, the sky started to boil with light: the Fires of Guilt were coming. I closed my eyes and braced myself for visions of madness. No more mad than what is happening to me now, I thought. The roiling flames hit the car with a thundering whoosh, but the visions did not come with it. I opened my eyes again and looked around. The Perceptionist was sitting next to me peacefully and Marlowe was driving along as normal. I shifted vision and looked down, to see once again the same golden light of rational thought surrounding my heart.

"How do you protect against the visions with the elements of rationality and knowledge?" I asked, looking back to The Perceptionist. "I don't understand why the visions would cease because of it."

He turned to me.

"Look around at the fires," he said. "Tell me what you see."

I searched the inferno surrounding the car. There were red fire elements whipping about it a fury. Laced within them were all of the lights of emotion as well, with fear and hate the most prevalent, brown and black. The rest of the spectrum was there also, with different colors of thought mixed in. It was hard for me to decipher it all.

"I see emotion," I said. "I see memory, decision, regret. What does it mean?"

"They are the ingredients of Guilt," he replied. "Guilt is a powerful emotion, just like hate, anger, love and happiness. Your heart is the seat of all human emotion and where you feel the most intense passions. Pushing these molecules inside you amplifies any doubt that resides within you. The weave of guilt traces back inside your history and plucks out the darkest emotional charges within you. It then multiplies the intensity of lament a million fold, to crush away reason and just leave unadulterated culpability. While these emotions all interact as twins with human thought, the purest form of knowledge and rationality destroys it."

"Why?"

"You can rationalize emotional guilt, because you completely understand why the choices were made. All actions which cause pain can be justified because they were the actions of an emotional being that did not understand everything. Once you truly comprehend why decisions were made or not made, there is no regret, there is just understanding. You know that things cannot be changed. You know that all is even and equal in the universe, that action and reaction is the way of seeking balance. Everything finds equilibrium in the end. Good and evil do not exist; there is just knowledge and ignorance. Pure knowledge negates emotion. By surrounding your heart with this element, you don't have to make the reasoning yourself, it repels it automatically."

I didn't understand. However, I don't think I really wanted to. The Perceptionist sighed next to me.

"If I could feel the emotion of loneliness, this would be the time to experience it," he said. "One day you may understand and we will be united. For now, accept the protection as my parting gift. Many of Asmodeus' old minions still retain the gift he gave them. It is only fitting that you are equal in that."

That explained why the demon jurors of the Tenth Circle had the same golden light about their hearts. How many others were not ruled by a forced sense of morality? I hoped I was able to control them. As I had the thought, a burning feeling welled in my ears. I reached up and felt them. They had grown larger, and the point was more refined. I was glad my longer hair covered them. But why had they changed?

The slowing of our vehicle interrupted my contemplation. I looked outside. We were at Kingsford Aviation: the home of my dear friend, Smithy.

15

MARLOWE STOPPED THE CAR in front of Smithy's rickety office. The scrap metal of decrepit planes was littered about the site around us. The figure of Smithy appeared on the porch ahead. He was holding a large, double-barrelled shotgun almost as big as he was.

"Who are you and what do you want?" the old man shouted, without even a hint of fear is his voice.

I realized that we'd just arrived in an all black vehicle with tinted windows, unannounced. I wound down the glass and poked my head out, with as big a smile as I could muster.

"Smithy!" I yelled. "Is that anyway to welcome a fellow soldier who helped you do battle with Moloch?" He squinted toward me, lowering his shotgun.

"Michael?" he ventured.

"I'm sorry I didn't call ahead. I've been a bit caught up with some trouble. Do you have time for a cup of tea?"

"Michael!" He launched off the porch and half hobbled, half ran to meet me. I opened the door and got out. I put my hand out to shake his, but he pushed it away and gathered me in a big bear hug, clapping me on the back heartily.

"How have you been, old boy?" He laughed. "You look well, you look really well. Don't worry about calling ahead, friends are always welcome here!" He stopped and looked at me. "You've grown your hair, mate," he said. "I'm not sure about it; you look like a bit of a hooligan. But that's alright, that's okay. How have you been?"

"I've been, ah, well, maybe it's better we talk inside," I

replied. I rapped on the front window of the Jaguar and with a low buzz it opened.

"This is my friend Marlowe," I said.

Smithy stuck his hand inside the car.

"Pleased to meet you, my Nubian friend. I'm Smithy," he said, shaking Marlowe's hand.

He looked behind Marlowe into the back seat where The Perceptionist was sitting. Smithy jumped back slightly, startled by the multi-eyed elemental's appearance.

"Oh, sorry," he said. "I've never seen the likes of you around before. What are you?"

The Perceptionist turned toward Smithy. "I am seeking perfection," he answered.

Smithy looked from The Perceptionist, to me, then back again.

"Well, mate," he said. "I'm sorry to say you're looking in a hell of a place for that. There's nothing but flawed old men and rusty planes here. I can show you my helicopter if you like, though. It's quite nice."

"It's okay," I said in Smithy's ear. "They're just dropping me off."

"Oh," he said, a little disappointed. "Alright then, nice to meet you both. Anyone associated with Michael is fine with me. I'm sorry I pointed my gun at your beautiful car. You're welcome back any time you like."

Marlowe looked at Smithy and smiled.

"Thank you, Mr Smith. I hope to see you another time. You too, Michael." With that he wound up the window and rolled away. I waved as they pulled out of the airfield, wondering if I ever would truly cross paths with them again.

I turned to Smithy. "Shall we?" I asked, pointing toward his office.

"Do you take milk and sugar?" he asked.

We entered his office. It was decorated with old war memorabilia, flags and photos of vintage aircraft. Smithy led me around behind his desk and into the back room. It was a cozy space, with two soft seats and a coffee table arranged in the middle. He walked over to a stove in the corner and clicked it on, putting a black, cast-iron kettle on the flames to heat.

"You'd think water would come ready boiled in Hell wouldn't you?" He winked at me, arranging two cups as I took a seat. "So how have you really been, Michael? Last time we parted you were on a mission that involved that father of lies, Asmodeus. I hope you managed to stay out of his sticky web?"

His directness caught me a little off-guard. Unsure what to say, I looked around the room. He stood there, waiting for me to answer. The silence hung in the room, pushing me to fill it with something.

"Not quite," I finally said. "The trouble I mentioned earlier is partly to do with him. But I think it's better if I start from the beginning."

He raised his bushy white eyebrows.

"Sounds like this should be quite a yarn! Is this a two or a three biscuit story?" he asked, rattling a jar of shortbreads.

His jovial tone dimmed the nervous edge of what I was about to tell him. If I was going to preach about truth to demons, I would need to start by hiding nothing from those I called friends. I would tell him everything.

"Better bring the whole jar," I said.

16

I'D SPOKEN FOR CLOSE TO FOUR HOURS straight by the time I finished. Smithy had not interrupted once. He did not judge. He did not offer opinion. He listened and occasionally made a fresh cup of tea. Once we'd arrived at the present point he sat back in his chair and exhaled loudly, staring into space.

"You know," he said after a few moments of silence, "I've done some horrible things in my life. You may not know it to look at me, but I was an evil man and I deserve to be here."

I started to interrupt but he held his hand up to silence me. "Nothing you have done is worse, so I cannot condemn you. In fact I commend your honesty. I will follow you, Michael. I'll fight with you into the depths of Hell if it means you will get your love back. We all have something to gain by the destruction of Asmodeus. But you need to promise me something."

I looked at him openly, tears almost brimming in my eyes at his blind acceptance of my faults and ills.

"Name it."

He started to say something, but a roaring gush of heat rushed into the room. The Fires of Guilt were upon us.

I watched helplessly as Smithy collapsed back into his chair and started lurching in agony. I knew the golden light of rationality protected me from the torment, but my friend was wailing and crying before me. He was screaming incomprehensible apologies. I decided to do something about it. If I could be free of these visions, then so could Smithy. Gathering as many golden lights of knowledge around my palm as I could, I thrust my hand into his chest, protecting his heart. Without warning, I was blown clear of his body and the world caved in about me.

***

* * *

"We're at an altitude of ten thousand feet and climbing," I said, turning the dials and adjusting the controls in front of me. "Are you okay back there?"

My crew all voiced in the affirmative.

"A-OK, Captain Smithy," the rear-gunner, Allan replied last. He was a green one, baby faced and fresh out of the academy. He was the only soldier on board I hadn't flown with yet. There was no way he was eighteen. But then, I'd lied about my age when I had first joined up in World War I. That was a long time ago and many battles had been fought and won for freedom since then. Today would be no different. Our target was Hamburg. As part of Operation Gomorrah we'd been pummelling the city relentlessly for the best part of a week. We were cleansing the evil Nazi regime from an unjust land. If the people of Germany wanted to support a monster like Hitler, then they deserved the end that our bombs delivered. This would be our final run to rain fire on the Nazis' heads. The young sprite in the back would be fine with me at the deck. The belly of our four-engine Halifax was packed full of incendiary bombs, designed to burn rather than explode.

With the engines purring smoothly around us, we levelled out at twenty thousand feet. My navigator, Jack, tracked our course to the city. He was a brute of a man, crass and hot tempered, but he was one hell of a navigator. It wasn't like we needed him tonight though. There were almost six hundred bombers in formation ahead, leading the way. They spread toward the horizon and out of sight. We trailed in their jet stream, with another hundred or more planes behind. Even in the dark of night it was easy to see. A full moon hovered like a silver balloon above the clouds at our feet.

The half hour flight went by in what felt like a few heartbeats. As we approached from the north-east, we increased our speed. The other planes far ahead had already begun to dart downward. The hum of our engines turned to a roar as we surged ahead. My heart started to beat faster. Just like that, it was time for battle.

We burst down through the clouds. I could see pillars of smoke rising up from the burning debris that was once one of the proudest cities in Germany. The metropolis was a sea of flames. A line of fire crept backward in a widening v from the initial target in the center of the city. Bombers swept down, dropping their load of death before pulling up again. I could hear the rattle of Browning machine guns echoing up to us. Sparks of light flew from some planes as they shot more lead down to the ground. Against the burning red of the city, I could easily make out a handful of German Nightfighter jets below. Their odd-shaped, scaffold nose was easy to distinguish from those of our planes. They were engaged with a large group of Stirling Bombers. I swept to the side to avoid the fracas. The boys would handle them.

"Keep a close watch at the tail, Allan," I said loudly through the mic. "Those Nightfighters always attack from below and behind. They try to creep up on you like the spiders they are."

The whooshing sound of fire, dropping bombs and clattering guns reverberated all around. I kept altitude as German flak started to explode just below. We were now in the thick of the black smoke, which carried up the stink of burning human flesh. I set focus to find an untouched target. There! Just past the fires.

"Gunners, ready!" I yelled.

"Ready," I heard.

"Bombs ready!"

"Ready!"

"Let's wipe out these Nazi swine!" Jack spat next to me.

I pushed forward fast. We wound up to top speed, almost three hundred miles an hour. The city blurred below as I headed toward an untouched area, just past the boundary of the fires.

I narrowed my eyes to see through the thickening smoke. The heat of the inferno below warmed the metal cabin of the plane, so that sweat was dropping off my nose. I could see a clean building up ahead. That would be ours. Suddenly, from above, a deep thud sounded. With a crack, the controls were wrenched from my hands and we dropped down.

"Shells!" Jack screamed next to me. "What did you do? We're hit!"

I grabbed at the flailing joystick in front of me, and hauled it up. There was little effect. Our rapid descent threw me back against my jump seat. Smoke began to billow inside the cabin.

"Parachutes on!" I yelled, wrestling for control of the Halifax. "Jump! Jump!"

Straining my arms, I levelled the plane just enough. Jack unbuckled himself next to me.

"Go!" I yelled. "Go!" His thick-chested body moved out of sight behind me. The ground was approaching at terminal velocity.

"I'm stuck! The turret's jammed!" I heard a voice in my headphones. It was Allan's panic-stricken voice. I couldn't answer. All I could do was try to slow our descent. I clenched the controls tighter and did my best to save us.

I tried to pull up. We kept dropping. With the nose up and tail dragging, we careened downward. I tried all I could to slow us but the ground raced up to meet us. A split second before the bone-jarring impact, I wrenched back on the controls. Our tail hit first, smacking into a heaped pile of charred bricks. The force of the impact whipped the nose of the plane down, tearing the fuselage in two. I heard Allan screaming through my headphones. The back of the plane came whirling past the front, whacking the side of the cockpit hard as it went. Strapped tightly in my seat, I was spun around. Smoke, fire and metal whirled in my vision. My legs and arms rag-dolled, my head whiplashed. The side of my helmet cracked into something, the noise screeching into my ears. For a moment things went black, but I refused to go under. I blinked and held onto consciousness.

Abruptly, everything rattled to a halt.

The thump of bombs dropping around the city still sounded in the distance. After the terrifying noise of the crash, it sounded like a faint heartbeat. My ears were ringing. I reached up to my face. My nose was bleeding slightly. I looked down. My legs were fine. My body was whole. I had a deep gash in the top of my right hand, but that was all. It was a miracle I was alive. I should be in pieces! I was sitting in what was once my cockpit. The roof was caved in to just a few inches above my head. The windows had been blown out, and shards of glass lay scattered all around me.

Ahead, through the crumpled windows I could see the wreckage of the back half of the plane. Red gore dripped from within what was left of the twisted cabin. There wasn't even a whole body left of my crewmen. I hoped some had gotten out. I wanted to vomit. I wanted to cry. Instead I fumbled with shaking hands and unclasped myself from the pilot's seat.

Wriggling forward carefully, I squeezed out through the gap in front of me. Slowly I clambered to the ground. My boots crunched down on uneven rubble.

There was relative silence around me. My brain felt numb. The world seemed dull, like it was coming to me through a plastic filter. I looked up to the skies. The clouds were illuminated with the red fires from the city. Hundreds of British bombers roared overhead. I could see German Wilde Sau fighters swooping down from above them. They normally attacked from below! That was why we were taken so off guard. I tried to shake the shock from my system. I needed to think. Where was I going to go? What was my next move?

I limped over to the back end of the plane to search for survivors. All I could see was blood. Almost gagging, I climbed back toward the tail turret where Allan was stationed. As I neared I could see his face, clear of dirt.

"Allan," I said in a hoarse whisper. "Are you alright?" I moved closer. There was no life in his face. Allan's dead eyes looked to me with terror. He was just a kid. I reached out and pushed his eyelids down. I would have said a prayer, but it didn't seem that God was anywhere near us. I looked at his face. In the sleep of death, he looked even younger. There is no justice in this world, I thought.

I heard a dragging noise from outside of the plane. I whirled around and peered out. My bleeding right hand dropped instinctively to my hip, where my standard-issue revolver was. My grip on its handle loosened once I saw the source of the noise. It was a young blonde girl, maybe twelve years of age. She struggled to drag the body of a limp woman through the destruction. She had the woman by the armpits and was pulling her slowly over the burnt ground.

I stepped out of the plane into sight.

She looked up at me with glassy eyes. "Bitte helfen," she said in German. "Please help."

Mentally I knew this was the enemy, but instinctively I saw two flesh and blood humans in trouble. I scrambled down to where she was. I knelt down and took the woman from the girl's hands, laying her on the ground.

From the smell and look of the woman's body, it was clear to me that she was dead. I looked back up to the girl who was squatting at the woman's head, stroking her hair.

"I'm sorry," I managed in broken German. "Dead."

Her bottom lip started to quiver and her eyes dropped down, back to the woman who was probably her mother. I reached out to the girl and pulled her into my chest, hugging her. She started to cry into me. I just held her, looking around dumbly at the chaos our planes had caused. The little girl shook in my arms, until finally her crying subsided. She then pushed herself back away and stood up. She pulled a handkerchief out of her grubby dress and went to wipe her face, but before she did she looked down at my hand.

"Wehtun," she said, pointing at it.

The blood from the gash was dripping off my fingertips onto the ground. The girl quickly took the handkerchief in her hand and wrapped it over the wound, holding it tightly. I smiled at her.

As she smiled back, there was a gunshot to the side of us. Blood misted into the air. The girl's smile turned to a look of shock. She looked down at her side, where a bloody wound seeped. All color drained from her face and she collapsed into my arms. I held her, looking into her ashen face, which was covered in soot. I shook her, fumbling to cover the wound in her side. The blood flooded around my fingers.

"Little girl. Little girl," I said pathetically.

I was unable to say her name. I didn't know what it was. She looked up at me questioningly. With one last bubbling gasp she closed her eyes, dead.

In a daze I looked over to where the gunshot had sounded. My navigator, Jack stood there with a smoking pistol in his hands. He smiled at me gruesomely.

"One less Nazi swine in the world."

I looked back down to the girl. She wasn't a Nazi, she was a child caught up in an old man's war. Numbness enveloped my body. Was this what we had become? Child killers?

I stood up slowly. Letting the girl's body fall, I faced Jack. I couldn't say anything. I couldn't call my body to action. I just stood there, staring at him mutely.

"Smithy!" Jack said, his voice coming at me from far away. "Are you alright, man? That crash must have rattled your brain. We've got to get out of here. We're in enemy territory. It's kill or be killed. We have to go!"

I stayed where I was and looked back down at the girl's body, which had fallen on top of her mother's. I watched as blood flowed out of her body and made the black ground even darker. The blood started to seep toward me, the puddle of it touching the toes of my boots.

I felt a tug at my arm. It was Jack. "We've got to go, Captain!" he said. "None of the others got out. It's just us. We'll head back to the edge of the fires and follow the creep-back line out of the city. Come on!"

He pulled me again and my feet clumsily moved, one over the other. I hazily followed him, past the wreckage of our plane, over a mound of broken bricks and into a long, deserted street. Down the far end, I could see the blaze of fire burning brightly. We crept towards it together, hugging the shadows of buildings to the side of the street, walking towards hell on earth.

As we approached the carnage, I could see people frantically moving in and out of what was left of the buildings. They scurried through the inferno, carrying possessions or bodies. Men ran with buckets of water, trying to quench the flames in vain. They were yelling in German. I couldn't understand their words. Jack pushed me into a dark crevice in the wall to avoid being seen. We watched as a team of men passed buckets to each other, dousing the buildings so that the fires wouldn't spread. One man, covered in ash, threw a large spray of water onto what appeared to be a pile of mud in front of him. As the steam hissed I could smell the stench of burning hair and skin. It wasn't mud. It was people. The fog in my brain began to lift, seeing clearly all of the horrors around me. Women ran from the flames, trying to group their families together through the roaring fire. Some ran past our hiding place bundling children away from the terror zone. One crying woman who passed at a quick walk was talking to a bundle in her arms, seemingly reassuring it. I glanced as she hurried by, only to see she was holding the body of her dead baby.

I almost gasped, but stopped myself lest we be discovered. I have been a fool, I thought. I had sat, up in my plane and dropped bombs on these people who I knew nothing about. I'd been separated by the distance of air into believing what I was doing was right. I'd believed I was holding up an ideal of freedom. Now I saw the reality, right in front of me. I knew in my heart we'd been terribly mistaken. This wasn't an evil race; they were men and women just like us, with families and lovers. I saw no soldiers, only men trying to save their homes. The only oppression I saw was the oppression of our attack. How many others were there like this? Every mission I had flown over the years would have caused the same devastation.

"Smithy," Jack whispered beside me. "We need to make a break for it across the street. I'll cover us. On three."

He pulled out his gun. As a family of three approached, he swept out and shot. A young boy dropped dead to the ground. His father spun to look at Jack. Jack blasted him in the face. The woman screamed and Jack grabbed her, wrapping his arm around her neck, using her as a shield. The gunshots brought the attention of the men fighting the fires. They dropped their buckets clanging to the ground and rushed towards Jack, who was now in the middle of the street, holding the struggling woman with a gun to her head. The men running at him stopped as they saw he had a hostage. One of them pulled out a pistol and Jack shot at him. The man crumpled, as the rest of the men watched in impotence.

"Smithy!" Jack yelled. "Get your sorry ass across the street!"

I pulled my gun out and exited the nook in the wall. The men saw me and backed up more, toward the flames.

"That's right!" Jack screamed at them, with bloodlust in his eyes. "We'll kill you all." He pulled the trigger, and with a bang, the woman in his arms dropped dead at his feet. He opened fire on the group of unarmed men, who scattered. I raised my gun and shot as well, but not at them.

Jack fell to the ground.

I walked over calmly towards him. I looked to his stomach where I had shot him. He was clutching his gut, trying to hold his gizzards inside. He looked up at me.

"Traitor!" he spat. "You'll burn in Hell for this."

"Then I'll see you there," I said and shot him dead.

I looked around at nothing but destruction. The sea of flames welled up and consumed the city. There were no more people around me, only corpses. My body started to grow numb again. No ideal was worth this kind of suffering. For my whole adult life I had been a good soldier, a faithful one. I had not questioned our actions and for that I was as much at fault as the ones who gave the orders. We had killed women, children, and civilians. I had killed them.

Where was these people's freedom? The only freedom we had delivered was freedom of death, and that hadn't been their choice. However it would be mine. I took the gun in my bloody right hand, pressed it against my temple and pulled the trigger.

*****

Heat. Burning. Paralyzed. I was a plagued tree of torment in the forest of lost souls. Unable to do anything but reflect on the hideous actions which had bought me here, I was frozen in gnarled sorrow. As much as I philosophized and reasoned, the same conclusion scorched inside me: I was responsible for my actions. My choice was to kill. Even though I had believed in the reasoning of my leaders' that the pursuit of freedom was just, there was no justice in ending the lives of those who had no choice. Killing soldiers who fought to aid oppression I could justify, but there is no collateral damage of the innocent that can be reasoned away as acceptable.

A kind voice wafted into my chaotic thoughts, diminishing the dying calls of the souls I had murdered.

"Would you like to be free of your prison, and work towards redemption?" the spirit asked.

"I would do anything to gain true atonement for what I've done."

"Then follow me," he said. "I will help you reconcile the evils you committed in life. My name is Asmodeus; I am the only true redeemer in this Hell."

A silver light enveloped my soul. I was free to move once more.

*****

I opened my eyes to see Smithy looking down at me, concerned.

"I didn't think you had to endure the visions any longer," he said.

I sat up slowly, blinking my eyes and shaking the grogginess from my brain. My intention of shielding him had gone badly awry. Instead I had peered unwelcomed into his innermost secrets. I felt like I had violated a sacred trust.

"I do not," I answered solemnly. "I didn't lie to you, but I have just made a terrible mistake, which I hope you can forgive me."

He looked around the room.

"Everything seems okay in here," he said. "Did you break a teacup or something?"

"No," I answered, crawling up into the chair close to me, still shaking from the intensity of the sorrows I'd just experienced.

"I tried to shield you from The Guilt," I stammered. "I reached inside to protect you, but I was drawn into you instead. I now understand your pain Smithy. I witnessed firsthand your actions and your regrets. I'm sorry."

He looked at me with wide eyes, which quickly seeped clear tears.

"Oh no," he said. Sobs started to wrack his body. He flopped down onto the floor shuddering in tears. "I'm sorry, I'm sorry," was all he could say.

I bent down and gently hugged him.

"It's alright," I said soothingly. "You've done wrong, but you are remorseful. It doesn't make anything right, but I forgive you, Smithy, even though I know you cannot forgive yourself. I see good inside you."

His sobs continued.

"I'm a monster. I took what wasn't mine to take. I'm a monster. I'm sorry."

"I forgive you," I repeated.

Finally his tears died down. I continued to hold him in my arms. He felt so small and frail, yet I could feel the strength of his life inside him.

"You're still my friend, Smithy. I understand. I'm sorry I intruded on your thoughts. I didn't mean it. Will you forgive me?"

He pushed lightly away from me.

"Why would you do such a thing?" he asked, not loudly but forcefully.

"It was an accident. I didn't mean to read your thoughts."

"That's not what I meant," he said, rubbing the streaked tears from his face and standing up. "Why would you try to stop me from feeling the guilt? I deserve it! You have no right to make that choice for me."

I was taken aback.

"I didn't think."

"No, you didn't think." His usual genial face had turned into that of a furious man. "You're just like Asmodeus. You just presume that I don't want to repent for my actions. You say you forgive me, you say that you don't want to see me in pain, but you're not the one I seek forgiveness from. The women and children I burned alive, they are the ones who I should ask forgiveness from. There is no proxy sin-taker for murder, not you, not Asmodeus, not Jesus. I accept my responsibility. I will live with it for eternity. I am guilty, so I feel that way. It is my rightful duty, and you will not take that away from me."

I sat in silence. I had completely misunderstood. I had offered forgiveness, but it was not mine to give. I was the one who had done

64

wrong. He was not sorry I'd seen what he had done, he was sorry for the acts he had committed, wholly and unreservedly. If only I had half the honor of the man before me then I would be a great man.

I stood up, looking Smithy in his burning eyes.

"I am sorry," I said. "I mean that. It is all I can offer, but it is the truth. You're right. There should be no forgiveness unless it comes from those to whom you have done harm. I have done you harm. Can you forgive me?" I asked.

His eyes softened.

"Of course," he said. "You are as human as the rest of us, Michael. That is what I love about you."

"How can I be a great leader?" I asked. "How can I do what is right?"

"The greatest leaders I ever followed as a soldier were the reluctant ones," he answered. "They were the ones who served the people because they were asked, not because they had an ambition to rule them. They are the leaders who fight for an ideal, even if they think it may not be achievable."

"You were about to ask that I promise you something, before the visions," I said. "What was it?"

"It was this," he said. "If the time comes where you have to make a choice between yourself and the people, choose the people."

"I will," I said solemnly. "Now, can I ask you something?"

"Of course."

"Can you promise to be my moral compass? Can you promise that if I stray off the track of good that you'll speak up? I need an honest friend, not a follower."

"You have my word," he replied with gravity. "Is there anything else?"

"Yes," I said. "Will, you fly me up to Mount Belial, one last time?"

17

THE BLADES OF THE HELICOPTER HUMMED above our heads as we took off from Smithy's airfield. His office fell away to a pinprick. The savage jungle of Hell spread out below. Roiling clouds sparked lightning just above us. The city in the middle of the landscape reached up like concrete fingers, wanting to pull us down into its grey fist. One building stood out more than the rest. It was where I hoped Clytemnestra would be now, gathering all the demons and souls in this domain, to make their pilgrimage and hear the truth about Asmodeus. They will come, I thought. The mountains and lakes surrounding the landscape encased the city on both sides. Far behind stretched a desert of black sand, with its endless dunes and valleys flowing into the distance. In between the desert and the city was Mount Belial. A molten river bled down its side to run through the center of the city then forked to form an island in the center, dividing the suburb of Smoking Gun from the rest of the districts.

"Is Moloch still lurking in her territory around the mountain?" I asked Smithy, remembering our first harrowing trip to the peak where Casa Diablo sat.

"No-one has spotted her in over a year," he replied. "Not long after we met the dragon, she flew up into the clouds, never to come down again."

Relief washed over me. I didn't want to have to expend too much energy until my sermon. Even with The Perceptionist's injection of vigor into my body, my head was still aching from my efforts in The Tenth Circle.

Buzzing forward unhindered, we didn't take too long to see Satan's old abode appear on its mountainous perch. The building was dark, no lights coming from within.

We floated down smoothly to land on the same cleared space as our first visit, but this time no one came to greet us. Smithy switched off the engine of the helicopter; we sat in silence amid the large green field as the blades whirred to a halt.

"What now?" he asked.

"I was hoping you'd know." I looked at him.

"You're supposed to be the leader. Why did you want to come here?"

"Because it's a bastion of power," I explained. "It is the one place no one in Hell would dare to come unless summoned, or felt it was their right. I see I wasn't wrong. This place is deserted."

I looked up to the building. The warped spires and jagged ramparts were indeed absent of any signs of life.

"Maybe we should go inside?" I ventured, realizing that I'd have to take possession of the citadel if I was to show that I was the ruler of Hell I was claiming to be.

Smithy blinked slowly and turned to look at the castle before us. "After you."

I jumped down from our aircraft onto soft grass. Moving toward the castle I could hear Smithy just behind me. We walked forward in silence. A large set of open steps led up to the main entry. Beside each of the carved oak doors were granite gargoyles. It was just how I remembered it, except this time the gargoyles remained in their stony silence. I leaned in to push the doors open. They didn't budge.

"Maybe you should knock," Smithy ventured behind me. "It would seem polite."

I wrapped my knuckles against the hard wood. Nothing. I looked from side to side. I couldn't see any levers or locks that would help me open the doors. It was time to try another approach.

"Step back," I told Smithy.

He practically ran halfway down the stairs as I walked back a few paces. I steadied myself and began to pull a gale of wind elements in front of me. Whipping them together into tornado force, I pitched them into the door. The hurricane belted into the wood like an invisible fist. A terrible smacking noise erupted as the wind hit, but the doors didn't move an inch.

I stopped. I hadn't wanted to use fire, since I needed the place intact, but I was left with little choice. Reluctantly I brewed red about my person. I heard Smithy gasp in wonder behind me, but ignored it. Shooting the fire ahead, I braced myself for the explosion I thought would follow. However, instead of a crackling of wood, there was no noise. The blaze simply glanced upward into the air, like a fan of light. I cut my efforts short.

"You've learned some great things," Smithy said, panting behind me as he re-climbed the stairs."

"Apparently not great enough."

I studied the door, from base to tip. This was clearly not just oak. I peered into its molecular makeup and was surprised to see the form of myself looking back. It was as if someone had placed a mirror over the surface of the entire building. Impossible! I thought inwardly.

"Maybe we'd better search for another entrance," I said outwardly. "You look over to the right. I'll search this way."

Without another word I started to follow the outward wall of Casa Diablo, looking for something. Anything. It was no use looking in the view of the elements. All I saw was the same mirror effect as before.

I searched with normal sight. It was an incredible building: there were modern twists to its overall gothic construction, like swimming pools encased within golden barred gates, and tennis courts rimmed by a spider-web of hedge work. Nowhere I looked, though, could I see a way into the building itself. The windows were shuttered in, the doors bolted. I came around to the back of the building, where there was an overgrown garden. There were statues scattered about with moss growing over them; rose bushes grew in huge tangled messes of thorns and flowers; white column fountains sat dry beside each statue, as dead as the figures next to them. I walked past each effigy. The figures were vile. Demons scowled outward from inanimate rock, baring teeth and looking at me with unknowing eyes. Some of the sculptures were only half finished, so the bodies looked like they were chipping themselves of the stone that encased them.

I came to a statue I thought I recognized. It had rams' horns winding out of its round head, with lines around them at half- inch intervals. There was a cement tuft of hair sticking straight up between the horns. The dead eyes of the statue had three tiny pupils carved in the middle of them. I leaned back to study it. Where had I seen this statue before? The figure was standing on a square podium of rock, from which under the moss, half an inscription emerged. I wiped the green slime away to see what it said. It wasn't in a language I knew. It looked like Latin. Slowly I tried to read the words out loud.

"Cedo Cessi Cessum Libertas Azazel Cedo Cessi Cessum Licentia."

As I spoke the final words, the statue began to shake. The whole garden started to breathe, puffing air in and out. Weeds retracted beneath my feet back into the ground. Flowers bloomed from the bushes beside me. With a roaring hiss, water spurted from the fountains around the garden, showering moisture over the stone statues. The white of the figure before me started to turn red, forming a crumbling crust about it. Suddenly the statue detonated in an explosion of bloody mortar. I was thrown down onto the ground, but scrambled to my feet quickly to see a demon emerge from the haze in front of me.

"Welcome to your new home, Master Michael. We're glad you have finally come."

I looked up at Satan's old manservant, Azazel. I knew I had recognized the statue! He had been living last time I had seen him. Azazel had been the demon that had met us at the helicopter upon my first visit to Casa Diablo. He watched me unthreateningly as I brushed dust from myself.

"Asmodeus said you would come to claim your castle," Azazel declared. "I have spent a year in stone, awaiting your arrival. I'm pleased to be able to serve you as I served him."

I eyed him suspiciously. Anyone who had worked for Asmodeus for so long was bound to have some allegiances still held within. That is, if he was treated kindly.

"Do you still serve Asmodeus?" I asked, not really expecting a truthful answer.

"I never really served that devil," he said humorlessly. "And even if I do call you master, it is, in truth, this house I serve. I am tied to it. It hurts me that it has been disused. It's meant to be lived in! Now if it should please you, I'd like to set about maintaining her."

He went to walk past me, but I called for him to stop.

"You will have all you need to re-establish this place to its rightful glory," I said, hoping that by using his obvious passion for the grounds, he would help me in return.

"But?" he said, freezing in his tracks.

"First you must show me inside. I need to prepare for a gathering tomorrow: I will need a large office space with two bedrooms adjoining it. I am planning a sermon to the inmates of Hell, to inform them of my rule."

"You'll need the war-rooms then," he replied, continuing his walk.

As he made his way through the overgrown garden, he tapped the feet of statues he passed. Upon his touch they came to life, morphing from antique bleached rock into colorful animation.

"Trim, weed, sculpt, hoe, rake," he yelled.

The garden burst alive with movement as the statues became real demons, jumping out of their rocky confines to run about fulfilling Azazel's orders. Garden tools appeared from nowhere in their hands and they began manicuring the plants adjacent to them. Azazel continued his march toward the castle, while I followed. When each of his steps fell onto the ground, pulses of blue light rippled out toward the castle. As the light touched the walls, gates opened, shutters rolled up and water burst from fountains to fill sparkling pools. The deadness of Casa Diablo immediately fell away to reveal a lively splendor. Azazel walked faster and it almost seemed he grew taller. He bounded up the steps and nearly collided with a running Smithy, who had rounded the corner, looking up at the building in fright.

"It's alive!" Smithy yelled to me, as he sidestepped Azazel. Then turning back to look at the demon, "Where did he come from?"

"I found him in the garden," I answered. "It seems he is Casa Diablo's keeper."

"Oh, I remember him now!" Smithy said. "Old Rammy, I used to call him on account of his horns. He is nice enough, if a little stuck up."

I smiled at the old man's frankness.

"Let's go," I said. "He's going to show us to our new home."

"Our new home?" Smithy muttered. "What's wrong with the airfield?"

"Nothing," I answered, as I started up the steps to the quickly disappearing Azazel. "It's only temporary. Until we know what we're doing."

By the time we had reached the oak doors, they were wide open. The gargoyles had disappeared and Azazel was standing in the foyer of the building, waiting for us.

"Now," he said. "Until I can get this palace up to standard, I suggest you keep to four rooms. This foyer is one."

He turned and strode across the space toward large black doors, which sat in the middle of a staircase that wound down both sides from above. The door had carvings of a mighty battle on it, with dead struggling bodies below and fiery angels flying above them. Above the door was a sword and hammer crossed together.

"These are the war-rooms," said Azazel, throwing the black door open.

Inside was a large conference room. A long rectangular metal table stretched from end to end with six plain, wooden chairs arranged on each side of the table. A throne perched at the head; it was gold, with red cushions and a white canopy that hung from four serpentine support beams. There was a door at each end of the room.

"Inside each of those doors is a private bedroom," he said. "One has beds to accommodate twelve people. The other is for one which, I assume, will be yours, Lord Michael. Each will be cleaned within the hour. If you would like to sit here and talk I can have some food prepared."

"No food," I replied. "Please go about your work and take any liberties you think necessary with the house. If I need anything I'll call. Tomorrow we host a large gathering. I'll need to consult you on some things later."

"Very good." Azazel left Smithy and I alone in the room. "Let us prepare for war, then," I said to Smithy, taking one of the plain wooden chairs closest to me.

18

SMITHY DID NOT SIT.

"War?" he asked. "I'm sorry, Michael. When I told you I would follow you to get your love back, I had no intention of fighting an immediate war."

"What?" I asked, baffled. "You said we could all gain something from destroying Asmodeus."

"And I spoke the truth. But you will not gain the support of the people by rushing headlong into a bloody battle that is likely to destroy most, if not all of us," Smithy told me. "You must first work for the people. You must unite them somehow."

"But what about Charlotte?" I asked. She was the reason I was striving ahead. I could not and would not abandon her, no matter what the consequences.

"Charlotte is our priority," agreed Smithy. "And I promise that our first mission will be to find a way to get her back. However, your first act must be to quell the sense of unrest that is out there. You told me you've declared in public that Asmodeus no longer rules. If you don't give those demons a good reason to follow you, there will be chaos. They followed Asmodeus because he promised them a ticket to Heaven. Are you going to promise the same false hope? I personally have only seen a handful of souls pass over to the realm of light in my time here. You must help the people. In doing so, you may help yourself."

"Then what do I do?" I asked. "What do I say to them?"

"I do not know," admitted Smithy. "I'm just an old soldier. It is a riddle to me how to lead."

"A riddle?" I repeated. "Then we must solve the riddle. How can we calm the people of Hell, have them wanting to prepare for a war against their enemy and rescue Charlotte all at the same time?"

Smithy just shook his head and stared into space. "It seems impossible. I can't solve a riddle that large."

"We must," I said. "Maybe I need to take a walk."

"Where are we going?" Smithy asked. I was warmed by his willingness to come with me blindly, wherever I wanted.

"You stay here and rest," I told him. "The visions are coming soon. I'm not going anywhere in particular. I just need to think, and I think best on the move."

Smithy looked at his watch.

"You're right," he said, "The Guilt will be here in less than an hour. I'll be here when you get back."

I nodded and left the old man to himself.

I walked back out into the foyer of Casa Diablo. Beautiful paintings hung on the walls all around; the height of renaissance talent was on display in the room. I could easily get used to staring at Rafael, Michelangelo and Caravaggio, but beauty would have to wait for now. The doors of the castle remained open. I walked out onto the steps to see scores of demons, scrubbing, cleaning and polishing everything in view. Azazel had not wasted any time in bringing his joy back. I descended to the lawn and walked straight ahead, along the grass path towards the place I had told Clytemnestra to bring every soul she could muster for my sermon.

The Forest of the Damned encroached on the south end of the grounds of Casa Diablo. Between the fringes of the forest and the castle was nothing but a field of grass, spanning, from east to west, at least a mile across and half that long. The space would be enough to hold over ten million bodies and would look gigantic if any less than that turned up. As I walked across the expanse, I took in my surroundings. I needed to see what they would see. I needed to think like they would think if I was to control them.

To the far left there were the flourishing gardens which led to a wall of hedges. To the right, steam rose up into the air from a hot lake which bubbled endlessly. Below that, lava bled out of a crater in the ground. The constant leak created the river which flowed down to the city.

The trees of the forest came into view ahead, the black trunks reached out with knotted limbs for the sky above. I moved toward them. The green grass beneath my feet began to turn brown, then grey, before leaving only ashen dust for my footprints. The first of the barky trunks of the forest stared back at me as I continued to walk. The closer I got, the more I started to feel an overwhelming sense of sorrow emanating from the forest into me. It was a sadness I could only start to grasp when I thought of losing Charlotte forever. I reached the first tree, close enough to touch it. I leant out and felt the bark. It was sticky with sap. I looked at the tacky substance that was on my fingers. It was a deep blue. I peered at the tree more closely and saw that the sap was dribbling down from above. Following the trailing lines of liquid to just above the first set of branches, I could see distinctly two alive eyes looking down at me, rolling from side to side in anguish. I jumped back startled. Looking closer I could clearly make out a gnarled face of roots and wood. The mouth was open in a silent scream, the nose a bulging knot of ebony. Above the nose were the eyes. They streamed blue tears, which slowly oozed down to the base of the tree. This was once what Smithy had to endure. I had an immense feeling of pity for it.

Shaking my head, I peered down through the forest. There were endless souls trapped here. The wood was so dense in places that no light at all shone through. There must have been over a hundred million suicides, stuck for an eternity, weeping in grief. I spotted a narrow path to my right. A brief feeling of urgency prodded me in its direction. Sucking in a deep breath, I tried to block out the sorrow in the air and focus on my own dilemma: How was I to capture the minds of all the souls in Hell. Would I be able to make them follow me as they had followed Asmodeus at the height of his reign? How could I be even better than him?

Painstakingly, I picked my way through the forest, walking down the narrow pathway and doing my best not to look up at the faces encased in the trunks of the trees. I walked forward, down into the forest.

How could I succeed where Asmodeus had failed? I asked myself. What was the origin of his evil?

I could see a clearing opening up ahead of me. The feeling of need, which had made me take the path, grew stronger still. I squeezed in between two thick trunks to emerge into a wide clearing. Right in the center was a solitary tree, standing alone. It was no taller than the rest of the forest, but was twice as thick and wide. It had twisted branches that reached both up and outward. On each branch hung a swinging noose and tied to the bottom of each noose were rosary beads, swaying without any breeze to blow. At the bottom of each set of beads was a white crucifix of bone. The feeling of sorrow in the forest increased and I was drawn in right next to the evil looking growth. I looked up and the sky flashed. The Fires of Guilt began to shoot over the heavens of Hell and down into the forest. Intense grief washed over me from all around. Although I didn't experience the visions myself, the feelings of melancholy forced me to my knees. I reached out to the tree in front of me to steady myself. As my fingertips touched the trunk, a voice pleaded loudly inside my head.

"Save us! Free Us!"

Startled, I pulled my hands away, but the voice echoed again. "Save us!

Free Us!"

Horrible images of trapped faces trying to push themselves out of the trees erupted into my head. All the sorrow-filled eyes looked at me, begging for me to help them.

I pulled myself to my feet, blocking out the images that kept trying to force themselves into my mind's eye. If I didn't leave, I was sure I would be overwhelmed, sucked into their sorrow never to return. In fear, I fled the clearing. Frantically, I pushed through the black trees, scratching past limbs that cut into me in my haste to be free of the forest. The haunting voice continued to call after me until I ran from the woods and climbed the steps to the safety of Casa Diablo.

Reeling, I sat on the steps. My head sunk into my knees, as I panted and gasped for air. Blood seeped out of the scratches in my face from where the branches had cut me. Finally, I calmed myself as the Fires of Guilt subsided.

I looked back toward the forest. Every soul trapped in there had been failed by its creator. God had deserted them. I promised myself that I would not fail where he had.

A slow movement far below the mountain caught my eye. I stood up, looking down the mountain to the city of Hell below. There seemed to be a moving flow of light exiting the streets and heading for the mountain. It was like a tide of radiance rising towards the base of the foothills.

"What is that?" I wondered aloud.

"It's your pilgrims," Smithy's voice said from behind me.

I looked back up to him. He was staring down into the distance.

"There are an awful lot of them to be able to see the group from here," he said. "I hope you know what you're going to say."

"I do," I answered, following his gaze back down to the mass of flickering lights wandering towards us. "I will tell them the truth."

74

19

THEY CAME FROM WITHIN THE FOREST. Soul upon demonic soul poured onto the great lawn in front of Casa Diablo. Clytemnestra and the five remaining demon jurors of The Tenth Circle were at their head. I stood on the balcony above the stairs while they gathered. Smithy and Azazel stood at my back. It took hours for the multitude to assemble within the space, and still more came. I watched the entire time, as twice The Guilt swept through their pitiful mass. It was a torment just to see that many people in pain. Whether they deserved it or not, for me, was beside the point. Millions upon millions of people gathered, until the grounds were choked with souls and even more flowed down into the Forest of the Damned. Finally, after each of the pilgrims had awoken from their second wave of Guilty Visions, I spoke.

"You are here," I began, amplifying my voice with the elements so all present could hear, "You are here, because you seek the truth. You are here because you have all been deceived for your entire lives into thinking that you may one day redeem your souls and pass to paradise. I am here to tell you, the one who made those promises has misled you. The one that some of you know as Satan, some as Asmodeus, has deserted us. He himself has fled to Heaven."

A murmur of anger rose up from the crowd. I continued. "He cares not for our souls. He cares only for himself. Asmodeus is not who he claimed to be. He was never opposed to God as he said. He is in fact the God you have despised all along. He himself is the creator. His has lied to you and I am here to deliver the reality: that he has created this Hell especially for our pitiful souls because we are not good enough for him."

Another burst of shouting rang from below. I could see some of the heads nodding in agreement, others shouting that I was the one who was the liar. I pressed on.

"God Asmodeus does not want the wretched; he does not want the weak. He does not even want the strong, or wilful. He wants sheep. He wants us to entertain him with our pathetic lives and follow the rules he has designed for us. He says he has given us freewill, but we have no freedom. When we act out of ignorance, he does not show us the way; instead he sends us to Hell! When we act upon the impulses he has given us, he punishes us! Is this the sign of a loving creator?" I bellowed.

Shouts of "No!" came up to greet me.

"No!" I repeated the cries. "He has created us to learn, but to learn slowly. He has given us the chance to disobey his will, but when we do he takes away our other freedoms. Asmodeus has trapped us here against our will!"

"Yes!" "Trapped!"

Voices rose from below.

"I am like you all," I said, feeling the support of the crowded swelling below me. "I am human like many of you were or still are. I am just as much a poor creation as you. I am a fellow child of Asmodeus. I have done evil things. But I am truly sorry for them. I have seen the harm that they have caused me and others. I am now willing to fight for each and every one of you to recognize your own humanity and your own right to live in freedom without fear of being hurt. I believe that inside all of us is the capacity for good without the threat of eternal fire. I believe we can learn to bring equality to this world. We are brothers and sisters and like siblings we will fight together to end this oppression."

A roar of approval went up from the mass before me.

"This fight will not be easy," I continued as the shouts settled down. "It will not be quick. It will be bloody. There are some who think that their right to morality is above all others. At the top of this hierarchy of evil is Asmodeus and it filters down to demons that even live among us. These demons prey on those weaker than them and serve only their own interests. I am here to say that those of unrepentant and unremitting evil will be destroyed by my hand!"

The frenzy below began to boil at my words.

I deliberately lowered my voice, so as not to enflame the gathering into a riot.

"However, my friends, the biggest battle will not be fought against a tangible opposition. It will be a battle fought within ourselves. We must fight within ourselves. It is a war to rise above our evolutionary instinct to kill or be killed. This is an eternal life. We now have that knowledge and, because we know this, we understand that time is with us. We must be patient. Freedom will be ours!

"I ask you now to go back to your daily lives with this knowledge: that from this day forth I will do everything in my power to save you. I will do all I can to free you from the barriers that Asmodeus has built between us. These walls of greed, sin and guilt!"

Another roar of approval rang out from the gathering.

"The largest barrier that divides us all is my ultimate target. These are the walls between Heaven and Hell. Why should we be thrown down here when others are rewarded for servitude? I will find a way to tear these walls down. When I do, we will all be able to live wherever we like in this ethereal existence. There will be space and abundance for all and we will no longer have to fight to survive. We will be able to search for the true ideal of a free and peaceful existence!"

The people and demons below cheered in a frenzy of support. I pressed my advantage.

"To show you I am intent on pursuing this promise, I give you a sign of my power. It is time we freed our brothers who sit trapped upon this very mountain. I'm talking about our fellow tormented souls who suffer in a prison that Asmodeus has created for the most wretched among us; those who would take their own lives."

While my voice echoed above the heads of the audience before me, I looked down to the forest, singling out the one lonely tree in the central clearing. Looking into the elemental structure of the tree I sought what I hoped I would find. The root system of the forest all branched toward that one growth, like veins linking into one heart. Concentrating with all of my skill, I began to uproot the tree. I divided the glowing soul I could see within from the molecular prison of wood and emotion which held it. As I tore the tree from the root system there was an earth shattering reverberation which shuddered through the mountain. The demons who were standing within the forest cowered on the ground, holding their arms over their heads in protection. Radiance sparkled as the atoms of wooden oppression were separated from the souls they encased. As I ripped their souls free, light exploded up into the sky toward the clouds of Hell.

Slowly the dust and wood of the cosmic event settled down. I peered down into the forest to behold my work. Every tree in the forest was now once more a naked human. The demons who had come from the city stood around them, watching in wonder. Each newly released soul slowly got to their knees and looked up the mountain, at the crowd of millions staring down at them. There was one figure amongst the uprooted forest who was unique in his radiance. He stood to full height, red curling hair flowing to touch his shoulders. A yellow and grey bruise around the middle of his neck stood out clearly against his alabaster skin. The power flowing from him was unmistakable. A faint white aura glowed about him. The naked man began to walk up the mountainside, and a sea of people parted before him. He worked his way over the green field and then paused at the bottom of the staircase of Casa Diablo. A circle of space formed wide around him as spectators looked on to see what he would do. Looking up at me, he got down onto both knees, and shouted with a voice that flooded the air around as mine had.

"You have freed my soul, Michael, son of Asmodeus. Just as you will free the rest of those in Hell who seek it. I am Judas Iscariot and I am now your devoted disciple. I am here to bear witness to your greatness and ensure those who oppose you will feel the wrath of my hand."

Judas spread his body out prostrate below me. Everyone around followed suit and began to bow. The effect rippled out in a circle until everyone was on their knees.

"Stop!" I yelled.

Everybody looked up from their worship.

"You will never bow on your knees to any god again! Follow me on your feet with equality in your hearts and I will deliver the freedoms I have promised."

20

I TURNED AWAY FROM THE CROWD of millions who had come to see
the new master of Hell. I had done my part to keep them under control, for
the time being. I had delivered what I believed to be a good speech, but
now it was time to start working towards delivering my promise. If I could
somehow bring down the barriers between Heaven, Limbo and Hell, then
not only would I free all of these creatures from their suffering, I would
have Charlotte back.

"Please bring Judas, Clytemnestra and the five revenge demons with her
to the war room," I instructed, as I walked past Smithy and Azazel who
were still peering out at the mass of people. "Spread word to the rest of the
crowd that they are free to go back to their normal lives for now. Is there
food and drink in the cellars here?"

"There is always plenty kept on hand, Lord Michael. In fact it is almost
endless."

"Good," I said. "Once you have brought my guests inside, send out food
and drink amongst the pilgrims. If they wish to stay on the grounds to
celebrate for the night then they are most welcome. Be generous with the
food and frugal with the drink. We don't want a million intoxicated
demons running out of control out there."

"Very well," Azazel said. He walked inside and disappeared down the
stairs.

I turned to Smithy.

"Well, what did you think?"

"I think you are either brilliant, or insane, or both," he said. "It is a fine
ideal to be working towards. But, ideals never come easy if they come at
all."

"I agree," I replied. "It's best we get to work. Meet me downstairs in
ten minutes." I forced a smile as I pushed past him.

The exertion it had taken to free the suicidal souls from the forest had almost broken me. My legs were shaking as I made my way down to where my bedchambers were. I sat down on the bed, leaning my elbows on my knees. Once again I was working on a wing and a prayer towards my aims. I closed my eyes. Sweat covered the dark suit I was still wearing from Oresteia. I needed to change. I got off the bed and walked to a cupboard on the wall closest to me. Sliding open the doors, I found what I was looking for: clean shirts, pants, jackets and shoes. Ever since we had arrived in Casa Diablo, it seemed Azazel somehow knew instinctively what I would need before I needed it. He had suggested the balcony for the sermon. He had put these clothes here. He had also given me a room with a private bathroom. I picked out some suitable clothes and took them into the ensuite with me. Since I had no time to sleep or rest, I did the next best thing. I showered with hot water to clean myself and then cold to wake myself back up. I scrubbed efficiently and quickly. I had guests arriving.

After I was washed and dressed, I looked myself up and down in the mirror. Only hints of the exhaustion I felt showed in my eyes. I still had a few light scratches from the forest on my face, but otherwise I looked presentable.

"Okay," I said to myself. "Don't ask too many questions; let them do most of the talking. They will provide the answers you need. They have been in Hell much longer than you. Surely they will know what to do."

I opened the door to the large conference room. Smithy was sitting, talking genially with the rest, who either hadn't offered to speak, or couldn't get a word in.

"As I was saying," Smithy said, "It really is a shame to waste more than two spoons of sugar in your tea, since that's all that will actually dissolve in the water. The rest simply stays at the bottom of the cup!"

I suppressed a smile and cleared my throat.

Those present all looked over to where I stood. Clytemnestra and the demon jurors were assembled on one side of the table. Smithy and Judas were on the other. Someone had given Judas a white robe which hung loosely on his shoulders. His chest was still bare and white beneath; the yellow of the bruises on his neck had faded. I deliberately passed the throne at the head of the table and took an empty seat next to Smithy.

"Thank you all for coming," I said as I sat down. "No doubt you have many questions for me, but I ask that you please hold them for the moment. I have already explained all I can during the sermon. Essentially, Asmodeus sits in Heaven while we remain in Hell. As much as I despise him and his actions, he has appointed me the new ruler here. Life in Hell needs to move on with as little disruption as possible."

"But what about war?" one of the red demons across from me snarled.

I looked at him with sharp eyes, but said nothing and pressed on.

"We are now fighting a battle within ourselves. We must contain the evil urges each and all of us have and stop harming each other. It is the only way forward. There is no war to fight with God at this present moment because we cannot reach him in Heaven right now. Our first step is to seek information on how to destroy the barriers between Heaven, Limbo and Hell. Only then will we be able to march on our oppressors. Learn about the force you are against before you attack. It is the first rule of war and until we know more, we cannot be the first ones to strike. In the meantime, there is the more pressing problem of new souls. Every day the dying from Earth are sent here, helpless and unprepared for the afterlife. We now have the added pressure of the souls from The Forest of the Damned. They will need homes and they will need orientation in their new surroundings.

"Clytemnestra," I said, turning to look at her. "Firstly you have my deep thanks for leading the pilgrimage here to Mount Belial. In doing so you have not only earned my trust, you have earned my respect. Only someone very powerful could succeed in such an endeavor."

She sat upright in her chair at my positive appraisal.

"Thank you. It was my humble duty and honor to serve someone so powerful," she replied in her gravelly tone."

"You know more about Hell and the organization of this domain than any other," I pressed on, "I herby appoint you High Chief of Lost Souls. You are now responsible for every person and demon in Hell, second only to me." There was an uncomfortable rustling about the room. "It is a job you have already been performing, and now I want you to be recognized for it. Take the main office in The Satanic Tower."

Clytemnestra beamed, her black gums contrasting with her red lips. It looked more like a sneer than a smile, but I could tell she was incredibly happy with her appointment.

"What else will you need to get the job done properly?" I asked.

"I'll need assistants," she replied. "I will need the ability to pay staff and full legislative rights to direct souls to create new buildings and suburbs for recent immigrants."

"You have it," I confirmed quickly. The day-to-day running of Hell would only prove a distraction to my main aim of finding Charlotte. "I assume Satan had bank holdings for such things?" I asked. She nodded an affirmative.

"Then you will control those also. Azazel, who keeps this house, will be second signatory, I the third. You only need my third signature should any extraordinary expenses need approval." I knew that Azazel would protect the money of Satan prudently. If it were to run short, it would affect the upkeep of Casa Diablo. He would come to me immediately if anything was awry.

"There is something else I might need other than money," she added.

I thought this might be coming. I waited for her to go on. "The Dark Lor… ah, Asmodeus, would offer his employees to be spared The Guilt in exchange to work for him. It was one of his lures to make sure he had the best people in Hell in his employ. By offering protection from The Guilt as an incentive, we'll be able to save on wages as well."

"No!" Smithy cried next to me. "Without The Guilt, demons will run crazy all over Hell!"

I put my hand on his arm to steady him.

"But you can't, Michael," he insisted. "The Guilt not only helps control evil here, it also helps reform souls to give them a chance to go to Heaven."

"Then why aren't you in Heaven, old man?" Clytemnestra spat from across the table. "If you enjoy your suffering so much, why aren't you in Paradise?"

"Silence!" I yelled.

Smithy was right, I couldn't spare people The Guilt just yet, but not because I wasn't willing. It was because I didn't know how. I wasn't about to admit any weakness in front of these demons, however.

"When we achieve our goal of tearing down the walls of Hell, then we will all be free of Asmodeus' forced visions. Until then, I would prefer to use The Guilt as a reminder for all that The Creator does not love us, and until we work together to bring down the walls which separate us all, we will remain in Hell. I am aware that some have already been spared The Guilt, and I will not presume to take away something that has already been bestowed. But understand this," I said, looking around the room. "If any of these privileged few abuse this gift, it will be swiftly removed."

I turned to the five jurors sitting next to Clytemnestra to steer the conversation away from debate.

"What are your names?" I asked. The demon who had spoken out earlier took the lead quickly.

"Lord Michael. I am Marax, this is Astaroth, Empusa, Barbas and Lamia. We will serve you with the ferocity you deserve."

"I have no doubt," I said, despising Marax and his companions for what I had witnessed in The Tenth Circle. I did not need him or the others stirring up wrath in what I hoped to be a new Hell. I realized only too well that they would need a strong hand to hold them. I would have liked to destroy them all then and there, but it wouldn't be a fitting action with someone who had just espoused freedom and equality to all the souls in Hell. I would have to hold my hand, at least until they did something publicly to deserve it.

"You are now the first of Clytemnestra's assistants," I told him.

A low growl rumbled in his throat.

"Unless there is a problem?" I asked, almost hoping he would resist me.

"Of course not, Lord," he said evenly, while fire burned in his eyes.

"Good." I looked back toward Clytemnestra and addressed her again.

"You now have five powerful demons to assist you. If there are any issues, let me know. What is your first step from here?"

"Once we leave here," she said, "I will gather the pilgrims outside and lead them back to the city. All will resume smoothly with Marax and his team behind me. While they may not have the glowing approval of the populace here, they certainly have fearful respect." She eyed Marax sideways after her comment. "We will find a site for the souls of the forest and commence construction, although I'm at a loss to say where."

"Why not use the empty space where the trees once were?" I offered. "Build all the way down into the city. I would prefer a road from here to having to walk anyway."

"Great idea!" she said.

"Anything else?" I asked, looking around the room. Only silence answered me.

"You're free to go then," I said to Clytemnestra. "I'm sure you will be kept busy enough. I will come and see you when I can."

Clytemnestra and her five new assistants stood. They looked from me across to Smithy and then to Judas, who had puzzlingly still not yet offered a single word. Each filed out of the room in silence. I did not trust any of them but at least they would be too busy with their new jobs to plot anything significant.

As the last demon exited the room, Clytemnestra closed the door behind her. There was now just Smithy, Judas and I sitting next to each other in a row of three.

"Do not trust her," Judas said firmly, looking at me with emerald-green eyes.

I stood up and walked around the other side of the table so I could talk to him face to face, instead of looking down the table.

"Why?"

"I can sense betrayal in her soul," he said with an unwavering stare which unnerved me.

"Coming from you, the person most known for his betrayal, that is a strange thing to say," I said to Judas, not offering that I still didn't trust

Clytemnestra completely.

"She has murdered all those she loved," was his cryptic answer. "She only serves herself."

"Then power should become her," I answered. "But tell me, Judas, why should I trust you? I have offered you your freedom and you have offered your service before all in Hell in return. We both know that promises are only words until they are delivered. Why should I trust your word?"

"Because you hold within you the ideal that I once followed in a lifetime past. You hold a love for people within your broken shell."

I was startled by his words.

"Oh yes," he continued, "I can see within people just as you can see other things. I see truth where others are deceived. It is the painful burden that I bear, for the truth is often uglier than the lie that covers it. Do you want to know the truth of my story?"

Now he had piqued my curiosity. His was the worst story of treachery in human history; Judas Iscariot was the one who delivered Jesus to be crucified by the Romans.

"I always want to know the truth," I answered honestly.

"Then take my hand," he said, holding it out across the table, "and I will show you."

I looked the red-haired man opposite me in the eyes, concentrating to see if there was any deception. I could not sense anything. I changed my vision to view his elemental makeup. Around him shone a white aura of peace. Looking at his hand I could see a surge of elements flowing from his heart and head into his fingertips. There was emotion, memory and thought woven together to create a silver tendril of time. I reached out and took his hand in mine. As his fingers wrapped around my palm, a blinding light flashed about me and I was transported to another place.

21

JUDAS WALKED DOWNHILL through rocky countryside towards a white walled city. His red hair swept like unkempt flames down his back. Ahead was a bearded man atop a donkey, following a dusty trail. His saddle was a heap of holed blankets folded across the animal's back. The air was dry and, with little shade from the scattered trees about us, the midday sun scorched the land. A heat haze led the way into the distance.

"Where are we, Judas?" I tried to ask my companion. No words came out. He went on without breaking his stride. It was as though I was an unheard angel, looking down on a scene I had no control over. I was confused as to where we were, but it was certain that Judas was showing me this for a reason. I was drawn along with him, walking down the trail at a steady pace.

"Judas!" the man on the donkey called, pulling to a halt. "Is this heat making you so delirious that you fall behind so easily? Come, have a rest. Ride the beast and I shall walk beside you." The man jumped down from his blanket saddle.

"No thank you, I'm fine, Jesus. It's but a few miles to Jerusalem. The others aren't far behind us. Maybe we should wait for them."

"Do you think word of what happened with Lazarus will have reached the city before we arrive?" Jesus asked, patting the donkey on the neck.

"I'm certain that word of a man being raised from the dead will have flooded down Mount Olive like a flowing river," Judas said seriously. "My concern is that it either will not be believed, or that you'll be accused of trickery."

"Trickery?" Jesus chuckled. "I've been accused of worse, my friend. We will receive the welcome of the people in Jerusalem, of that I am certain, but it is not the people I worry about."

"The Pharisees?" Judas asked.

"It's time those faithless men in Jerusalem stood up and took notice of us."

Jesus waved his hand, looking back up the hill past Judas. I turned to see a group of people making their way down from where we'd come. There were twelve of them in total: the Apostles.

"Tonight after we eat," Jesus said to Judas quietly, "I would like to talk over a serious matter with you. I have a favor to ask that you will not like, but it is one I must ask nonetheless."

"What is it?" Judas asked.

"Later," Jesus answered, "they're almost back with us. Please, get up on this donkey and rest your weary feet."

"My Lord, you know that I will not. You must be the one riding once we get to Jerusalem. The message of the King of the Jews come in peace must not be spoiled because of my blistered feet. I'll have no argument."

Jesus nodded and climbed back onto the donkey, just as the trailing party pulled up to meet us.

"We're not far from the city," Jesus said to the group. "Take some water now and walk again, contemplating God rather than your thirst. We shall be there before you realize."

He handed down a leather water pouch and the group passed it around. Including Jesus and Judas, there were thirteen men, and one woman. She was a breathtaking redhead who, despite wearing the same road-worn robes as the men, oozed unearthly beauty. She was the last to take a drink from the pouch, swigging a healthy gulp before returning it to Jesus. As she passed it back, their fingers brushed and lingered for a few moments.

"Thank you, Mary," Jesus smiled down at her.

"Thank you, Lord," she said, and began walking up ahead.

The procession moved forward once more. Judas walked in between the group, having quiet conversations, as we wound through the rock and sand-strewn landscape. Flies buzzed about the sweating group, along with an air of excitement. I was able to put names to each of the people as we progressed. Peter was a large solitary man, with a constantly angry look on his face. Matthew was silent and contemplative. John and James both wore blue robes and walked together, smiling as they spoke of the glory of God and the coming Passover feast.

As we approached Jerusalem, the trees rising out of the dry soil become slightly greener. Ahead were a woman and young child of around ten years old, resting in the shade. The child jumped up and ran over to us.

"Who are you?" he asked innocently, looking up at Jesus on his donkey.

"He is the Lord Jesus and the messiah of mankind." Peter scowled at the urchin.

"Peter, please," Jesus said quietly. He looked down at the boy and threw him a loaf of bread from a bag which hung at his side. "I am a friend," he said to the child. "If it's alright with your mother, you run ahead and tell the people at the gates of the city that Jesus of Nazareth comes in peace with his flock. I will give you a fish to eat with that bread if you do it well."

The boy looked over to his mother who nodded eagerly. With the bread in his hands, he sprinted off towards the walls of the city at top speed, yelling the news.

"Jesus is here. Jesus of Nazareth is bringing some sheep to the city. Make way."

Smiling, Jesus urged his mount onward.

As we entered the gates of the city, a small crowd had gathered to watch. Peter pushed up ahead of the group and called to them.

"Welcome the Lord and savior, Jesus Christ, messiah of the people!" The crowd called and cheered a warm reception. Two women came forth and laid a blanket down in his path. Others in the throng threw down small olive branches as a welcome before him. He waved as our group continued through the people, into the city streets. A lady approached the group with a bundle in her arms. Paul went to step in front of her, but Jesus motioned to let her through. She came to stand beneath Jesus.

"I have heard you can perform miracles," she said, holding out a crying baby. "My son is sick, can you heal him?"

Jesus jumped down from his mount to stand next to the woman. He looked down at the child in her arms and reached out to touch it on the head. He closed his eyes for a few moments, and his hand shuddered slightly. The baby's cries quieted down.

"His fever will break tonight," Jesus said, opening his eyes again to look at the woman. "Take him home now and give thanks to our Lord God in Heaven."

"Bless you." She nodded her gratitude and scurried off into the crowd. The young boy who had gone ahead of us caught up to the group. Puffing, he still clutched his loaf of bread.

"Mister Jesus, Mister Jesus," he called. "Can I have my fish now?" "But you already have your fish," said Jesus with a smile, pointing to the child's hands.

The boy looked down to see a large carp, flipping alive in his fists. In shock he dropped it to the dirt. The crowd around us all gasped in astonishment and began talking furiously amongst themselves. Jesus bent down and picked up the fish, which was now slowly gasping in his hands. He handed it to the boy.

"Take this home to your family," he said. "They have fresh bread on the table."

Jesus turned and continued through the buzzing masses, leading the donkey behind him.

"Let us now go to temple, to give thanks," he said, and pushed up the street, leaving the people in wonder behind him as the Apostles followed closely.

The streets were packed full of people as we neared the large temple. Worshipers were pouring in and out of the archways, which led inside the large grounds. We passed through into the courtyard. Rather than praying pilgrims preparing for Passover inside, there were tables set up for trade. Livestock was gathered into reeking pens in the middle of the space. Booths were set up for changing money around the more shaded edges. Our party came to an abrupt halt. I could hear each of the Apostles voicing their disgust at the state of the temple. Jesus was furiously untying the rope from around his donkey's neck, and began winding it with a piece of leather from his belt into a cord. Anger burned in his eyes and his normally serene demeanor became wilder with each of his hurried movements. He was looking around, shaking his head as he bound the rope and leather together. I heard John whisper into James' ear behind me.

"What is he doing? I've never seen him like this."

After tying off the ends of his lash, Jesus walked quickly over to the closest stall, where money was changing hands. He kicked the table roughly. Coins clattered to the ground and the man who sat behind the table fell backwards onto the ground. Jesus swiftly kicked him in the ribs before pressing his foot down onto the man's neck. People all around stopped what they were doing to see what the commotion was about. Jesus unfurled the rope in his hand and whipped the man in the face with it. He cried out in pain and some other men to the side began to step in.

"Stop!" Jesus yelled loudly. Everyone fell silent to behold this furious man who held a whip in his hands. "This is Herod's Temple, is it not? This is a place of worship, not a place of commerce. You are all sinners by letting this revolting act of blasphemy take place within the walls of my Father's house! It is written: my house shall be called the house of prayer, but ye have made it a den of thieves! Do you not love God? If you do not, then you should fear him!"

Once again, Jesus unleashed the whip down onto the man's face before running into the middle of the courtyard and ripping down the pen which held in the livestock. Whipping the backs of cows and sheep he sent them bleating, running out toward the exit. Pandemonium broke as the animals stampeded out of the temple, knocking over tables and booths as they went. One cow crashed through a stack of birdcages which held a flock of doves. As the cages fell to the ground, they opened and the doves went cooing into the sky. Some of the people scurried out of the way, while others scratched on the ground in a bid to gather up the scattered coins that lay in the dirt. Above the din of confusion, Jesus' hoarse voice continued to rant.

"Leave this place, you thieves! You rob my Father of his glory. Do not come back until you wish to praise him. In his name, I put an embargo upon all trade in this place. When you return, return to a place of sanctity and peace!"

Incredibly, the people listened to his command. While the dust that had been roused up still hung in the air, everyone filed out of the courtyard until there were no animals or customers left. Just a few hawkers hurriedly packed up their wares so they could escape before the man with the whip attacked them as well. Jesus and the Apostles were the only ones left when a priest came storming out of the church into the yard. His robes flew behind him.

"What are you doing?" he yelled. "How dare you disrupt our prayers?"

"How dare you let this sacred place fall into the darkness of trade?" Jesus roared back, holding his whip high in the air.

The priest stopped in his tracks, face red, spluttering with indignity. "What right do you have to make judgment on what happens in my temple?"

"Your temple?" Jesus yelled, stepping forward. John and James quickly moved in to hold him back. "This is the temple of God!" Jesus fumed. "Are you claiming divinity?"

The priest looked like he had been slapped in the face. "You would insult a Rabbi so?"

"I would insult an old man who knows nothing of the true word of the Lord! You will burn in Hell!"

"This is outrageous!" the Rabbi said, turning from red to purple.

"High Priest Caiaphas will hear about this!" He then turned and marched back into the church.

As the Rabbi disappeared inside, Jesus threw his weapon to the ground. "Let us leave this soiled place and find somewhere else to pray," he said.

The Apostles all followed Jesus out of the courtyard in stunned silence, back into the crowded streets of Jerusalem.

We continued to roam the city as Jesus talked to the people, preached upon steps, prayed, and attended to the sick where he saw them. The entire time, his Apostles simply walked behind, listening when he spoke. Upon nightfall, the group gathered inside some simple lodgings to rest for the night and eat.

While Judas was alone, rolling down his blankets for the night in a quiet corner, there was a light knock at the door.

"Judas?"

I turned to see Jesus enter the room; Judas straightened stiffly before turning to greet Jesus with a smile.

"It was an interesting day today," he said, as he hugged Jesus and kissed him on the cheek.

"Yes it was," Jesus agreed, shaking his head and looking to the ground. "I'm sorry I let my temper get the better of me, Judas."

"You cannot always be meek and mild. Even God is wrathful, mere men cannot hope to escape anger."

"They should try," Jesus said. "But I have not come to justify my actions, Judas. I have come to seek a word."

"Ah yes," Judas said. "The favor I may not like. You know I would lay my life down for you if you asked me to, my Lord."

"I know. But would you lay down my life, if I asked?"

"What?" Judas said. "I would never do anything to harm you!" Jesus nodded slowly, still looking at his feet.

"I know you wouldn't, Judas. You are my closest and dearest friend. You, who understand my teaching of God better than all others. You, who realize the potential that lies within all of God's children to be divine. What I am asking is something that I know will hurt you a great deal, but I will ask it anyway. I have foreseen that this is needed to deliver all of mankind from their sins."

Judas stood silent and waited.

"In two days from now, after the feast of Passover, I need you to give me up for arrest to the authorities."

"You wish for me to betray you?" Judas asked, aghast.

"There is no betrayal if I know it is happening," Jesus said to him, finally raising his eyes from the ground to meet those of Judas. "Tomorrow I will speak out against the established church in public. It will enflame great resentment from those in power, not because it is challenging to them, but because they know the truth of their hypocrisy and will seek to hide it. They will charge me for treason and for heresy."

"Impossible!" Judas whispered fiercely, looking out the door to make sure nobody overheard. "You would never speak out against God! But, if you are arrested and found guilty of such a charge, you will be crucified. The crimes you speak of carry the penalty of death!"

"I know," Jesus pressed. "But it will be a death of the body, not my divine spirit. It will mean the rebirth of the glory of God in this world. People do not understand simple words, they understand sacrifice, and there is no bigger sacrifice than martyrdom. It will arouse the passion of God within the populace once more. You can see this is needed. The biggest temple in this holy city was trading animals today! Is that my Father's will? No! He must be worshipped above all else." Jesus looked Judas deep in the eye. "Above all else, Judas! Above my life, above your pride. You must do this for the good of man. Will you?"

"What about my soul?" Judas asked. "Will God in Heaven forgive me this betrayal?"

"He has already forgiven you," Jesus said, putting a hand on Judas' shoulder. "You will become the apostle cursed by all others. It's still possible for you to reach Heaven, but you will struggle a great deal. This is God's will, my friend. Will you do what I can ask no other to do?"

A tear slid down Judas' cheek as he nodded. "Yes my Lord, I will do as you ask."

"Thank you," Jesus said softly, the words barely passing his lips. "Now rest. It will be another eventful day tomorrow. Sleep well." He turned and walked quietly from the room.

Judas slumped down onto his blanket and began to weep softly. As his tears fell, the enormity of the conversation welled up in me.

Jesus was orchestrating his own death. Judas had not truly betrayed him as The Bible taught, he was asked to give up Jesus to the Romans. It made sense. Without the crucifixion there could be no resurrection and therefore no Christianity. Jesus was pushing himself onto the cross to unite the world under a new religion. As Judas wept, I stared into space, wondering what other surprises were in store in the coming days.

***

The courtyard of the Temple of Herod had been cleared. There were no longer animals or moneychangers. It had been transformed once again into an area for preaching. Jesus had come back with his Apostles and set up an area in the most shaded part of the yard. Many had gathered to hear him speak, as word of his miracles and teachings had circulated throughout Jerusalem. The courtyard virtually hummed with religious fervor. Men stood shoulder to shoulder throughout the yard, arching onto their tiptoes to get a glimpse of the so-called Messiah.

"The Kingdom of Heaven is great, and we all want our spirits to go there," Jesus said, from an elevated step above the crowd, his back to the western wall of the temple. "Praise God and worship him, forsaking all others. Treat your fellow man with love, respect and kindness. We have all heard of the rewards of Heaven, but I am now here to tell you of a different place. A place you will go, should you not heed my Father's word." There was a murmur through the crowd. What was this? They had only heard of one afterlife, that of Sheol.

"The charlatans inside this house would not tell you of this place," Jesus preached, "because they are not the real prophets of God. But I am here to reveal to you that if you are evil you will be cast down into burning pits of brimstone and sulphur. You will writhe in agony, and weep, gnashing your teeth in pain. God has given these pits a name. They are called Hell and all of the sinners of this earth who have rejected God will dwell there for all of eternity."

"What can we do to avoid this Hell you speak of?" a man yelled from the crowd.

"Observe always the commandments that Moses handed down from Mount Sinai," Jesus answered. "In this there can be no compromise. For those here who may have sinned, do not fear; you still have a chance at redemption. We are all flawed, for we are human. If you have not lived a pure and holy life until now, you can still reach the Kingdom of God. Admit your wrongs. If, truthfully in your heart you are sorry and promise to never be led into temptation again, then God will forgive you! God loves each of you present, without exception."

Again there was a ripple of approval from the crowd. From the back, there came a shout. A group of people were pushing through, yelling and shoving people out of the way. It was the Chief Priest of the Temple who had clashed with Jesus the previous day. With him were six elders, all bristling with anger.

"On whose authority do you say these things?" the priest challenged loudly.

Jesus looked down and replied evenly, "I will also ask you one question. If you answer me, I will answer you. John's baptism—where did it come from? Was it from Heaven, or from men?"

The priest looked to the elders around him, puzzled. He was about to open his mouth, when Jesus cut in.

"You are hypocrites. All of you! Look at you old men, full of self-importance. You clothe yourselves in ostentatious robes and encourage people to call you Rabbi! You take the place of honor at people's banquets, when you have no honor yourselves!"

The priest began to open his mouth again, but Jesus yelled loudly over the top of the crowd.

"You say you teach about God, but you do not love God, you love the power your position gives you. You do not enter the Kingdom of Heaven in your prayers, nor do you let others enter. You preach a dead religion, making those converted to your word twice as much the sons of Hell! You covet the gold of the altar more than the meaning it represents!"

"You're breaking the law!" one of the elders shouted from beside the priest.

"You speak about law!" Jesus replied. "But you do not practice the most important laws: justice, mercy and faithfulness to God! You obey the tiniest of laws like the tithing of spices, but this is not the real meat of what God commands! You appear clean because you have bathed, but you are dirty within. Everyone here can smell the stench of your greed. You are like whitewashed tombs, beautiful on the outside, but full of dead men's bones!"

A burst of shouts of approval went up from the gathered people. The priest and his companions began to shrink at the words of Jesus.

"You say you have a high regard for the dead prophets of old and claim you would never persecute and murder prophets. Really, you are cut from the same cloth as the persecutors and murderers! You too have murderous blood in your veins, you who would challenge me, who speaks the true word of God Almighty!"

The people around voiced their approval of Jesus' vehement speech. Someone from the crowd threw a small rock, which struck the priest on the side of the head. He fell down, and was picked up by his friends.

"You have not heard the last of this, you blasphemer!" the priest yelled, blood trickling from his temple into his beard. His friends steadied him on his feet and ushered him out from amongst the turbulent mass of followers, back toward the shelter of the inside of the temple.

"Go back to your house of woe!" Jesus yelled after him. "While the real word of God is delivered at its doorstep!"

A shout of approval went up from the crowd as the group of men retreated through a doorway into the temple proper. As they moved inside, Judas stirred next to me, inching backward from where Jesus stood toward where the priest and his followers had withdrawn. With all attention focused on Jesus, who had begun preaching once more, we slipped unnoticed through into the cool exterior of the shadowy temple. A few priests shuffled about, not paying us any attention, while others sat immersed in reading scrolls. I could see the Chief Priest sitting on a wooden bench next to the main alter, being tended to by another man, who was wiping the blood from where the rock had struck. The priest was fuming with rage, his chest heaving with deep breaths. Judas made his way unobtrusively over to the two men.

"Hello, Rabbi," Judas said quietly.

"I do not have time to hear your troubles," the rabbi said brusquely, waving Judas away. "Can't you see I've just been attacked?"

"That is why I approached," Judas went on in the same soft manner. "I have come to offer a solution to the trouble the man called Jesus presents you and the Holy Church. It was his incitement that caused that stone to be thrown at you. I witnessed everything."

The rabbi suddenly became more interested. He sat up straighter in his chair, took the cloth the man was using to wipe his blood and held it firm over his wound.

"You were there to listen to him preach?"

"I was. I have been following him as a close member of his party for some time now."

"Then why would you help me?"

"At first I was enchanted by his words, but I have now grown to understand that inside his humble exterior lies a false heart."

"He is a violent criminal!" the rabbi burst out. "He attacked merchants in the square outside yesterday, he blasphemes against God. There isn't a humble bone in his rotting body." He winced in pain, as he stood up and stepped closer to Judas. "What is this solution you speak of?"

"I will help you lead the authorities to where he is staying, so that he can be arrested for heresy," said Judas, licking his lips nervously, his eyes flitting from the rabbi's face back to the ground.

"I could just get the authorities to arrest him now!" the rabbi almost shouted.

"If you did it in public there would be a riot," Judas answered carefully. "He has the support of the people; you saw that with your own eyes. He is swaying them away from the teachers who are sanctioned by the law. He must be arrested in secret, away from a group of supporters large enough to stop it."

"Yes," the rabbi said, starting to nod. "His preaching without the Emperor's authority could be considered treason! I will take this to High Priest Caiaphas. Are you sure you can lead us to him?"

"Of course," Judas said. "The night of Passover he has prepared a banquet. After this banquet he and his Apostles will go to rest. I can come and find you here. I will lead you and the soldiers to arrest him."

Judas screwed up his eyes at the explicit mention of his betrayal. The Priest noticed the facial twitch, and peered at Judas more closely.

"I can see this matter troubles you a great deal," he said. "It takes courage to set aside personal loyalties for the good of The Church. I'll ensure you are rewarded for your courage. Thirty pieces of silver will help you establish yourself as the moral citizen you are, yes?"

Judas simply nodded.

"Good," the priest said, smiling maliciously. "Then at midnight, after the Passover meal, I will meet you at the door of this building. Agreed?"

Judas nodded again, and turned to go. As he started to leave, the priest called out to him.

"I haven't yet received your name."

"It is Judas," he said, and walked away.

"Judas!" the Priest called after us. "Your name will become synonymous with loyalty after this good deed."

***

The day leading up to Passover, Judas largely avoided Jesus and the rest of the Apostles. His time was spent in quiet reflection, sitting on his blanket in the shade of the walled city. When night came, we sat down to the meal of Passover. Jesus asked Judas to sit at his side. He accepted gracefully and moved into his place with a melancholic air about him.

The beauteous Mary Magdalene sat on Jesus' other hand, while each of the Apostles were seated about the table. Chatter was lively amongst the party; it was a night of celebration. Smells of roasted meats and freshly baked bread wafted from the kitchen. Red wine flowed freely and the talk grew louder. As the food was brought out to the table, Jesus stood. The conversation fell quiet. Jesus reached out and picked up a loaf of bread from the table. He began to break the bread into even pieces, which he passed around the table.

"This is my body, which is given to you," he said as the bread was taken from his hands. "Eat it in remembrance of me." The Apostles each placed the bread in their mouths and began to chew.

"I now pass to you a new commandment," he continued as they ate. "You must each love another, even as I have loved you dearly." He placed a hand on Mary's shoulder and smiled down at her. "In this way, you will show other men that you are my disciples and lead by example to spread love in the world."

Jesus picked up a pitcher of red wine and poured a glass to the brim. "This cup is the new covenant in my blood, that which is poured out for you. Take this and divide it among yourselves; for I say unto you, I shall not drink henceforth from the fruit of the vine, until the kingdom of God shall come." He lifted the chalice and drank from it. He passed it down to Mary who took a small sip and passed it to Luke who sat next to her. As the wine made the circle around the table, Jesus uttered the fateful words:

"One of you who sit at this table shall betray me."

It was as if all happiness had been sucked from the room.

"Surely it is not I?" Luke said.

"Nor I!" Peter added.

Each of the people present voiced their protests and asked who would do such a thing. Judas remained silent. Jesus interrupted the din by holding up his hands.

"As I have foretold, it shall be so. By the hand of one of those closest to me, I shall be delivered to death."

Everyone present sat grim-faced and solemn, no longer talking. They just stared ahead, trying to come to terms with what had been revealed. However, Jesus remained smiling. He looked to each of the Apostles in turn pointedly, nodding to each of them as he spoke.

"This is not something to be mourned. I have been teaching you my Father's word for a long time now. No good pupil repays his teacher by remaining a pupil. In your future lives, I ask that you too become teachers. You must go out, like sheep amongst the wolves, and spread this new gospel of love and tolerance to man. The divine spark of God lives in all of us. I shall prove this by rising from the grave before ascending unto Heaven. It is now your duty to enflame this divine spark within your fellow man. Now, I would ask: are there any of you here that can now unleash that spirit? Let the perfect spirit within come out and face me."

All of the Apostles remained quiet and seated. They looked from one to the other. Finally it was Judas who stood up, next to Jesus. Still with his eyes to the ground, Judas slowly began to shiver slightly. Gradually, a beautiful white light shone out from him, encasing him in a wonderful aura. All in the room gasped and abruptly the light began to fade again.

Jesus clapped Judas on the shoulder, grinning through his dark beard. "It is your star that will lead the way, my dear friend." He looked around to the others. "You all have what Judas has shown within you. Now please excuse us while I speak to him of a new lesson, which only he is ready for."

Jesus then leaned in to Judas' and whispered in his ear, "Come. I will tell you the mysteries of Heaven."

As they exited the room, excited talk erupted between the Apostles at what they had just seen. If Jesus wasn't the only one who could perform miracles, then maybe they were all indeed divine inside.

I shadowed Judas and his master outside into the cool night air. The city was lit brightly by the moon, and we could the hear festivities for Passover all around. Jesus walked down into the middle of a stairway and sat down with Judas.

"Tonight is a hallmark night in the history of mankind," Jesus said. "Generations will be telling this story for thousands of years to come. From just fourteen small people in a room, we will change the world for the better. However, neither of us is long in this world of men. The mortal life is but a blink of an eye compared with the eternity of the divine soul." He continued, "We will be together in the Kingdom of God. It is a great and boundless realm, which no thought or heart could ever understand."

"I don't want to have to do this," Judas said, interrupting Jesus' speech. "There must be another way. We can convince the world of God's love through the power of truth, not through a deception of martyrdom. I cannot understand how the betrayal of a friend can spark something good."

"That is because you are still only human, Judas." Jesus smiled at him. "Even I cannot fathom everything while I am encased in this mortal shell. I welcome the impending day when I am not restricted by its limitations. Do not fear my friend. As I said before, your star's brightness will eclipse all others. You will exceed all of them, for you will have sacrificed the human shell that holds a god. You will reveal the divinity they cannot yet see."

Judas' only reply was a sigh.

"You have finally accepted the truth of the soul within," Jesus said. "Now that you have the power to grasp its significance, you will be able to peer within the hearts of men and see their deepest wishes. You have become a powerful prophet in your own right, Judas. Use that power to look within yourself and know what you are doing is right."

Jesus stood and patted Judas once again on the shoulder as he got up. "It is best that you make your way to Herod's Temple, to rouse my accusers," he said. "We will be camped in the Garden of Gethsemane."

Judas looked up at him in horror, but said nothing. Jesus turned and walked back up the stairs, his steps light and easy.

Judas made his way unhindered through the night time streets of Jerusalem as I followed. Passover celebrations had moved entirely indoors and we met only the odd drunken pilgrim, stumbling home to bed. By the time we made it close to Herod's temple, it was almost midnight. Judas paused momentarily in a doorway. He leaned against the wall for support, silent tears running down his cheeks.

"This has to be done," he said to himself. "This is for the good of mankind. This is God's will." He wiped the tears from his face and stiffened his back. "This is God's will," he repeated, and walked forward again, moving to the entrance of the temple not far ahead.

"I'm glad your courage did not fail you," the Chief Rabbi called out to Judas. He was standing amid a small army of Roman guards, who each held a burning torch in one hand, the other resting on the hilt of their sheathed swords. Next to the rabbi stood another man, dressed in fine silken robes.

"So this is the savior of the church?" the man said, raising an eyebrow at Judas. "I am High Priest Caiaphas. I have come to meet firsthand the person who would bring us to this Jesus, who threatens Mother Church. You are doing something brave and just tonight. I thank you."

Judas nodded his head slightly. He then looked around at the soldiers gathered with their weapons.

"You will not need your swords tonight," he said. "Your presence will be enough to make Jesus come peacefully."

"We'll take him as we see fit!" Caiaphas said haughtily. "Then we'll then hand him over to Pontius Pilate for judgment."

"Only God can judge us," Judas said and turned away. "Come, I will lead you to him."

He set off at a march down the street, leaving the priests and soldiers no choice but to follow quickly. Judas did not pause or hesitate as he led them. It was as if he was creating a sense of momentum within himself that couldn't be stopped. He tracked through the dusty streets, past homes and buildings, winding towards a mount of olive trees. Judas pushed through the midst of the trees to emerge with the priests and soldiers into a garden. Ahead, there was a shout and a group of men stirred from the ground. Through a mix of flaming torchlight and the moon, I could see it was Jesus and his followers.

As Judas stepped forward, Jesus held out his arms and welcomed him with a warm hug. Judas kissed him on the cheek and pulled away.

"That's the sign!" Caiaphas said. "Seize him!"

One of the guards right next to Caiaphas strode in to take Jesus, but Peter ran forward and struck him in the face with his fist. The guard toppled to the ground dropping his sword. Peter swept up the weapon and hacked downward. The soldier wailed in agony, rolling away, clasping the side of his head. His ear sat bloody on the ground. Peter advanced again and the other soldiers moved in.

"Enough!" Jesus called loudly. "Those who live by the sword will die by it." His voice sung clearly through the garden as if it were a clarion from God. All present froze in their place. Peter dropped the sword in his hand to the earth.

Jesus walked forward. He spoke loudly toward Caiaphas.

"You come out here with an army, like you would against a hoard of thieves?"

He knelt down next to the wounded soldier who still lay moaning on the ground. With a steady hand, Jesus touched the man on the ear. The guard sat bolt upright and gasped. Holding his whole ear he stood once more.

"You have healed me!" he said. "He has healed my ear!" He turned to Caiaphas. Blood was still caked on his head, but the bleeding had stopped. The soldiers moved back a pace at the sight.

"It is of no consequence!" Caiaphas said. "This man uses the powers of evil. Take him!"

"I will come peacefully," Jesus said, holding out his fists to be tied.

As the guards moved in to take Jesus, Judas pushed past the gathering to leave the garden in disgust. Priest Caiaphas stopped him by grabbing his arm. "You have done well," he said. "Take your reward and spend it wisely." He pressed a small jingling pouch into Judas' hand.

Judas looked down at it with numb eyes and exited the scene of his treachery. He fled through the streets at a run, his breathing ragged and heavy. Each breath he let out was a rattle of misery. He turned blind corners in the dark, winding and weaving without seeming direction, until he came to a dead end alley. He stopped at the wall and turned. Looking up to the sky, he cried, "Why? Why like this? Why me? No good can come of treachery. Have I been deceived by the Devil? Will you forgive me?"

The night sky shone back down at him in silence. He collapsed on the ground, a wretched heap of weeping. Dust covered his red hair as he pushed his head into the ground, clawing at the earth with his fingers until they became bloody. He was delirious with grief. He lay in the dirt, continually tearing at himself, punching the ground, hitting his head against the stone walls around him, until he finally lapsed into an unconscious state of unrest.

The light of dawn crept upon Jerusalem. Pale blue light slowly rose above the horizon, pushing back the black of night to herald the coming of the morning sun. As the grey predawn air sparkled, Judas stirred on the ground. He opened his eyes to look up at the disappearing stars. Recollection slid across his face like the slice of a razor. He let out a low wail of sorrow and brought his hands up to cover his face. He lay there, shaking silently for a few moments, before his tremors abruptly stopped. Pulling himself to his feet, he looked around with red eyes. Holding out a hand he leaned against a wall. Once again he looked to the heavens and exhaled a long, stuttering breath. Pushing himself off the wall he stumbled out of the alley. We were at the exit gates to the city. Outside, along the walls of Jerusalem there was a market setting up for the morning trade. Judas stumbled to the nearest stall.

"Rope," he croaked. "I need a length of rope."

The man setting up his wares looked at the dishevelled Judas and shrugged his shoulders.

"I don't have rope to sell, only rugs," he said, pointing at the Persian carpets he had hanging behind him.

"They are hanging from a rope," Judas said determinedly.

"But how will I display them?" the man asked, shaking his head. Judas reached into his robes and pulled out the small pouch that the Priest Caiaphas had given him the night before. He poured its contents onto the dirt at his feet.

"Are thirty silvers enough?"

The man looked down at the coins strewn in the dust. He quickly ran back and pulled his carpets from the cord they were dangling from. Once he had untied it, he eagerly thrust the rope at Judas.

"Thank you," Judas said, and turned away. As he walked with purpose away from the city, the hawker behind him collected his payment from the ground.

Just out of town, Judas came to a field beyond a small patch of trees. The sun was pushing above the mountains ahead of us. As the blazing orb of light began to dawn, Judas made his way over to a gnarled tree in the middle of the field. Hitching the rope over his shoulder, he began to climb. Nimbly, he rose up into its twisted branches. Once he was about ten feet up, he inched outward over a thick branch which reached out from the trunk. Taking the rope from his shoulder, he furiously wound it around the branch, tying it off tightly. With shaking hands he started to tie a noose.

"Judas!" I tried to yell to him. "Judas, you don't have to do this. I've seen enough!"

"If Jesus can free his divine spirit of life by walking to his own death, then so can I," he said to the air. He pulled the noose over his head and looked up to the sky once last time.

"Forgive me. I will wait for you in Heaven, Jesus. We will be together again my Lord and friend."

With those sad words, he let himself fall off the branch. With a shudder, his feet jerked to a stop a few feet from the ground. As his choking gasps died out, the sun finally cleared the horizon to mark the beginning of a new day.

***

There was darkness where there should have been light. Terrified breaths rasped in my ears. I was trapped. Encased in a wooden prison. I could not move my body an inch, yet I could feel the suffocating heat of Hell all around me. More repressing than the searing temperature was the knowledge that I had betrayed my best friend and in turn had been betrayed. This was not the Kingdom of Heaven I had been promised.

A chilling voice whispered in my ear. It was the unmistakable tone of Satan.

"Hello, Judas," he said, with sinister mirth. "Welcome to your reward. You have forsaken your life on earth and therefore you have forsaken your divine soul to me for eternity."

No! I thought. This couldn't be. I had sacrificed my honor for God. I sacrificed my name. I was the true follower, doing the Lord's bidding. There has to be a mistake.

"There is no mistake," Satan whispered again, wriggling inside my head. "You took your own life. It is something that God cannot ever forgive you for, you traitor. Jesus is bleeding on his cross right now. It's most wonderful to watch."

I thought I was releasing my soul. I was supposed to meet Jesus in the Kingdom of Heaven.

"You cannot willingly release your soul, and expect to go to Heaven. If you could, then there would be nobody left on earth. Everyone would commit suicide to join with God. It could never be what he wants. He wants people to suffer through life unhappy. Only then does he reward with never ending bliss.

But his martyrdom was a willing one. Isn't that a kind of suicide? Will Jesus not end up in Hell, with me? I've made a terrible mistake.

"Yes you have made a mistake." The Devil laughed horribly. "But your error was trusting in God to do the right thing. Jesus will go to Heaven, to reunite his soul with his Kingdom of Grace. But he has forsaken you, Judas. He has betrayed you, his greatest ally, to an eternity of suffering. It brings me untold joy to know I can torment his closest Apostle. He must have known you would end up here, yet he did nothing to stop it. He said nothing to save you from your fate."

You are wrong, I thought. *He will come and save me, and I will be delivered from sin.*

22

I SAT UP, GASPING FOR BREATH. We were back in the war room. The wood of the chair dug hard into my back and I knew that we'd been out for some time. I sat up panting, letting my eyes focus. I looked over at Judas who was lying unconscious across the table, his hand extended toward me. The bruise around his neck had reappeared. Dark purple blotched from where the rope had cut into him, staying there as a physical reminder of his death while he was imprisoned inside his wooden body.

There could be no deceit in what I had just witnessed. The vivid final days leading up to the Last Supper and the arrest of Jesus by the authorities spun in my head. Everything I had learned during my life about Jesus and Judas had been turned upside down. I sat contemplating what this meant for us.

With a groan, Judas began to stir. He tried to sit up, but slumped back down onto the table. Blood was seeping from out of his ears, mixing with the already crimson tinge of his long hair. The power of the memory had produced an intense physical effect on him.

"Good God, what happened to him?" asked Smithy, rattling into the room with a tray of cups. "Is he alright?"

Smithy placed the tray roughly onto the table and went to Judas' side, real concern in his eyes. I stood up and went around to help Judas sit up in his chair.

Judas groaned again as we pulled him upright. His eyes opened briefly before closing again, his head lolling backward.

"Judas!" I said, holding the back of his head gently. "Judas, can you hear me?"

"Jesus never came for me," he answered weakly, through cracked lips. "He left me. After three days the Devil returned, to bring news of Jesus' resurrection and ascension to Heaven. It was a knife in my heart. My spirit was broken. What kind of a loving God would abandon his companion to cover himself in glory?"

Judas coughed and a bloody splinter of wood came out of his mouth. Smithy wiped it away, looking at me in fright. Judas continued.

"Periodically, through the darkness, Satan would visit to whisper in my ear. He tormented me with visions of the revolution of Christianity. All over the world, people whispered my name in hatred: Judas, the accursed Apostle, the betrayer, the traitor.

The Devil delighted when the crusades came, thousands upon thousands of deaths in the name of God, because of what I had done. My sacrifice had meant more souls had been sent wailing into Hell."

He straightened a little in his chair. Pushing our hands away softly, he opened his eyes to look at the two of us weakly. I stood, holding my hand on his shoulder in case he slumped again. Judas put his hands on the table to steady himself before looking up at me again.

"The worst moments where when other suicides came burning down to the forest beside me. Their roots were lodged into me. I felt their suffering on top of my own. Over two thousand years, uncountable souls penetrated my consciousness with their own sorrows. Soon, even Satan forgot about me. He no longer came to whisper in my ear, but seemed content to leave me frozen in agony forever. Forsaken by all and loved by none.

"Until one day, through the darkness, a bright spirit wandered into the forest. He touched my tree and I was able to peer into his soul, using the power Jesus had bestowed upon me. I saw his painful past and his bitter thoughts of revenge, but deep within I saw something else, the white spark of hope: Love. Truth. He had come to free me from my prison, and for that I will be his follower forever. That man is you, Michael. I am your true apostle."

Judas took my hand and kissed it. The green fire in his eyes had returned.

"Do you trust me now?" Judas asked with passion. "Do you see why I should want to continue the fight for the truth I believe in? Do you understand why I may feel wronged to have been cast into Hell, despite my sacrifice?"

"What happened?" Smithy asked beside me. "What did you see?"

"I saw that Judas was betrayed by Jesus," I said to him, "not the other way around as you might think. I saw that he is a true fighter for the ideals of love and freedom, and that he is now with us in this fight."

"You've earned this, then," Smithy said cheerily, handing Judas a hot cup of tea.

Judas held the cup in both hands. Shakily he brought the tea up to his mouth and slurped the hot liquid inside. By the time he had drained the cup he seemed revitalized. The faint white aura of power had returned to surround him.

"Where do we go from here, Michael?" he asked.

"I was hoping you'd provide some guidance," I answered. "In your time with Jesus, did he mention anything about the walls that separated the worlds of the afterlife? Do you know how we can dismantle the barricades between Hell, Limbo and Heaven?"

"No," Judas replied, running his fingers through his hair with a steely look in his eyes. "But I know someone who may be able to help us."

"Who?" I asked expectantly.

"Mary Magdalene," he paused, before adding softly, "my sister."

"What?" I said, standing up in shock. "Mary Magdalene is your sister?"

"Yes," Judas answered, studying the back of his hands. "It was a secret we kept from everyone except Jesus. I'm not sure how the others never saw the family resemblance; red hair wasn't common in Judea. She fled our family when she was just a girl, to escape our abusive father. I finally tracked her down in Magdala once I'd joined Jesus. She was working as a whore, but we saved her from that life."

I studied his face closely. He did indeed have similar features to the Mary who sat at Jesus' side during the last supper. It wasn't just in the hair, it was the eyes.

"Jesus fell in love with her," Judas continued. "She became his wife in secret. I was the one who wed them. Jesus wanted to keep their union secret, because he thought the others might judge his love for her as greater than his love for God. He couldn't be seen to be favoring anyone more than the Lord. We were quite a holy trinity, the three of us. I'm not sure what happened to her, even now. I'm sure the bride of Christ would be in the Kingdom of God with him, but she may still have an allegiance to me if I can get word to her somehow."

"Mary is not in Heaven," I cut in. "She is here in Hell. She has returned to the life you rescued her from. She runs a brothel in the city, Magdalene's Mansion."

Judas looked up to me, his penetrating glare boring into me to see if I was telling the truth.

"Are you sure?" he asked, rising to his feet.

"I'm fairly sure," I said slowly. "I've been there myself, but I never actually saw her with my own eyes. Asmodeus went to meet her, while I was having guilty visions," I said, avoiding his gaze.

"How could this be?" he gasped. "Why had she not come to me in the forest? I don't understand."

"I don't either," I said cautiously. "Maybe we should visit her to find out."

"Oh bugger," Smithy said next to us. "It's going to be one thing after another with you isn't it, Michael? I'll go and get the helicopter ready."

23

WE LANDED ON THE ROOF of the towering glass brothel. Smithy kept the rotor spinning. We had agreed that he would go to check on Clytemnestra while Judas and I met with Mary. I wanted to keep their family reunion as private as possible. I didn't know what was going to happen, but I was sure some uncomfortable truths would have to be faced.

I stepped down from the helicopter, ducking my head as I walked out from underneath the blades. Judas followed not far behind.

As Smithy took off, two large demons came out from a door ahead of us and waited as we approached. One was a blue lust demon covered in pus-filled sores. He wore a loose pair of denim shorts, to thankfully cover his nether-parts. The other demon was a deep orange color, his belly swollen with the gluttony of his sins. His bulbous head was even larger than his stomach, giving him a top-heavy sway as he stood beside the door.

"Hello," I said, holding up my hand in salutation. "I am..."

"Lord Michael," the lust demon said. "My name is Forneus. I was at your sermon, and so was Wharton here."

The orange monster nodded slightly and he wobbled off balance. "We support your cause. We hope that someday soon we can be free of Hell as you've promised. How can we be of service to you?"

"We've come to see Mary," I said, happy inside at our good fortune. "Can you take us to her?"

"Of course. Follow me."

We passed through the door into a cool, well-lit corridor. Descending a small flight of metal stairs we continued down the passageway, trailing behind Wharton's swaying gait We were led to an elevator, which opened as we approached. All four of us fit inside easily and Forneus tapped a button with a golden 'M' inscribed on it.

"I admire what you're trying to do," Forneus said, to me as we descended. "We're all trapped within our own desires. It is time we started to think more of each other and help find a way out of this hellhole of guilt. Truly, in my heart of hearts I believe that."

As he said the words, I noticed a few of the weeping sores on his chest closed up. He didn't seem to perceive the change, but to me it was incredible how a body could transform so rapidly as the philosophy of will shifted. I nodded my agreement and smiled.

The elevator stopped and the doors slid open silently. What appeared to be a bathhouse stretched out before us. White tiles paved the ground. A red-carpeted pathway led us forward. Pools of water rippled on both sides of it. On the left side, the pools gave off hints of steam from their heat. The ones to the right had small ice blocks floating in them. Around the pools there were green plants, sprouting directly from the floor. Some of the plants bloomed with strange, multicolored flowers which wafted a beautiful potpourri scent. The end of the room was curtained off with white flowing drapes. Wharton and Forneus walked ahead, along the red carpet between the pools, toward the white curtains. We pushed through into a wide room. It also had white tiles with two marble fountains bursting with water on each side. In between the two fountains there was a staggering emerald desk which sparkled green light. Sitting at the desk, talking on the phone, was Mary Magdalene.

"Yes," she said through the receiver, flicking her red curls out of her eyes with an air of dignity. "Business continues as planned. We perform a valuable service."

She placed the phone down and looked up at us as we walked into the room. She looked from the demons in front of us to me and then to Judas. As her eyes locked with his, her mouth dropped. The dignified aura around her disappeared and she looked almost like a little girl. Her emerald eyes brimmed with tears as she got to her feet. She ran out from behind the desk, pushed the demons out of the way and launched herself at Judas. She clung to him in a teary embrace.

"You have no idea what I've been through," she sobbed. "Oh, Judas! Finally, you're free, you're free," she blubbered over and over again.

Judas hugged her back tightly. I could see his eyes were also glassy with tears, although they didn't fall as freely as Mary's. I let them hold each other and bask in their reunion. Finally, Mary pulled her face away from Judas' chest, which was now wet with tears. She looked over to me and parted from her brother. She then embraced me in a fierce hug and kissed me full on the lips.

"Thank you, thank you, Michael. For doing what I could not achieve in all these hundreds of years of trying. You have freed the only soul in existence that I care more about than my own. I wasn't at the sermon, but I have heard the rumors. I was just preparing to come and find you!" She stepped back and wiped her eyes. Mascara ran black down her cheeks, but it did nothing to dim her beauty.

"I don't know where to start; what to say," she said, looking from Judas to me and back again.

"Start with why you are here and why this is the first time I've known of your presence in Hell." Judas said. His face turned stony with barely contained anger. "You seem to be doing very well for yourself."

She nodded, looking down at her feet.

"Yes" she said, "you deserve an explanation, and you will have it." She turned to the demons who stood back behind us silently. "Wharton, Forneus, thank you for bringing me my brother and master. Please go and help Oba. She is at the front desk and has been inundated calls about Lord Michael's sermon. I have briefed her that we continue to run as normal; all services must be completely consensual. What we do here helps stem the desire of Hell's souls. What they would have to take by force, we can deliver through transaction. Oba needs help to answer phones, so she can continue to welcome guests."

"Very good." Wharton said and both demons turned to leave.

"Oh and," Mary said to the departing pair, "if you tell a single soul that you just saw me crying, I'll have you both on clean up duty for a decade."

"Yes ma'am." Forneus nodded.

"You shift from emotion to business with the ease of The Devil." Judas commented sharply as soon as the demons left the room. "Have you gone back to your old ways so easily?"

She stared at Judas with a hard face, before it softened again. "I deserve that." She nodded. "I deserve a lot of things. You will have your explanation Judas. There is something downstairs I need you both to see. Why don't we walk and talk?"

"You always were efficient." Judas said harshly.

"And patience was never your strong suit!" She snapped back.

They stared at each other, two flame-haired, green-eyed visions of power. The tension between them was a mangled knot of unanswered questions. Mary shook her head and looked up to me.

"Only a brother can talk to his sister like that and get away with it," she observed. "We'll take my private stairs down. It's time both of you understood the work I've been doing here. We're going to bring down Asmodeus and his Kingdom of Lies once and for all."

108

24

MARY PRESSED A BUTTON under her desk. It split in the middle and the ends rose up to form two emerald walls. Between the walls, the floor slid away to reveal a black staircase.

"Follow me," she requested. "I'll speak as we descend. I must ask you to promise that you won't interrupt me at all while I tell my tale. I'll try not to get lost in the details, but some are very important. Do you promise?"

We both agreed and so she began to step down into the stairwell. At first we trailed behind, down a square cut set of stairs then caught up to her and were able to walk comfortably side by side as we went down. Mary began her story.

"On the night of the Last Supper, Jesus came to me," she began. "He came to me with a startling revelation, that the person who was to betray him was you, Judas. He explained that he had asked you to do it and that you had agreed. He went on to reveal my part in his plan. Once he had been crucified he would resurrect himself from the dead before ascending to Heaven. I was to witness this and ensure the word was spread: that Jesus was the true Son of God and had died on the cross to save man from his sins. In the shedding of his blood he would give mankind a chance at redemption, and enflame the passion for God in humanity as never before. He said that I would have to let you go into exile, away from the accusers of your betrayal, but before you left I should help assuage your guilt. I was to let you know that I too knew the truth; that although you'd be hated by your once close friends for the rest of your life, you would still have my and God's love. He said that you would be rewarded in Heaven even more than the rest of the Apostles. I was devastated the next day when your body was found. The others rejoiced shamefully at your suicide, for Jesus had been arrested and sentenced to death. They did not know the truth. I looked on as the Romans tortured the love of my life and my dear brother's name was desecrated. It was unspeakable to behold, even though I had been forewarned of what was to come.

I clung to the hope that God's plan was a righteous one. I prayed that despite your ungracious departure from this world, your sacrifice would be enough to keep you in the Kingdom of Heaven. I did as Jesus asked and spread word of his resurrection, keeping your true part secret. The effect was as he desired: all those who believed the story became zealous converts. We were still a small group, but the gospel of Jesus and his sacrifice resonated with all who heard. The followers grew. I kept the secret of your part in the plan buried inside me. I lived a guilty life until the end of my days, but I stayed true to Jesus. I lived a good life. Unlike many, I lived what I preached. When my time came I died and went into the graces of Heaven. It was a wonderful place. Everything you could want was there. It was true rest. You didn't have to struggle against desire. You need not worry about any harm coming to you. It was bliss. But still things were missing: you Judas. You were not there."

Mary looked at her brother and a single tear fell down her cheek. She clasped Judas' hand. He held tightly and she continued.

"The man I knew as Jesus had also essentially disappeared. He had reunited his soul with God Almighty and so both of my true loves were lost. God was kind to me, but he was not a companion, He was a master to be worshipped. I walked with God in the bountiful gardens of knowledge, but I didn't understand how you could be left to suffer in Hell alone. When I asked God why, he explained that he viewed suicide as a slight against His gift of life. Your body is a temple, and you had soiled that temple willingly. He said that if anyone could murder themselves and expect to come to Heaven, everyone would kill themselves before they could be corrupted. Human life on earth would cease to exist. He had built Hell to redeem souls, but the sin of suicide must first be punished by ten thousand years penance of imprisonment within a petrified forest. He was unwilling to revoke his binding creation, even in your case. God maintained that his decision was perfect and therefore could not be contradicted. I was uneasy with the explanation and even more distressed that you should be tortured in Hell for so long before coming to us. I felt impotent to do anything. Anyone who challenged God outwardly was expelled to Hell immediately and if I were to speak out in direct opposition to Him, we would both be hopelessly trapped. I knew there had to be a better way.

"I watched and waited. Over time I grew troubled at the lack of souls that seemed to pass into Heaven from Damnation. Any unrepented sin on Earth, no matter how small, would send a soul to Hell. It seemed that, although Hell was designed to help redeem souls, it would actually

110

corrupt most of them further. It seemed the temptation that dwelled here in abundance was too much to resist for many. The tales of Hell I heard from some of The Converted seemed to confirm my suspicions. I was told many souls deeply despised God for sending them to Hell, the worst place for the worst evils, when they felt they had lived justly in their hearts. Even if people weren't completely evil to begin with, they learnt over time that goodness doesn't pay in the savage jungle of damnation.

"After centuries of seeing the trickle of souls coming from Hell dwindle almost to nothing, I approached God one day with a proposal. We would create a middle ground, where dead souls who were close to being able to enter Heaven could go to perfect their intentions. Initially, God rejected the idea. He wanted perfect obedience to His will in Heaven or nothing at all. But I persisted. God craves love like we all do. He wants souls to bask with him in Heaven. I began to slowly convince Him, over centuries of cautious debate, that my way would help allay the bitterness of many souls. If they didn't have to experience The Guilt in Hell and did not feel condemned by Him, then they could understand more clearly their own small imperfections without feeling resentment at being punished. Of course, the truly evil people would still go to Hell and feel the remorse for their sins, but the essentially good could have the mercy of realizing their errors through quiet reflection. I dubbed this middle ground Purgatory. Many since have called it Limbo.

"Through long debate, God grudgingly accepted my logic. His concern now was that there was another hurdle in creating this Purgatory. God had made Heaven and Earth in six days, but Hell was more complex. It had taken him centuries to perfect the formula for its construction. If we were to build something in between, he would first have to build a new wall between Purgatory and Heaven and then alter the barrier of Hell without destroying it. This would take a colossal amount of time and energy. I pressed him. What is time for God? What is energy for the infinite one? Finally he agreed on one condition: that I was to be the supervisor of this Purgatory once it was created. I had questioned his word, so in a sense it was a punishment, but I accepted it for the good of others. The bargain was struck. I was hopeful that once I was able to control Purgatory, I might somehow be able to find a loophole to help speed your passage from Hell to Heaven.

It took God half a millennium to finish the task. He worked day and night and paid attention to nothing else. Earth fell into the dark ages without his divine influence but, in the end, he succeeded. There were now three realms to the afterlife: Hell, Purgatory and Heaven."

We reached the bottom of the stairs. Mary cut off her story and stopped at a golden door with a sculpture of a circular eye at the top of the frame. The pupil in the center was a picture of Earth, surrounded by an iris of grey. Above the iris, the space to the top of the circle was white, while below the iris the space was black. Mary opened the door and we were bathed in a soft light. She walked inside; we followed behind her into what appeared to be a revolving dome. The roof stretched up high above our heads, the arc of the walls a gentle curve. We looked down to see we were walking on glass flooring. Rolling black clouds struggled to rise against the clear level at our feet.

"This room is a representation of the sum of God's creation." Mary said, continuing to move to the center of the room. "I had it built so I can educate my employees about the reality of their predicament. I can use it to show you where we stand in the universe."

She stopped at a bench in the middle of the room, which sat in front of a slowly spinning globe. The top half of the globe rose above us, around ten feet in height, while the other half sunk into the floor. Clouds shifted above its surface, constantly moving and spinning.

"This is, of course, Earth," said Mary. "It is an exact replica, which changes as Earth does. Weather, developments of man and environmental movements are all recorded moments after they happen."

I looked in amazement at the globe. It was an incredible feat of engineering. Before I could voice any questions, Mary pressed on.

"If you look upwards you will see the Heavens. They are forever expanding to be in essence infinite. I don't have the resources to map any changes, but they are created from my memory of my time in the Kingdom. Heaven is perfect to God, so the only change would be to repeat what exists, to allow more room for his wanted children. This model is a poor substitute, but at least it gives you an idea."

Above us shone galaxies of stars, suns and planets. Gold and silver tracks of light spun into swirling nebulae, which were joined by fine rainbows of illumination. The detail was remarkable. From my vantage point I could only make out a portion of what was there, but I was sure that if I were able to move up into the sky that I would discover new worlds, new splendor.

"Below," Mary interrupted my enchantment, "is the basin of Hell." I looked down and the black clouds parted. The fires of doom spread at our feet. Indeed the city of Hell shone beneath us. Mount Belial framed the metropolis, with the lakes, deserts, rivers and seas beyond that.

"It's so big," I said.

"Bigger than you think," Mary replied, "yet not big enough to maintain the perpetual growth of population we're experiencing. If something isn't done, then eventually Hell will become so choked with souls that it will be even worse than it is now. This is why Satan worked tirelessly to try to cleanse souls as best he could. Ultimately the task was impossible for him. But I digress."

She pulled a switch on the bench before us. The ground started to rise and curve.

"What I have shown you so far is what God created before we inserted Purgatory in the middle. This is what the universe has evolved into now."

As the floor rose underneath us, higher into the air, I could see that it had pushed into a curving bulb below as well. Small, grey mountains began to grow inside the cavern it created. Grey rivers started to flow and grey trees sprouted. Buildings rose up between the landscapes. It was totally colorless. Finally we were standing on the ceiling of Earth, looking down to this new world of Purgatory. The new realm surrounded the atmosphere of the model of Earth. I looked down to take in the detail and Judas did as well. Mary stayed at the bench, which was positioned right above the North Pole of the green and blue planet.

"God didn't want any spectacular beauty to foreshadow the purpose of the souls from their reflection while in this state of Limbo," she went on. "He created landforms, so people are able to move about with a sense of bearing. However, he refused to bring any potential joy into the realm. He was afraid people would settle for freedom in Purgatory, rather than come across to love and serve him in Heaven. The real mercy he showed to the souls was that there was to be no forced visions of guilt while there. Also, since most of the souls that arrive in Purgatory are basically good, there is no fear of harm coming from other deep evils like anger, lust or greed."

Judas and I both looked up back at Mary. She pointed to a sketch of the realms on the desk in front of her.

"It's easier to understand how each realm related to the other when it was smaller. Come and see."

We moved back to her side. The sketch showed the same figure I had seen on the door outside. It was a large circlular eye with a pupil of the earth in the middle. Around Earth was an iris of grey; purgatory. Above was a white Heaven, below was a black Hell.

"All of the realms of afterlife are connected to Earth through the rite of death. Heaven brushes the top tip of Earth, Hell the bottom. Purgatory surrounds. It means that souls can go directly to their intended realm once their mortal body dies. It is a perfect arrangement. The only way you can exist on Earth is if you are alive inside a flesh casing. Once that shell releases your soul, you are sucked towards whichever afterlife you belong. At the time of death, the barriers of the realms sense your soul's deepest emotions, your dominating thoughts. They gauge your past actions and your potential future intentions to determine your destination. The walls between Hell, Purgatory and Heaven act the same way. Once your intentions form and change to true conviction, once you have conquered desires that pull your freewill away from the obedience of God, then your soul will be drawn through the filter towards Him. Your ethereal body in the afterlife comes with you wherever you go, but of course it can change just as your mind can. If you regress back toward sin or give in to your desires, you are sent plummeting back through the filters. It is possible to float from Hell to Purgatory and then to Heaven, once your soul becomes light without the burden of desire."

I stepped back and looked once more around at the universe. It was stupendous. All of this had come from the hands of one creator. There was beauty and form that could only come from the mind of incredible artistic genius. However, it sickened me. The whole creation was a system designed to enslave us. We were bound to obey the rules of that system or suffer as a result. The divisions between realms were walls of tyranny, blocking our path to freedom. Freewill had no place in this universe, yet it had been given to us anyway; that was the cruellest joke of all. I opened my mouth to say so, but Mary continued her story.

"Once Purgatory was complete, God handed me the keys to the gates between my new realm and Heaven. The gates work almost like service doors. They allow the keepers of the universe to move between the realms, as they desire. My keys are like Saint Peter's keys between the Kingdom of Earth and the Kingdom of Heaven. The keepers of the keys can use them to unlock the gate and pass through into the other kingdom. They are then allowed three days in the visited realm before being drawn back to where they belong. If I needed advice on how to tend the souls of Purgatory, I could always return to God for a short time. Because in my heart I still questioned God's decision on Judas, I would always be drawn back to Purgatory eventually. It was a caveat which I was content with since I held the ability to visit Heaven using the keys at my own freedom. I asked God whether there were keys to the barrier between Purgatory and Hell but he denied their existence. He said there could be no reason that anyone other than The Devil would want to pass back and forth from the realm of Hell at will. I knew better than to openly question his judgment, and felt my heart sink at his declaration. However, I still held his word in doubt. I continued to hope that I might be able to pass through and find you one day.

"Once in Purgatory, I threw myself furiously into the task set for me. All kinds of souls washed into my domain. Those with a slightly altered perception of God's word came, along with kind-hearted atheists, mildly corrupted teenagers and almost reformed sinners. I welcomed them all with open arms, and was surprised with how quickly some of them accepted the true love of God and passed to Heaven. It was a resounding success. God congratulated me wholeheartedly for my accomplishments. However, over the centuries it became evident to me there were still some souls who had taken up what seemed a permanent residence in Purgatory. Those who had been murdered violently, and couldn't accept that it was part of God's plan, made up many of this group. There were also others who enjoyed small sins; often their desires would escalate and I would lose these souls to Hell. I grieved each passing like I were losing a child. I knew that these people didn't really deserve to be punished, just like you did not, Judas. They were just using the freewill they were given by God. They were simply giving in to desires which he had built into their makeup. Still I continued with my task. I frequented Heaven less and less and finally kept the keys of the realm locked safe within my apartment. They were secure there, since if anyone had the true intention of stealing them from me, they would be sucked down into Hell before they could break the seal of the safe I had constructed.

"I asked every soul who entered Purgatory from Hell if they knew of your plight, Judas, but none had. It continued to eat my soul that you should be damned.

"One day an intensely interesting being made his way into my realm. He had come from Hell. His name was Zoroaster. When I asked if he had heard of you, he said he knew your story well. He declared with great gravity that many things had been hidden from us, and that is was his purpose to battle for truth in the universe.

"Zoroaster told me that once he had been a Prophet of God, but had disagreed with the plan of Jesus and Christianity, so had been thrown into Hell. There he pondered for years on the real purpose of things. He decided that God was hiding things from us and that it was his soul's meaning to expose as much truth as he could to anyone who would listen. He hoped that through absolute truth would come order and eternal knowledge. Zoroaster became a powerful magician. His talents grew so that he could compel the forces of the elements with his will. Preaching his ideal of truth, he converted many demons to his new religion. He embraced demons that were true to their desires, as long as they never lied about their intent or actions. It was a revelation in Hell. Many followers joined him. Finally, Zoroaster led a revolt to Satan's palace to demand their freedom from The Guilt and insist he free the trees in the Forest of the Damned. Zoroaster had known the truth of Judas and wanted to expose the lie to everyone. Satan used all of his power and influence to quash the rebellion. Demon was pitted against demon. Zoroaster fought against Satan himself. The war was bloody but swift. Satan was able to defeat Zoroaster's forces by weight of numbers and the magician was no match for the Lord of Hell.

"In defeat, Zoroaster and the last seven of his followers fled to the outreaches of Hell. He set up a small monastery there, and continued to reflect on his internal search for truth and how to spread it throughout the universe. He built a bridge up into the sky to the barrier between Hell and Purgatory: the Chinvar Bridge. He studied the barrier's construction, and saw how he could work the system of its function by controlling his own thoughts and desires. Zoroaster was able to push away his grudge against God and his desires for revelling in the pleasures that God deemed impure. He left his seven demons and passed over to Purgatory.

"Zoroaster spoke freely about all of this. He never covered up his wrongdoings. He was incredible to speak with, this man who had no duplicity or pretension. He knew exactly who I was and what I had done in my life. He could see inside me. He understood my want to redeem souls, and my deep longing to be reunited with Judas once his penance was complete.

"I told him of my suspicion that there might be a hidden gateway which would allow us to pass into Hell from Purgatory at will. He said he would find it if it existed. Returning to the barrier, he studied it closely from end to end. Finally he found a small chink in its façade. There was indeed a door. It was sealed up by elements he had never ever seen before. I had no ability to see what he could, but I trusted his word without question. It was so refreshing to be able to take someone at face value and know that he hid nothing. I showed him the keys I had for Heaven and he told me they were made of these same unique elements that sealed the doorway tight. With painstaking effort, Zoroaster was able to unpick these elements from the archway around the door between Purgatory and Hell. He then melded them into keys of a shape that could turn the gate's lock. We now had the ability to pass between the realms of the afterlife as we wished.

"I wanted to go to Hell to see you right away, but Zoroaster advised me to think it through. What if, when I got there, Satan discovered me and took these keys? It would be a disaster. It could mean the spread of more falsehood and chaos into Purgatory and even Heaven. If we dared go into Heaven, God would know right away what we had done and would take the keys from us forever.

"Zoroaster came up with a plan. We would travel to Hell together, but first we had to create protected hiding places for both sets of keys. He left me in Purgatory and, using the keys to Hell, went to his monastery at the base of the Chinvar Bridge. He returned quickly with his seven demons before Satan could discover he'd entered the realm of the damned. In the safety of Purgatory, Zoroaster performed a dark rite. He drew out the souls of the seven demons and wrapped my keys to Heaven inside a weave of their spirits. He then encased the knot of their souls inside my own soul. He hid it deep within my body, impenetrable to see or feel by anyone but me.

"The demons willingly sacrificed their conscious ability to stay in their bodies in the hope that one day we could use the keys to bring truth to the universe."

Judas had been weeping as Mary told the story. She kissed him on the cheek and took his hand. I looked away, down into the universe at our feet. It was hard to imagine that all of this had happened. Eternity held so many secrets that I might never know.

"Zoroaster then opened the door to Hell again and we went inside," Mary continued. "Taking the seven empty shells of his demons with us, we locked the gate. We were now in the realm of Hell. Zoroaster took two full days to create a safe for his keys at the Chinvar Bridge Monastery, far away from the city of Hell. On the third day, we travelled in secret to visit you in the Forest of the Damned. Zoroaster wrapped us in an invisible shroud of elements and we approached your prison. Satan was there, whispering evil things in your ear. It felt like I had been gutted. I could only stand by and watch in horror. Zoroaster said there was nothing he could do to free you. He had already tried and failed.

"We returned to the Chinvar Bridge ready to pass back through to Purgatory, but I could not. I refused to leave you, Judas. The seven demon souls which dwelled inside me would ensure I could stay in Hell. There was enough collective sin sown in my soul to keep me from ever passing back. Zoroaster made me a promise that he would leave the keys to Purgatory safely hidden in Chinvar Bridge Monastery. He would take my place in Purgatory and help cleanse souls so they could pass to Heaven. I would keep the Keys to Heaven safe within my being. "I went back into Hell and found Satan. He was intrigued by me. He could see within my soul seven perfect sins, yet I remained outwardly a human. The weave of the knot was so rendered that he was unable to read my thoughts. My true soul was hidden deep within. He asked who I was and I told him. I was Mary Magdalene. He laughed, and called me 'The Whore of God'. I told him that I would do anything for him to release you, Judas. He said he would never, ever do it. He said I had nothing that he could desire and that he wanted to keep us both in Hell, away from God, for we had once walked beside him arm in arm. Satan then made a proposal: he would build for me what he called 'a house of song' to help relieve souls of their desires and move out of Hell. I would manage this place and in return he would give me wealth, status and security. Most importantly, he promised to leave you to your grief, never to whisper horrible things in your ear again. I agreed. It was the only way I could keep you safe and work on a way to free you.

"The 'house of song' Satan built is this brothel. I went back to my original profession and helped create Magdalene's Mansion to help stop lustful souls going out and stealing humanity from their victims through vicious rapes. I fulfil fantasy in order to turn desire into realization and realization into the truth: that there is no lasting happiness in physical pleasure alone. There must be a deeper connection.

"All of the men and women who work here are treated well. I teach them about the ways of the universe; I show them the truth. A high percentage of them pass over to Purgatory where I hope Zoroaster still resides, guiding them into the restful peace that lies in the Kingdom of Heaven. I have worked for centuries to turn this house into a place which can help rather than consume.

"Satan would come here sometimes when he wanted unalloyed sexual pleasure. I would not unleash him on my girls, so I took his lustful burdens on myself. I thought that maybe my service would convince him to release you, Judas. I was wrong. He would never commit. But I refused to let him break me. I make my own decisions, I am truthful about them and I am not sorry.

"One day, Satan came to me. I could tell that he was changed somehow. He began calling himself Asmodeus instead of Satan. He started asking me if I knew anything about a set of keys which could lead him into Heaven. The only way he could know of their existence was if he'd spoken to Zoroaster or God. Neither option seemed likely, but there could be no other explanation. I had told nobody the secret of my reason for being in Hell, and I was certain he couldn't read my thoughts.

"I denied the keys' existence. I went against my philosophy of Zoroastrian Truth to keep them safe. He demanded I give them up to him. He said that if I handed them to him he would free you. I did not trust him and continued to deny any existence of the keys. I know now, because of Michael, that Asmodeus is God reunited with his evil side. Before, I saw him as always kind and wise, even if I didn't fully agree with him. Asmodeus is a different being altogether. He is perverted. He must be stopped. He must not be allowed to continue a reign of lies in Heaven."

Mary turned and took me by both hands.

"Michael, you have freed my brother. I believe in your vision of a life without boundaries with all my heart. I have been waiting for someone like you to come along for almost two thousand years and finally you have arrived. You are the real messiah of mankind. I will do anything I can to help you achieve your goal, even if it means tearing down the walls of Purgatory that I wanted to create in the first place. I am your follower forever."

She then turned back to Judas, holding out her arms to him. "Now do you understand, brother?" she asked tearfully. "I may not have done all of the right things, but I have done my best and I have done it with honesty. Can you find it in your heart to forgive me? I have lain with The Devil, but I have done it willingly to have us back together. Here we stand. All of my work has been worth this very moment."

Judas looked at her with stony eyes. "Maybe you would have been better to stay in Heaven. I would never ask you to become a whore for me. Not ever."

"Judas," she cried. "I know you would never ask anything of me. I did it willingly. I may have given up my body at times, but I have never given up my divine soul. You have always said that is worth more than anything else in this existence. You are part of that soul, Judas, my only family. I beg you, look past all the lies and understand the truth. I love you with all my heart. I would do anything to make you happy. I want nothing but good for everyone in this universe."

Judas' face softened.

"I missed you, Mary. You were always the heart of the family."

They embraced, shaking in each other's arms; reunited after so many years. I held onto that moment and stored it inside me. It was what I would feel when I found Charlotte again.

"Where do we go from here?" I asked finally.

"We gather the keys," Mary said, pulling away from her brother's arms. "And we use them to tear down the walls that bind us."

25

MARY PRESSED A BUTTON under her desk. It split in the middle and the ends rose up to form two emerald walls. Between the walls, the floor slid away to reveal a black staircase.

"Follow me," she requested. "I'll speak as we descend. I must ask you to promise that you won't interrupt me at all while I tell my tale. I'll try not to get lost in the details, but some are very important. Do you promise?"

We both agreed and so she began to step down into the stairwell. At first we trailed behind, down a square cut set of stairs then caught up to her and were able to walk comfortably side by side as we went down. Mary began her story.

"On the night of the Last Supper, Jesus came to me," she began. "He came to me with a startling revelation, that the person who was to betray him was you, Judas. He explained that he had asked you to do it and that you had agreed. He went on to reveal my part in his plan. Once he had been crucified he would resurrect himself from the dead before ascending to Heaven. I was to witness this and ensure the word was spread: that Jesus was the true Son of God and had died on the cross to save man from his sins. In the shedding of his blood he would give mankind a chance at redemption, and enflame the passion for God in humanity as never before. He said that I would have to let you go into exile, away from the accusers of your betrayal, but before you left I should help assuage your guilt. I was to let you know that I too knew the truth; that although you'd be hated by your once close friends for the rest of your life, you would still have my and God's love. He said that you would be rewarded in Heaven even more than the rest of the Apostles. I was devastated the next day when your body was found. The others rejoiced shamefully at your suicide, for Jesus had been arrested and sentenced to death. They did not know the truth. I looked on as the Romans tortured the love of my life and my dear brother's name was desecrated. It was unspeakable to behold, even though I had been forewarned of what was to come.

I clung to the hope that God's plan was a righteous one. I prayed that despite your ungracious departure from this world, your sacrifice would be enough to keep you in the Kingdom of Heaven. I did as Jesus asked and spread word of his resurrection, keeping your true part secret. The effect was as he desired: all those who believed the story became zealous converts. We were still a small group, but the gospel of Jesus and his sacrifice resonated with all who heard. The followers grew. I kept the secret of your part in the plan buried inside me. I lived a guilty life until the end of my days, but I stayed true to Jesus. I lived a good life. Unlike many, I lived what I preached. When my time came I died and went into the graces of Heaven. It was a wonderful place. Everything you could want was there. It was true rest. You didn't have to struggle against desire. You need not worry about any harm coming to you. It was bliss. But still things were missing: you Judas. You were not there."

Mary looked at her brother and a single tear fell down her cheek. She clasped Judas' hand. He held tightly and she continued.

"The man I knew as Jesus had also essentially disappeared. He had reunited his soul with God Almighty and so both of my true loves were lost. God was kind to me, but he was not a companion, He was a master to be worshipped. I walked with God in the bountiful gardens of knowledge, but I didn't understand how you could be left to suffer in Hell alone. When I asked God why, he explained that he viewed suicide as a slight against His gift of life. Your body is a temple, and you had soiled that temple willingly. He said that if anyone could murder themselves and expect to come to Heaven, everyone would kill themselves before they could be corrupted. Human life on earth would cease to exist. He had built Hell to redeem souls, but the sin of suicide must first be punished by ten thousand years penance of imprisonment within a petrified forest. He was unwilling to revoke his binding creation, even in your case. God maintained that his decision was perfect and therefore could not be contradicted. I was uneasy with the explanation and even more distressed that you should be tortured in Hell for so long before coming to us. I felt impotent to do anything. Anyone who challenged God outwardly was expelled to Hell immediately and if I were to speak out in direct opposition to Him, we would both be hopelessly trapped. I knew there had to be a better way.

"I watched and waited. Over time I grew troubled at the lack of souls that seemed to pass into Heaven from Damnation. Any unrepented sin on Earth, no matter how small, would send a soul to Hell. It seemed that, although Hell was designed to help redeem souls, it would actually corrupt most of them further. It seemed the temptation that dwelled here in abundance was too much to resist for many. The tales of Hell I heard from some of The Converted seemed to confirm my suspicions. I was told many souls deeply despised God for sending them to Hell, the worst place for the worst evils, when they felt they had lived justly in their hearts. Even if people weren't completely evil to begin with, they learnt over time that goodness doesn't pay in the savage jungle of damnation.

"After centuries of seeing the trickle of souls coming from Hell dwindle almost to nothing, I approached God one day with a proposal. We would create a middle ground, where dead souls who were close to being able to enter Heaven could go to perfect their intentions. Initially, God rejected the idea. He wanted perfect obedience to His will in Heaven or nothing at all. But I persisted. God craves love like we all do. He wants souls to bask with him in Heaven. I began to slowly convince Him, over centuries of cautious debate, that my way would help allay the bitterness of many souls. If they didn't have to experience The Guilt in Hell and did not feel condemned by Him, then they could understand more clearly their own small imperfections without feeling resentment at being punished. Of course, the truly evil people would still go to Hell and feel the remorse for their sins, but the essentially good could have the mercy of realizing their errors through quiet reflection. I dubbed this middle ground Purgatory. Many since have called it Limbo.

"Through long debate, God grudgingly accepted my logic. His concern now was that there was another hurdle in creating this Purgatory. God had made Heaven and Earth in six days, but Hell was more complex. It had taken him centuries to perfect the formula for its construction. If we were to build something in between, he would first have to build a new wall between Purgatory and Heaven and then alter the barrier of Hell without destroying it. This would take a colossal amount of time and energy. I pressed him. What is time for God? What is energy for the infinite one? Finally he agreed on one condition: that I was to be the supervisor of this Purgatory once it was created. I had questioned his word, so in a sense it was a punishment, but I accepted it for the good of others. The bargain was struck. I was hopeful that once I was able to control Purgatory, I might somehow be able to find a loophole to help speed your passage from Hell to Heaven.

It took God half a millennium to finish the task. He worked day and night and paid attention to nothing else. Earth fell into the dark ages without his divine influence but, in the end, he succeeded. There were now three realms to the afterlife: Hell, Purgatory and Heaven."

We reached the bottom of the stairs. Mary cut off her story and stopped at a golden door with a sculpture of a circular eye at the top of the frame. The pupil in the center was a picture of Earth, surrounded by an iris of grey. Above the iris, the space to the top of the circle was white, while below the iris the space was black. Mary opened the door and we were bathed in a soft light. She walked inside; we followed behind her into what appeared to be a revolving dome. The roof stretched up high above our heads, the arc of the walls a gentle curve. We looked down to see we were walking on glass flooring. Rolling black clouds struggled to rise against the clear level at our feet.

"This room is a representation of the sum of God's creation." Mary said, continuing to move to the center of the room. "I had it built so I can educate my employees about the reality of their predicament. I can use it to show you where we stand in the universe."

She stopped at a bench in the middle of the room, which sat in front of a slowly spinning globe. The top half of the globe rose above us, around ten feet in height, while the other half sunk into the floor. Clouds shifted above its surface, constantly moving and spinning.

"This is, of course, Earth," said Mary. "It is an exact replica, which changes as Earth does. Weather, developments of man and environmental movements are all recorded moments after they happen."

I looked in amazement at the globe. It was an incredible feat of engineering. Before I could voice any questions, Mary pressed on.

"If you look upwards you will see the Heavens. They are forever expanding to be in essence infinite. I don't have the resources to map any changes, but they are created from my memory of my time in the Kingdom. Heaven is perfect to God, so the only change would be to repeat what exists, to allow more room for his wanted children. This model is a poor substitute, but at least it gives you an idea."

Above us shone galaxies of stars, suns and planets. Gold and silver tracks of light spun into swirling nebulae, which were joined by fine rainbows of illumination. The detail was remarkable. From my vantage point I could only make out a portion of what was there, but I was sure that if I were able to move up into the sky that I would discover new worlds, new splendor.

"Below," Mary interrupted my enchantment, "is the basin of Hell." I looked down and the black clouds parted. The fires of doom spread at our feet. Indeed the city of Hell shone beneath us. Mount Belial framed the metropolis, with the lakes, deserts, rivers and seas beyond that.

"It's so big," I said.

"Bigger than you think," Mary replied, "yet not big enough to maintain the perpetual growth of population we're experiencing. If something isn't done, then eventually Hell will become so choked with souls that it will be even worse than it is now. This is why Satan worked tirelessly to try to cleanse souls as best he could. Ultimately the task was impossible for him. But I digress."

She pulled a switch on the bench before us. The ground started to rise and curve.

"What I have shown you so far is what God created before we inserted Purgatory in the middle. This is what the universe has evolved into now."

As the floor rose underneath us, higher into the air, I could see that it had pushed into a curving bulb below as well. Small, grey mountains began to grow inside the cavern it created. Grey rivers started to flow and grey trees sprouted. Buildings rose up between the landscapes. It was totally colorless. Finally we were standing on the ceiling of Earth, looking down to this new world of Purgatory. The new realm surrounded the atmosphere of the model of Earth. I looked down to take in the detail and Judas did as well. Mary stayed at the bench, which was positioned right above the North Pole of the green and blue planet.

"God didn't want any spectacular beauty to foreshadow the purpose of the souls from their reflection while in this state of Limbo," she went on. "He created landforms, so people are able to move about with a sense of bearing. However, he refused to bring any potential joy into the realm. He was afraid people would settle for freedom in Purgatory, rather than come across to love and serve him in Heaven. The real mercy he showed to the souls was that there was to be no forced visions of guilt while there. Also, since most of the souls that arrive in Purgatory are basically good, there is no fear of harm coming from other deep evils like anger, lust or greed."

Judas and I both looked up back at Mary. She pointed to a sketch of the realms on the desk in front of her.

"It's easier to understand how each realm related to the other when it was smaller. Come and see."

We moved back to her side. The sketch showed the same figure I had seen on the door outside. It was a large circlular eye with a pupil of the earth in the middle. Around Earth was an iris of grey; purgatory. Above was a white Heaven, below was a black Hell.

"All of the realms of afterlife are connected to Earth through the rite of death. Heaven brushes the top tip of Earth, Hell the bottom. Purgatory surrounds. It means that souls can go directly to their intended realm once their mortal body dies. It is a perfect arrangement. The only way you can exist on Earth is if you are alive inside a flesh casing. Once that shell releases your soul, you are sucked towards whichever afterlife you belong. At the time of death, the barriers of the realms sense your soul's deepest emotions, your dominating thoughts. They gauge your past actions and your potential future intentions to determine your destination. The walls between Hell, Purgatory and Heaven act the same way. Once your intentions form and change to true conviction, once you have conquered desires that pull your freewill away from the obedience of God, then your soul will be drawn through the filter towards Him. Your ethereal body in the afterlife comes with you wherever you go, but of course it can change just as your mind can. If you regress back toward sin or give in to your desires, you are sent plummeting back through the filters. It is possible to float from Hell to Purgatory and then to Heaven, once your soul becomes light without the burden of desire."

I stepped back and looked once more around at the universe. It was stupendous. All of this had come from the hands of one creator. There was beauty and form that could only come from the mind of incredible artistic genius. However, it sickened me. The whole creation was a system designed to enslave us. We were bound to obey the rules of that system or suffer as a result. The divisions between realms were walls of tyranny, blocking our path to freedom. Freewill had no place in this universe, yet it had been given to us anyway; that was the cruellest joke of all. I opened my mouth to say so, but Mary continued her story.

"Once Purgatory was complete, God handed me the keys to the gates between my new realm and Heaven. The gates work almost like service doors. They allow the keepers of the universe to move between the realms, as they desire. My keys are like Saint Peter's keys between the Kingdom of Earth and the Kingdom of Heaven. The keepers of the keys can use them to unlock the gate and pass through into the other kingdom. They are then allowed three days in the visited realm before being drawn back to where they belong. If I needed advice on how to tend the souls of Purgatory, I could always return to God for a short time. Because in my heart I still questioned God's decision on Judas, I would always be drawn back to Purgatory eventually. It was a caveat which I was content with since I held the ability to visit Heaven using the keys at my own freedom. I asked God whether there were keys to the barrier between Purgatory and Hell but he denied their existence. He said there could be no reason that anyone other than The Devil would want to pass back and forth from the realm of Hell at will. I knew better than to openly question his judgment, and felt my heart sink at his declaration. However, I still held his word in doubt. I continued to hope that I might be able to pass through and find you one day.

"Once in Purgatory, I threw myself furiously into the task set for me. All kinds of souls washed into my domain. Those with a slightly altered perception of God's word came, along with kind-hearted atheists, mildly corrupted teenagers and almost reformed sinners. I welcomed them all with open arms, and was surprised with how quickly some of them accepted the true love of God and passed to Heaven. It was a resounding success. God congratulated me wholeheartedly for my accomplishments. However, over the centuries it became evident to me there were still some souls who had taken up what seemed a permanent residence in Purgatory. Those who had been murdered violently, and couldn't accept that it was part of God's plan, made up many of this group. There were also others who enjoyed small sins; often their desires would escalate and I would lose these souls to Hell. I grieved each passing like I were losing a child. I knew that these people didn't really deserve to be punished, just like you did not, Judas. They were just using the freewill they were given by God. They were simply giving in to desires which he had built into their makeup. Still I continued with my task. I frequented Heaven less and less and finally kept the keys of the realm locked safe within my apartment. They were secure there, since if anyone had the true intention of stealing them from me, they would be sucked down into Hell before they could break the seal of the safe I had constructed.

"I asked every soul who entered Purgatory from Hell if they knew of your plight, Judas, but none had. It continued to eat my soul that you should be damned.

"One day an intensely interesting being made his way into my realm. He had come from Hell. His name was Zoroaster. When I asked if he had heard of you, he said he knew your story well. He declared with great gravity that many things had been hidden from us, and that is was his purpose to battle for truth in the universe.

"Zoroaster told me that once he had been a Prophet of God, but had disagreed with the plan of Jesus and Christianity, so had been thrown into Hell. There he pondered for years on the real purpose of things. He decided that God was hiding things from us and that it was his soul's meaning to expose as much truth as he could to anyone who would listen. He hoped that through absolute truth would come order and eternal knowledge. Zoroaster became a powerful magician. His talents grew so that he could compel the forces of the elements with his will. Preaching his ideal of truth, he converted many demons to his new religion. He embraced demons that were true to their desires, as long as they never lied about their intent or actions. It was a revelation in Hell. Many followers joined him. Finally, Zoroaster led a revolt to Satan's palace to demand their freedom from The Guilt and insist he free the trees in the Forest of the Damned. Zoroaster had known the truth of Judas and wanted to expose the lie to everyone. Satan used all of his power and influence to quash the rebellion. Demon was pitted against demon. Zoroaster fought against Satan himself. The war was bloody but swift. Satan was able to defeat Zoroaster's forces by weight of numbers and the magician was no match for the Lord of Hell.

"In defeat, Zoroaster and the last seven of his followers fled to the outreaches of Hell. He set up a small monastery there, and continued to reflect on his internal search for truth and how to spread it throughout the universe. He built a bridge up into the sky to the barrier between Hell and Purgatory: the Chinvar Bridge. He studied the barrier's construction, and saw how he could work the system of its function by controlling his own thoughts and desires. Zoroaster was able to push away his grudge against God and his desires for revelling in the pleasures that God deemed impure. He left his seven demons and passed over to Purgatory.

"Zoroaster spoke freely about all of this. He never covered up his wrongdoings. He was incredible to speak with, this man who had no duplicity or pretension. He knew exactly who I was and what I had done in my life. He could see inside me. He understood my want to redeem souls, and my deep longing to be reunited with Judas once his penance was complete.

"I told him of my suspicion that there might be a hidden gateway which would allow us to pass into Hell from Purgatory at will. He said he would find it if it existed. Returning to the barrier, he studied it closely from end to end. Finally he found a small chink in its façade. There was indeed a door. It was sealed up by elements he had never ever seen before. I had no ability to see what he could, but I trusted his word without question. It was so refreshing to be able to take someone at face value and know that he hid nothing. I showed him the keys I had for Heaven and he told me they were made of these same unique elements that sealed the doorway tight. With painstaking effort, Zoroaster was able to unpick these elements from the archway around the door between Purgatory and Hell. He then melded them into keys of a shape that could turn the gate's lock. We now had the ability to pass between the realms of the afterlife as we wished.

"I wanted to go to Hell to see you right away, but Zoroaster advised me to think it through. What if, when I got there, Satan discovered me and took these keys? It would be a disaster. It could mean the spread of more falsehood and chaos into Purgatory and even Heaven. If we dared go into Heaven, God would know right away what we had done and would take the keys from us forever.

"Zoroaster came up with a plan. We would travel to Hell together, but first we had to create protected hiding places for both sets of keys. He left me in Purgatory and, using the keys to Hell, went to his monastery at the base of the Chinvar Bridge. He returned quickly with his seven demons before Satan could discover he'd entered the realm of the damned. In the safety of Purgatory, Zoroaster performed a dark rite. He drew out the souls of the seven demons and wrapped my keys to Heaven inside a weave of their spirits. He then encased the knot of their souls inside my own soul. He hid it deep within my body, impenetrable to see or feel by anyone but me.

"The demons willingly sacrificed their conscious ability to stay in their bodies in the hope that one day we could use the keys to bring truth to the universe."

Judas had been weeping as Mary told the story. She kissed him on the cheek and took his hand. I looked away, down into the universe at our feet. It was hard to imagine that all of this had happened. Eternity held so many secrets that I might never know.

"Zoroaster then opened the door to Hell again and we went inside," Mary continued. "Taking the seven empty shells of his demons with us, we locked the gate. We were now in the realm of Hell. Zoroaster took two full days to create a safe for his keys at the Chinvar Bridge Monastery, far away from the city of Hell. On the third day, we travelled in secret to visit you in the Forest of the Damned. Zoroaster wrapped us in an invisible shroud of elements and we approached your prison. Satan was there, whispering evil things in your ear. It felt like I had been gutted. I could only stand by and watch in horror. Zoroaster said there was nothing he could do to free you. He had already tried and failed.

"We returned to the Chinvar Bridge ready to pass back through to Purgatory, but I could not. I refused to leave you, Judas. The seven demon souls which dwelled inside me would ensure I could stay in Hell. There was enough collective sin sown in my soul to keep me from ever passing back. Zoroaster made me a promise that he would leave the keys to Purgatory safely hidden in Chinvar Bridge Monastery. He would take my place in Purgatory and help cleanse souls so they could pass to Heaven. I would keep the Keys to Heaven safe within my being. "I went back into Hell and found Satan. He was intrigued by me. He could see within my soul seven perfect sins, yet I remained outwardly a human. The weave of the knot was so rendered that he was unable to read my thoughts. My true soul was hidden deep within. He asked who I was and I told him. I was Mary Magdalene. He laughed, and called me 'The Whore of God'. I told him that I would do anything for him to release you, Judas. He said he would never, ever do it. He said I had nothing that he could desire and that he wanted to keep us both in Hell, away from God, for we had once walked beside him arm in arm. Satan then made a proposal: he would build for me what he called 'a house of song' to help relieve souls of their desires and move out of Hell. I would manage this place and in return he would give me wealth, status and security. Most importantly, he promised to leave you to your grief, never to whisper horrible things in your ear again. I agreed. It was the only way I could keep you safe and work on a way to free you.

"The 'house of song' Satan built is this brothel. I went back to my original profession and helped create Magdalene's Mansion to help stop lustful souls going out and stealing humanity from their victims through vicious rapes. I fulfil fantasy in order to turn desire into realization and realization into the truth: that there is no lasting happiness in physical pleasure alone. There must be a deeper connection.

"All of the men and women who work here are treated well. I teach them about the ways of the universe; I show them the truth. A high percentage of them pass over to Purgatory where I hope Zoroaster still resides, guiding them into the restful peace that lies in the Kingdom of Heaven. I have worked for centuries to turn this house into a place which can help rather than consume.

"Satan would come here sometimes when he wanted unalloyed sexual pleasure. I would not unleash him on my girls, so I took his lustful burdens on myself. I thought that maybe my service would convince him to release you, Judas. I was wrong. He would never commit. But I refused to let him break me. I make my own decisions, I am truthful about them and I am not sorry.

"One day, Satan came to me. I could tell that he was changed somehow. He began calling himself Asmodeus instead of Satan. He started asking me if I knew anything about a set of keys which could lead him into Heaven. The only way he could know of their existence was if he'd spoken to Zoroaster or God. Neither option seemed likely, but there could be no other explanation. I had told nobody the secret of my reason for being in Hell, and I was certain he couldn't read my thoughts.

"I denied the keys' existence. I went against my philosophy of Zoroastrian Truth to keep them safe. He demanded I give them up to him. He said that if I handed them to him he would free you. I did not trust him and continued to deny any existence of the keys. I know now, because of Michael, that Asmodeus is God reunited with his evil side. Before, I saw him as always kind and wise, even if I didn't fully agree with him. Asmodeus is a different being altogether. He is perverted. He must be stopped. He must not be allowed to continue a reign of lies in Heaven."

Mary turned and took me by both hands.

"Michael, you have freed my brother. I believe in your vision of a life without boundaries with all my heart. I have been waiting for someone like you to come along for almost two thousand years and finally you have arrived. You are the real messiah of mankind. I will do anything I can to help you achieve your goal, even if it means tearing down the walls of Purgatory that I wanted to create in the first place. I am your follower forever."

She then turned back to Judas, holding out her arms to him. "Now do you understand, brother?" she asked tearfully. "I may not have done all of the right things, but I have done my best and I have done it with honesty. Can you find it in your heart to forgive me? I have lain with The Devil, but I have done it willingly to have us back together. Here we stand. All of my work has been worth this very moment."

Judas looked at her with stony eyes. "Maybe you would have been better to stay in Heaven. I would never ask you to become a whore for me. Not ever."

"Judas," she cried. "I know you would never ask anything of me. I did it willingly. I may have given up my body at times, but I have never given up my divine soul. You have always said that is worth more than anything else in this existence. You are part of that soul, Judas, my only family. I beg you, look past all the lies and understand the truth. I love you with all my heart. I would do anything to make you happy. I want nothing but good for everyone in this universe.

Judas' face softened. "I missed you, Mary. You were always the heart of the family."

They embraced, shaking in each other's arms; reunited after so many years. I held onto that moment and stored it inside me. It was what I would feel when I found Charlotte again.

"Where do we go from here?" I asked finally.

"We gather the keys," Mary said, pulling away from her brother's arms. "And we use them to tear down the walls that bind us."

26

WE WALKED INTO THE FOYER of Satan's tower. The revenge demon, Marax, was at the front desk frantically answering phones. He paused as he saw us enter and stood to greet us.

"Lord Michael," he said, letting the phones ring endlessly around him. "How can I be of service?"

"I need to speak with Clytemnestra," I replied. His face grew dark at the mention of her name.

"She's upstairs in her office with your friend Mr. Smith. I can ask her to come down to you."

"We'll go up, thank you, Marax." I offered, continuing past him toward the elevator.

He moved back to his desk quickly and resumed answering calls.

We travelled upwards to floor 666. The doors opened. Smithy and Clytemnestra turned to see who was entering. The old pilot broke into a huge smile.

"Michael!" he said. "Nessy and me were just having a great chat."

"Nessy?" I raised an eyebrow at her. She rolled her eyes, but smiled. "How are things progressing?" I continued. "I hope Smithy has been of some service."

"I must admit, I never thought an old man could be so insightful," said Clytemnestra. "Things are progressing well with the new suburb on the mountain. Souls are being filtered through orientation, although there are so many more with the Forest of the Damned. It's taking longer than expected."

"I trust your judgment," I told her. "Actually, I've come to ask a favor, something that could prove very useful to our cause against Asmodeus."

"So soon? Are we marching?"

"No, we're a long way off that. We need a priest. One who is wholly human."

"A priest?" She choked. "That's...impossible. I'll certainly search for you, but they are almost invariably demons by the time I reach them; that or they pass over to Heaven."

"I understand it will prove difficult, but nothing is impossible. We have to be vigilant. It's very important."

"Of course." She nodded. "I will do my best."

The phone rang on the desk in the far corner of the room. Clytemnestra excused herself to answer it. "This had better be good Marax," she snapped. "I'm with The Master."

I turned to Smithy while she spoke on the phone.

"How is everything here?" I asked, putting my hand on his shoulder. "Really."

"It's all going well," he whispered, leaning to my ear. "She isn't very tactful with the staff. In fact she is downright rude if she thinks someone ranks below her. But she is getting the job done. The positive is she has been an angel to me. I suspect that's because she knows you sent me."

"Thank you," I whispered back in gratitude. "And you're calling her Nessy?"

"I can't say her real name," He admitted, turning red.

"Don't worry, Smithy, I find it hard as well," I chuckled.

The sound of the phone slamming down made us spin around. Clytemnestra stood there looking at us, white as a ghost, her hands on her cheeks.

"We have a problem," she said. "We need to go downstairs, now."

27

THE DOORS OF THE ELEVATOR OPENED on the bottom floor of the building. We were met with carnage. Rocks and other missiles were being thrown into the windows all around. People outside were screaming.

Marax ran over to us.

"I've secured the doors," he said. "It was all I could do to stop them stampeding in."

"What's going on?" I asked calmly. Inside, my stomach was churning.

"I'm not sure. Just after you went upstairs, a march started rumbling down the street. Demons and humans with knives were cutting themselves open as they came towards the building," he explained with worry etched into his face. "They were screaming to be freed from their existence, or something. They were coming for the doors so I barricaded them shut. That's when they started climbing the walls outside. I didn't know what to do, so I called you. I'm sorry if I have failed you." He bowed his head toward his feet.

"You've done nothing wrong here," I assured him. "Are you sure they can't get in?"

"I'm sure," he said, raising his head again. "This building is completely fortified against any attack. They can climb all they like; they won't find a way in."

Sickening thumps started sounding outside. It was like people were beating wet bags of sand on the pavement. I moved closer to the windows to peer out. They weren't bags. The people who were climbing the building were throwing themselves off onto the street. Their bodies would explode on the ground, bleeding out onto the street, creating a river of blood. The red tide was seeping beneath the doors onto the foyer floor. I watched aghast as their bodies healed again. The mangled messes of bone and blood would then start scaling the walls again to plummet once more to

133

the street.

"What on earth are they doing?" I asked, barely containing my emotion.

Smithy walked over to stand at my shoulder. He looked out of the bloodstained windows.

"It seems to be a protest," he said. "Some of the people out there are holding signs."

I followed his line of sight and could see the same thing. Thousands of demons and people were crowded outside, waving banners. Some said "We Want a True Death"; others read, "Release us from this Hell".

"We have to do something." I turned and pointed to Marax. "You. Stand ready to open the doors. Judas," I said turning to him. "You're coming outside with me. We need to make some sense of this. Everyone else, stay here."

Mary moved forward. "Let me come," she pleaded. "I might be able to help."

I nodded. The three of us stood in front of the doors.

"Ready, Marax," I yelled. "Now!"

He opened the doors and I sent a strong wind blowing in front of us. Blood and bodies scattered onto the far end of the street. I pushed the gale outward further, to clear a wide circle.

"Stop!" I yelled, cutting off the wind of elements. "What is the meaning of this?" My voice rippled like thunder out into the crowd.

The demons gathered themselves quickly and started marching back toward the building. They were all screaming at us; everyone was yelling at once, over the top of each other. I couldn't make sense of it. Another body splattered onto the ground at our feet, covering Judas in blood. One of the protestors threw a rock at Mary's head. In the nick of time she ducked and it went clattering into the doors behind us.

"Stop!" I boomed again. "You have my undivided attention. Do you have a spokesperson? Anyone who can explain on your behalf exactly what it is that you want?"

The crowd looked confused. They froze and slowly fell silent. The demons all looked around at each other, unsure how to react to my question.

"Do you have a leader?" Mary repeated beside me.

An older man pushed his way forward. He looked either Indian or Pakistani, had white hair and wore thick frame, black glasses. He was clothed in black pants and a black shirt with a clerical collar.

"I can speak for them," he announced. "My name is Bishop John Joseph."

A Bishop? I thought, bewildered. I covered my shock and cleared my throat.

"Please ask them to rest and we can talk about this together inside."

"Very well," he said.

He turned to the crowd, holding up his arms.

"Please," he asked. "The Lord is willing to listen to our demands. We will be heard. Wait for me in peace and I will return with answers."

Again, the crowd looked around confused. Their momentum had been broken for now. I hoped I could help solve this problem, but I was more curious about this priest before me. Where did he come from and how had he gone unknown until now?

28

MARAX OPENED THE DOORS for us and we ushered the Bishop inside. The protestors all began to sit down peacefully on the street. The blood from the burst bodies was quickly coagulating in the heat of Hell. A deep stench rose up from the puddles of red and black muck. The doors sealed behind us, and we were enveloped by the cool air-conditioning of Satan's Tower.

"Thank you for coming in to speak to me, Bishop," I said, as we gathered in the foyer.

"Thank you, Lord Michael for your time. Please call me John," he answered softly and politely.

"Ok, John," I said wearily, trying to keep my anger at what had happened outside in check. "Would you prefer to speak one on one, or can I bring some advisors with me?"

He looked around at the group of people gathered about him. If he was overwhelmed, he didn't show it. He nodded and smiled to each of them in turn before looking back to me.

"I'm happy for Master Judas to be present," he said. "And the elderly man in the pilot's cap. Otherwise, I'd prefer a small audience."

"Of course," I said, and then looked to the others. "Clytemnestra, please send someone to clean up the mess outside. Make sure they're careful to be cooperative with the people out there. They must be courteous at all costs. Is there somewhere on this level where we can speak with John?"

"There is a door next to the elevator, which leads to a small conference room," she told me, pointing to the right.

"We should offer him something to drink as well, as a sign of hospitality," Smithy came to my side and whispered in my ear.

I asked the priest what he would like in the way of refreshment and he requested a cup of tea.

"Bring a pot," Smithy chimed in, as we made our way toward the meeting room, and Marax went in search of it.

Once inside, we all sat at a small round table. Settling into a black office chair, I looked over to Bishop John. He sat comfortably, smiling at us all. I tried to sense any kind of unusual emotion from him, but, with my own apprehension and anger boiling inside, I found it hard to focus. I forced myself to stay calm and laid my hands open on the table.

"John," I said quietly. "Firstly I have to say I am both shocked and angered at the protest outside. I've heard no whispers of unhappiness from anyone since my sermon on Mount Belial. I was under the impression that I made it clear if anyone had any issues, they could approach me on even terms. I am sorry if I get to the point too quickly, but what in Hell is going on out there?"

John looked at me, nodding and still smiling. His ease of character in such a volatile situation was beginning to get on my nerves.

"I have tried to approach your office on several occasions this last few days," he said. "I was told that you were busy with other matters and that I would have to wait. Unfortunately, my comrades outside are tired of waiting. They insisted we march. We thought that a radical display would be the only thing to move you to the action desired."

"Which is?" I asked, slapping my hand on the table.

"We want you to kill us," he smiled again.

"What?" I thundered. "That's ridiculous."

Smithy tugged at my arm and I realized that I was on my feet. I closed my eyes and took three deep breaths before sitting back down. When I opened them again I was a touch more subdued.

"I'm sorry," I said, pausing again for a moment. "It's been a tiring week. I don't quite understand what you mean. You're already dead. You're in Hell. I'm working day and night trying to find a way to free you all from this place."

"But you already have a way to free us," he replied. "Everyone in Hell has heard you can tear a soul apart at will. The group outside wishes the same blissful oblivion for themselves. We are sick of being tortured with Guilt and Fire. We are sick of centuries of unfulfilled promises of redemption that will never come. We have waited for what seems an eternity, but we will wait no more." He placed both of his hands palms down on the table softly. "Even if you can bring down the walls between the realms, Asmodeus will never let us rest until he is destroyed."

"But that's what I want: to kill Asmodeus," I said in anger. "You don't understand. If I destroy a soul, it is irreversible. There's no coming back. The hope of a better life is here. I just need time."

"We've had nothing but time in this existence," John replied in the same friendly tone. "But we cannot see an end in sight. For many of us, an eternity of consciousness, no matter how blissful, seems a horror in itself."

"He's right," Smithy said quietly beside me.

I turned to him, unable to believe what I'd just heard.

"I've been where John and the people outside are," he said looking at me. "I know how they're feeling. For them it seems like their pain will never end. Sometimes it starts to get better, but then life plummets back down. I was in that frightful space for a long time. It is only recently that my thirst for life has been renewed."

I blinked, trying to let what Smithy was saying sink in. "Why do you want to live now?" Judas asked him curiously.

"Because I have a purpose," Smithy said, looking at me. "I have friends who talk to me. I am no longer a lonely old man wallowing in his guilt each moment I breathe. I can see a chance at making things right. But this isn't about me. My point is, these people do not feel that. They can see no way to crawl out of the darkness, and so they simply want it to end. Nothingness would be a mercy to them."

"But it's not right," I repeated. "It's too final."

"Maybe there is something else we can do," Judas said.

"What?" I asked, exasperated. "We can't just let them stand outside, throwing themselves off buildings forever."

"Oh, they won't do that," John said, his voice barely audible, as if he were really talking to himself.

"What then?" I asked.

"If they don't get what they want, they will attack you. If you don't kill them in peace, then they will force you to do it in violence. They are desperate, and for them this is the final play."

Marax clattered into the room with a large teapot in one hand, several cups in the other. He placed them on the table in front of us with a rattle. Smithy smiled a thank you at him as he picked up the teapot and poured hot liquid into the cups. He pushed it over to John, who accepted it with a nod. John started heaping sugar into his teacup. I stood and started to pace around the room while the others sat in silence. I rubbed my hand over my face, trying to think of some way to avoid having to murder more than a thousand souls. I neither wanted to do it, nor was I sure how long it would take or the toll on my energies it would require. What if more souls saw the opportunity and embraced nothingness? It seemed wrong to me, but was I wrong to take that choice away from them?

"What if we can give them something to look forward to?" Judas finally asked. "What if we can ask them to give us a reasonable timeframe for coming up with a solution?"

"I'm happy to hear any suggestions you may have," John said, stirring his tea easily. Smithy was watching him with intense interest.

Judas looked up at me. I nodded. I was just as eager to know what he was thinking.

"War," he said.

"What are you talking about?" I snapped. "We're not ready to go to war with Asmodeus."

"We're close though," said Judas. "Closer than many realize." He looked at Bishop John sitting across from us. "Bishop John, are you a Catholic?" he asked.

"Yes, of course," he answered. "And are you human?"

"Yes."

"Why are you in Hell?" I asked.

"I committed suicide," he said. "It was a protest against the cruel treatment of Christians in Pakistan. God sent me here. Even after my sacrifice I was condemned. I am angry about how I was treated, maybe enough to hold me here, but not enough to turn me into a demon. I don't really know. I was only freed from the Forest of the Damned a few days ago, so I'm new to this place."

I drew in my breath sharply at his words. He paused to look at me quizzically before continuing.

"I have since then heard the story that God and Satan have united into a being called Asmodeus. I hold doubt in my heart that I want to go to Heaven to be with such a creature. That's when I joined the group who were talking about petitioning for a true death. I just want it to all end," he finished, with tears in his eyes.

Judas looked over to me. I knew what he was thinking because the same possibility had entered my mind as soon as I saw the bishop.

"Have you ever performed an exorcism?" I asked. "What? No."

Smithy looked up from his tea, confused at the strange turn of conversation.

"Do you know how to?" Judas pressed.

"Well," John said slowly, looking from Judas to me then back to me again. "It's all a matter of procedure. I suppose if I had a copy of the Vatican Rites at my disposal and some holy water, then I could do it. But what does this have to do with freeing our troubled souls?"

"There may be a way that we can bring down the walls that separate Hell, Purgatory and Heaven soon," I replied carefully. "It may only take weeks to pull the necessary elements together. I would need your help, however. Do you think your fellow protestors outside could be persuaded to wait just two more weeks for the walls to come down? Would they wait two more weeks for freedom?"

"It certainly would be worth staying around to watch," John mused, rubbing his chin. "What if it doesn't work?" he asked.

"Then I will concede to your request to assist in euthanizing any soul who truly wants it."

"And if we succeed?" John continued. "What if people still want to die?"

"Then they can be the first to attack Asmodeus and their wish will be granted either way," I answered.

The bishop sat pondering the option while he sipped his tea. "Alright," he said finally. "I think I will be able to convince them to wait two weeks, but no more." He looked up at me. "If you think you can deliver what you are promising, then I'll do whatever else you require."

"Good," I said, suddenly energized with the thrill of possibility this priest presented. "There is a silver lining to any situation."

"Indeed," John said. "I will go and tell my comrades the good news."

I stood up to leave with him, but Smithy touched me on the arm again.

"May I have a word?" he asked. I could tell by the look in his eyes that it wouldn't wait.

I turned to Judas. "Can you please escort John outside and be my representative?" I asked. He nodded and the pair left Smithy and me alone.

I sat back down and swung the chair to face Smithy. He had a serious look on his face.

"I'm not sure what's going on, with all of these questions about exorcisms," he said, "but I do not trust that man."

"Why not?" I asked, puzzled.

"I don't know." He picked up his tea and sipped it thoughtfully. "An old man's gut feeling, that's all. We cannot trust him."

I nodded slowly. He had to give me more than that.

"We don't have a whole lot of options here," I told him. "We need his help badly. It's time I brought you up to speed with our plan to break down the walls of Heaven and Hell."

29

SMITHY LET OUT A LOW WHISTLE.

"That's one heck of a story," he said. "So once we have the keys, we can go up there and basically blow the place sky high!"

"Something like that. We're really not sure what will happen, but it's our best chance to achieve a true balance between realms." I paused and sat back in my chair. "So what do you think? Are you still with me?"

He nodded fiercely.

"I promised you I would. I'd say I'd follow you to Hell and back, but we're already there," he smiled. "I still don't trust this bishop, though." Smithy's face turned dark. "He's not right. I can't put my finger on it, but it's something. I just know it."

"What can we do?" I asked, wanting my friend's full support.

"Maybe we can test him," he said slowly. "Let's hunt for Zoroaster's keys first. We take the priest with us. If he proves loyal, then I'll eat my words."

"Okay," I agreed. "It's better to play this safe anyway. We'll go together: you, me, Mary, Judas and the priest. Let's rest first for the next coming of The Guilt, and then regroup in the foyer in an hour."

"You're a born leader, Michael," Smithy said. "Thanks old timer," I replied fondly.

We moved back out into the foyer and briefed the others on the plan. Judas and Bishop John reported that they had managed to sway the crowd to the two-week truce, although there was still some unrest about the circumstances. If nothing happened soon they would gather at Casa Diablo and renew their protest.

The group split to rest for the impending fires of The Guilt. I went up to Clytemnestra's office and lay on the couch, trying to get some rest for the journey ahead.

I tossed and turned. My mind would not sleep, even though my body was drained. Thoughts of Charlotte plagued my consciousness. Would she be happy to see me once we reached Purgatory? Would she see the same man she fell in love with? So much had happened since we had been torn apart. As I slowly fell into a doze, my mind swung to the impending task. If we tore down the walls, what would really happen? Galaxies spiralled through my vision, whipping toward a white nucleus of light. I came close enough to touch the blazing sun, but before I could reach out, it exploded into a shower of blood.

I jerked awake, sitting up on the couch. Clytemnestra sat at her desk nearby. She looked over.

"The others are ready downstairs," she said. "I told them we were having a meeting about building permits first. You were twitching while you rested. My husband used to do that only when he was dead tired."

I wiped the sleep from my eyes.

"Thank you," I said gratefully. "I did need the rest."

I pushed myself off the couch to my feet. I felt revitalized from my short nap. I was ready for the next step: the hunt for Zoroaster's keys.

30

THE FIVE OF US BUZZED THROUGH THE sky in Smithy's helicopter. I had decided it was best to keep travel simple and conserve my elemental energies in case I needed them. We soared over Hell, crossing beyond Mount Belial into territory I had never seen. Mary sat in the front, helping navigate the route. We traced the path of a crystal blue river which bubbled through a pestilent jungle. The jungle receded into black-grass plains before they turned to desert. At the far edge of the desert I could see a straight beam of light shooting into the sky.

"That's it!" Mary exclaimed with excitement. "That's the Chinvar Bridge which leads up to the gates of Purgatory. At the bottom is the hiding place that Zoroaster created for the keys."

As we drew closer, the glow of the bridge became brighter. From a distance it had looked a mile wide; up close it became clear that it was really a fine laser point, razor thin. The intensity of the beam radiated illumination past its actual borders to flood the whole area with pulsing light.

"That bridge thing is messing with my instruments," Smithy yelled, tapping a dial on his dash. "I can't take us too close. This'll have to do."

He set the helicopter down a few miles before the light, at the base of a large sand dune.

"This is fine," I said. "You've saved us a long journey."

"Where to now?" Judas asked as we grouped outside our aircraft.

"We head to the bridge," Mary said. "At the bottom is the monastery. There is an outer circle and an inner circle in the building. The outer circle represents the falsehood of chaos. The inner circle is the order of truth. You have to pass through the outer circle to get inside where the keys are stored. Zoroaster warned me that there is a test to be passed on the outer circle. Once inside, the keys are suspended in a liquid which should not be touched."

"Or what?" I asked.

"I'm not sure. His exact words were: 'If you touch it, you will touch nothing else for a thousand years'."

I looked around at the group. Everyone seemed ready to press ahead, no matter the consequences. I knew I was.

"Smithy, you stay with the helicopter," I told him, "in case there are sandworms or something."

"Sandworms?" he asked, suddenly looking at the sand around our feet.

"Or something. The rest of us will go to the monastery. Please wait, for as long as it takes."

Smithy dragged his eyes off the ground and nodded, smiling weakly.

"Aye, Aye Captain," he said.

Mary led the way across the scorching sands.

"There aren't any sandworms out here," she said, once we were out of earshot of Smithy. "There's nothing out here. There never has been since the dawn of time."

"I know," I smiled at her. "I just wanted to keep him on his toes. He likes sleeping too much."

She shook her head and we continued to march in silence toward the sharp light of the Chinvar Bridge. The air around us hummed with energy as we pressed forward. I kept my eyes on my feet, to stop me from going blind from the brilliance ahead. We almost walked headlong into the monastery. It was made from plain grey brick with a red tile roof. The windows had no glass in them, and were black within. Now that we were right next to the Chinvar Bridge, the surrounding glow seemed to have subsided somewhat. I could now see it was a finger-width beam, pointing arrow straight into the endless clouds of Hell above. I had no idea how you could use it to climb up into the sky, but right now it was a distant obstacle. For now, we had to enter this monastery, unprepared for the unknown within. We circled around the building walls and found the entry. There was an archway that led to the interior; no door blocked the way. I started to walk inside, but Mary stopped me.

"We need to be cautious," she said. "Zoroaster is a powerful and intelligent man. We have to be ready for something difficult."

"She's right," John agreed. "Maybe one of us should stay out here, just in case. Three can go in."

"Mary, Judas and I will go," I told John. "You sit tight for now. If anything happens, or you're concerned we're taking too long, then come and find us."

I paused and turned back to Mary: "Ladies first," I said, waving her through the entrance.

She stepped through; Judas followed right behind.

"We'll see you when we have the keys," I said to John and walked into the archway.

31

I WALKED FORWARD IN BLINDING DARKNESS. I tried to ignite some fire elements to shed some light in the room, but they wouldn't mould together. It was as if the air inside the room was stopping them from bonding. Everything felt slippery. I couldn't see the others at all, so moved ahead in darkness. I kept walking for what seemed like hours. Surely I would be at the inner circle by now, I thought. I yelled out to Mary and Judas, but there was no answer. Finally, I saw a faint glow ahead. It was a blue-grey hue and grew brighter as I moved forward. I realized it was a door. I pushed through it without hesitation, thinking it would lead me to the inner circle. I stepped into a softly lit bedroom. Rose petals were scattered on the floor in front of me, leading to a soft bed. Candles were lit all around the room, and the air smelled of sweet perfume. It was the same perfume Charlotte used to wear.

I felt a tap on my shoulder and turned around. Angelic blue eyes met mine. I stood back to behold a grinning Charlotte, dressed in her favorite blue jeans and white singlet.

"Surprise!" she said, laughing.

My heart stopped. It was my love. It was her! She wrapped me in a warm hug. I just stood there astounded.

"I've missed you!" she whispered in my ear and then kissed me on the lips. "I knew you'd come though; Zoroaster told me. He sent me to you."

I pushed her away, bewildered.

"Where are we?" I asked, suspicious that this was a trick.

"We're in Purgatory, silly," Charlotte said, tapping me on the nose with her finger. "You crossed the Chinvar Bridge. We're here, together at last!" She moved in and kissed me again.

She smelled so good. She tasted just like I remembered, her mouth soft with strawberry lip-gloss. I kissed her back, inhaling her scent. She was

146

warm against me. Relief flooded into me. She was OK. She loved me. It was her. We were together! I hugged her tight and started crying with happiness.

"Lotte!" I cried into her neck. "You have no idea what I've been through. Oh God, it is you."

She clung onto my back.

"I know, baby, I know. It's okay. I've been waiting for you. I'd wait for you forever. Now we can stay here, happy!"

I looked her in the eyes again. Happy? Happy didn't even begin to describe it! Joy, elation, relief and love all surged inside me. Nothing mattered any more. I had what I was searching for. Asmodeus, Hell, Heaven, none of that mattered now I had Charlotte back.

"The others!" I blurted. "Where are the others?" I pulled back from her slightly.

Charlotte clung back onto me and pushed me slowly back toward the bed.

"It's okay, Michael," she said, kissing me more intensely.

"They came out before you. I've asked them to give us some space. We can go and see them once we've had a little time together." She pushed me on the chest and I feel back onto silk pillows. The soft candlelight wrapped around the image of my gloriously beautiful wife as she teasingly peeled off her singlet. I moved to kiss her supple skin, my tongue gliding up to her neck where I showered her in tender kisses.

"I missed you," I whispered. "I missed you so much, Lotte."

"I missed you too, my darling Michael. I love you," she said, wriggling on top of me, pushing my shirt over my head.

Hands started pulling my boots off as I lost myself in the warm press of Charlotte's body.

Abruptly, the hands grabbed me by the feet and started pulling. I was wrenched off the bed. Charlotte screamed behind me. I twisted around, trying to get away from the set of hands. I started flailing, reaching out to Charlotte to pull me back. She sat on the bed, crying, just out of reach. I turned and kicked wildly at the hands. I was screaming and kicking, delirious with rage. Finally the hands let go. I got to my feet and looked around. I was back in the darkness. I could still make out the faint light of the blue-grey door. I started to run back towards it, but was tackled by a phantom. We rolled on the ground. I started punching up at it.

"Stop it!" I heard a familiar voice yell. "Stop it, Michael. It's me." I opened my eyes and saw a bleeding Bishop John sitting on top of me, panting.

"It's me, Michael. It's John. It was a deception. It wasn't real."

I twisted out from underneath him.

"No!" I screamed. "It was real! Let me go back. It was Charlotte!"

"It was a lie," I heard Mary's voice say behind me.

I turned to see her and Judas standing in front of an egg-shaped case which was filled with green gel. Floating inside were two dull silver keys. We weren't in the darkness, we were in the inside circle. Somehow we'd made it through. We'd done it. But I didn't want that now. I just wanted to go back.

I dropped to my knees, my head in my hands.

"No," I said weakly, tears welling inside me. "Lotte. No."

32

I SAT WITH MY HEAD ON MY KNEES, WEEPING. The wound of having been torn away from Charlotte had been opened again and my soul was bleeding out.

Mary came to my side and started rubbing me on the back, consoling me.

"I know, Michael, I know. We all had to face a deep desire we held within. Zoroaster always said that the most beautiful lies are the ones that cause the most chaos once revealed. But no matter how beautiful, in the end they are just lies, Michael. They are not the true way things are. You will be back with her soon, I promise you that. It must have been even harder for you than us. Judas and I have each other now. Your aching longing for her is stronger than anything we could have experienced in there."

I felt numb. I was with her. I held her in my arms. It was all that I had wanted with every breath since I met her. Burying my head in my hands, I tried to shake the feeling of hopelessness. It had been so real. Trying to gather my senses I looked up to the others.

"How did you find me?" I managed to ask.

"I heard shouts from outside," John said softly, kneeling in front of me. "I could hear Judas and Mary calling, but I couldn't hear you. I knew something was wrong, so I came inside. My most urgent desire at that moment was find you, so I suppose it overshadowed any other visions that may have appeared to me. I searched and found a blue light leading into a room. I looked inside and saw you, Michael. I saw the bliss on your face and almost left you, but I knew it couldn't be real. I'm sorry I had to pull you out, but reality is always more precious than illusion."

John rested his hand on my knee. I knew he was right. Despite this, it didn't make me feel any better. I sighed. How could I have been fooled so easily? I had wanted it so badly to be true that it had blinded me to reality.

I stood up slowly. John helped me to my feet. I put my hand on his arm to steady myself. There was still a task to be done.

"I'm glad you pulled me out of there, John. As happy as I was in that moment, you're right, it was a lie. Better you got me early than if I had been even deeper into the illusion. The true Charlotte is still out there, waiting. It's her happiness that I truly want more than anything else."

"This is the essence of true love," John said to me. "Giving all that you can without asking anything in return."

I looked into his giving eyes. He had saved me. I owed him. Mary came to my side and held my hand. It felt good to be comforted by someone who understood the pain of my loss. My heart was still heavy, though.

Judas was circling around the egg-shaped case, which sat in the center of the small temple interior. He was studying it at a short distance, looking to see if he could find any niches or cracks that could open a way within. The case itself was almost as tall as Judas, and appeared to be made entirely of thin glass. The oval case balanced precariously on its curved base on a small, raised circular disc of stone. A clear green fluid filled the egg; tiny bubbles of air floated in place within the gel. Right in the middle were the keys. They didn't look like much. They were about the size of any normal key and a flat silver color.

"I can't see any way inside," Judas said, after completing a full rotation of thorough searching.

I shifted my perception to see if I could discern anything that couldn't be noticed normally. It looked entirely different when I beheld it as an elemental whole. The case was not made up of glass; it was actually made up of water. It wasn't frozen into ice, but was held still by a perfectly balanced arrangement of molecules. It was like an intricate house of cards. To upset even the tiniest element in the structure of the case would send it flooding down around us. The liquid inside was an ocean of dark atoms. They actually pulled any movement of light around inside them and changed it into stillness. Within, the keys shone outward brightly. They were made of a pure element I had never thought existed. It was as though I was staring into the molecules of God's soul.

I caught a small hint of movement out of the corner of my eye.

"NO!" I yelled.

I was too late. Judas had reached out and touched the case. In an instant, the water case poured over him. Instinctively I threw up a barricade of earth in a circle between the rest of us and the flood of elements. The gel of the egg washed over Judas and crashed into the floor, but was stopped by the bank I had made.

"Judas!" Mary screamed, and tried to leap over the wall of mud that protected us. John reached up and pulled her back. She tried to break free, but he hugged her tight to his chest.

Judas lay paralyzed on his back, covered in the green plasma. Spread onto the floor it was just a thin layer of fluid. They keys now sat above the puddle, on top of the circular stone disc, which had held up the case.

Mary was crying into John's chest as he looked over to Judas' prone body.

"Is he dead?" he mouthed softly.

"No," I said, shaking my head as I looked closely at him with elemental vision. "His soul is intact, but the gel has washed through him. Every molecule in his body is coated in it. It's like he's asleep: no thoughts or emotion can form within him. He's in a complete coma."

Mary pulled her face away and turned to Judas, tears in her eyes.

"Can we help him?" she asked tearfully. "What can we do?"

"Let me try," I said.

I formed a cushion of air beneath him and lifted him up, out of the fluid. Creating a flat table in front of me, I floated him over to us and placed him gently upon it. Mary rushed to his side.

"Don't touch!" I warned her, taking her hand gently in mine. "I'll see if I can get the gel off him first."

Lightly, I washed elements of water over him, cleaning his exterior of the fluid. I tried to push more water inside him, to clean him internally. The gel repelled my attempts. I tried air. I even tried a light amount of fire. Nothing would move it. I peered inside him and studied the gel even more closely. It was fizzing ever so slightly all about him. It appeared to be slowly dissolving. I watched in silence, trying to gauge the rate at which it evaporated. It was impossible to come up with any guess of how long it would take. I explained to the others what I saw. Mary looked numb as she stared at him.

"A thousand years," she said.

"Sorry?" I asked, unsure what she meant.

"It will take a thousand years," she repeated. "Zoroaster said if you touch it, you will touch nothing else for a thousand years. That's what he meant."

We all stood in silence, looking at the still body of Judas. I reached out and pulled Mary close to me.

"At least he is at peace," I said. "We will welcome him back dearly when he wakes."

She buried her head into my chest and cried.

"I'm sorry." I could find no other words. It was a harsh thing to have lost her brother again so soon.

John came to stand close to us.

"Let his sacrifice, not be in vain," he said. "Let us embrace what he has given us: a chance at freedom. We now have the keys." He pointed to them in the center of the room.

I nodded. Closing a fist of air around them, I brought them to me. They were cool to touch. I handed them to Mary.

Taking a knife out of her pocket, she cut a lock of Judas' long red hair. Threading the hair through the loop at the tip of the keys, she tied them around her neck.

"I'll keep them safe for now," Mary said.

"Can you help her outside?" I asked John. "I will carry Judas with us."

"No!" Mary said, fire blazing in her eyes. "I will carry him." Before I could say a word, she had picked him up in her arms, and begun trudging into the outer ring.

33

MARY CARRIED JUDAS all the way to the helicopter. Each time we offered to help, she refused, saying "I will never leave him again."

Smithy ran up to greet us.

"Oh thank God," he puffed. "I was beginning to get worried you might never come back."

"Don't thank God, thank Judas." I said sadly.

"Oh, no," the pilot whispered, seeing Mary trailing behind with his body. "What happened?"

"He's asleep," I said. "For a thousand years."

"How?"

"The keys were inside something Zoroaster had created to make anyone who touched it fall into a coma. Judas was the first one to try to get them out, and this happened. He has sacrificed himself so that we can move forward."

"Did you get the keys?"

"Yes," I said softly. "They are hanging from Mary's neck." He looked over to her.

"Is that it?" he said, furrowing his brow. "I was expecting something a bit more impressive. They look like the keys to my hangar."

I patted Smithy on the shoulder and walked past. I was still upset at the loss of my new friend. Judas was the last person who deserved to forfeit what he had just gained. It was a small consolation that at least he would survive in the end.

Smithy fired up the helicopter and we rose into the air. I sat staring in silence as the desert flew past beneath us.

Soon, Hell city came into view and I snapped out of my desolation. I turned to look at John.

"You have proven a trustworthy ally," I told him "How can I repay you after we've exorcised the other keys from within Mary?"

"You can repay me with this," he replied, pulling a small glass vial from inside his jacket. It was filled with the light green gel from the temple.

"Where did you get that?" I asked, suddenly angry.

"I took a sample from the floor before we left. Everything in that temple was a gift to us from a greater being. This is the answer to my prayers. I could not leave it behind."

"But it's dangerous! It should be destroyed! We can't play with something we don't understand."

"No," John said softly. "I do understand it. You said yourself, if you tear a soul apart so that it can embrace nothingness, it is irreversible. This is the solution to all of the souls who want to sleep. If you help me create more of this, then I can dispense it to the souls who would seek oblivion. We can make a waterfall to wash away consciousness. When they wake, they can make the choice to rejoin the living they have left behind, or chose to drink the waters of mercy once more."

I looked at him. He seemed resolute.

"You have been thinking about this the entire way back," I said.

"I have been thinking about this since I've been in Hell," he replied. "This is a perfect solution. You cannot deny it."

"What about our deal?" I asked. "We were going to let the souls witness the bringing down of the walls and lead them to war."

"Some may still choose that path," he said, "but many will fear the horrors of conflict that may await. Would you deny them the freedom to make the decision on their own?"

"I won't hand the people in Hell a weapon to destroy themselves with. What if the wrong person gets their hands on it and attacks others?"

"You could set people to guard it," John pressed. "You have the resources. There are fortresses that could easily keep others away. You could also use it as a weapon when you move against Heaven. It is a solution for everyone."

"It's too powerful!"

"If you follow my design, I promise it will be an aid in your mission. Those who want to embrace nothingness can. You speak about truth and freedom. This is a chance to deliver it to those who crave it, before you launch headlong into battle. This is real choice. Would you take that away from them? The ability to use their own freewill? If you do, then you're just as bad as Asmodeus, who you oppose for his lies."

I looked to Smithy for assistance, but he was staring ahead, concentrating on flying into the city. I looked to Mary.

"It is an honest answer." She nodded. "We must pursue truth above all else."

I couldn't believe she was taking John's side in this.

"But how do we do it? Where would we put it?" I asked them, searching for a reason to at least delay the process.

"You could put it at Casa Diablo," Mary suggested. "It's a fortress that no one would dare attack."

"Yes!" John jumped in, seeing his advantage. "When I was freed from the forest, I saw that the back end of the castle was blocked off by high gates. Maybe there is a spot in the grounds there that could be used to build what I need. People can pass through the waterfall into a cave to sleep on the other side. You can build it using your elemental powers. I know you can."

I looked out of the window of the helicopter. The last thing I wanted was to hold back the souls of Hell in their ability to make their own decisions. Stifling something like this opportunity was just as bad as putting control in place like Asmodeus had. If I wanted true freedom for all, then giving this chance to someone who asked for it was a step in that direction. I turned back to face John.

"Once you have performed the exorcism for us and we have the last set of keys, I will do what you ask," I said reluctantly. "Your friends will have their choice."

34

WE STOOD IN THE BOWELS of Magdelene's Mansion. Mary had created a crypt beneath the floors of her home. The bodies of the seven demons of Zoroaster were around around us in seven white coffins. Now placed in an eighth open coffin was the sleeping body of Judas. Bare rock walls surrounded us, giving the room an oppressive feel.

In the middle of the circle of coffins was a large stone table altar in the shape of a crucifix. On the roof above the altar was a glass figure of a white dove emerging from a painted sunburst which pulsed white light. The light streamed directly down onto the altar, while shadows clung to the edges of the room.

Bishop John entered through an opening carved in the rock face furthest from Judas' coffin. He was dressed in a full-length black cassock and white surplice with a purple stole draped over his shoulders, hanging loosely along the length of his torso. He carried a jug of water in one hand and a book of scripture in the other. Mary stood next to me, beside Judas' peaceful body. She was clothed in a plain white dress, her hair pulled back in a ponytail. She held a thick candle in each of her hands; a crucifix around her neck dangled next to Zoroaster's keys.

John came forward and asked Mary to follow him to the altar. Next to the altar sat a small table where he placed the jug of water and book of scripture. John then took the candles from Mary and placed them beside the water. Unclasping the crucifix from around her neck, he laid it neatly between the two candles.

At John's request, Mary lay on the altar. She rested her head at the top of the cross, closed her eyes, and arranged her hands neatly over her chest. As soon as she was in this position, the temperature in the room dropped. Both John and I breathed vapor from sudden the chill in the air. I looked around but could see no reason for the cooling of the crypt. I felt there was a presence there with us, as if the demons inside her knew that something was about to happen. John motioned for me to stand close to Mary.

"If I ask you to restrain her, please do so, but only using your hands," he said. "Do not use any elemental hold on her during the exorcism. She will be stronger than you think possible while the demons possess her. She may try asking us to stop or use any tactic to keep the demons inside her, but it's not her talking; it is the demons looking to fool us. Inside this jug is holy water, which I have blessed according to custom. Should anything in the room start rattling or moving, please take some of the water and flick it on the object. I don't know what is going to happen here, but we must be prepared for some strange occurrences."

"I've have experienced nothing but strange occurrences recently," I said, trying to lighten the mood.

John looked at me blankly and went back to pick up his book from the table.

He traced the sign of the cross over Mary, over himself and then over me. Taking some holy water he sprinkled some on each of us, before beginning to chant over Mary's body.

"Save your servant. Who trusts in you, my God. In the face of the enemy, let the enemy have no power over her. Lord, send her aid from your holy place. And watch over her from Sion. Lord, heed my prayer. And let my cry be heard by you. The Lord be with you."

He then made the sign of the cross over Mary. Her eyes snapped open and she turned to smile at John innocently.

"You don't know what you're doing, John Joseph. What kind of a Bishop kills himself anyway? You're nothing but a wolf in sheep's clothing. This isn't going to work."

John looked at me with a grimace.

"That is not Mary speaking. The demons are already trying a ruse. Do not engage her in conversation even if she speaks with you directly. We must strive ahead with purpose or the demons inside will divert us."

He flicked the page in his book and continued.

"God, whose nature is ever merciful and forgiving, accept our prayer that this servant of yours, bound by the fetters of sin, may be pardoned by your loving kindness."

Mary started to giggle.

"God blah, blah, Jesus blah, blah. They have no power down here in Hell! This is a waste of time."

John pressed on, over the top of her.

"Holy Lord, Almighty Father, everlasting God and Father of our Lord Jesus Christ, who consigned that fallen and Apostate tyrant to the flames of hell, who sent your only begotten Son into the world to crush that roaring lion, hasten to our call for help and snatch from the clutches of the noonday devil this human made in your likeness."

"I look nothing like that ugly old cunt," Mary snarled.

I jumped, startled at her language. John seemed not to hear as he prayed.

"Strike terror, Lord, into the beast now laying waste your vineyard. Fill your servants with courage to fight against that reprobate dragon, lest he despise those who put their trust in you. Let your mighty hand cast him out of your servant Mary Magdalene!"

Mary turned her head to face to me, her eyes rolling in her head.

"Stop this, Michael. You're the kind one here. This won't work anyway. Even if we get the keys, we won't be able to bring down the walls. Who do we think we're kidding?"

Before I could answer, John cut in.

"Who is speaking now? Who inhabits this body of Mary Magdalene? Answer me, you demon, in the name of Lord God and his Son in Heaven."

Mary swung around violently to John and spat in his face.

"I am your slut," she croaked in a voice that wasn't hers. It was a deep, subhuman howl. "I am your willing whore, your wet pussy. I am pure sin. I am the lust you bury inside, you unholy bishop. I am ready for you. Come and fuck me." She licked her lips and looked at him with a terrifyingly inviting stare. "Come and fuck me like you fuck those little altar boys. Come and violate my ass with your shrivelled little cock. I know you want to ravage this beautiful temple." She rubbed her hand down her body, pressing it between her legs then spat at him again.

"Hold her down," John said to me sternly, brushing off her obscene insults as if they were nothing.

I moved in, taking her arms and pinning them back into the stone altar. I avoided all eye contact. She writhed beneath me. I was at least double her size, yet incredible strength vibrated through her body. It took everything I had just to hold her down.

She started shrieking in the same animal voice as before. It churned out of her. Her syllables started long and drawn before rambling over each other. A rancid stench wafted up from her skin. It assaulted me, thick and pungent. I gagged, but held my breath as John's voice grew louder behind me.

"I command you, unclean spirit, whoever you are, along with all your minions now attacking this servant of God. By the mysteries of the incarnation, passion, resurrection, and ascension of our Lord Jesus Christ, by the descent of the Holy Spirit depart this holy body!"

Mary began to convulse beneath me; her spine arching in pain, her mouth babbling a string of incomprehensible words. Her shoulders lifted so violently upwards that I was thrown back. I steadied myself on one of the white coffins, before moving back in to hold her. In between her grunts, more loudly, I could hear: "I am Lust, I am Greed, before she choked and spat, I am Gluttony, I am Wrath," and on and on.

John rushed to her side. He crossed Mary over her brow, lips and breast and then flicked more holy water on her. At the water's touch she began to scream. Her limbs wrestled against mine and I pushed my weight down to try to keep her in place.

John turned the pages of his book and began to read once more.

"Jesus once drove out a demon, and this particular demon was dumb. The demon was driven out, the dumb man spoke, and the crowds were enraptured. I now drive out similar demons as tools of Beelzebub. Let my cry be heard by you. The Lord be with you."

Mary began to bash her head back against the altar, so hard I was afraid she'd crack her skull open. I let go of her arms and cradled her head. As soon as I let go of her she jerked up and bit me on the ear, growling. I pulled away and my ear tore off into her mouth. She spat it out at me, blood seeping on her lips.

"You'll never get her back, Michael," she smiled cruelly. "Never! God will destroy Charlotte's soul before he'll let you touch her again."

I felt myself rushing in to attack her. But John held his hand out to stop me.

"It is not her," he muttered. "It is the demons trying to distract us. Pay no mind and hold her down, man!"

I slammed Mary's shoulders back into the stone in anger and held her fast.

"Keep going!" I yelled at the Bishop.

"Depart, you devils!" he pressed on. "Let God's power now fall on you from heaven like lightning. Let that power spear you out of Mary. I ask this through you, Jesus Christ, our Lord and God, who are coming to judge both the living and the dead of the world by fire. Amen."

Again he made the sign of the cross over himself and then Mary. He leaned in and pressed his purple stole onto her neck. Burning flesh crackled beneath it. Mary's screaming turned to girlish whimpers.

"No, Michael," she sobbed. "In the name of Judas, make him stop."

John placed his hand on Mary's forehead and pushed her back down.

"See the cross of the Lord! Begone, you hostile powers! I cast you out, unclean spirit, along with every satanic power of the enemy, every specter from Hell, and all your fell companions. In the name of our Lord Jesus

Christ, begone and stay far from this creature of God. It is He who commands you, He who flung you headlong from the heights of Heaven into the depths of Hell. It is He who commands you, He who once stilled the sea and the wind and the storm. Tremble in fear, Satan, you enemy of the faith, you foe of the human race, you begetter of death, you robber of life, you corrupter of justice, you root of all evil and vice, seducer of men, betrayer of the nations, instigator of envy, font of avarice, mentor of discord, author of pain and sorrow. Fear Him!"

John made three signs of the cross, then dipped his hands in the Holy Water, tracing a cross on Mary's forehead. The water sizzled and popped on her skin. Bloody foam bubbled from out of her mouth.

"Begone, then!" John bellowed. "In the name of the Father, and of the Son, and of the Holy Spirit. Give place to the Holy Spirit by this sign of the holy cross of our Lord Jesus Christ, who lives and reigns with the Father and the Holy Spirit, God, forever and ever. The Power of Christ compels you! The Power of Christ compels you! The Power of Christ compels you! Begone from this body of Mary. Begone!"

At the last word, seven colored spirits burst out of Mary's body. They wailed into the air. Her body arched and twisted in convulsions as they gushed out of her chest. John fervently continued his chant as the demons spewed into the air.

"I cast you back into your cursed bodies, where you should dwell forever more. Leave this woman and do not return. In the name of God the Almighty, I banish you to your rightful body. Amen!"

A shower of light exploded above Mary and the twisted souls roared toward the seven coffins placed around her. I was sent sprawling to the ground by a hot wind as the souls flew past me to crash with a burst of sound back into their ethereal shells.

Dazed by the spectacle, I shook my head clear. I was on my knees next to the altar, gasping for breath. With effort, I held the edge of the stone table and pulled myself upward. Mary now lay back on the altar. Her eyes were closed. A small, white alabaster jar was clasped between her hands on her chest. There was not a mark of blood or a bruise or a scratch on her. I couldn't believe my eyes. Where there had been violence there was peace. I reached up and touched my ear. It was whole.

Father John looked over to me and nodded, before slumping to the floor, exhausted.

35

MARY'S EYES FLUTTERED OPEN. She smiled.

"How do you feel?" I asked, shakily.

"I feel... lighter," she said, with a contented look on her face, as if she'd just awoken from a long and peaceful sleep. She raised her head cautiously and sat up, cradling the white alabaster jar in her lap. Twisting the top off with care, she peered inside. She breathed a sigh of relief and replaced the lid.

"They are there. They are safe."

"Good," I said, catching my breath. "You keep them that way until they're needed."

I heard a stirring at the foot of the altar. Bishop John's head peeked above the stonework.

"Is everything in order?" he asked. "Yes," I said. "You did a fine job."

Another noise growled around us. The rumbles grew stronger, coming from within the coffins which surrounded us.

"It seems your children are awake," John said, looking about at the boxes with fear in his eyes.

"Don't worry," Mary said. "I'll calm them."

She walked around the circle, sliding the lids off each of the coffins with one hand. As each lid moved to the side, she showed the small white urn cradled in her other arm and nodded. After she had completed a full circle of the room, the growling subsided to a low hum. Slowly, each of the demons sat up from its deathly bed. Silently, they swung their legs in unison over the side and eased down onto the floor. They walked over to form a line in front of Mary who was now standing at the entrance to the crypt. As each came to her, she kissed them on the lips and whispered thank you. They formed a semi-circle behind her and looked at us with suspicion in their eyes.

"These are the Pure Seven," Mary said to us. "Thus known because they are the ideal embodiment of their chosen vice."

I looked to each of them, studying them for the first time. They were not ugly in the slightest; in fact, they were beautiful to behold. They were perfectly formed, female angels with silver hair and wings. Their skin was the color of their chosen sin, but in every other way they were identical. They had flawless features, high cheekbones, perfect proportion. The only hint that they represented some kind of real evil was their hands. They were clawed. Long curved fingernails forked into deadly knives at the end of each finger.

"This is our new Lord, Michael," Mary said to them. "He is sworn to uphold an ideal for freedom in the universe. He pursues truth much like we do and he has a battle that requires our assistance."

"Whatever you desire, Lord Michael," they said as one. "We will serve you as long as you hold genuine truth within your soul."

I nodded my appreciation.

"This is Bishop John Joseph," I told them. "He helped free you from within Mary's soul. He is a friend and ally."

"Hello," John said weakly next to me.

"Maybe it's time we all got some rest," I suggested. "Mary, is there somewhere John can recoup after his efforts?"

"Yes. Follow me. I'll show everyone to a private room."

We filed behind Mary out of the crypt up into the regular levels of the building. She kept a steady yet slow pace. She must have been totally drained from that ordeal, yet her strong will that kept her walking without so much as a stumble. After many twists and turns we came to a circular foyer which had multiple doors around the walls.

"Choose whichever one you like," she said. "They are all comfortable and clean."

"You remember your promise, don't you, Michael?" John said to me, holding my arm.

"I do, John, and I will keep it. First let's rest. I will meet you in the main reception downstairs in eight hours. In the meantime, get some sleep."

I watched him walk to a door and pass through before I turned to Mary.

"You too Mary," I said. "Please get some rest. Everything has happened so fast. We need to pause and take stock of where we're headed before we rush through the gates. Will you also meet me downstairs once you've had a chance to recover?"

"Of course," she replied. "What happened in there? I can't remember anything between lying on the altar then waking with the jar in my hands."

"It was… interesting," I said, not wanting to go over the horrible details of the exorcism. "What about your friends?" I looked at the Pure Seven who still stood just feet behind her. "What are they going to do?"

"They have had enough rest," she responded. "They would like a chance to go out into the world of Hell and see how it has evolved in the last thousand or so years. With your permission."

"You may go at your own will," I said to them. "Please keep the peace though. We don't need any more protests out there to distract us from our cause."

"As you desire," they answered in chorus.

"Please meet us all up at Casa Diablo, atop Mount Belial within the day," I requested. "We may need your help."

I then turned and walked to the closest door and let myself inside. The room was indeed comfortable. Through the dull light I could see a king-sized bed pushed against the far wall. A large plasma T.V. was secured opposite. I flicked what I thought was a light switch and the curtains whirred open. Outside blazed the world of Hell. It never stopped moving, never slept. People bustled down in the streets endlessly. I flicked the switch again. I had to block it all out for at least a few hours. I had a big task ahead. I knew it would take a massive amount of energy to build what Bishop John wanted. I worried that I might not be able to create the whole thing, but hoped I would be able to use the small scrap of liquid he had taken and reproduce it by repeating the formulae. I had to at least try; I had promised John. Otherwise, I might face a revolt of souls before our true battle would even begin. It was an unwanted delay, but it was necessary.

I lay down on the bed. What was going to happen when we walked through those gates to Purgatory? What would happen when we tore them down? All I knew was that it meant there would no longer be anything separating me and Charlotte. It was selfish of me. I prayed it wouldn't end badly. True freedom. Did that really mean order or chaos? By pulling down every barrier there was and letting souls run free, was I setting up the universe for disaster, or would the endless bounty of Heaven spread through the realms and calm our spirits into harmony and peace?

The risk was worth the possible reward.

I closed my eyes and the last thought I had was something The Perceptionist had said to me.

"There is no good or evil, there is only knowledge."

36

MY EYES FLICKED OPEN. Someone was tapping at the door.

"Come in," I yelled. Rolling myself upward, I got to my feet and shook the depths of sleep from my mind. It had been the rest I needed. I'd slept in my clothes, exhausted from the day's events.

Mary slipped inside the room. She was wearing a crimson dress, a few shades darker than her hair. Between her breasts sat both sets of keys to the realms of the afterlife.

"It's almost been eight hours," she said. "I thought I would come and get you myself. Smithy is downstairs with John, waiting for us. That pilot is a unique man."

"That he is," I said, looking at her a little puzzled. "Why? What did he do?"

"Nothing," she said, smiling. "He's just really obsessed with drinking tea, isn't he? He forced John to have two cups downstairs just now."

I shook my head.

"I'm glad he's here," I said, "otherwise things would get too serious. Shall we?"

Mary didn't move. She stood in front of the doorway, looking at me uncertainly with her beautiful emerald eyes.

"Is there anything else?" I asked.

"Yes," she said slowly. She loosened one set of keys from around her neck. "I have held on to these long enough. I want you to take one for me, Michael. Both sets are too much of a burden for a single soul to bear. Please."

I lowered my head so that she could place them about my neck. I let our foreheads touch. We stayed there for a few moments, letting the warmth of platonic friendship pass between us. Mary straightened after a short while. She then turned and led me out into the circular foyer. We veered left and made our way toward the main lift.

"What do you think will happen when we destroy the walls?" I asked.

"I honestly don't know," she answered. "But I do know it's something which needs to be done. The barriers didn't always exist. We're merely going back to the original state of life and afterlife. It will be simpler."

"Yes, but will it be better?" I asked.

"It will be better for two thirds of the realms," she replied. "Only those who already exist in Heaven may feel that it's a regression to something they don't like. I do think it's for the greater good. It's more truthful."

I nodded. We stepped inside the main elevator and descended into the foyer. Smithy and John were there. John had a cup of tea in his hands and Smithy was watching him closely. *He really is a little odd*, I thought with fondness.

We approached them and John put down his cup with a look of relief.

"Are you ready?" he asked me.

"I am," I said. "We're going to Casa Diablo. I want to make the waterfall there. It will be easier to keep secure."

"Agreed." John nodded. "How will we get there?"

"My helicopter," Smithy said. "I parked it outside."

"What? On the street?" I asked.

"Why not?" he winked. "If the friends of Lord Michael can't have a few extra privileges, then why be his friend?"

Shaking my head, I walked for the doors. Mary, John, Smithy and I came out onto the footpath in front of Magdalene's Mansion. Traffic was backed up on either side of the aircraft, which sat right in the middle of the road. Horns were honking, but silenced once I strode into sight. Smithy waved at the cars with a smile as we climbed up.

"See," he said. "They don't mind."

We took off, floating straight upward into the sky. Around us, the lights of Smoking Gun flashed brightly, drowning out the normal black and red glow, which came from the clouds above. Once we had cleared the tops of the buildings, Smithy took us forward toward what I supposed was my home. I didn't really know anymore.

Azazel came out to greet us as we touched down on the great lawn. Works for the new suburb were grinding away down the mountainside, where the Forest of the Damned had once stood.

"These constructions are driving me crazy," he said as I jumped down from the aircraft. "Dust is blowing into the castle day and night. It's impossible to keep it all clean."

"Never mind," I said calmly, trying to placate him. "They'll be finished soon. It is something that you know is needed."

165

"Very well, master." He bowed his head as the others grouped behind us.

"I need your help, Azazel," I said, and he looked up at me again. "I'm going to be doing some other alterations on the other side of the castle today. Is there a secure area that is blocked off from any possible intruders?"

"What kind of alterations?" he asked suspiciously.

"It's a waterfall. One that needs to be kept from prying eyes."

"They are your grounds," Azazel said grudgingly. "At least it will be better than the view of concrete on this side. I can show you a place that may suit." Azazel turned and marched off, leaving us to follow.

"There is a large space around the very back, toward the sheer side of the mountain," he said as we walked, catching up to him. "Entry is blocked by a set of gates that Satan designed himself. Only the ruler of Hell and the keeper of the house can open them, meaning you or me."

We moved around to the far side of Casa Diablo, through the lively garden from which I had freed Azazel. We came to a long set of barbed gates which towered out of the side of the castle and ran all the way over the edge of the mountain. Azazel reached out and touched the silver metal of the fence. An opening hissed away around his hand, spreading out to a hole big enough for each of us to file through one by one. Ducking my head through, I passed inside to see that this part of the mountain overlooked the jungle, which eventually led on to the desert and Chinvar Bridge. The ground in front of the castle was flat, green grass the size of a football field. There was another set of gates on the far side, with a few trees scattered along the perimeter. The field spread outward to the side of the mountain, which cut away sharply at the edge.

"There is a steep overhang of oil-rock which drops thousands of feet down. It is impossible to climb," Azazel told us. "Gargoyles patrol the rim day and night. No one can get up this side without us knowing."

I surveyed the area. It seemed to be the ideal spot.

"Thank you, Azazel. That will be all for now. I'll call you if you're needed."

"Yes sir." He turned and passed back through the gates.

I walked out into the middle of the field, gauging a proper distance to start from the castle. I then looked toward the edge. The waterfall would need to be right in the center, to make sure there was enough room.

"I'll want you by my side for this, Smithy," I said. "I might need someone to steady me."

"Smithy is still at the gates," said Bishop John beside me.

I turned around, confused. I'd assumed the others had all followed me out, but Smithy and Mary were still back at the fence, talking to each other. Smithy was pointing into the sky and then at the ground. He then turned, looked up to us and waved happily.

"I can assist," John said, drawing my attention back to him. "It's only proper that I help with something I asked to be created."

"Thank you," I said, "I'd appreciate it. This is going to take a vast amount of energy to achieve. I'll need first to create the landscape we need. We'll have to make a steep rise for the waterfall to cascade off and a cave within so the souls who pass through can sleep inside."

"After that we'll need to go to the top of the cliff and pour the liquid down," John added.

"I'll have to grow more of the gel from what we already have. It's a lot simpler to replicate an existing thing, than to create from nothing."

"I can agree with that," John said.

"Okay," I said, steeling myself and planting my feet into the ground. "The others are probably better back there for safety. Let's get started."

With John at my side, I focused on the elements of earth at our feet. I tore the ground apart in front of me by wedging gas inside and expanding it. The sounds of cataclysm rent the air as I worked. Building mounds of rock and dirt on top of each other, I grew a steep precipice out of the earth. Using liquid fire I then burrowed a deep cavern inside it, cleaving stone apart to drill a shaft deep into the mountain. Pushing my mind downward, I funnelled a pathway which led right through the earth to an opening near the base of Mount Belial. I pushed elements of water down through the tunnel to wash out the grime and sealed the bottom with a complex sieve of air. The only way through the sieve would be to pass from the inside out. I stopped for a moment to catch my breath. Letting the ground settle, I focused my attention back to the lip of the cliff I had made. Sucking in air again and grunting with effort, I formed a wide basin at the top which would feed the waterfall. At the base of the cliff I formed another pool and connected the two together with a linking duct which would recycle the gel of sleep up to the top again. It would be able to fall forever in a perpetual cycle, cleansing tormented souls by sending them into a thousand year slumber. The final finishing touch was a floating stone path I created at the base of the pool so souls could walk over it to get to the waterfall's curtain. This meant that one person could easily guard the entry.

I stopped my toils and let the dust settle. Gathering my breath, I turned to see Smithy and Mary coming over to join us. They both looked up in awe at what I'd just created. Even I was daunted by the extent of my power. I had never moved so many elements together at one time before. It had drained me, but not so much that I couldn't continue. It was now time for the hardest part.

I stood for a few moments looking up to the top of the cliff. This Fount of Mercy would be beautiful once it was finished: beautiful and dangerous. Water would fall from above to cover the cave within. Souls would be able to pass through the curtain of water and then sleep inside. The steep floor of the cave meant their bodies would slide down to the bottom of the shaft through the mountain while they slept over the years. When they awoke, they would have the choice to rejoin humanity by passing out of the mountain. Otherwise, they could choose to sleep again by climbing back to the top of the cave and drinking from the waterfall.

The Bishop stood patiently next to me.

"By the saints!" said Smithy, walking closer to us. "I've never seen anything like that in all my many days."

Mary followed behind him.

"It's not finished yet," I said. "It's time to add the most crucial part."

"Now?" Smithy asked.

"No point in waiting," I said.

Smithy looked over to John who was gazing up to the peak of the cliff.

"No, I guess not," he said, eyeing the bishop. "May we come too?"

"I'd prefer it," I said.

We climbed carefully around the side of the cliff, winding up through a narrow pathway I had created for the purpose. It was a welcome rest to be climbing physically, rather than concentrating my mental energies.

Sweating in the heat, we made it to the overhang. I surveyed the basin. It was just as I had hoped, round and lightly sloped so that the fluid I put inside would flow easily over the cliff edge. I asked Smithy and Mary to stay at the side of the empty bowl while John and I climbed inside.

"Are you sure I can't do anything?" Smith asked after us.

"We can finish it, my friend." I smiled back at his offer. "Just stand back and watch the show."

"I'm sure I can do something!" he said, climbing down.

"No, Smithy," I said, firmly, knowing he was only trying to help. He reluctantly turned and rejoined Mary on the banks of the basin.

"Are you ready?" I asked John.

He nodded and took from his pocket the small vial which held the green gel of sleep. He handed it to me. I looked inside, viewing the molecules that danced within. The weave was one I knew I could replicate, but it would take intense concentration to get it right.

"While I pour it out," I told John, "I will expand it. As the pool fills, lead me backward out of the hole. I'll be looking at the fluid the whole time, so will have to trust you to be my eyes."

"You can trust me," he said quietly.

I pulled the stopper off the vial and gently poured the gel out. The fluid, with its thick consistency, slowly dribbled out. I pulled my attention within its elemental fabric. I became one with it. The spirit and thought mixed inside joined my soul. I could feel how it was made. I could sense it.

Focusing on growing the droplets, I attracted the same elements toward each other. They bonded as each came near to their cosmic twin. As the rush of atoms intensified, they took on a life of their own. I could barely feel the outside world as John guided my steps backward.

The trickle of gel soon became a steady stream from out of the vial. It increased to a spurting fountain and then a flood. It surged forth, away from me, like a fire hose, filling the basin rapidly. I felt myself stumble, but strong hands lifted me up again. I was drawn toward the liquid, which I felt partnered with. I tried to step forward, but John pulled me out, away from the shimmering gel which sprung all around. With a mighty effort I tore myself out of my concentration and snapped the tap shut. I tumbled backwards onto the ground, spent completely from the strain.

Black swirled around my vision as I struggled to maintain consciousness. My heart hammered in my ears. I was close to falling into oblivion, but was jolted to my senses as I felt a boot crush down on my throat.

I opened my eyes to see the face of Asmodeus looking down at me. The Keys of Zoroaster were dangling from his clawed fingers.

"Thank you, son," he said, as I choked for air. "I've been waiting a long time to get my hands on these."

37

I WRESTLED WITH THE FOOT, which pinned me on the ground by the jugular. Asmodeus laughed malevolently at me, swinging the keys to Purgatory into his palm and placing them in his pocket. He must have taken them from around my neck. But how?

This was impossible. What had happened? Where was John? Where were Smithy and Mary? I heard Smithy shout and Asmodeus thrust out a fist. Elements crackled from out of his hand, forming a force field around us.

"That's close enough, my pilot friend," he snarled.

I was shaken, barely able to understand what was happening. I drew into my reserves of power, but they were tapped out. I had used the last of my vitality on making The Fount of Mercy. I was like a rag doll, helpless beneath a powerful dragon.

"My dear Michael," Asmodeus clicked his tongue. "So easy to manipulate, so predictable! You have been so single minded in your task of getting to Charlotte all this time, you didn't see what was right in front of you. A bishop in Hell. One that stayed human? It's so ridiculous it's almost laughable." He threw his head back in mocking laughter before looking down back into my eyes. "You have grown in power, though, I have to give credit where it's due. If I had not let you drain yourself making this fountain, you might almost be a match for me. Almost. Your real weakness lies in that dull mind of yours. Do you really think that a path of fate was laid out before you that would lead you directly to both sets of keys? Do you think I wouldn't know about this way to split the realm's walls apart? I am the engineer of this universe. I know all the loopholes. Do you think you could achieve something so difficult with so little effort? Oh, I let you stumble on a few hurdles along the way. I helped give you the opportunity to find what has been hidden from me for so long. You did all the hard work for me. It was so perfect! In the end it was Providence which led you here, Michael. It was a fate that I created. The Lord giveth and The Lord taketh away. I'll take away now, my son," he growled. "I'll have my other keys back. I can easily travel through my own realms already, but I do not need anyone else playing God with my creation!"

Asmodeus kicked me hard in the ribs and stamped his foot downward. A shuddering earthquake shook the ground. I was able to roll over onto my side to see both Smithy and Mary scrambling to keep a foothold. Mary lurched to the side and Smithy rushed in to hold her up. Asmodeus shot from beside me. With unearthly speed, he scooped Mary into his arms and pushed Smithy to the side. She thrashed about, clawing at The Devil's face. Her fingernail caught his eye and he yelled, throwing her to the ground. She landed only inches away from the pool of deathly gel.

A fearsome screech sounded above and a blur of green, purple and violet thundered into the body of Asmodeus. He was tossed to the ground as three dark angels rolled about him in a struggle. Four other angels slammed down, pounding into Asmodeus, screeching in rage. It was the Pure Seven! They tore at his body with their fearsome claws, ripping at his flesh. He tucked in tightly as they shredded spiked fingers across his back, exposing ghastly white flesh. All seven sinful colors piled on top of Asmodeus, overwhelming him with force of numbers. They were slowly dragging him to the edge of the cliff, looking to throw him off in the water of sleep below.

I looked on like a helpless child, trying to pull myself off the ground. My legs kept collapsing underneath me. I struggled to sweep the confusion from within me. I tried to gather energizing elements around me, but I had no strength left inside.

The battle raged on. The seven vengeful demons of truth thumped their wings into the inert form of Asmodeus, biting him, wounding him. Just as I thought they would topple him over the cliff edge, a blue light started to glow from within him. It started warping and growing, the air hissing about him. With a sonic detonation, the blue orb about his soul shattered into a million fragments, sending the angels of death screaming away. Their wings were on fire, burning from the heavenly discharge which Asmodeus had sent bursting from within him. Asmodeus stood up calmly, looking about while he brushed the dirt from his clothes. He spotted Mary, crouched over the still body of Smithy, who must have been knocked out from the blast. In one smooth movement he swooped in and grabbed her by the foot, lifting her in the air, dangling in his grasp. He whirled around to see me, still flailing on the ground. Without even taking a step, he pulled me in the air toward him with the elements. In an instant he had both me and Mary by the ankles, hanging out over the cliff.

Asmodeus stood there, holding one of us in each of his powerful hands, his chest heaving. He stood above the turgid green waterfall which roared down to the pool below.

"Stay back!" he snarled loudly. "All of you who would attack me, cease your assault or I will cast these two into a sleep which will last an eternity. They will never be washed out of the pool. They will be lost to you forever!"

Hanging upside down, I could see each of the Pure Seven, wings smouldering, their eyes blazing with hate as they looked from us to Asmodeus. Smithy still lay unconscious on the ground behind them. I was powerless to do anything, the waterfall of sleep surging inches below my face.

"Please," Mary said weakly, in the other hand of Asmodeus. "Set Michael free. I will give you the key. If you don't, I will drop it in the waters, and even you won't be able to save it." She took the key, which was hanging about her neck and held it threateningly ready to drop it into the depths below.

"You always were one for a bargain," our captor sneered while he held us. "Compromise is for the weak!"

Mary let the key slip lower, toward the waterfall. Asmodeus threw his head back and laughed.

"Have it your way, Mary," he said, and tossed me, like a puppet, skidding to a halt at the feet of the still seething Pure Seven.

"No," I managed to say feebly. "It's our only hope, Mary. Don't trade it for me!"

With tears in her eyes, Mary took the key and held it up to Asmodeus. She looked over to me, and mouthed softly, "I'm sorry."

Asmodeus snatched the keys from her hand and thrust it into his pocket in an instant.

"Now what should I do with you, my lovely little whore?" he asked, grinning wickedly down at Mary, who still hung in his clawed fist.

"Drop me," she said. "I welcome sleep."

"No." He shook his head. "It would be too good for you, to be reunited with your filthy brother. You should live with the knowledge that you not only caused his demise by leading him to the Monastery of Zoroaster, you have destroyed Michael's chance of ever seeing his love, Charlotte, again. I'll let my son deal with you."

With a grunt he flung Mary hurtling down toward the tanks far below. Two of the angels rushed forward to catch her. The other five screamed in rage and propelled themselves toward Asmodeus. He spun around like circular lightning, whipping his arm around as he did so and imploded out of existence with a loud bang. Five raging demons shot through the space where he had been. Just a small puff of white mist lingered in the air where he had disappeared.

Asmodeus was gone, the keys with him. He had destroyed any hope of accomplishing what we had worked so hard to achieve. I let the darkness rip my mind away from the conscious world.

38

I LAY IN A SOFT BED. Light sheets covered me in the darkness. There was no noise. I struggled to remember how I'd come to be there. I stared up into the darkness. With a spark of realization, memory roared over the top of me like a train bearing down on the tracks of time: my promise of freedom to the souls of Hell, our quest for the keys, the betrayal of Bishop John who was not a Bishop at all. My father Asmodeus had taken our one chance at revenge. I sat up gasping. I'd fought a losing battle.

But how did I get here?

Struggling out of the knot of sheets around me, I leapt up. I fumbled in the darkness before I had the sense to bring the elements of light around me.

Familiar surroundings. I was in my bedroom at Casa Diablo, dressed in a black pair of loose pants, naked from the waist up. I traced my hands over my body, checking for damage. I was clear of any wounds but ached all over. It was my mind that suffered. Everything was lost. The keys we had fought so hard to find were now lost to Heaven. Our plans to bring down the walls between the realms were dashed. My hope to reunite with Charlotte had been torn away once more.

I rested my hands on my knees. I was back to the same situation when Asmodeus had first left: no ideas, no plans, just anger and frustration. I now had a choice to make: wallow in that anger as I had done before, or use it to create something. I needed to clear my head. Straightening up, I walked to the bathroom and turned on the shower.

I stepped inside and cool water washed over me. Closing my eyes, I let the refreshing liquid cover my head. Faces jolted into my mind. Mary. Smithy. Were they okay?

I punched the tiled wall of the shower hard. Splinters of ceramic stuck into my knuckles as I punched again and again. I had let my friends down.

174

My first thoughts upon waking had been of myself, not of them. Was I so selfish? A well of self-loathing crawled inside me. Leaving the tap running, I stepped out of the shower. Without even drying myself I pulled my pants back on and rushed out of the room.

As I burst into the war room, Mary and Smithy jumped out of their seats. They were sitting at the large metal table with The Pure Seven. Their presence caught me completely off guard.

"Michael!" Smithy yelled, running over to me. "You're okay! We were worried. You've been out for days. We've been waiting for you." He paused and looked me up and down. "What are you doing? You look like a drowned rat!"

I looked at myself. I was dripping in water, in nothing but black pants, blood seeping from my hand. In my haste and confusion I hadn't thought things through.

"I'm..." I searched for words within. "I'm sorry."

"There's nothing to be sorry about," Mary said behind Smithy.

She got up from her chair and walked over to us. Leaning in she gave me a big hug, not worrying that I was soaking wet. She kissed me lightly on each cheek before pulling away. I simply stood there, dazed.

"You have nothing to be sorry for," Mary repeated. "We were lucky that no one was lost. We were even luckier that we have one man with us who questioned what we did not."

"What?" I asked, trying to grasp what she was saying.

"Smithy. Smithy guessed that John was not everything he appeared to be. It was his quick thinking which helped us save one set of the keys."

"What?" I asked, the fog of hopelessness beginning to lift from my mind. So many questions came jumbling to the fore. All I could say was, "What?"

"Well," Smithy said, puffing out his chest a little. "I told you I didn't trust him. I couldn't put my finger on it at first, but when you were in Zoroaster's Monastery I started to think about it. It didn't sit right with me that he had asked both Judas and me to come into the meeting with you at Satan's Tower. It seemed an awful big coincidence that we happened to be the only two souls out of the group in the foyer who had both committed suicide, yet he had singled us out to join the discussion. How could he know that we would be sympathetic to his arguments?"

Why hadn't I noticed that too? I thought. I seemed so obvious now that Smithy brought it up.

"It wasn't just that though," he continued. "There was something about the way he drank his tea that got to me. I really couldn't understand it. It was only the next time, when we were in the foyer at Magdalene's mansion, that I realized it. He drank his tea exactly like Satan used to: six spoons of sugar followed by six stirs clockwise, six stirs counter. It used to make my skin crawl watching Satan drink his tea. I got the same feeling from John."

"He told me his suspicions once we landed here at Casa Diablo," Mary joined in. "While you were talking with John, Smithy pulled me aside. At first I thought he was talking nonsense, but it raised some questions of my own. How had he managed to find you in the monastery? It really didn't make sense to me, but our focus at the time was on the keys and then Judas. Everything had happened so quickly. Neither Smithy nor I knew what to do about it, though. We had no proof of our accusations. Had we confronted him directly we didn't know what would happen. You were already involved in making the waterfall with John when we arrived and we thought maybe we could buy some time until later. Then, everything tumbled out of control."

I ran events over in my head. I had been rushing forward so hard that I hadn't stopped to think about anything else but our goal. I hadn't given anyone a chance to voice concerns.

"But the keys," I asked. "You said you saved the keys. I saw you hand them to Asmodeus!"

"They were the keys to my hangar!" Smithy laughed. "That old goat was so busy fighting off The Pure Seven that he didn't notice the keys around Mary's neck had been swapped for fakes. These are the real ones." He pulled a jingling ring of keys from his pocket. Singling out two, he pulled them off the ring and handed them to me. I changed my perception and looked down in amazement at the molecules of light shining up at me.

I looked back to Smithy and Mary in wonderment. I grabbed both of them in a big hug. Possibility and hope rushed into me. All was not lost! I squeezed the two as hard as I dared. When I had been blinded, these two had been my eyes.

I pulled myself away from their friendly embrace.

"So what does this mean now?" I asked. "What's our next step? What's best for everyone?"

"We've been talking this over since we regrouped," Smithy said to me. "And we've come up with a plan I think you'll approve of."

39

I WAS NOW FULLY ALERT AND EXCITED at the potential that lay ahead. We might have lost our first real battle, but from defeat had sprung a galvanized unity of purpose I had not ever felt before.

Smithy stood at the head of the table, mapping out his strategy with Mary, The Pure Seven and me. His act of saving the keys from Asmodeus had given him new confidence. He now spoke to us with the authority of a general.

"We have to assume that, before too long, Asmodeus will discover that one of the sets of keys he has are counterfeit - if he hasn't already. He was distracted at the time of his attack, but now he's back in Heaven we have to assume he has inspected the keys," Smithy said, his hands clasped behind his back as he paced around the table. "He'll know that we're now on our guard for any kind of deception he may throw at us. He would not risk another frontal attack with Michael back at full strength, but we can trust no one. Only we were present at the attack, so only we know what really happened. No one else can be told the truth just yet lest word get to him somehow. I'm sure he has spies placed in Hell. We need to act fast and we need to act in secret. They keys we still have in our possession are the keys to the gates between Hell and Purgatory. Our mission is to journey into the middle realm. Mary and Michael will take the keys and approach Zoroaster with word of the fight we are waging. With his help we'll unite the souls in Purgatory to our cause and use the keys to tear down the walls between Hell and Purgatory. It will increase our numbers to an army that Asmodeus could never defeat. We will then make a final assault on the walls of Heaven."

"So what you're saying is that we make Purgatory and Hell one realm? We remove the barrier and bring all of the souls there to our side?" I asked, to confirm I had heard correctly.

Smithy nodded.

"All in Purgatory want to go to Heaven just as much as we do," Mary added. "It will be easy to convince them that our fight is a noble one. Zoroaster will also be a powerful ally. Together you two will be a match for Asmodeus himself."

"But what if Zoroaster doesn't take our side?" I said. "What if he's not even there?"

"The Master will be there," The Pure Seven spoke together. "He promised he would continue Mary's work in the Limbo realm. His word is truth and cannot be perverted."

"I believe he'll help us," Mary continued. "If we're honest in our intentions with him then he will aid our cause. He has fought against both God and Satan before. He will continue to oppose them until all is equal. He will help us."

"But if he doesn't?" I pressed.

"We need him to. Only he knows exactly how to join the keys together to create the proper block. If he doesn't, then we'll have to try to bring the wall down ourselves," she said fiercely, "but it won't come to that. I know he'll help. While Zoroaster may work in absolutes, he understands that action must move ahead in increments. Our worst case scenario is that he'll remain neutral until he sees we're working in the right direction. We are in the right here, Michael. You know it and so do I."

I nodded and Smithy continued.

"While you're gone, I'll run interference in Hell city. I'll tell Clytemnestra to spread word that Michael is safe at Casa Diablo and that The Pure Seven are guarding him. I'll feed her the details of the battle, and say that Lord Michael is planning his next move. This will buy us a few days at least. I'll ask her to use her contacts to seek knowledge of ways we might be able to return Earth."

"Earth?" I asked.

"It's a distraction," he said excitedly. "We spread word that you're planning to attack the realm of the living. Our hope is that any spies Asmodeus may have here will pass the misinformation on to him. He would never assent to a perversion of his favorite plaything. Just the threat of an attack on Earth will divert any attention away from Purgatory until you're able to complete your mission."

"We do not like using lies as a weapon to pursue truth," the Pure Seven chorused.

"We've been over this already," Smithy said to them calmly. "This is war. I don't like it either, but as Mary explained, to achieve an absolute you must move in steps. These are not explicit lies that will create oppression;

they are diversions, which will aid in destroying it. You will not have to lie yourselves; you will only have to keep silent."

"Exceptions to an ideal make the ideal worthless," they responded.

"Please," Mary said. "You all know me. I am just as much a student of Zoroaster as you. If we begin to stray too far off the path of truth, then I trust you will be here to stop it. Michael and I will seek Master Zoroaster's advice. I believe with all my heart that he'll join us in this fight. Do you promise to hold your allegiance to me until we can meet him?"

"We promise with our souls," they said in unison. "Thank you, Mary replied softly.

"Are you ready for this, Michael?" asked Smithy. "I won't be able to take you to the desert in my helicopter this time. You'll have to take Mary there yourself without giving yourself away."

I was wary of the idea. We had already rushed into our first plan too quickly to see the trap that Asmodeus was setting. Who knew what he had up his sleeve still. How he had snuck into Hell undetected was something that gnawed at me greatly. If he had done it before, he could do it again at any moment. It felt like he held all the cards. It felt like I couldn't trust anyone except the people in this room who had helped in the battle against him. I racked my brain for other options. If we admitted anything to the outside world, we would be admitting weakness. It would risk word getting back to the enemy. Yet this seemed to be the only option. Where swiftness had been our downfall before, it could prove to our advantage this time. We had to work before Asmodeus could make his next move. We had to act immediately.

I looked from Smithy to the Seven and then to Mary.

"I'm ready."

40

I WENT BACK TO MY ROOM and changed for the trip: all black as usual. I tied my hair back to keep it from getting in the way. I noticed my ears were still a deep red, but hadn't grown any worse. I was nervous about the trip to Purgatory. It wasn't just because of the danger; the hope of seeing Charlotte lingered inside as well. Our mission was to go straight to Zoroaster, no questions. Deep down I prayed we would be able to see Charlotte before we tore down the walls. I wanted to explain our plans to her. I wanted to let her know that once the walls were down, we would be together.

I met Mary back in the war room. She stood waiting, dressed in blue jeans and a black t-shirt. It was the plainest I'd ever seen her dress. She smiled at me as I entered. Her emerald eyes showed a sweet innocence inside despite everything she'd been through in her long and troubled existence.

"Is everything set?" I asked.

"The Seven are preparing what you asked. They should start at any moment."

We waited silently and then heard a wailing scream outside. I smiled to myself and waited for a few more minutes. The clattering and yelling grew louder and louder, then faded away to silence. I got up and moved to crack open the door of the room. In the foyer, a trail of carnage led outside and down the steps. The room was empty except for broken paintings which had been ripped off the walls and scattered between splintered chairs and upturned tables.

I locked the rooms behind us and we quickly moved outside to the top of the stairs. Looking to the right I could see the Pure Seven. They were going berserk: tearing rosebushes from the ground, smashing fountains and screeching unearthly cries into the air. Azazel was flailing underneath them, trying to group his demon helpers to stop the angels of sin from destroying the grounds.

With all attention diverted away, Mary and I hurried around the opposite side of the castle. As we rounded the back wall, I put my hands onto the silver gates that hemmed in the Fount of Mercy. At my touch, the steel melted away to let us through. The field before us was a dark reminder of the battle that had taken place. The green waterfall of sleep plummeted down from the cliff I had constructed into the pool below. We moved towards it carefully. In the center, the floating stone pathway I had constructed bobbed above the water.

"Be careful," I said. "One at a time."

Stepping out onto the stones, I lightly padded my way across. As I did so, I created a thick shell of air all around me. When I came to the waterfall, the gel parted, cascading over the barrier I'd made for myself.

I turned and expanded the air barrier, making a clear pathway for Mary to wade through. She saw my signal and ran deftly over the stones and into the cave next to me. I let the elements fall back and the waterfall roared and tumbled again over the opening.

Green shimmered all around us in watery shadows which rippled up and down the walls. The roar of the rushing curtain of water echoed all around. I turned to the steep shaft at the back of the cave which burrowed through the mountain.

"This will take us almost to the foot of the jungle below," I said to Mary. "We can then fly low, over the top of the canopy. I'll create a camouflage around us, just in case anyone is looking down from Casa Diablo, but we should be fine."

"Wouldn't it be better to travel through the jungle?" she asked. "To save your strength?"

"I have no idea what's in there," I answered. "There could be creatures of unimaginable horror for all we know. I don't want to risk it. This way is quicker. I shouldn't need to use the elements in Purgatory and flight doesn't take up too much energy."

I stepped forward to climb downward into the earth. The descent was steep, but not so steep that you couldn't walk down carefully, steadying your hands on the low roof. Our footsteps sounded around us as we scratched down the shaft. The roar of the waterfall above faded to a whisper as we went. Soon we could make out a red light below which signalled that the opening wasn't too far ahead.

"Do you have the keys safe with you?" I asked Mary. She patted her chest and nodded.

The opening wasn't large, barely head height. It looked over the green jungle below us. We were slightly above the height of the trees. I searched into the distance and could only just make out the glowing light of the Chinvar Bridge over the horizon.

"Hold on tight," I told Mary. She moved to the back of me and hugged me around the chest, nestling her head between my shoulder blades.

"I've always wanted to know what it's like to be a bird," she whispered in my ear.

I pulled a swirl of molecules around both of us. Raising us just off the ground, I gathered a tornado at our backs. With a burst of wind, we flew out of the mountain like shot from a cannon.

41

WE ROCKETED IN A BLUR over the teeming jungle, the wind at our feet. I put up a mirror of elements around us to reflect outward movement. Any probing eyes watching from above or below would see just a smudge running across the sky. It wasn't perfect invisibility but it was the simplest to maintain.

Mary giggled in my ear as we flew, her hair ruffling me on the neck. She clung to the back of me, her arms wrapped under my armpits, her legs around my middle. She wriggled forward so her head was next to mine. Her hips squirmed over my back.

"This is incredible!" she yelled above the wind. "I feel like a little girl in an amusement park!"

I swooped lower toward the trees to give her a thrill, pushing the elements of air faster behind us to accelerate. She yelped as we almost touched the leaves below. In minutes we'd cleared the jungle and were whipping along the desert sands, shooting toward the Chinvar Bridge.

I undulated our flight up and down, hugging as close to the ground as I could without disturbing the surface of the dunes. As the illumination of the bridge came closer, I slowed down, squinting into the rays. Almost blind, we floated over the last small rise of sand before the bridge. The light subsided back to a healthy glow and my vision returned in blurry dots. Keeping a straight line, I pulled up and wafted gently to the ground. My feet touched down next to the Monastery of Zoroaster.

Mary jumped off my back. Her normally porcelain skin was flushed from the flight. She smiled a big grin, bouncing on the balls of her feet.

"Wow. Wow!" she exclaimed, bursting with energy. "I thought war missions would be all serious business." She was flicking her hands up and down, her eyes wide.

I couldn't help but smile back briefly.

"I'm glad you liked it, but the fun's over, Mary. We have to figure out how to get up this bridge to the gates. We need to be careful now we're so close. We can't have any other setbacks. Maybe we should just fly up and follow along the row of light to the gates?"

My tone sobered her mood somewhat and she looked up into the sky. The thin ray of light beamed up uninterrupted through the black storm clouds that were ever present in the sky of Hell. She shook her head.

"No, the light fails in the clouds. We would be hopelessly lost without the guide of the bridge. We have to use it the right way. It's safe."

"Do you know how it works?" I asked. "I always thought a bridge was something you walked over."

She nodded slowly, moving a little further toward the beam. "A bridge is just something that joins two things together. It can be anything. This Chinvar Bridge is something like you've never known. You have to focus on a single truth while you're touching it," she said looking at me. "It might sound easy but it's not. If any other thoughts enter your head, any doubts, then your grip on the bridge will begin to fail. You need to create a clear vision of something in your mind and cling to it. You then reach out and hold onto the beam. Once you attain the right clarity, the beam will draw you upward. For me, before, my single thought was my desire to get Judas back. I always held onto that with all I had. I used it when we came down here and realized that in truth it was my only driving purpose. I would picture the face of Judas in my mind. That was the one thought I could keep without any distraction."

"Charlotte," I said firmly. "I will focus on Charlotte. There's nothing more powerful than my love for her."

She looked up to the bridge grimly. All of the light in her eyes from before had vanished.

"Judas," she said quietly. "I just want you to wake up and be happy. I want us back together for good."

She turned back to me.

"Come and put your hand on the beam. Wrap your fingers around it and start to breathe slowly. Let the image of Charlotte arrive in your head freely. Don't force it. Once you have it, the beam will become solid in your hand and draw you up inside it." She put her hand over the beam and closed her eyes. I walked next to her and clasped my fingers around it, just below hers. It was like trying to hold onto a rushing jet of water. My hand bumped up and down with the current. Closing my eyes, I let air fill my lungs, steadying my mind. I breathed, in and out, feeling the scorching air rush into my nose, through my throat and into my lungs.

Mary's body brushed past me as she lifted off the ground. I sucked air into my lungs again picturing Charlotte's face. Her white teeth sparkled beneath full, pink lips. Her eyes locked into mine and she became more than a face. She became a person: my wife, my love. Vaguely, I could feel myself rising into the air, as I smiled back at Charlotte.

We looked at each other. She blinked a few times. Her face was warm and kind. I floated upward in bliss. I wanted to talk to her. She seemed so real.

"I love you Charlotte," I said.

Charlotte opened her mouth and, in the voice of Mary, screamed: "Michael, help me!"

42

A BODY CRASHED INTO ME FROM ABOVE. Hands fumbled to hold onto my legs as I tried to hold on to the vision of Charlotte.

"Michael," I heard Mary scream again.

I opened my eyes and looked down to see Mary's face mixed with a vision of Charlotte looking up at me in desperation. We were still encased in a white light. Black mist swirled around us. Piercing thunder rumbled in my ears. Mary was grasping onto my leg, her hair swirling around in the wind. The keys to Purgatory dangled around her neck. She looked up to me again, pleading.

"Help me, Michael. Pull me up!"

The memory of Charlotte flickered out of my mind completely and the light around us gave way. The bridge shrank back to a rushing torrent of light in my hand. We started to slide downwards as my grip began to fail. I clasped my hand tighter, reaching right into the middle of the beam. Touching a hard surface within, sharp edges of heat sliced deep into my skin. I clenched my teeth and wrapped my fingers around the surface as hard as I could. The central chord of the bridge cut through to the bones of my palm. I let out a cry of agony and we shuddered slowly to a halt. The blade of light burnt into my hand. I squeezed tighter, but it just made the pain worse. I thought about using the elements but didn't, lest I lose grip of the bridge completely and get lost in the clouds. The weight of Mary pulled down on me. I reached up and clasped my other hand over the one that was holding on to the bridge. Blood was seeping between my fingers and down my forearms.

"Climb up!" I said between gritted teeth.

"I can't!"

"You can!" I screamed back. "Get onto my back."

She started to claw up my leg, clinging around my thighs. "I can't get any further!" she yelled.

I closed my eyes at the torture throbbing in my arms. I had to reach down to her. I couldn't lose her. We were so close. Holding with all my might, I dug the fingers of one hand into the beam and swung the other hand down. The heat of the Chinvar Bridge burned into my bones. Our combined weight started to pull us down slowly again, the blade cutting at what was left of my shredded palm. I reached down with extended fingers. Mary stretched up and clasped my hand. Wrapping my fingers around hers tightly, I wrenched her upward. She reached up with her other hand and grabbed my forearm. I pulled her up so she was able to grasp onto my torso. Lightning flashed and a ghastly crack of thunder almost threw me off the bridge.

"Hold on!" I yelled. "I'll take us up!"

I swung my free hand up and clasped it over the one holding onto the beam again. Struggling to push the pain from my arms, I worked to regain the vision of Charlotte. As Mary pressed into me tightly, her weight eased.

I grimaced and recaptured the light of Lotte's eyes in my mind. Her smiling face came back in the haze of agony.

"Help me, Charlotte," I begged her. She nodded and closed her eyes. Warmth encircled my being. I was with her again. We started to move back toward the heavens.

"Thank you, Charlotte. Thank you, Charlotte." I was saying over and over again.

"Thank you, Michael." Mary said into my ear. "We're here. We've made it to the gates."

43

I OPENED MY EYES AND LOOKED AROUND. Purple lightning forked below us. We were perched on top of a ledge of light, inches below a swirling black and white vortex. It was enormous. I looked out across the spinning filter and could see no end. Chaotic eddies of emotion twisted around and around in an endless cycle. Thunder crashed about our heads. The black and red clouds stewed underneath us. We were right in the eye of the spiral. Currents of power crackled mere feet above us. The flow of the elemental hurricane churned out from the center in a white chord and came back inward as a black river of power. It all converged on the spot directly above our heads. The convergence was a shimmering purple dot, barely the size of a clenched fist. The entire force of the whirlpool channelled into the dot on one side and burst out on the other.

I looked to Mary at my side. She held the keys in her hand with tears in her eyes.

"What happened?" I yelled to Mary above the thunder. I looked at my lacerated hands. They were healing painfully.

"I'm so sorry! I lost my focus. Judas' face turned on me."

"To what? What happened?" I asked, not understanding what she meant.

She cast her eyes downward in shame. After a few moments she looked up again.

"Thoughts of revenge on Asmodeus invaded the space I held for Judas. I'm sorry. I almost ruined everything."

"We're here! It's enough. What do we do now?"

She took one of the keys off the ring in her hand and passed it to me.

"Do you see the gap there in the gateway?" Mary asked, pointing upward.

I nodded. If I put my hand in the air I would be able to touch it.

"Reach up and place your key inside. Once it's in, turn the key clockwise. When the lock clicks you'll be drawn with the key into Purgatory."

I held the key steadily between my fingers and raised it upward, slotting the end into the chink above. As I turned my wrist, I felt the metal vibrate between my fingers. With a deafening howl of wind I was ripped upward into darkness. Voices of every language screamed in my ears. My eardrums almost split with the assault. The physical force of the noise speared into my gut. As quickly as it began, everything fell silent. I was standing in a calm grey meadow, wobbling on my feet. The ground about me looked as though it was made of the tops of clouds, yet it was as solid as rock. Those rocks gave way to dull grey blades of grass a few feet away that continued into the distance in every direction. With a hiss, one of the bubbles of rock next to me turned into a glowing, red, molten puddle. The form of Mary shot up out of it. I had to blink it was so fast. The cloud-like rocks were now solid at her feet again and there she was, teetering for balance at my side. I reached out and steadied her. Mary looked at me. With shame still in her eyes she handed me her key.

"Take it. I don't ever want to jeopardize our mission again. I can't believe I was so stupid!" She hung her head.

"Forget it," I said, taking the key. Securing it with a sticky set of elements, I hid it inside my pocket. "We made it, Mary. None of this could have been possible without you. Now, we need to focus. We have to keep on track. Where are we and how do we get to Zoroaster?"

She peered around. There wasn't a breath of wind. Everything was completely still and grey. The dullness of the place sifted around me like a worn out soul. It was tranquil, although nothing about it brought me any sense of peace. Grey wispy clouds hung in the sky, layered over the top of each other to create a dense wall of mist above.

"We're in the Far Reaches. There's nobody here. It's isolated from the city by these fields. This is where any soul who comes from Hell to Purgatory ends up. We need to head north," she said, pointing ahead of us. "We'll come to a hill and then once we get to the top of that, in the distance we should see the city. It's quite a journey by foot."

No use in delay, I thought. I picked my way carefully over the short space of uneven rocks to the safety of the grass. Mary came close behind. Without pausing, I led us with purpose through the vast grey meadow of boredom.

We trudged on. I resisted using the elements. My body had healed, but the effort had made me tired. The dreary feeling of Purgatory tugged at my brain. Even the air seemed to pull passion away from me. The sky was morbid. The ground was monotonous. The only ray of color around was the beauty of Mary next to me.

"It's all so dull," I said to her, hoping conversation would nudge my brain out of the doldrums.

"You're only feeling that because we're out here," she replied. "God made it like this on purpose when he built it. I told you, he didn't want natural beauty to distract the souls here from their real intent of passing to Heaven. That's one thing Hell has over Purgatory; it's savage, but it's still striking. Once we get into the city, the people will help lift you out of what you're feeling. The souls light up this place."

We lapsed once more into silence. The meadow stretched on and on. There weren't even any more rocks to break up a sense of travel. We'd been walking for hours and it felt like we could very well be in the same spot. The light around us wasn't dark, but it wasn't bright either. It was like the few minutes before dawn, where you can see everything perfectly fine, but there's no real brilliance about the world. Whereas with an earthly dawn there is the anticipation of a new day about to break over the horizon, here I knew it would stay this way forever. I reached out with my mind to Mary and sensed love emanating from her. It heartened me to be travelling with a true friend.

"How far do we have to go until the main city?" I asked. She looked ahead and then back to me.

"It's hard to get a bearing, but I think we're a half day's walk. It's flat, so it shouldn't be difficult. That's if it's still the same as when I left."

"What do you mean?"

"It's been almost five hundred years since I left for Hell. At lot has changed there since. I imagine it may be the same here. As technology moves on Earth and generations develop ideas, they bring them to the afterlife. People change over time in many ways. In others they stay the same."

Five hundred years. She had been alive for over two thousand. I had only been alive for just over thirty and already I felt weary. It was hard to imagine someone living for so long and still looking so young.

"What are the big changes you've seen?" I asked, interested as well as wanting to keep the conversation going to help pass the time.

"It's mostly in technology. If you had told me about the Internet or even a computer a thousand years ago, I would have laughed. Cars, planes, skyscrapers, everything."

"It must be strange."

"Yes and no. It's like living with someone who grows their hair out. Because the change happens slowly, you are accustomed to the changes.

They're gradual. The real challenge would be if you slept for a thousand years and then woke up. It amazes me that Judas wasn't completely overwhelmed when he was freed from the forest."

I nodded my head. The mention of Judas dampened my spirits.

"Is there anything that hasn't changed?"

"People mostly. Thoughts and ideas might change, but emotions don't. The big motivations for existence are the same as when I was a girl so long ago. People seek love, they seek wealth. Above all they seek happiness. They seek to matter. There is always conflict, though. One person wants one thing and another person seeks something different. This is why there's so much pain in the world; everyone lives within their own personality. Two people might agree on something, but there's always a third party who thinks their's is a better way to do things. Always. That's why I believe it's so important to work towards an absolute truth. If everyone was able to see things exactly how they are, with no opinion, then there would be no conflict."

"Is that possible?"

"There's always hope," she said. "I really don't know, though. It's a wonderful idea, true peace."

We walked on and I turned the concept over in my head. True peace. No conflict. Would it become boring? Would no opinion mean that we were all really dead in a way? Would no variance take away individuality, take away color? I looked about at the grey world of Purgatory. Maybe conflict was something that the human mind needed in order to keep an interest in life. Had we been created that way on purpose as another one of God's cruel jokes? I hoped that someday I would have the intelligence to know.

"What do you think will happen when we destroy the filter between Hell and Purgatory?" I asked.

"I'm not certain." She paused. "But I have thought about it quite a lot in the past. Zoroaster and I would talk it over for days on end. Our most promising theory was that it will simply open up the two realms to each other.

"But how?" I asked.

"Right now, we are walking over the swirling barrier. The crust at our feet is solid, but below is moving. The barrier we saw at the top of the Chinvar Bridge is like a huge tectonic whirlpool that shifts constantly. Where we came up, you can see the power of the filter trying to bubble through."

"The cloud rocks."

"Yes." She smiled. "That's the same point we'll return to once we can bond the keys together. If we can jam the power flow of the barrier, then it

191

will create a reaction that should cause something like a gigantic earthquake. The filter will solidify quickly, and because of the heat and pressure it will crack. With an elemental push from you and Zoroaster, the ground we stand on now will give way. The sky of Hell will fall in over the desert below. In essence it should open a celestial porthole the same size as the filter. It will then be easy for people to travel through at will. Souls will be able to move up to the city here, or vice versa. The space of Hell will be doubled, but because there are fewer souls in Purgatory, there will be more room for everyone."

"Yes, but will it make things better for those souls?" I asked.

"I hope so," she said slowly. "At the very least it will improve the overall balance in the universe. The reason there's so much conflict and untruth is that no one is on even ground at the moment. We don't have the same experiences, the same lives. We see what someone else has and want it. When I heard about the political vision of communism, I thought it was a wonderful idea. However, the human mind took hold of it and corrupted it. It became useless, evil even. It shows how something perfect in the mind can become imperfect in reality. There is always someone worse off than us, but there is always someone better off as well. Until we can create a true balance, the universe will tip from side to side."

Mary's intelligence and insight had rattled me. I had never really thought of the world in that way. I had just been selfish, looking within myself for answers. She had had more than several lifetimes to ponder these things, but did that mean she was right? I knew she meant well in her heart.

"Do you think how people are will corrupt what we want to achieve?" I asked after a few moments.

"Not if the powerful are willing to lay down their might for the greater good." She stared at me pointedly.

I looked down at my feet and continued in silence. There would be a fight, no matter what we did. Power meant nothing to me; I would willingly let it go. If I could subdue Asmodeus, then there was true hope for peace.

As we walked, my mind kept wandering back to Charlotte. It helped a real smile spark inside me. She was here. She was so close. Butterflies crept into my stomach and fluttered madly. I let myself fall into daydreams of our old life on Earth together. I thought about how we'd met on a plane and hit if off instantly. I remembered my proposal on the cool sands of Greece when she had cried tears of joy. Everything I did was to see that same happiness in her eyes one more time. A reunion with her would be worth all the suffering I'd been through.

I was so lost in my thoughts that I hadn't even noticed we were walking up an incline. One moment it seemed like endless meadow still laid out in front. The next, we rounded the top of a soft peak.

We stopped and looked down over a bleak city. Lackluster buildings rose into the sky. The metropolis spread out toward us, but gave way to lifeless trees before turning into the meadow we were in. We walked down towards the small wood. The trees were sparse, but seemed to be a marker for the beginning of the city. We pressed through the grey forest. As we drew towards the middle, I spotted a person.

"Hello!" I yelled. The man looked up to us. He was sitting beneath a tree, his legs crossed. His hands were resting on his knees, palms up in a pose of meditation. He appeared Middle Eastern and had a white turban wrapped around his head. His being sparkled with light. It made me glad that we were with another living form.

"Hello," he said. "I thought I felt a shift out there in The Reaches. It's good to see you, Mary. Who is your friend?" I was startled that he knew Mary's name.

"His name is Michael," she said next to me. "Michael, this is Zoroaster."

44

"ZOROASTER?" I BLURTED INVOLUNTARILY, surprised that this was the prophet we'd come to find.

"Yes, Michael, that is what Mary called me," he replied, still sitting. "Maybe if you've spent some time with her, you already know who I am. I don't know who you are yet, but we'll have time to talk. Your aura looks very strong. I wonder if I could beat you in a fight. Maybe if the fancy takes us we can try later. First I want to talk with Mary." He turned to Mary with a smile.

His strange manner took me aback. He seemed to jump from one thought to another as they formed is his mind. These were very weird things to be saying; yet I sensed no malice in him at all. He had an easy grin on his lips and, even when he said I might know of him, it was said candidly rather than with any kind of pride.

"It's very nice to see you, Mary," Zoroaster continued. "It's been a very long time. When I felt that small breath of hot wind coming from the direction of the gateway, I hoped it would be you and not someone else. You haven't lost an ounce of your wonderful beauty. I'm disappointed you've come with a man. I felt a stirring in my loins when you first approached. I haven't been with a woman in many weeks. He is more handsome than me, so I can understand your choice would be easily with him. We have a lot to catch up on. Are you still practicing the way of truth?"

Mary blushed and flicked her eyes to me before looking back at Zoroaster.

"Yes, I'm doing my best – although I'm still not close to your standard! I'm not romantically together with Michael; we've come to seek your help."

"Oh?" Zoroaster said. "My help with what, Mary?"

She paused and looked at me before continuing in a slow voice.

"We're here on a mission to seek your help in creating more freedom in the universe. Michael is the new Lord of Hell. There has been a revelation that Satan and God were two sides of the same being. He has now reunited those halves into an entity we call Asmodeus. Michael wants to end his reign of lies. Our first step in the plan is to bring down the barriers between Hell and Purgatory."

"Oh!" he said again, his eyes growing wide. "That's all very interesting. Very interesting! I'm glad you still practice the way of truth. It always brings you to the biggest things on your mind first. Maybe we should go to my home and you can explain this to me some more. I'd like to know the whys and hows and whos. I had heard whispers of a revolution in Hell, but the details have been thin until now. I'm reluctant to help you attack what God has created, but I could be persuaded if I think your intentions are worthy and any hidden motivations are in the open."

He narrowed his eyes and looked at me. I felt naked beneath his stare. He then glared the same way at Mary.

"I can see both of you have the chaos of hidden lies within. They can wait for the moment. For now let's take a walk through the city and I can bring you up to date with how things are progressing here. We've made many breakthroughs during your absence."

Zoroaster unfolded his legs and reached out a hand to Mary. She leant down and helped him stand. He was short, only coming up to my shoulders, and was even a little shorter than Mary, albeit a lot wider.

He took off at a brisk walk through the trees.

"He's like no one I've ever met," I whispered to Mary as we started to follow behind him.

"Most people take a while to get used to undiluted honestly," she whispered. "He often appears a little manic because he says whatever jumps into his mind. When he's focused he is a sight to behold."

"I can hear you talking about me," called Zoroaster. "No need for whispering. There are no secrets, only truth. I know I can appear unusual to outsiders, Michael. Come, come, don't dawdle."

We emerged through the trees to a road. There were no cars to be seen, but there were crowds of people. Everybody was on foot, walking in the middle of the street with an easy pace. I could feel the warmth of their souls. My weary mood from the meadow had entirely lifted to an invigorated sense of spirit. It was as if we were in a black and white movie, but all the people were still in color. The contrast made their souls dazzle even more than usual.

"I've recently managed to convince the people to take away most modern conveniences from Purgatory," Zoroaster said, as we crossed the road, winding through the bright people. Many of the passersby said friendly hellos to us as he spoke.

"It was a lot of work at first, but now with no cars or televisions people have been brought back towards inner contemplation. Instead of rushing forward to nowhere, where they can get lost in an alternate reality, people are turning within. The most interesting reality is here," Zoroaster pointed to his own chest. "The spark of awareness is the truth of things. It's rather amazing really. With less distraction from trivial amusements, more and more are passing over to Heaven! I actually think God was onto something when he made the surrounds of this realm so lifeless."

Mary nodded.

"You're right Zoroaster, He did have a point. But beauty is still important for people, is it not?"

"Of course! It is a powerful driving force. That's my point exactly." He laughed. "If there is no external beauty surrounding you, there is a desire to cultivate the beauty inside yourself and others. Unfortunately, some of the people have painted their buildings different colors to satiate that desire for the beautiful instead of looking within. Those people tend to be the ones who regretfully stay here because what they seek is superficial only. I haven't asked anyone to repaint back to grey yet, but I'm toying with the idea. I really hope they will come to the realization on their own. I don't want to force anyone to do anything. Often I wonder if I should, though. The suggestion of removing the pursuit of technology alone has worked wonders."

I looked around. Indeed there were a few buildings of color. The overwhelming majority of them were still grey, but there were brilliant exceptions. One house near us was all blue, with white trim around the windows. It was a beautiful flower amongst rows of uniformity. The streets were overflowing with people. I was surprised at the amount of them. There was no disorder, though, no one in a hurry. Men and women were moving along at ease around us, talking with each other as they went, or sitting around quietly. There were seats on the pavement, butted onto all of the buildings, so if people wanted to stop and rest they could at their leisure. The thing that struck me most was that almost everyone was smiling. They seemed quite happy, even animated in conversations. It was a world away from the streets of Hell, where scowls reigned and souls surged to their next appointment with little regard for the others around them. I searched among the people, hoping I would see Charlotte. She was nowhere to be seen.

"Incredible," Mary said, looking around her. "Although I have to remind you, there weren't televisions or cars around when I was here. It has been almost half a millennium, remember?"

"Really? I knew it had been a long time, but so long! Well, we've peeled it back to something close to what you began with then. I remember you saying how successful it was at first. Of course the difference is now that the people who come here are already used to those material things. It takes some weaning off the technological teat until they understand the culture. It seems that over the centuries people have become obsessed with a life of convenience. My mother always told me that nothing good comes easy. She was a mean old lady, but I think I understand her a little more, finally. You would think by making life easier with inventions that humans would be able to remain focused on the goodness of the soul. But it appears the opposite has happened on Earth. Convenience has become an obsession. The easier things become, the more people demand a lazy life. They start to crave instant amusement instead of lasting happiness. I can't blame them; it's hard to differentiate between the two when life on Earth is so fleeting. Of course now they know there is an eternity, people calm down much more easily."

We stopped in front of a squat structure with a wide entrance and wide windows all the way along the front. A black and white sign above the entrance read: Veritas Splendor. People were milling in and out of the doors. Everyone coming back out seemed to be in a contemplative frame of mind, looking either into space or intensely at the ground.

"This is my school," Zoroaster said, walking up the pathway set over grey spikes of grass. "I won't take you in for too long, we'll just peek inside."

We picked our way through the crowd to sidle up to the open entrance. Zoroaster and Mary stood on one side of the doors and I moved to the other. Inside the building there were rows of people sitting cross-legged on mats facing the front of the large square classroom. An elderly woman standing at the front was speaking to them. I could hear her mature voice over their heads.

"We are now going to do an exercise," she said, clasping her hands at her waist. "I want you to turn to the person behind you and tell them a secret you kept during your life. It doesn't have to be big, just something no one else knows. As the secret comes out, feel the burden inside lift within your spirit."

Students turned to each other and there was a murmur of conversation. After a few minutes, beaming smiles resonated on the faces of everyone present. They looked to each other with a united aura of achievement.

"Very good," the elderly woman said. "Now think to yourself: if the truth of something so small can make me feel so good, how light will I become when I reveal my darkest deeds?" She turned to a whiteboard behind her and wrote in black on it: What are my Darkest Secrets? She then turned back to her students and stood there a moment, looking at each of them seriously.

"I want all of you tonight to contemplate what your darkest secrets are. What are you least proud of doing in your life? It may take some days until you're honest with yourself, but when you are, then you are ready to be honest with others. I am always here to listen to those confessions, but remember I am not being told them in confidence. I am being told so that it is common knowledge. The real truth is when nothing is hidden from even someone who barely knows you. It's like being famous in a way, people can read the tabloids of your misgivings just like on Earth."

There was a titter of laughter and everyone started to rise. Some stretched their limbs as they stood in place and chatted to one another.

"This school has been another great help in cleansing souls," Zoroaster said. "These people are more honest than you could believe. I hope their truth spreads into Heaven when they pass over. We're chipping away at chaos, one lie at a time!"

The prophet turned to us with a smile. "The truth will set you free!"

"You haven't changed," Mary smiled.

"We all change," Zoroaster said. "Our only hope is that we change for the better."

He took Mary by the hand and turned to lead her back down the pathway. I followed close behind. We pushed past people who were coming up to the school and turned right again, walking up the hill, along the bustling street. Zoroaster patted Mary's arm fondly as they walked. I strode forward to keep up. We turned a corner and a group of children came running down the street, laughing and playing. One of them bumped into my leg. He looked up, with big brown eyes. A scar ran from the corner of his mouth to his ear, disfiguring him hideously.

"I'm sorry mithter," he said with a lisp, and kept running down the street.

Zoroaster turned to me.

"You look like you've seen a ghost," he said. "His scars weren't beautiful. They are a hangover from his personal perception of body in life. Don't let it bother you."

"It's not that," I said, shaking my head in dismay. "There are children here. I thought all children would be in Heaven."

"That's quite naïve of you, Michael," he replied as we walked on. "There are children in Hell too if you cared to look, although if nothing's changed they are normally turned into fully fledged demons quickly. Young minds are easily influenced, positively or otherwise."

"But they're children!" I said. "Surely God would have given some grace when he created these filters for them?"

"A soul is a soul, Michael, young or old. What age would you set to become an adult? Eight, ten, fourteen? It's different for everyone, that kind of level of maturity. The ability to tell the difference between right and wrong can come much earlier. If you're stealing candy from your parents, it is still a sin in God's eyes. What's to stop you stealing other people's things in Heaven? Hmmm?"

"But..."

"But nothing," he kept on. "Stealing candy is only a minor sin, so those children thankfully come here. But 'children', as you call them, can still murder or torture. Some wage wars, some are soldiers. Maybe you've lived a sheltered life, Michael, but surely you can see that even if you're little, you can become a brute. It's a grace from The Lord in Heaven and Mary here that many of those young souls come to Purgatory now. Before, they would have gone straight to the flames."

I shook my head.

"It's one of the reasons we need to create more freedom in the realms." Seeing an opportunity to plead our case, I continued, "God, as you call him, has lost grip on what's good and evil. The Asmodeus I know is nothing but a brute himself."

"You don't understand much then, do you?" Zoroaster said, still with an easy smile. He wasn't attacking me, simply making a comment. Nevertheless, anger prickled inside me.

"I understand that freedom and truth are not things that Asmodeus holds dear."

"Maybe so," Zoroaster said. "But matters of good and evil aren't so simple. You aren't ready for this conversation yet, though, Michael. Maybe after some more time to learn and reflect we can pick up this discussion."

"I want to discuss it now," I said, my face getting hot with embarrassment at his words.

"No, it will be useless. Tell me. Would you kill one child so that you could save two?"

"I would never kill a child!" I said defensively.

"Not even to save two? What about two million?"

I stood there, dumb.

"If I knew that by killing one child it would save two million lives, then I would do it," I said sullenly.

"Would you?" Zoroaster said in surprise. "What if it was your own child? What then? Would you stand and watch while other children devoured your baby for sustenance? Wouldn't that make you a monster? Forsaking your own flesh and blood like that?"

I stood and thought for a few moments. If it was my own child, I wasn't sure I could make that decision.

"It doesn't matter anyway," I finally said. "It's not a choice I would ever have to make. We're just talking rhetorically."

"Life is rhetorical. I told you that you're too young for this conversation." Zoroaster frowned. "God, the Asmodeus that you despise so much, has to make those kinds of decisions all the time. That is one of the biggest misconceptions about Him. People think He's evil because He takes the lives of innocents, but in the end He is doing it for the greater good."

"Who is to say what the greater good is?" I countered. "It is the natural order of things."

"There is no natural order when a supernatural being pulls all the strings," I said. "He should leave us to determine what is natural for ourselves. Our lives are our own; we should be the ones who decide."

"You aren't qualified to make those decisions of what the greater good is," Zoroaster said.

"More evil has been committed under the auspices of 'the greater good' than almost any other!" I snapped, losing my cool. "Religion, efficiency. It's all the same. They take the faces away from the people and treat them like meat on a chopping board." I had raised my voice passionately to put forward my argument. Some people had stopped around us and were staring.

"It's easy for you to make moral judgments," Zoroaster said calmly, resuming our walk. I had no choice but to follow. "Many people think utilitarianism is a bad thing because it takes the focus off the individual." He turned back to me as he made his way up the street. "We all want to be viewed as individuals, but how can you separate one leaf from a tree?"

"How can you take away an individual's unique contribution or potential by lumping them into a group?" I said.

"I can't," Zoroaster continued. "But God has to. He is forced to look at the bigger picture because he is the bigger picture. Like I said, you aren't ready for this conversation. I don't expect you to fathom Asmodeus' reasoning without having been in his presence for at least a few hundred years or more and seen history's mistakes with your own eyes."

"Asmodeus is my father!" I said stupidly. It was a last ditch attempt to stay in the debate.

"That doesn't change much. Unless he raised and nurtured you with his ideas?"

I remained silent.

"We are all God's neglected children in a real sense that he created us," Zoroaster went on. "I have problems with The Father just as you do, but his ethics on the treatment of unclean souls isn't one of them. It's his inability to act in absolute truthfulness, which disturbs me most. Now, where is this building we're looking for?"

He glanced from left to right. I wanted to jump into the conversation again, but he was concentrating on looking up and down the street.

Mary touched me lightly on the shoulder.

"Don't take anything of this personally, please. He can rub people up badly when they don't like the truth they hear."

"It's a problem that there are sometimes two versions of the same truth," Zoroaster interrupted us. "Perspective and experience can split the same concept radically either way. I don't mean any offence, Michael. Please listen to Mary. I'm not trying to make you angry. You have to understand, I'm more than a thousand years older than you. With age comes perspective, if not wisdom. What's more important right now is that we find my home so we can really sit down and discuss thoughtfully and rationally what it is you are really seeking from me."

He was spinning around, looking at the buildings around us. There was no color at all in this area of the city. Each building was the same size, dull and grey.

"Do you know where we are?" he asked Mary.

"We're on the corner of 8th Avenue and 10th Street," she said, pointing to a road sign near us.

"Ha!" Zoroaster said. "I'm glad we haven't done away with all conveniences! Although maybe those signs are a necessity, I'm not sure. I'll have to meditate on the truth of that later. We're not too far. Only three more blocks."

He took off once more at a brisk walk.

Rather than be drawn into conversation again and risk losing Zoroaster's respect, I decided to look at the people, as we walked, to calm myself. The streets were a melting pot of every different race, age and sex. There was no discrimination by Asmodeus in sending people to Purgatory – by physical appearance at least. It buoyed me to see the pedestrians passing and smiling. I felt a connection of brotherhood with them all. *No matter who we are, we are joined by our humanity. We have been cast down here together*, I thought. Our desires aren't split between nationality or language or generation after all. A smile is a smile anywhere. A sin is a sin to Asmodeus, no matter who you are.

A man with dirty-blue eyes and a hooked nose walked past. He did a double take as he brushed by.

"Michael?" I heard him say. "Saint Michael, is that you?"

45

IT TOOK ME A FEW MOMENTS to register who the man was. He was wearing a grey, holey beanie on his head, pulled down to meet his high arching eyebrows. A scraggly teddy bear was tucked tightly under his arm.

"Dante!" I said, recalling the bum I'd once met on the winter streets of Las Vegas.

"Michael! It is you! You remember Virgil as well, don't you?" He held up the bear and wiggled it a little.

"How could I forget?" I smiled. Abruptly, my smile clouded to a frown. Was this another one of Asmodeus' tricks? I looked to Zoroaster, who was just ahead. He had turned to see what was happening.

"Zoroaster," I called. "Is this man supposed to be in Purgatory? Do you know him?"

The prophet waddled back towards us and studied Dante who was grinning, looking from Virgil to me and pointing.

"Ah yes, I know him," Zoroaster confirmed. "He's been here a few months. We are dragging him slowly out of the chaos of insanity in his mind. His biggest hurdle is to admit that the bear isn't actually a living being, otherwise he's perfectly sane and fit."

Dante looked up to Zoroaster angrily.

"You're not a living being! Why would you speak of Mr. Virgil that way?"

"Would you give us a few moments?" I asked Zoroaster quietly. He nodded and rejoined Mary, who was standing patiently a few paces away. They began a conversation of their own and I turned back to my friend.

"What are you doing here, Dante?" I asked, looking him up and down. He was identical to how I remembered from when we first met on the cold night streets of Las Vegas. "I thought you'd be in Heaven!"

"Oh, I'm trying, Saint Michael," he said. "I died not too long ago. I'm told that it will take only a small time until I get used to my new body here, and that my mind will adjust to proper working order again. I'm very much looking forward to it. I'm excited to go to Heaven and see my wife. I miss her so much. My daughter will be there one day too, I'm sure. We can be a family again. That's all I've ever wanted in this life. To be with them again."

I reached up and held him on the shoulder. There was so much sadness in his eyes.

"I'm glad to see you're okay." I said. "Everything will work out. I'm trying to make sure of that. It's why I'm here, actually. I'm trying to find a way we can all go to Heaven."

"That would be fantastic!" he exclaimed excitedly. "Everyone's so nice in Purgatory, but it's incredibly boring! If only we could all go to Paradise together, the afterlife would be so much better. I'm relieved I'm not in Hell, though. Earth was bad enough."

Dante hugged Virgil close to his chest and stared into space for a few moments. I thought he would ask how I was going to get him to Heaven, but he did not.

"I wanted to say I was sorry," he said finally.

"What for?" I scoffed. "You did nothing wrong to me. If anything, I should be thanking you. You helped me."

"Helped you?" He screwed up his hooked nose. "If I remember, you were the one who pulled me off the freezing streets for a night and fed Virgil and me a hot meal. Then we stole your beer and left your skipping rope in the fridge. I was going to say I was sorry for acting so strangely. It wasn't a way to return the kindness you showed us."

"Nonsense," I said. "Your act spurred me to start living life properly again. I started training again because of the note you left me. I became great. It led me to meet the love of my life."

"But you're still not in Heaven. I obviously didn't help you enough," he said sadly. "What happened to that love of yours?" My heart sank.

"She was murdered," I admitted reluctantly, not willing to go over the whole truth with him.

"Well, maybe that was my fault for leading you in that direction. Fate works in funny ways."

I shook my head. "You're not at fault. I am."

"Admitting your mistakes is the first step in amending them. That's what they say at the Veritas School I'm going to. They're lovely people. Just lovely."

I smiled.

"I'm glad." I looked back up to Mary and Zoroaster who stood waiting. "I'm sorry Dante, but I have to go. I'm happy to see you. Is there anything I can do to repay the favor you did me once?"

"Yes. You can get us all to Heaven like you said. You, me and Virgil. He's been my only trustworthy companion through all of my hardships. He never left me, and I will not leave him behind, ever. We just want to see my wife."

"I promise you," I said sincerely, "I'll get you to Heaven."

I turned, heavy in my heart, and walked back up to Mary and Zoroaster. Dante was here. So was Charlotte. I ached to find her, but time was of the essence. We needed to convince Zoroaster to help us before Asmodeus was alerted to what was happened. Then, I'd find my love.

"Everything alright?" Mary asked.

"Yes," I said. "Dante was a ghost from the past. He tends to make me see things the way I should. Shall we go?"

"We're here," said Zoroaster, pointing up to an open doorway just in front of us. "Let's hear what you have to say."

46

WE SAT DOWN IN A SPARSE WOODEN ROOM. It was circular, constructed out of what looked like a grey version of pine. There were white cushions spread over the floor, and a plain futon mattress tucked into one corner. Zoroaster sat down on one of the cushions and crossed his legs. He sat unmoving and listened while Mary and I told him exactly how we came to be in Purgatory asking for help. We left out nothing, from the explanation of how Satan and God had united into the same being, to my desire to have revenge on him. Our hope was that Zoroaster would fully understand our case if we were as honest as possible. He bowed his head in silence during our tale and displayed little to no reaction. We ended our story by recounting the battle at the Fount of Mercy and how Asmodeus had stolen the keys to Heaven from Mary.

"Our plan from here is to tear down the walls of Purgatory and Hell," I summarised in conclusion. "We ultimately seek an even state in the afterlife, with no borders or filters. We want equality and freedom for all. Once we have brought down the first wall, we will gather the souls from both realms and rally them to attack Heaven head on. It will not be an unplanned assault. It may take decades to execute, but this first action is a step in the right direction. We're heading towards a freedom and truth in the universe we all deserve. If people wish, they can remain living in Hell, but they will have the choice to travel to Purgatory or Heaven without having to suppress their desires or leaving their sins at the door. They will be true to themselves wherever they are and we will accept each other for what we are, imperfect but striving to be good. We don't want to change the landscapes of the universe, just to bring down the barriers which separate us."

Zoroaster looked up once I had finished. He sat staring at the both of us for a long time.

"I think there are some admirable qualities in what you are looking to achieve," he finally said. "I once fought Satan for similar reasons. I wanted him to take away the controls he had put in place. I strove to reveal his lies. He resisted strongly. I'm sure that as Asmodeus he will do the same. The difference now is that he has more power at his disposal. He has God's might within him. It's a dangerous combination. I'm afraid of the consequences for those who resist him. If he cannot cast those souls away from him into a prison, you leave him with little alternative but delivering a true death. Are you ready for that?"

"I am ready to die," I said with conviction.

"That wasn't my question. I asked if you are ready for others to die. Are you ready for Mary to die? Judas to die? Smithy to die? Your wife to be ripped apart before your eyes? Truly?"

"That's not a decision for him to make," Mary cut in. "I am ready. We will only lead those to battle who are willing!"

"Will you?" he asked. "Most of the wars I have seen have been waged with a mentality that you are either with us or you are against us. That is false logic. You can be neutral. How will you treat those who are neutral?"

"How will Asmodeus treat them?" I replied hotly. "He won't let souls in Heaven sit idly by. He will make them take up arms."

"He won't have to force them, Michael," Zoroaster said, adjusting his legs on his cushion. "Every soul in Heaven is obedient to His will over everything else. They believe in him, in his goodness. By attacking the gates of their realm you are forcing them to fight you. They will not remain passive. Every last soul in Paradise will fight to defend what they have. That brings a ferocity you cannot anticipate. However, yet again you have diverted from answering the real question. Will the people in your new joined realm of Hell and Purgatory have a choice when it comes to battle?"

"I will give them the freedom to choose," I answered truthfully. "I will do all I can to persuade them, but in the end, the choice is theirs to fight or not."

"You give them a bitter choice," he said softly. "If you pull down the barrier which separates Purgatory from Hell, then the Fires of Guilt will rise up into this realm. The dominant characteristics of Damnation will envelope this place. The landscape may remain mostly intact, but in essence all that constricts those in Hell will constrict the souls here as well. You would invite them to feel the same torment as you, and then ask them if they would like to stay, or go to a better place? That is not a truthful choice at all."

"Then what would you have me do?" I snapped at him, frustration bursting from me. I got to my feet. Zoroaster remained calm and seated.

"Sit down, Michael, please," Mary pleaded.

"What do you want from me?" I asked Zoroaster, still standing.

"I told you from the beginning. I want the truth. I think you are basically heading in the right direction, but may be heading there for the wrong reasons. I have looked inside both you and Mary and seen secrets inside. You must both reveal exactly what it is you're hiding before we can come to the correct action."

I was shaking with rage. I looked down at Mary, but she avoided my eyes. Zoroaster stared up at me from his crossed legged position.

"Tell me, Michael," he said slowly. "Why are you really here?"

"I've told you why I'm here," I seethed through gritted teeth, doing my best to remain calm.

"Please. I can see you hold a lot of anger inside you. Sit."

I forced myself to sit down. The action helped to settle me a touch.

"Please," Zoroaster said again. "I am no enemy of yours. I am simply trying to locate the honest truth. Now look inside yourself and ask, what are my motivations? Why do I truly want to bring down this wall of Purgatory? As great as all of the effects are - stepping towards freedom, equality, justice, truth – what is the thing you look forward to most once the walls come down?"

Guilt smothered my anger. If I asked myself that question, truly, I was ashamed at how selfish the response was. I wasn't the leader I wanted to be. I wasn't a fighter for freedom.

"I will get to see my wife, Charlotte," I said, hanging my head.

Zoroaster tipped his head in acceptance. My stomach churned with emotion.

"That is not an evil motivation," he said. "It is all I wanted to hear: the truth. You are human after all, and it makes me want to help you more, not less. That is the real issue I have with Asmodeus. He can sit behind his ideals and justify the greatness of his actions, which are indeed great. However, in the end he does not admit his imperfections. He lies to himself and so he lies to others. It is a hypocrisy, which I cannot reconcile. I promise to help you, Michael."

I looked up to him in disbelief.

"But," he continued, "only after you go to see your wife here in Purgatory. Knowing that once your first motivation has been fulfilled, you must come back to me and honestly say you're still willing to risk your happiness and the happiness of others to pursue an ideal you say you hold. Her name is Charlotte? I know of one particularly fine young woman who has said her husband's name was Michael. She has been helping at my school. She should be at Veritas Splendor right now, teaching the children's class."

The cloud of shame that swirled in me lifted into hope. "Charlotte St. Claire?" I asked.

He nodded.

My spirits soared. I couldn't believe it. In admitting my hidden motivation to Zoroaster I hadn't been condemned. I had been rewarded. I was to see Charlotte! I jumped to my feet, ready to rush from the room to see my wife.

"Wait!" Zoroaster commanded. "First we must hear Mary's confessions."

I looked to Mary, torn. I wanted to run out of the door then and there. The look on her face made me freeze in my tracks. She seemed terrified and wouldn't look either of us in the eye.

"The chaos inside her is darker than even yours," Zoroaster said grimly. "It's better she tell two people what she is hiding, rather than just one. The greater the lie inside, the more people who should bear the truth of it."

A brick of doubt formed in my chest. Had she betrayed us somehow? Was she helping Asmodeus? Had she delivered us into his evil hands?

"Mary?" I said. "What have you done?" She looked up at me and burst into tears. "I'm so sorry, Michael. I'm so, so sorry."

Knots of tension gripped my body. I looked to Zoroaster, who sat there, calm as ever. I braced myself to hear the most horrible acts of evil. Mary looked to Zoroaster in despair.

"Please, Mary," he said. "Let out your secret." "What have you done Mary?" I shouted.

She looked up as me with glassy eyes.

"I'm sorry, Michael. I've fallen in love with you."

47

I WAS ROCKED. The brick of doubt that had hung in my chest grew into a boulder of tension. My stomach felt hollow. My fingers twitched.

"What?" I managed to say softly.

"I love you, Michael. I'm sorry. I shouldn't have told you. That was the real reason I fell at the Chinvar Bridge. My mind wasn't just on Judas, it was on you."

I slowly sat back down, staring into space, trying to make my mind work. This was completely unexpected. Mary was my friend. She was a fellow fighter. This couldn't be happening. Mary cried softly next to me, but said nothing more. Zoroaster adjusted his legs.

I reached out and took Mary by the hand. She hung her head, looking down into her lap.

"Mary," I said, still not able to look at her directly. "You're like a sister to me. I'm in love with Charlotte, and only Charlotte. I love you too, but not in a way that could ever see us together."

"I know. I know," she said softly, cutting back her tears. She raised her head and met my eyes. "I don't expect you to change anything for me. I know your soul is for another. That is why I didn't want to tell you. I didn't want this. It just happened."

"How?" was all I could ask, looking at her.

"I don't know." She let my hand drop out of hers and stared away again. "Maybe it was you saving Judas. Maybe it's the conviction I see you have for Charlotte. I want someone to feel the same for me and I know you have that inside you. You're kind. You work towards what you believe. I know that none of this is reasonable, but love isn't reasonable sometimes. I'm sorry, I shouldn't have said anything."

"Yes you should," Zoroaster interrupted quietly. "Good people hold onto lies because they think if they tell the truth it will cause chaos. Like

210

now, the truth can create disorder for a short while, but the outward chaos only matches the struggle you held within yourself. As realities are revealed a balance is met and things settle. You have released that uncertainly from within you, Mary. Things will find a balance, I promise. You have met the truth, and all that can come from this is eventual harmony."

I heard Zoroaster's words, but I couldn't agree with them. I wished Mary had kept this truth to herself. I wasn't angry at her; I couldn't be. I was upset that Zoroaster had forced her to say something when she knew better. I couldn't see how good could come of this. I wanted to get up and leave to go to Charlotte. I wanted to run away, but I knew I couldn't. Mary deserved more than for me to up and desert her when she had just poured her heart out. She was still a friend, after all.

I looked into Mary's tearful eyes and took her hand again.

"I don't know what to say, Mary. What do you want me to do?"

"Nothing," she said. "It's enough that you know the truth. I want you to be happy and I know you're happy with Charlotte. Go to her, please. You deserve her love. Just don't forget us when you see her. Don't forget our cause, our fight. There is more to this than just love. This is about freedom for every soul that suffers in the world. We have to continue, regardless of our personal struggles. I believe that, and I hope you do too."

Her emerald eyes blazed with passion as she said the last words. I nodded. I squeezed her hand one last time and got up. I would not fail her. I would continue the fight. But first, it was time to see Charlotte.

48

I EMERGED FROM ZOROASTER'S HOUSE onto the street. Before I rushed headlong down to Veritas Splendor, I was careful to take note on exactly where I was: three houses downhill from a daffodil colored shack on 8th Avenue.

Moving down the street, I half walked, half jogged. I didn't want to fall over myself to get there. I was excited, but nervous at the same time. Mary's revelation had also tempered my enthusiasm. She was back there, sitting in tears and confusion with Zoroaster. I hoped he might be able to talk some sense into her. It seemed to me that all he spoke were theoretical philosophies, not things that would work in the real world. A knot still clutched at my chest. Whether it was apprehension at seeing Charlotte or worry for Mary, I wasn't sure.

I pulled my hair back and tucked it into my shirt, but then remembered my ears. I pulled it back out again and let the black curls spill around my shoulders. Dare I smile when I see her and reveal my wolf teeth? I needed her to love me. If she rejected me for some reason, I wasn't sure what I would do.

There were still a lot of people walking along the pavement, but I didn't register their presence. I pressed ahead, through the blur of bystanders. I almost knocked someone down and realized I was running. I forced myself to slow down. I didn't want to explode into the classroom, puffing and panting. The school appeared in sight down the street. I could see souls standing and talking out front. Searching their faces, I saw none of them were Lotte. Without pausing I pushed past, up the path toward the building. My heart was hammering so hard in my chest I thought it might bruise my ribs. My hands were trembling uncontrollably. I came to the entrance of the school where the wide windows lined the front.

Peering through the window, I saw her. An angel. It really was my perfect Charlotte. I stood there transfixed, watching her through the glass. She was laughing and smiling, talking to a group of children who sat on the ground crossed legged in front of her. She wore a white cotton dress with black buttons that went from the neck of her dress down to the hem at her knees. Her stunning blue eyes shone like sapphires. Lotte tucked her blonde hair over her ears then started clapping her hands, singing a song. I knew the tune. It was called Baby Bumble Bee. She used to sing it to the kids at the hospital she worked at. I mouthed the words as she sung.

I caught a baby bumble bee, won't my mommy be so proud of me.

Once the song was finished, the children all laughed. I wanted to walk inside but was glued to the spot. I couldn't make my feet work. With tears clouding my vision, I brought a shaking hand up and tapped lightly on the window. I was crying so hard I couldn't see. I wiped the tears from my face to see if she'd noticed. Everyone in the room was looking up to me. I didn't see any of the children's faces; all I saw was Charlotte. Her mouth was open in shock.

"Michael?"

The words didn't reach me, but I could see them on her lips. She looked down at the children and then back up at me. I waved at her foolishly. I didn't know what else to do.

Lotte held her hands out to the children, motioning for them to stay seated then, almost tripping, she ran around them towards the doors. I moved quickly to greet her. We collided into a fierce embrace. Her momentum pushed me backward to the ground. She was crying. Lotte buried her face in my chest as I held her tight against me. There were no words to express the flood of emotion pouring out of me; I simply wrapped her in my arms tightly and squeezed.

"I knew you'd come, I knew you'd find me," she cried into me over and over again. "I knew you'd come."

I held her in silence, my heart smiling. I rested my chin on top of her head while I hugged her. It was as though the sun had risen over my world again. I could have stayed like that forever, basking in her warmth. She loosened her hug and I pulled back to look in her crystal eyes. They were filled with love and relief. She buried her head back into my chest with renewed sobs.

"I was so worried, Michael. Oh, Michael!"

Holding her tight, I cried with her. Right now, nothing needed to be said. It was just enough that we were together again.

"Miss Charlotte?" a child's voice said next to me. "Are you okay?"

I looked up to see that the whole class had come out of the door and was standing in a circle around us. One taller boy had stepped forward.

"Is this man hurting you, Miss Charlotte?" he said bravely. Lotte pushed away from me softly at the noise. Brushing the tears from her face frantically, she looked to the children. She was straddled on top of me, her knees either side of my stomach. She looked from the children to me and then back to the children again.

"No, David," she said, smiling at him with tear-glazed eyes. "This is my husband, Michael. We thought we had lost each other, and I'm happy to see him again."

"But you're crying." he said, in an Irish accent.

"My mum said it's okay to cry if you're sad or if you're happy," a girl said to him.

The boy looked down to me with some doubt, but stepped back.

"It's okay, David, really." Charlotte said.

She looked back down at me and beamed. She leaned in and kissed me lightly on the lips. I tried to pull her back in to a hug but she resisted gracefully. Pushing my chest down playfully, she climbed off me back to her feet. I got up quickly, not wanting to move even an inch from her side. I took her hand in mine and squeezed it lightly.

"Now, children," she said. "Please go back inside and play sleeping lions. I'm going to talk with my husband, but I will be watching from out here. Remember you have to keep as still as you can and keep your eyes closed. No cheating!"

With grins on their faces, the children obeyed Charlotte and skipped back inside. Some were whispering to each other, sneaking looks back at us as they started to lie on the floor and pretend to be asleep. Charlotte watched as they went inside, but reached out and took my other hand without looking. We stood hands clasped. She watched the children, but I only had eyes for her. I studied her skin, her hair, her eyelashes. This was no illusion. It was my love.

Once she was satisfied the children were settled, Lotte turned her head back to mine. She leaned in and kissed me deeply. The Perceptionist had taught me that thought and emotion were elemental twins. I understood now that my wife and I were also twins. We were two souls that found context in each other. Without the other at our side we were just fragments of a greater whole. She pulled out of the kiss.

"I don't even know where to start," she said with wide eyes, looking me up and down. "What happened? Your hair? What..."

"It's a long and complicated story," I said, rubbing my head. "I was so scared. I didn't know if you were alive or dead, in Heaven, or Hell, or..."

"That can wait," I said, stopping her short. "What about you? Are you okay? Are you safe? What happened when you died? What happened when you came here?"

Her eyes flickered in pain. She held my hands again and looked me deep in the eyes.

"It was horrible, Michael." Tears welled in her eyes again. "You were there; you saw what they did to me. Those monsters. I couldn't stop them. That is the last memory of my life, that brutality." She swallowed a lump in her throat and continued. "I woke up here in Purgatory, that final memory of my life still lingering in my brain. It wasn't what had happened to me that hurt me most though, Michael. It was not knowing what had happened to you; not knowing why. I was alone in the grey fields away from the city. I could see it far in the distance. I walked and Zoroaster was there to greet me, at the edge of the city in the wood where people come out of The Far Reaches. He helped calm me. He explained to me that I was indeed dead and that there was an afterlife. I was in Purgatory. I had so many questions, Michael, but he couldn't answer them. He told me as much truth as he could, but all I wanted to know was about what happened to you. Zoroaster explained that just as Earth has no real knowledge of the afterlife, Purgatory is blocked off from the other realms."

"You cannot see Earth like we can in Hell?" I asked, shocked. I had never taken up the option because I had no interest in a world without Charlotte, but souls in Hell were able to watch the drama of the living unfold if they so desired.

"No." Lotte shook her head. "Zoroaster told me that this is not like Heaven or Hell, where the dead can look on the living. We are locked in the unknown. It was made like this on purpose so that we are motivated to make it to Heaven to find out the fate of our families. That is the real torture of this place; not the grey boredom, but ignorance of where our loved ones are."

I hugged her tightly. I knew the same torture. Not knowing if Charlotte was safe was the hardest part of being in Hell; the rest was a mere shadow of that pain.

"I know that must have been hard," I said to her.

"It was so hard, Michael," she continued. "I didn't know what to do. Zoroaster was a great councillor, though. He drew me out of my shell of suffering. He was candid about my options. I could stay here and wait, or I could go to Heaven. He warned that if I tried to go Hell by committing sin I might never make it out again. My best chance was to stay here and hope you passed through one day. When that day would come I could not know, but it was my only real choice. So, that is what I've done, my love. I have stayed here and waited for you. I didn't want to go to Heaven. I know that you question everything before you accept it, so would never go straight to Paradise. While I settled here in Purgatory, Zoroaster advised me to stay busy while I was here. He said it might be centuries before you arrived, if ever. I knew you would make it here, though. I had faith in you, Michael. I had faith and I was right. You have found me - and even sooner than I had hoped!

I leaned in and kissed her again. She was safe; Lotte was with me. I had faith in her as well. I knew she would wait for me.

"Now please, Michael," she said, pulling away from our embrace. "You need to tell me. What happened to you? What happened to us that day? Do you know?"

My face fell. I wasn't ready for this. All I had thought about since finding myself in Hell was getting back to Lotte, yet I hadn't thought about what I would do when I did. All I had wanted was to be close to her again. What was I supposed to say to her? The initial relief that had flooded out of me at seeing her was slowly being replaced with dread. I was the ruler of Hell. I was becoming a demon. She had accepted my imperfections before, but maybe this would be too much. Her death at the hands of Gideon, the truth about Asmodeus and his relationship with me: it would all sound so ridiculous. How could I tell her that she had been murdered because of me? That I was the son of Satan? That all she had been put through was my fault? I held her by both arms and leaned in to kiss her on the cheek.

"I am okay," I whispered in her ear. "It will take a long time to explain properly. Can we go somewhere and talk?"

She pulled back again and looked inside at her students. "They won't stay quiet for too much longer. There's nearly another hour left in the class. I'm sorry, I can't leave them." She locked my eyes with a pleading gaze.

"Then I'll wait," I said. "I waited my whole life for you, Lotte. I would wait for my afterlife as well if you asked."

"You're a sweet, sweet man," she said, tears welling in her eyes. "Can you wait inside? I don't want to lose sight of you ever again. I need to know everything."

49

FROM THE BACK OF THE ROOM, I watched Charlotte as she taught. She had an amazing affinity with children that I would never understand. It was as if they could see the kindness within her and were drawn to it. They sat and listened to her, behaving like angels. Some had visible scars on their bodies, some were shy, some were loud. They were of every different color and race I could think of, about fifty or sixty in total. They sat on the grey carpet of the room watching their teacher, like cross-legged sunflowers.

Lotte stood at the front, not just delivering the lesson, but asking them questions and interacting. She drew them out of their shyness when they were unsure. She encouraged them, even when they grew bold and asked serious questions.

The Irish boy, David, who had stood forward to protect her outside, put his hand up in the air.

"Yes, David?" Charlotte asked.

"Why are we here and not in Heaven?"

Her eyes flicked to mine and I could see a look of melancholy in her eyes. She didn't lose her smile, however.

"That's a very good question, David," she replied. "Like all good questions, there is more than one answer. Since you've asked such a great question, could you come up to sit with me at the front of the class?"

He stood up like a rocket, puffing out his chest with pride, and made his way to the front. He had orange tinged hair and a freckled face. I tried to guess his age. He was taller than most of the younger children and very skinny. He could have been anywhere between six and ten. Charlotte pulled forward two wooden chairs and arranged them facing each other. Once he had made it to the chairs, she asked him to sit opposite her.

"Now," she said, clasping her hands over her lap. "I want you to help me demonstrate truthfulness to the rest of the class. Can you do that, David?"

"Aye." He nodded.

"I'm going to be truthful with you as much as I can, and I want you to do the same. Are you ready?"

"Yes, Miss."

"Okay. The hard part about telling you why you are here in Purgatory and not in Heaven is because it's different for everyone. Only you really know the answers, not me. I can help ask the right questions, but unless you are honest, then the real answer won't come out. Do you understand?"

"I think so," he said, looking a little uncertain. "Do you mean that I have to tell you things about me, even if I don't want to?"

"Yes. And if you tell me truthfully I might be able to help you understand why you're not in Heaven yet. Then if you understand, maybe we can figure out how you can go to Heaven as well."

"Okay." He smiled.

Charlotte looked around the room at the children.

"This is an important lesson, children, so please make sure you pay attention. When I ask David a question about something, ask the same question to yourself in your head. Think about your answer and see if it makes you feel good inside or bad inside. If it feels bad, then please come and see me after class and tell me. Now," she said turning back to the boy, "David, how long have you been here?"

"Two weeks," he replied.

"And can you remember dying?"

"No," he said. "The last thing I remember about being alive is that I was on my bike and a car was coming at me real fast."

Charlotte took in a deep breath. "David, I think maybe that car hit you and that might be what killed you. Do you understand that?"

"Aye," he said, looking up thoughtfully. "My ma always told me to stay off the road, but I liked riding on the road because I could go faster."

"And are you okay? Does thinking about the car make you feel bad?" Charlotte asked slowly.

"No," he said earnestly. "One minute I was on my bike, and the next minute I was sitting with Mr. Zoroaster. It didn't hurt. I just miss my ma and da." His face grew a little sad.

"You're doing very well, David." Charlotte told him. "I'm happy you're being so honest."

The boy's face brightened into a smile once again. "Have you ever stolen anything, David?" she asked.

"No." He shook his head.

"Please take some time and think about it," Lotte probed. "Have you ever taken anything that isn't yours? It's okay if you have. You're safe here. We're your friends."

He sat with his eyes shut for a while, screwing them up tightly in concentration.

"I haven't stolen anything," he said finally.

"Have your parents ever told you off for being naughty?"

"Yes," he said, nodding his head slowly. "I called my sister a bad word last month. My dad was really angry."

"Did he hit you?" she asked.

"No." David shook his head furiously. "He yelled a lot, though. He told me if he ever heard me call my sister that again, he'd send me away to boarding school."

"How did that make you feel?" He thought for a moment.

"Scared. I didn't want to go away from my family." He started to cry a little.

"It's alright David, it's alright. We don't have to keep going if you don't want to."

"No," he said, rubbing his eyes. "I want to keep going. I need to go to Heaven. My mum always told me that's where we'd go if we died. If she's trying to come and find me, that's where she'll look. I have to be there in case she's looking for me."

Charlotte swallowed loudly. It was clear she was trying her best to hold back from crying herself. She bowed her head for a few moments before continuing.

"Okay, David. Is there any other time you can remember your parents being more angry with you?"

"Never," he said instantly. "They were both so mad at me."

"What about another time. What about..." She paused and looked at him for a moment. "David, what did you call your sister?"

The boy went red in the face and shook his head. He crossed him arms over his chest in defiance.

"I don't want to say it, Miss Charlotte. It's a very bad word." She narrowed her eyes.

"It's alright, David. I'm an adult. We're all very truthful here. It might be a bad word, but it's only a word. It might be important."

David kept his eyes downward for a few moments, before he said softly, "Protestant."

"Excuse me?" Charlotte said.

"I called her a filthy Protestant and I said she was going to Hell." He burst into tears. "That's why I'm here, isn't it? I shouldn't have said it.

She's not a Protestant, she's a good Catholic girl." He was shaking in his seat, covering his face and crying into his hands. "I'm sorry, Jesus."

Charlotte leant over and rubbed him on the back. I was baffled, sitting at the back. Surely this wasn't why he was here. Charlotte was whispering into his ear as she patted his shoulder. I leaned forward, trying to grasp what she was saying. I reached out and I felt a strong sense of compassion coming from Charlotte. The remorse of the boy was buried beneath it. David composed himself, but remained in the chair. The rest of the children sat still with sad looks on their faces. A few of them had tears in their eyes at seeing their classmate upset.

"David," Charlotte said to him softly. "I promise that is not why you are here in Purgatory. But I think we're getting close to understanding why you are."

David straightened in his seat and stopped crying. I straightened up as well and so did the rest of the students. It seemed we were all as curious as each other to hear what Lotte was about to say.

Charlotte took a tissue from her pocket and wiped David's eyes. She mopped up a bubbly trail of snot that had seeped from his nose. Once he was calmer, she continued.

"David. Is your family a good Catholic family? Did you go to church and say your prayers?"

He nodded.

"And does Jesus say that you should love your neighbor?"

"Aye, miss."

"Were any of your neighbors Protestants?"

"No." He shook his head vigorously. "They live on the other side of the city. We stayed away from them; they're evil people."

Charlotte paused. She sighed heavily.

"Why do you think they're evil, David?"

"Because they follow Satan. They don't follow the Pope. They don't follow Jesus. They shoot Catholics and want to take our land."

"Who told you that?"

"Everyone."

"Who is everyone?" Lotte asked patiently.

"My ma and da, the priests, everyone."

Charlotte closed her eyes and paused. I couldn't believe my ears. Living in America, I had known of the centuries old enmity between the Catholics in the South of Ireland and the Protestants in the north, but had never really understood the depth of it. Children must have been indoctrinated into each side at such an early age that it became a part of them. They lived and believed the hatred of their parents and their grandparents.

"David," Lotte said, breaking my thoughts. "This is going to be very hard for me to explain, but I'm going to try. I think I know why you are in Purgatory and not in Heaven."

The boy's eyes went wide with wonder. A few of the children in the room gasped with excitement. Charlotte looked to everyone in the class but remained seated. She was wringing her hands nervously.

"What is it, Miss?" David prodded. "Please, I need to know."

"I'm trying to find the right words," Charlotte said, not looking at David.

"Please, miss."

"David. How old are you?" "I'm nine, miss."

"Okay," she said. "Have you ever known your parents to lie to you? To not tell you the truth?"

"No!" he said, angrily.

"Please, David," she said softly. "I'm sure your parents are very good people, I am trying to make you understand something."

David settled down somewhat in his chair.

"Do you believe in Santa Claus?" Charlotte asked carefully.

"No," he said, looking out to some of the younger children in the class. "Santa is for babies."

"What about the Easter Bunny?"

"It's the same thing."

"But when you were younger, you believed they were real?"

"Yes." He nodded. "My little sister still does. I have to keep it a secret so I don't spoil the fun for her."

"Who spoiled the fun for you David? Who told you the truth?"

"A friend at school told me," he said. "He told me to stay awake and watch my parents on Christmas Eve. He said that they were really the ones who put the presents in my stocking. I didn't believe him, so I asked my Da. He told me that I was old enough to know the truth, but asked me to keep the secret."

"But before you asked your dad about the truth, he was the one who had told you that Santa was real, wasn't he?"

The boy nodded. "Yes, but it was just make believe."

"And your mother, and the priests? When you were little they all told you the same fib, that Santa Claus and the Easter Bunny were real, didn't they?"

David looked at Charlotte shocked. Realization spread across his face.

"You cannot blame your parents, though," Charlotte added quickly, "Their parents told them the same little fib when they were young too. It's just a big trick to keep children happy on Christmas Day."

"But why would they do that?" David said. "We would be happy with just presents; we don't need a fairytale to keep us happy."

"Some people like fairy tales," Charlotte said. "Some fairy tales are lots of fun."

David smiled. "I did like Santa when I was little," he agreed. "But I also liked knowing a secret the other children didn't."

Charlotte nodded her head gravely. She looked to me at the back of the room again. I nodded knowingly and she pressed on.

"David, there are other secrets that adults like to keep from children as well. Sometimes they even believe the secrets themselves because no one has told them the truth. Sometimes only a few people know the real truth."

"What are they?" he asked, moving to the edge of his seat. In his interest, he'd completely forgotten about the rest of the class who all leaned forward expectantly as well.

"I don't even know all of them," Lotte said. "But I know some of them."

"Tell me," he demanded.

"David," she said in mock conspiracy, lowering her voice to a whisper. "Protestants aren't all bad people."

"What?" He sat back. "Yes they are, they put bombs in our pubs. They killed my uncle."

Charlotte nodded. "Yes, some Protestants have done bad things in the past and some are evil people. I agree with you. Some of them have hurt others in the name of God. What you need to understand is that not all Protestants are bad, just like some Catholics are bad people too. At the same time there are a lot of very good Catholics, but there are a lot of good Protestants as well."

"No there aren't," David said shaking his head. "My dad said all Protestants are scumbags. My dad said."

"Your dad said Santa Claus was real too," Charlotte pressed softly.

David hung his head.

"Did you know any Protestants, David?" Charlotte asked. He shook his head as he looked to his feet. Lotte reached out and took his hand gently.

"Then how do you know for sure that they're all bad people if you've never met one?"

He looked up sullenly and shrugged his shoulders.

"David, when you hate a group of people for no reason, without really knowing them, that is called prejudice. It could also be called racist. Have you heard that word before?"

David shook his head again. Charlotte looked back to the class.

"Does anyone else know what prejudice or racist means?"

A black girl at the front of the class put her hand in the air. "Yes, Ella?" Charlotte asked the girl.

"It's when white people call me nigger."

Charlotte nodded her head. "Yes, Ella. That is one horrible example, but it could be many things."

She looked at David, whose hand she was still holding, and then looked back to the children.

"It is very hard to understand, but sometimes adults can hate people even if they don't know them. Some white people hate all black people because they are afraid of them. Some people might even hate others because they have more money or land than they do. Others hate because they think they believe in a different God. When you hate someone without knowing them, it is called prejudice. It is one of the worst kinds of hate. This kind of hate creates a lot of violence on Earth. It helps very smart and very evil men trick others into killing each other. Not many people know this is a trick, so they believe what they are doing is right. Children, do you think it's bad to kill someone?"

"Yes!" they all said loudly, some nodding their heads.

"That's right," Charlotte said, turning back to David who still sat in his seat next to Charlotte.

"David. I think the reason you might be in Purgatory is because you hate Protestants. You don't really know why you hate them, but you still hate them with everything inside of you. If you went to Heaven and saw a Protestant, you might try to fight him, or hurt him."

David nodded his head again.

"Do you think God wants people fighting in Heaven?"

"No," David said. "But I wouldn't see a Protestant in Heaven because they don't believe in God and they all go to Hell."

Charlotte shook her head. "David, that is just another lie. Protestants follow the word of Jesus just like you do. They believe he was the son of God just like you do."

"How do you know?"

"Because I was a Protestant," Charlotte said, holding his hands. "And I never went to Hell."

David's eyes popped. He shook his head from side to side, refusing to accept what she had just said.

"Yes," she pressed. "Do you think I'm a bad person? Do you hate me?"

He shook his head again furiously. "No, Miss Charlotte. You're kind and smile a lot."

Lotte blushed at the compliment.

"I might be different from you, David, but I still love you. I believe in loving everyone," she said. "I don't care what they look like, or if they're Catholic. I love them."

"But why aren't you in Heaven, then?" David asked curiously.

Charlotte's smile dipped momentarily, but she recovered quickly. She looked down at David.

"I still don't know yet," Charlotte said. "But I hope I can go to Heaven one day, just like you will."

She reached out and ruffled his hair playfully. David laughed. She looked to the rest of the class.

"Everybody. This is something you should all try to understand. Please work your hardest to listen to what I'm about to say. God doesn't care if you are Catholic or Protestant. He doesn't care if you're a Muslim or a Jew. He doesn't care if you're Hindu or Buddhist or black or white or Asian or Hispanic. He does care if you love each other or not. He wants to know that you love everyone as much as you love Him. He doesn't want you to fight each other, or to hurt each other by stealing. This isn't what God wants. God wants peace. God wants love. If someone is wrong, you should forgive them, not hate them. Not many adults even understand this very well, but the ones who do will go to Heaven. If you believe this in your heart, then you will go to Heaven too. Please give David a clap for being so honest with us."

Everyone clapped and cheered loudly. I clapped as hard as I could from the back. He stood up off his chair with tears in his eyes and threw himself at Charlotte's legs in a hug. She hugged him back. As she clasped him in her arms, his body began to shudder. Slowly a white aura enveloped him and his body fused with it to become a brilliant light. His form flickered and morphed into a glowing orb. Charlotte stood up and watched in awe as the lightened soul of David floated up into the air. It hovered for a few moments before lifting again more quickly, through the roof and out of sight.

I got to my feet in wonder at seeing the soul of the child David pass over to Heaven. As much as I didn't believe in the goodness of Asmodeus, I knew deep down that he was better off there in the blissful rest of Heaven than suffering here in Purgatory or, worse, in Hell. I looked to Charlotte who was standing there radiating goodness. The other children were laughing and looking to the roof. They started to chatter excitedly, some jumping to their feet and pointing. I wanted to run up and hug Charlotte for what she'd just done. As I started to walk forward, she motioned for me to stop.

"Class! Class!" she said above the excitement. "It's been a good lesson today. We have seen a miracle. Everybody please stand up."

Those who weren't on their feet already got up.

"Seeing David go to Heaven was a great end to the day. When you go home tonight I want you all to really think about what we've talked about. Think about the truth of it. If you really understand, then you can be just like David and go to Heaven. Now, class is finished for today.

A few of the children groaned.

"Now, now! For some of you, your parents are waiting outside. Those who live in the boarding house please go back and report to your dorm leaders."

The children started to chatter again, walking to the front doors.

"Wait," Charlotte called. They all stopped to look at her. "What do we say before the end of the class?"

"The truth will set you free," they all chorused.

"Just as it set David free today!" she said.

The children all filed out slowly, talking and laughing. I waited for them to leave. I was now decided on what I would tell Charlotte. Once the final child had exited the doors, Charlotte came up to me and kissed me again.

"I was a good day today," she said. "For many reasons."

I nodded. It was a great day, but it would also be a hard one in the end.

"Do you really believe the truth will release us from our sins?" I asked her, hugging her again.

"I do." She smiled.

"Then it is time I set you free."

50

CHARLOTTE AND I WALKED out of Veritas Splendor hand in hand. There were groups of families at the entrance standing and talking with their children. The parents all greeted Charlotte with nods and smiles. One woman with darker skin and black curly hair waved as she held her daughter's hand. She quickly made her way over to us.

"Hello, Marie," Charlotte said.

"Charlotte." She smiled. "I just wanted to come and thank you for teaching Natalie here so much! She's even teaching me things about myself these days." Marie looked down at her daughter with pride.

"It's my pleasure," Charlotte said.

I stood back a little, not wanting to interrupt the conversation. I was going over in my head the best way to break our horrible reality to Lotte. Nerves shook my body. I felt physically weak, but was resolute in what I had to do. The truth: it was much harder to expose all than to simply gloss over the uglier parts. But I had to bare it, bones and all.

Charlotte came back to me and took my hand.

"Such a wonderful woman, that Marie," she said. "She's an amazing scientist, very intelligent. I'm so lucky to have met her."

I smiled and nodded weakly.

"Let's go before we get stuck talking to any others." Lotte winked at me. "I need to know what happened, Michael. My unit is only a few minutes away."

We walked up the hill in silence, through the colorful souls of Purgatory, in the same direction as Zoroaster's. After the first block, we turned a right hand corner and then stopped in front of a tall white edifice of an apartment block.

"This is me," said Lotte.

Still holding my hand, she led me up the stairs. There were no locks on

226

the front doors, she merely pushed them open and we went inside to the foyer. Straight ahead was a wide passageway. Everything was painted white. It felt like a hospital. Lotte took me down the passage and then stopped at a door a few feet in. Again, I noticed the door had no lock. She turned the knob and we went in. The room was small, but somehow Charlotte had made it look homely rather than cramped. There was a tidy kitchenette to the far side, a bathroom to the left and a single white bed, tucked in the corner. A two-seater couch sat in the middle of the room with a knee-high coffee table in front of it. All were white. The only splash of color was a light blue blanket which had been laid over the back of the couch in a folded triangle.

I could feel the forced tension of the unknown trembling in Charlotte's hand. We still hadn't said anything of consequence to each other since leaving the school. I released her hand and made my way to the couch.

I sat down and looked up to her.

"My love. Please sit, this is going to be hard for both of us," I said with a steady voice. Inside I was wavering with every breath.

Lotte sat down next to me. I looked her deeply in the eyes and pulled back my hair to reveal my twisted red ears. She gasped, but I laid my spare hand on her knee quietly to silence her. I then bared my wolf teeth at her.

"Oh, Michael!" she whispered, a trembling hand going to up to her mouth. "What's happened to you?"

"This physical deformity is nothing compared with what's inside me, Lotte," I said softly. "This is just easier to show you, but it is the tip of something larger. Will you promise to let me explain this to you fully before you judge me?"

"I would never judge you!"

"You just might, once you hear what I have to say," I said. "But please know I still love you will all my heart, no matter how you feel about me in the end."

"You're scaring me, Michael. Surely it can't be so bad?"

"It is worse than you can imagine, but it's the truth," I said solemnly, searching within myself for the strength to say what I knew I must. My tongue felt swollen and dry in my mouth.

"I'll start with the hardest parts first. I would soften the blow, but in the end the facts are so dark that, no matter how I say this, I will hurt you with the truth," I said, before pausing and drawing in a deep breath. "I am the one true son of Satan and I am the reason you were murdered."

Charlotte looked at me with utter confusion in her eyes. She had to know by the tone of my voice that I was telling the truth. "I had no knowledge of this until I died," I continued. "I was killed at the same time as you by an agent of Satan who called himself Gideon."

Charlotte started to look around the room frantically. Her hands were clutching at her knees. She looked at me again, before getting up and running to the bathroom, where she retched into the toilet bowl. I stood up and went to her quickly. Pulling her hair back, I held it while rubbing her back.

"I know," I said. "That is how I felt when I found out. I am sorry, but there's more."

She vomited into the bowl again, her body constricting. I continued to rub her back until she had finished. I helped her back to her feet. Without speaking she moved over to the basin and turned on the tap. Splashing water on her white face and washing it into her mouth, she finally spat into the bowl. She straightened and looked at me unsteadily.

"Surely this can't be right?" she said with cloudy eyes. "It can't be true."

"I'm sorry," I said. "If you had told me the same thing before we died, I would have thought you were mad. Please Charlotte, I wouldn't lie to you. I know it's far fetched. I know it sounds insane. Just think, if someone had told you about the reality of Purgatory or Heaven, would you have truly believed them without question while you were alive?"

She shook her head. I took her in my arms and hugged her. "My love for you hasn't changed this whole time, Lotte. You are the reason I've been able to press on through this nightmare. You are my reason for being and I would never do anything willingly to hurt you."

"I still don't understand, Michael. You said there's more? What is it? What?" Her voice trailed off.

I ushered her carefully back to the couch and helped her sit down. I propped her up with cushions and knelt in front of her. "I think it might be best to show you exactly what happened," I said to her. "If you are strong enough, I can show you how this came to be."

She looked at me, clarity starting to show in her eyes again. "I would do anything to understand, Michael. I need to. I love you."

I closed my eyes and concentrated on the elements within me. I worked to recall the exact weave of elements that Judas had displayed when he had shown his own memories to me. I pictured the first time I was in Hell, sitting with Asmodeus. I took the memory, the emotion, all the thoughts I had of that time and pushed them outside of me, pulsing down my arm until it throbbed with power.

"Then take my hand," I said to Lotte. "And you will know what I know."

My wife reached out and clasped my palm. In a silent blast we tumbled backward together, to the moment where my life began to unravel.

228

* * *

He preferred to be called Asmodeus. This was all I knew about the man standing before me. In fact, I wasn't even sure if he was a man. When I looked directly at him he appeared normal. But if I glanced out of the corner of my eye I could see something else, something intangible. It was as if his true self was hiding in his shadow, which loomed dark and menacing on the wall, flickering in the firelight.

Charlotte's consciousness sat at my shoulder. I was not alone in the nightmare this time. She would be there to understand that I was forced into this evil nature against my will. I had to relive this for her. I blinked my eyes and was swept into the memory, as if it was happening right now and I had no choice but to ride out this infernal repetition once more.

51

MY EYES FLICKERED OPEN. I was lying on the floor at the foot of Charlotte's couch. She looked down at me, curled up in a ball on the cushions, tears bleeding onto her cheeks.

My body was weak from reliving the experience. It was like waking up to reality at the exact spot where the dream had finished. My hand still clutched feebly onto Lotte's. I stared into her eyes, searching her for hatred, for rejection. There were only tears.

"What now?" I whispered to her softly. "Where do we go from here?"

Charlotte remained silent. Her grip on my hand grew tighter. Slowly, she raised herself to a sitting position. I also raised myself to half kneel between her knees, my hand clasped in hers.

"I understand now, Michael," she said finally.

I dropped my head. Was this the end?

"Thank you for showing me that part of you."

My head snapped up with questioning eyes. Thank you? I didn't understand.

"I know now that you didn't want any of this to happen to us. I know you more than I ever have. What I just saw was brutality, but it was the most intimate truth I've ever experienced, my love. To truly know who someone else is, to truly know where they come from, to live inside them. How could I not cherish that? Even if I hate some of the things I saw, I peered into your soul and have seen mostly light and love. We are together again, Michael. I am ready to come with you and fight this Asmodeus together. No matter what it takes."

I launched myself at her. I hugged her tight, unable say anything. I just held her. She understood. Against all my fears, she knew I meant only good things for her. Even the son of evil could have love. If I could get a second chance like this, then maybe there is goodness in the universe.

There could be balance. I started to kiss her; kiss her neck tenderly. She was perfect. She was redemption.

Lotte kissed me back, her lips pressing more eagerly against my skin with each one. She found my mouth and her tongue urgently wrapped with my own. Her passion pulled deeply on my soul. I kissed her back with all the love I had inside me. Clutching at my back, Lotte fumbled to pull my shirt up. The urgency of the moment lanced into me. I leant back and wrenched my shirt over my head before rushing back in to kiss her again. My lips locked with hers as I fumbled for the top of her dress. I found the first button. I tore the top of her dress open, exposing her perfection beneath me. I could wait no more. I ripped the buttons the rest of the way down and then kissed her hungrily again. Drinking in her hot skin, I licked her. My wet lips and tongue slid over her body, down to her breasts. Lotte's hands were pushing at my pants, her hot palm wriggling inside to find me. I was throbbing for her, my love mixing with lust for her body. Her hand started to move up and down my length as I searched her breasts with my mouth. We rocked together on the couch, moving with each other. A light moan escaped her lips as I bit her nipple gently. I felt I would explode with desire. I moved up again and kissed her hard on the mouth. Her hand squeezed tighter around me, working up and down. I pushed my hands between her thighs. Wet heat met my fingers. I slid them inside the warmth and Charlotte gasped. Her mouth clasped on my neck as I pushed inside her. I clamped my mouth over her breast again and swirled my tongue as I moved my fingers. Her palm heatedly stroked me with the same timing.

"I want you," Lotte's voice breathed in my ear. "I want you now."

I pushed her down onto the couch and moved between her legs. She guided me inside as my hips pressed into her. Lotte quivered beneath me as my length pushed deeply within her. I began to move my hips slowly, leaning in and finding her lips again with mine. My skin was tingling as I pushed deeper, harder, more urgently. Charlotte began to moan loudly; our breathing grew faster. I could feel the ecstasy welling inside me. Her fingers dug into my back, raking down my body. Lotte pushed her hips up to meet mine as I thrust inside her. Her hot moisture tightened around me as she let a deep moan escape her lips. The sounds of her pleasure tipped me over the edge. My body arched as I pulsed my love, my hips shuddering as I thrust one final time. Lotte's body throbbed with mine, her legs wrapping around me, pulling my buttocks tightly to her. We were locked like that, black stars twinkling around the edges of my vision as I poured my soul into hers. I pushed as deeply as I could and sighed in pleasure, looking down at into her eyes. She looked back. Her earlier tears were replaced with happiness. A wicked smile of pleasure played on her lips. I collapsed on top of her, every part of me spent. We were both panting and sweating, twitching with joy. I pulled my hands to the back of her head, cradling it as I kissed her. We let our lips linger and I dropped my weight completely onto her body. We lay there, kissing. We were at one again. Our bodies joined in bliss.

We lay in a silent embrace, our skin pressed against each other's. The warmth of the moment made me feel at peace for the first time since we had parted. I nestled my head in next to hers and stayed there, enjoying her touch.

"What now?' I whispered to her softly once more, but this time it was with hope.

"We bring down the walls of Purgatory and we go back to Hell, together."

52

CHARLOTTE AND I DRESSED QUICKLY. We had lingered long enough together. It was now time to do what I had set out to achieve.

Hand in hand we left her building. Lotte's footsteps were light and happy beside mine. She walked quickly, leading me without faltering toward Zoroaster's. My purpose was now hers as well.

People nodded hellos to us as we passed. Lotte answered them politely, but did not pause to talk. Children waved to us from across the street. The twinkling of their spirits shone outward to meet me.

I should have been happy. I should have been content. But I was not. A heaviness had crept into me that I couldn't explain. I was reunited with my wife and soon we would be one step closer to creating a balance in the universe, but as we passed through the people of Purgatory my soul grew darker and darker. I thought of Mary. Charlotte knew what had happened with her. Was that why I was feeling this way?

Lotte was almost skipping next to me. I looked at her and she grinned back. Her smile helped buoy my sinking spirits. We were one again.

I spotted the daffodil house near Zoroaster's and knew we had arrived. I stopped at the foot of his stairs. Charlotte tugged at my hand as she started to go up. She turned back down to me.

"What are you waiting for, Michael?" she asked, frowning.

"I don't know," I said, shaking my head.

"Come on!"

Lotte pulled my hand again and I followed her into Zoroaster's. He was sitting on his cushions talking with Mary who sat opposite, as if they hadn't moved since I'd left. Their conversation paused as we entered.

"Michael!" Mary said. Her initial smile turned quickly to a frown when she saw who I was with. She stood up and held out her hand. "And you must be Charlotte."

"Yes, Mary," she responded flatly. "Michael has told me all about you."

Charlotte left Mary's hand hanging in the air. Mary held it there for a few moments before letting it drop uncomfortably.

"Oh," Mary said.

"So," Zoroaster interrupted the tension. "You are together again at last. Is all well with you both?" He looked from me to Charlotte and back again.

"Yes," I nodded. "Lotte knows the truth of why we're here."

"And I'm willing to fight," she added next to me.

Zoroaster nodded, smiling. He searched me up and down again with his eyes and clapped his hands together at his chest.

"Fantastic! I can see you hold no secrets from each other. It is a wonderful thing to see."

"Does that mean you're ready?" Mary asked coldly, from beside him. "Are you ready to continue our mission, no matter what it takes?"

"I am," Lotte said defiantly.

"Good." Mary folded her arms across her chest. "Then we should make our way back to the gates of Hell so they can be destroyed. Are you ready, Zoroaster?"

"We will need some preparation first," he said, turning to me. "But are you ready, Michael? Are you intent on this plan?"

The heaviness in my heart crept toward a true realization of what it was I must do. The epiphany crushed my personal desire. I had come this far to recover Charlotte, yet when I looked at her, I understood I could not take her with me to the Fires of Guilt that plagued the souls of Damnation. It wasn't right.

"No," I said, clutching my fists at my sides and looking to my wife. "We cannot do it. It isn't right."

"What are you talking about?" Mary asked, halting her walk toward the exit.

"We're not going to bring down the barriers of Hell," I answered, not taking my eyes off Charlotte. "We're going to break the walls of Heaven instead."

53

LOTTE LOOKED SHOCKED AT WHAT I'D JUST SAID. She clasped
my arm at the elbow tightly.

"What are you saying, Michael?" she gasped. "What do you mean we're
going to break the gates of Heaven? We cannot. We only have the keys to
Hell."

"It doesn't matter," I told her, shaking my head. "We don't want to turn
the lock; we just need to block the flow of the filter. The keys we have will
do the same for either gate. Am I right, Zoroaster?"

"Yes." He nodded. "You are both right and just."

I could hear Mary shuffle uncertainly near the door, but didn't look. I
only had eyes for my wife.

"I don't understand," Lotte said, panic starting to creep into her voice.
"What about the plan? I thought we were going to build an army against
Asmodeus? What are you going to do?"

"He is going to sacrifice the one thing he loves more than anything else
for a greater purpose," Zoroaster said.

"What?" Mary and Charlotte asked together.

I looked to Zoroaster. For once he wasn't smiling. He face was set in
stone. His brown eyes were filled with both remorse and respect. He
tipped his head to me.

"It's okay," he said. "It will work. I will keep her safe."

"What are you talking about?" Mary asked again, stepping forward.

"What's going on?" Lotte added, frantically.

I turned to Charlotte, taking both of her hands in mine. My mind was
made up. I finally understood. Her questioning look almost made me
pause, but I knew what I had to do.

"We're going to leave the barrier to Hell standing for now and give the
souls here their dream of entering Heaven. The people in Purgatory do not

235

belong in Hell," I explained. "They do not deserve the burden of the fires. They deserve the peace of Heaven. Children, teenagers, people like Dante: none of them should have to feel The Guilt that we feel down there. The pure at heart should be embraced in eternity. As much as I don't believe in the goodness of Asmodeus, I know that Heaven is a better place for these souls. It is a better place for them. It is a better place for you."

"No," Charlotte said, shaking her head, tears welling in her eyes, her chin trembling. "I can't leave you again. I won't. What about Asmodeus? It's not safe for me there."

"It is safer than you think." Zoroaster stepped forward. "God cannot be seen to harm anyone who is not openly against him. His kingdom is built on pillars of faith and love. Should he do anything violent to you, it would shake those pillars. His kingdom could come crashing down. He would not risk attacking you without just cause in his safest of havens."

Lotte broke down. She dropped to her knees at my feet. "No! Please Michael, no," she cried. "I want to come with you. Why can't I come?"

I looked down at her. My heart was splitting in two. Every element inside me wanted to take her in my arms and tell her that I'd never leave her ever, that we could stay together forever and no harm would come to her ever again. But this wasn't just about us; this was the right thing to do. It felt horrible, as if I was strangling my own soul.

I sat down next to Lotte, putting my arms around her. I held her close and put my lips next to her ear.

"I'm sorry Lotte," I whispered. "This is the hardest thing I have ever had to do, but it's what I must do. Your soul is pure. Once the walls come down, you'll be taken to Heaven because you have committed no sins to forgive. You don't belong in Purgatory and don't deserve to be damned. You don't know Hell. You don't ever want to go there."

"Hell is being without you," she said, staring ahead, avoiding my eyes. Her words were like a dagger in my heart, but I continued.

"I promise we will be together again," I whispered, pulling her close. "I will come to get you when the time is right. The realm of Hell will no longer exist one day soon and the obstacles separating our love will be gone. We can live in peace one day, but for now I need you to be strong for me. I need you to be the pure soul that I love."

Lotte shook in silent sobs in my arms.

"This has to be done, Charlotte. It would be selfish of us to drag the rest of Purgatory into the fires because of our love for each other. Do you understand that? Do you understand why it has to be this way?"

Lotte's crying subsided. She nodded her head slowly. I squeezed her hard again and kissed her on the head. She looked up to me, her blue eyes almost melting my resolve to continue.

"Zoroaster," I said, tearing my gaze away from my love to look up at him. "How quickly can we get out to the gates? How quickly can we be ready to do this?"

"We can leave now," he responded. "I suggest we do not delay. The moment is with us. You will have my help. We can prepare as we move."

"No!" Charlotte whimpered next to me. "Why so soon? Can't you stay a little longer?"

"I wish we could," I said, holding her tight against me again. "We cannot risk Asmodeus finding out our plan. We've been here almost too long already."

"Can I come with you? I want to help," she asked pleadingly. "It's best you do not," Zoroaster interrupted. "We are bringing down the sky. You will be safer in the city, Charlotte. Wait for me here and I will come back for you. We can then lead the souls of Purgatory up into Paradise together. We can look Asmodeus in the eye and show him the truth in our souls."

Charlotte dropped her head in silence. I reached out tenderly and tipped her chin back up so she faced me.

"I need to go now my love," I said. "Before I do, can you promise me something?"

"Anything," she said, holding my gaze.

"Promise you'll stay true to our cause no matter how hard it might be."

"I promise," she said softly. "I love you."

She leaned in and kissed me. Our lips touched softly. I closed my eyes and felt a tear slide down my face. I forced myself to pull away.

"You're the reason why the universe will one day be free," I told her. "You're the reason I can do what I must."

She smiled at me sadly. All of our tears had been shed. It was time to go. I stood up, helping Charlotte to her feet. I hugged her one final time and then gripped her hands.

"I will see you again," I said. "We will succeed."

Reluctantly, I let our fingers slip apart. I turned for the exit and Lotte dropped again to her knees. Willing myself not to go back to her, I pushed past Mary and opened the door trying not to look back. Every step was a struggle against my soul.

Zoroaster came beside me and rested his hands on my shoulder as I lingered in the doorway.

"This is the right thing," he said.

"Then why does it feel so wrong?" I whispered.

I turned to around to Charlotte one last time. She was on the floor, with her head in her hands. Mary looked at me and then turned back. She walked to Lotte and carefully knelt at her side. She touched Lotte's back lightly.

"I promise you Charlotte, with every ounce of truth in my heart," she said to her with fire in her eyes, "Michael will remain yours as long as my soul lives. Despite what you think you know about me, I can see the true love between you and I respect it. I will do nothing to get in the way of that. I hope you understand. You have my word."

Lotte looked up from her to me and then back to Mary. "Thank you," she whispered to her.

Mary draped her arms around Charlotte and kissed her on the cheek. She whispered a goodbye in her ear. Zoroaster helped push me out the door. The pain of the moment threatened to consume me.

"We head back for The Reaches," he said as he guided me down the front steps. "The gates of Heaven are directly above the center of where you came in from Hell."

I heard Mary shut the door as she came out of Zoroaster's house.

"Charlotte said she will wait for you here," she said to Zoroaster as she joined us. "She understands," Mary added.

I wasn't sure if the last sentence was for me or Zoroaster. My heart was a bleeding piece of lead.

"Then let us go," said Zoroaster. "It is time to bring Heaven to the middle realm."

54

WE STOOD ON THE STEPS of Zoroaster's house. He looked up to the sky and began to move his hands in front of him, like a conductor of an orchestra. Through my misery I could feel a rush of elements moving about us. As Zoroaster conducted his silent symphony, a cloud of blue began to gather at our feet. It became firmer beneath us as the blue darkened to a navy hue. We rose off the ground. I looked down with an elemental view to see how the cloud was made. It was an exceptional weave of molecules that I'd never seen before: here was air, liquid and earth, all spun into a moving blanket of atoms. It was a self-sustaining creation, almost living. I understood the genius of it immediately. By creating something that had its own perpetual source of power, there was no need to concentrate on holding it together. Zoroaster could now save his energy and focus on something else. I'd have to learn that trick. We started to rise further into the air. The street dropped beneath us as we floated upward, above the buildings of Purgatory.

I looked back up to Zoroaster in grim wonder. Charlotte was still heavy on my mind. I had done nothing but seek her since I died. Now I was letting her go. It was unthinkable. Despite my personal desolation, I had to maintain my wits. We were heading to fulfil a destiny which was bigger than any individual. I did my best to push Lotte to the back of my mind.

"Please sit," Zoroaster instructed calmly.

Mary and I crouched down onto our magic carpet. Zoroaster sat at the edge of the cloud and faced toward The Far Reaches.

"Forward," he commanded, throwing his hand in front of him. A gust of wind propelled us ahead. As we sped to our destination, Zoroaster turned back to us. The misty clouds zipped past our heads as he spoke.

"This will take all of our wills combined," he said. "We'll be at the gates within the hour. Once we get there, Michael and I will need to build a blockade around the edges of the energy filter. The city must be protected from the fallout of destruction. If I'm right, the eternity of Heaven will rush in to meet us once the walls break. The vacuum will send you both crashing into Hell and rain new complexity onto the surface of the meadow below. This means we must build a wall right around the perimeter of The Reaches. Once we've built a sufficient dam, then I will hold it as best I can. If I can contain the surge of power from Heaven for a few moments, it will give you time to prepare yourselves for the fall. Mary, you'll have to push the key into place when we're ready. Michael, once the flow of the filter starts to back up, it will slowly harden. Cracks should start to appear. It will be your job to drive whatever you can into those cracks and split them further. Once we get it to a certain point, there will be no turning back. Are you ready for this? Really ready?"

I nodded my head in determination. Mary voiced her assent as well.

"Good," Zoroaster said. "There will be no room for error. Now, first we need to prepare the keys. Michael, do you have them?"

I reached into my pocket silently and found the cool metal with my fingers. Drawing them out, I handed them to him carefully. He took the keys from me and pressed his palms together flat over them, as though he was praying. He held his arms out straight so his fingertips were almost touching my chest.

"Place your hands vertically over mine," he said, "so we are forming a cross."

I reached out and pressed my palms on either side of his hands, my fingers pointing to the sky, his at my chest.

"Now," he said, "when you feel the heat of love in my hands, I want you to focus hate inside them."

"Hate?" I asked.

"Please. Do as I ask. A balanced bond of love and hate should meld these keys together enough to hold the pressure of the barrier's flow. It will be close to impossible to replicate the true God elements that make up the keys, but we can at least make something that will withstand the torrent of atoms it needs to. We have to make sure we lock the keys together as firmly as possible. If we work together we can do it."

I opened my mouth to question him, but Zoroaster closed his eyes.

"Hate," he said. "Every grudge you hold against Asmodeus rolled into one. It must be pure."

I felt him push his palms harder into each other beneath mine. He began to hum. Golden light and warmth started to grow into my hands. I closed my eyes and pictured Asmodeus. I could see his malevolent sneer in my mind. I despised him with everything I had. My blood curdled to acid in my veins. Cold enveloped my heart. I drew the darkness inside and pushed it out of me. My arms began to shake as I channelled the rage into Zoroaster's hands. The deathly cold of hate flowed out of me. My teeth were grinding with effort. The iciness of my hands shadowed the warmth of Zoroaster's. His humming grew louder, but the pulse of the angry heart in my ears drowned it out. I was grunting with effort. My throat was on fire and my arms were a blizzard of loathing. A knot of hate elements sliced out of me and into Zoroaster. Revenge plagued my being. Just as I felt as if the disgust inside would overwhelm me, Zoroaster pulled his hands from my grip. I snapped my eyes back open, my chest heaving. I looked at Zoroaster who was surrounded by a pink aura of love. I started to rumble a primordial growl.

Mary reached out to steady me. "That's enough, Michael!"

I stared at her angrily. She pulled back, putting her hand over her mouth.

"Your eyes!"

"What?" I asked, through gritted teeth.

"They're black," she said, before looking down at my lap. "Oh God, Michael, your hands."

I looked down. My fingernails had turned into points and were as dark as night. Red veins thumped over the back of my hands. Every muscle in my body was constricted into a knot of stress.

"Michael," I heard Zoroaster's voice say. "Come back to us." I felt his warm hand at my shoulder. The touch spread into me, making me slowly relax. I could feel the well of hatred subsiding back into my heart, being pushed back by Zoroaster. My breathing became normal. I flexed my fingers and the veins on my hands sunk back into my skin. The nails stayed as they were.

"Thank you," Zoroaster said, patting me on the back. "I know that took a toll, but we did a fine job. This will hold, I am sure."

He held up the keys before my face. They were shining their unusual godly glow. In between the keys sat slightly darker, but still dazzlingly brilliant elements. Their balanced weave held the two keys tightly in what looked like a sideways figure of eight. The beauty of them helped shake the last thoughts of hatred from my mind. I felt the platform of cloud beneath us begin to slow. Zoroaster and Mary must have felt it too, because we all looked as one down to the meadow below. Far beneath us I could make out the small circle of bubble-shaped rock which marked the center of The Far Reaches.

Zoroaster stood up beside me. He handed the keys down to Mary, who took them reverently in her hands. The prophet then raised his hands up to the sky, flicking his fingers in a circular pattern. Wider and wider the circles of his hands became. Elements danced at his will.

The wispy mist above us parted as Zoroaster pushed his finger to point directly upward. As the greyness split like an ethereal sea, the spinning vortex of the Heavenly filter came into view.

55

THE COLORS OF THE BARRIER TO HEAVEN took my breath away. Unlike the vortex in Hell, which was only black and white, this one had a sparkling metallic sheen to it. Silver and gold twisted in one direction while blue and red spun in the opposite. The four colors wound in and out of each other like a psychedelic braid of light. I could barely make out the spot in the center where it all collided into a single point. Coming from the distance of the city, the unmistakable form of a white soul drifted upward to the filter. It was shining against the grey backdrop below. As the soul drew closer, the gold current bulged downward and sucked it into the flow of power.

Soon, every person in the city of Purgatory will be able to follow that soul into Heaven as they wish, I thought

"Michael, we need to begin," Zoroaster said from next to me. "I will build the blockade to shield the city. It will run all the way around The Reaches. As I work, I need you to add the same elements to fortify its construction. Once the wall is complete we'll move closer to the gateway." He looked over to Mary who was still crouched down, holding the keys tightly in her hands. "You had better hold on," he said to her.

Zoroaster was perched on one end of the cloud, with me on the other. Mary lay flat on her stomach in the middle. We were ready.

Again Zoroaster started his frenzied hand movements. With a clasped fist he motioned down to the ground and then pulled it back up, his arms visibly straining. I looked down to see earth elements being drawn upwards into the wall. I did as Zoroaster had asked and followed his lead, pulling deep brown earth upwards with my will. With a low rumble, a mountainous divide grew from around the outskirts of The Reaches. It started as a peak in the middle and then began to spread across and out to the edges of each horizon. The growing mountain range towered higher and higher, blocking the city completely from view. My legs started to shake with the effort. I looked to Zoroaster. He appeared to be in a Zen state, carefully plucking invisible strings that charmed the elements in the air. I did my best to keep up with him, sending water, fire, love, rationality, air and knowledge down to mimic Zoroaster's creation. As the mountains rose in a circle around us, we rose higher and higher toward the eye of the vortex.

With a crackling hiss, like hot metal being dipped in water, the fortification reached the ceiling of Purgatory. We were encased within the area of the great filter, solid walls on all sides. The grey meadow of The Reaches shimmered with a dusty molecular residue that had been stirred up from our work. Our cloud had been raised so high that our heads were inches from the flowing swirls of power. A burning wind from the current buffeted our bodies. Right above us, the crystalline fist of rock in the center of the gateway sparked with energy. The roar of the vortex' flow echoed off of Zoroaster's blockade around us. I looked down.

"Mary!" Zoroaster shouted above the powerful din of the filter. "When I say, you must force the keys inside the eye of the gateway. I will do all I can to keep our barricade intact as the blockage pushes back. Michael," he said turning to me, "do everything you can to aid in crumbling the integrity of the filter as it hardens. You will have to use the most powerful of your emotions. Draw deep, this will be our only chance."

I nodded. Mary readied herself in a crouch, the keys locked in her fingers. Zoroaster raised the cloud beneath us a touch higher. "Now!" he bellowed.

Mary sprung upwards and thrust the key into the heart of the gateway. Purple forks of light encased her arm. Mary screamed in pain as the forks splintered down her whole body. She threw her head back and wailed in agony. I moved in to help, but with a bang she was thrown thumping back into our platform. The cloud wavered beneath us and I almost toppled over the edge. Scrambling to steady myself, I rushed on my hands and knees to Mary. She was out cold. Her limp body still sparked with electricity. I looked to her hand and the shape of the key had been burned into her palm. Black, blistered skin sizzled a figure eight of infinity.

"Leave her!" Zoroaster yelled. He was still standing, holding out his arms, throwing still more elements outward to the protective wall surrounding us. "Look!" he said, lifting his chin to the sky.

I gazed up. All about, the metallic light of the vortex was starting to slow. The middle no longer glowed purple, but throbbed a dull, pulsing, red light. I could see the end of the keys jutting out of it, like two holding spikes frozen into rock. The roar of the power flow started to subside.

Silence dropped around us. There wasn't a breath of wind, not a ripple of noise. I looked about in anticipation. The gateway was at a standstill. I crouched low, keeping my center of gravity steady. Zoroaster kept pouring layer upon layer of elements onto the wall of earth around us. A constant stream of energy came from his hands as he made the mountains thicker and stronger, so they shone like steel.

I returned my gaze up to the gateway, waiting for something to happen. The eye above us began to glow redder. Brighter it grew, until deathly heat began to seep from it. A deep groan started from all around. The sound intensified. It was like being in a steel mill. The noise of twisting metal joined with a hellish heat. If I hadn't endured the fires of torment for so long, I would have been consumed by it. I kept watch above as the groan deepened to a thunderous wail. Suddenly, a great splitting noise rent the air, like cracking ice. Spreading out from the center, hairline fractures splintered across what was once the spinning filter of Heaven.

"Quickly!" Zoroaster spurred me on.

I closed my eyes. I needed to do this right. Digging my feet into the platform below, I drew on my emotion. The misery at having to leave Charlotte rose to the surface. The hatred I felt for Asmodeus boiled. The fear I held at maybe never seeing my wife again, the regret of having to sacrifice our love, every dark vessel of doubt surged within me. I let it build and build. I let it fester. My body started to swell with evil thoughts. My skin started to blister from the inside out with the intensity of feeling trapped within.

Just when I thought I might burst, I unleashed it all upward with a shuddering scream. Opening my eyes, I funnelled the blast directly into the heart of the gateway. I spread it into the cracks and expanded it. I felt the dominance of my wickedness shoot out of me toward the pillars of Heaven. It tumbled forth. The depth of suffering inside me magnified stronger and stronger. My vocal chords turned into clarions of destruction. Black streamed out of me, roaring into the fissures of the great filter. The cracks began to widen as my will pushed them apart. Small splits became inverted canyons that stretched upward into a yawning darkness. I drew on every piece of energy I had inside and wailed it upward.

From the corner of my vision I saw the first chunk of the gateway fall. It struck on the side of Zoroaster's earth barrier with a crunch and then rumbled to the ground far below. Another brick tore lose, then others. From the outside inward, the walls of Heaven started to disintegrate. As each piece fell, it cracked down onto the elemental mountains around us, tearing our construction apart. I heard Zoroaster groan with effort beside me. I drew on his resolve and renewed the liquid death that flowed out of me.

A sliver of white light sparkled from above. It shone through the steaming rock of the gateway onto my face. It was glorious. I peered up and could see the beating of an angel's wings through the cracks. The sliver of light grew wider, then wider still. I could see them: the beautiful souls of Heaven, looking down at me in wonder. I grimaced up at them, remembering that this was all I was going to miss when I was tossed back to Hell. My Charlotte would be lost to me again. I roared up at them and the angels shrank back in terror. A chunk of rock swept down and almost knocked me off my perch. I swayed to the side, grasping for purchase. Another boulder slammed down beside me. I was flipped over onto my back and the energy soaring out of me was cut off. All above, beams of light were pouring through the walls of Heaven. We had done it! We had started the reaction that couldn't be stopped. I lay there, exhausted, with a numbed feeling of acceptance.

I heard Zoroaster cry out next to me, as a slice of rock hit him. He fell sideways. Reaching out, he grabbed the foot of Mary's still prone body. Our platform teetered wildly, almost tipping vertically. I held fast to the top edge above me with the last of my energy and tried to reach out to Zoroaster. It was too late. I watched in horror as Mary and Zoroaster slid off the cloud. They dropped down into the sky that was raining apocalypse. There was nothing I could do.

I swung my weight around, holding the edge of the cloud platform with both hands. Another brick struck my shoulder, almost throwing me off again. I strained through my exhaustion to stay balanced. I wanted to see this finished.

"Michael!" I heard a ringing voice from above.

I clung onto the edge with my fingers and smiled with grim satisfaction at the noise. Father. I forced myself to look upward. The shadowy form of Asmodeus blazed down at me in hatred. He stood directly over me, his feet either side of the wavering eye of the gates.

"What have you done, Michael?" my father boomed.

"I have done as you asked," I laughed insanely back to him. "I have brought you new souls. I have given Heaven all the soldiers you are going to need, because next it will be Hell that rises up to your feet."

"No!" he shouted in pure anger and frustration. "No!"

"Yes!" I spat. "And there is nothing you can do to stop us."

With that I let go of the platform and shot a final terrifying shudder of elements into the eye of the gateway. As I free-fell downward, the destroyed filter shattered completely. It blasted into oblivion with a blinding flash of white light.

The last thing I saw was my father's head thrown back in rage, as I tore back down to the flames of Hell.

EPILOGUE

I STARED AT THE BLACKNESS, flat on my back. I knew where I was. It was where I belonged: Hell. I moved my fingers over my palms. They were claws that scratched my skin. It didn't matter. I was who I'd become by choice.

Clytemnestra would come for me soon. She would have to know I was here, in this same room where I had begun my journey so long ago. It was my room, my cell of darkness.

I waited patiently, thinking of what my next move should be. I would gather my army of demon friends, my lost souls. We were now one step closer to equality in the universe. To freedom. The scales might be tipped towards Asmodeus for now, but we could not fail. Our power of strength would become unstoppable. The truth was our weapon, destiny our goal.

I did not feel any pride in what I had done in Purgatory. No lasting satisfaction. To sacrifice the only thing I'd ever cherished for the greater good was too bitter a pill to swallow. I sat up slowly, thinking of Lotte. Lost again. Waiting. Zoroaster would keep her safe. She would keep herself safe.

"I'm coming for you my love," I whispered into the air.

There was a knock at the door. I got to my feet and stood in the darkness, waiting for a few moments.

"Come," I finally said with authority.

Red light seeped into the room as the door opened. The silhouette of a woman stood in the entry, silent. I drew myself to full height and gathered white elements of light to illuminate the room.

"Get the war room ready," I said, as my sight adjusted to the light. "We have a battle to plan."

Mary stepped through the doorway, looking at me with her brilliant emerald eyes. I was surprised to see her and not Clytemnestra. She was in a long black dress which contrasted sharply with her pale skin.

"Mary!" I said with relief, letting my guard down. I moved in to hug her lightly. "I'm glad you're safe. I lost you in the storm in Purgatory. We did it. The barrier is gone. Their souls are now free."

"I knew you would finish it," she smiled, nodding.

I stepped back to look her up and down properly.

"Are you okay? Were you hurt in your fall back to Hell?"

"I'm fine," she said, holding up her hands. The scar from the keys was still etched firmly into her palm. I took her wrist and looked at the mark. It was dark pink.

"Oh that," she said as I studied it. "I imagine I'll have that scar forever. It hasn't healed fully since I returned to Hell. It doesn't hurt. I see it a badge of honor. A reminder of our quest."

I let her hand drop back down. Our quest. What was our next move?

"We need to assemble the others," I said. "We need to start planning for a new assault on Asmodeus."

"They're already waiting at Casa Diablo," she replied. "Your soul has been long in finding its way back here. It's been days since I returned."

"Then there's no time to waste." I moved to push past her. "Asmodeus won't be so idle."

Mary put out a hand to stop me. I stepped back again. She looked up at me, smiling brilliantly. The look in her eyes made me nervous.

"There is someone I want you to meet first," Mary said, looking behind her. "There is a new soldier here that I wanted to introduce before we leave. I want your approval."

I paused, wary of another deception like that of the Bishop. I needed people I could trust, not untested recruits. This was going to be a war against deception.

"Who is he?" I asked suspiciously.

Mary smiled wryly. "Actually, you know her," she said, stepping aside.

A vision of perfection came into the room.

"It's me," said the woman in a voice of pure innocence.

It couldn't be. I didn't know what to say. My mouth hung open. I stepped forward and pulled my hand up to touch the face of this angel. I needed to see if she was real or if I'd lost my mind in Purgatory. Her warm cheek felt soft to touch.

"Lotte?" I choked. "How?"

I carefully ran my spiked fingers over her arms, wanting to see that she was real, but trying not to hurt her with my claws. My heart thumped in my ears, my eyes roving all over her. Was it really her, my wife? She was supposed to be in Heaven.

"It's okay, Michael," she said softly, holding my hands steady in hers. She squeezed her fingers around my palms. "I'm here. With you."

"But, how?" I repeated, confused. Her perfect soul should have been taken to Paradise with the rest of Purgatory. I didn't know what to say.

"Mary whispered some advice before you left," she said softly, looking over to the woman at our side. "She told me that if I really wanted to be with you, then all I had to do was hold the same hate for Asmodeus in my heart as you have."

I stared questioningly into her eyes.

"It wasn't even a choice," Lotte continued quickly. "He has done despicable things to both of us, Michael. He needs to be finished. I am here for you, my love. We can do this together." She gripped my hands tightly.

I looked back to Mary. She nodded at me, smiling. "It's her, Michael. This is no trick."

I switched my view to behold the elements. I searched the room for deception. It was all as it should be. There were no veils or mirrors, just the natural weave of molecules that make up the universe. My vision snapped back to a worried looking Charlotte. I reached out with my senses and felt overwhelming love coming from her.

"Are you okay, Michael?" she asked. "Have I done something wrong? I just wanted to be with you."

I hugged her without further hesitation, pressing my body into hers.

"Lotte!" I cried. "No, you haven't done anything wrong. I love you. I just wasn't sure. Thank you. I, I –we're together!" I hugged back into her.

"We're together," she whispered back in my ear. She kissed my cheek and then found my lips. She kissed me hard before stepping away. Her eyes locked with mine, a vicious light shining in them that I hadn't seen from her before.

"We can now bring the tyrant Asmodeus to the end he deserves," she said fiercely. "We will kill our maker and free all the universe. Are you ready, Michael? I am here to help build your army."

She flashed a dark smile at me. The white light of the room glinted off her new, wolf-like teeth. It was the most beautiful thing I'd ever seen.

THE HELLBOUND TRILOGY CONTINUES WITH…

BOOK 3

DEICIDE

1

SITTING AT CASA DIABLO, my closest allies surrounded me. Could I trust them all?

Charlotte was at my immediate right, an angel fallen from Heaven back into my arms. To my left sat my most faithful adviser and friend, Smithy, the elderly pilot who was as wise as he was kind. Mary Magdalene, Clytemnestra, Marax and the Pure Seven made up the rest of the council. Twelve in total: twelve dark apostles, seated around a food-laden table for our meeting. An ostentatious throne sat empty at the head, its red cushions cold and dusty. I refused to sit there despite some protests from the others. Rather, I sat in the middle, so I could be amidst the discussion instead of directing it. All present had proven true to our cause so far, but their number unsettled me. Memories of the Last Supper spun in my mind. Jesus' words came back to me in a whisper: 'One of you will betray me'. Was I to have the same fate?

I shook my head. No; I was in charge of my own destiny. I was a creator and a destroyer alike. Asmodeus had made me in his image: his true son. I was powerful, able to control the elements that made up existence. Unlike my hated father, I was intent on creating truth and freedom in the universe. All he stood for were lies and oppression. We had to stop him.

Our first mission was successfully complete: the barrier separating Heaven and Purgatory had been demolished. With the help of the prophet Zoroaster, we destroyed one of the two filters, which separated the realms of the afterlife. Our initial goal had been to take down the wall between Purgatory and Hell, but I could not stand to bring more souls into this fiery pit of sin. We had freed the innocent souls of Purgatory and allowed them to enter Paradise against God's wishes: against Asmodeus' wishes.

He is not a God. I thought to myself. He is an abomination.

Only one more obstacle remained: we had to bring down the gates of

Heaven once and for all, so the lost souls of Hell could rise up to claim their own right of equality.

"Our only way to Heaven is to go through Earth," Clytemnestra growled in her demonic tone. Even now, the unearthly pitch of her voice seemed askew with her femininity. Were it not for her sharp teeth and black gums, she could have passed for human. She held a piece of uncooked meat in her hands, but did not eat. Shadows roamed up and down the walls behind her, where a row of fire torches cast their light about the room.

"We cannot ascend to Earth without bodies to be born into," she continued. "I have asked all the shamans and necromancers I can think of. They all say the same thing: there are Hellmouths where the entry to above is possible, but without an earthly vessel to contain our ethereal souls, we would just be sucked back down into the abyss."

"What about possession?" Marax said in his subhuman growl. "It has worked for others before."

"Only in rare cases," Clytemnestra replied matter-of-factly, "and it's too problematic. There are families, priests. We cannot hope to possess entire cities. Only weak souls who are open to total control accept possession for any length of time. We do not have that. Most would resist and we would be confined to wrestling with their spirits."

"Michael can make us bodies," Charlotte said confidently, leaning forward in her seat next to me.

I gently wrapped my clawed hands over her fingers. My body was part demon, part human: a sign of defiance against our creator. My fingers were sharp talons. My ears curved into sharp points, tinted red on the ends. My teeth were that of a wolf's. Charlotte's smile was the same as mine: fanged and deadly. It did not diminish her pure beauty. The change had happened when she decided to hold hate against Asmodeus in her heart, so she could come to Hell to be with me. I loved her all the more for her commitment.

"There are too many problems with this plan." Smithy got to his feet beside me. He let his old eyes linger on each of those present. "We can't take millions of hellish souls to Earth and hope to somehow sweep up to Heaven. There are too many innocents there that could be harmed."

"Most humans on Earth are far from innocent!" Marax snapped from his seat. The hulking wrath demon had once been the head juror in the tenth circle of Hell. His vicious pursuit of blind justice often clouded his thinking.

"But some are," Smithy pressed, raising his voice over Marax, "it's not right. We're not prepared. We would be marching into battle blind. And what do we do once we are in Heaven? Just charge the gates? It's madness!"

"Do you have a better plan?" Clytemnestra cut Smithy off. "Since Lord Michael returned, the barrier of Hell has been fortified even further from above. There is no way we can take a direct route to Heaven. We must use Earth."

"There is always another way," Smithy bristled.

"Then what is it?" Marax joined Clytemnestra's argument. "You do nothing but find fault in other people's ideas."

"Enough!" I said finally, slapping the table with irritation. After returning to Hell, I had enjoyed a blissful few days reuniting with Charlotte. Now the sharp reality of our situation hung in the air. We were all trapped here, hoping to somehow overthrow a powerful enemy, without any idea of how, or when, it would happen. On top of that, all of the demonic souls in damnation were restless. They had heard that the wall to Purgatory had been dismantled, but the ringing reply was not one of joy. The question being shouted loud and clear in the streets was: what about us? Something had to be done quickly, or the tension in Hell might boil over to something even more sinister. It was no environment in which to be mounting an attack.

Another problem remained too. In the past, Asmodeus had infiltrated Hell in disguise. He had made himself into a Bishop and gained our trust. How he had done it was still a mystery. The fact that he could do it again weighed heavily on my mind.

"Smithy is right," I said firmly. "A blind charge is not the answer. I cannot create millions of bodies for a mass resurrection to Earth anyway. Unless a soul is implanted into a womb it is impossible to fuse a soul with a new, fully grown body."

"But you were reborn to Earth when you went back for Gideon," Charlotte said softly next to me.

I looked at her, surprised. It was easy to forget that I had shown her my memories. My wife now knew me more intimately than I ever thought possible. She knew my thoughts, my desires. She even knew my greatest fears, ones I would never voice aloud. Her blue eyes shone with knowledge; they gleamed with certainty. She had been lost in Limbo for so long that I couldn't believe she was finally at my side again. Sometimes in bed I awoke with a start, grasping to make sure she was still there. I would never leave her again.

Mary shuffled uncomfortably, clearing her throat. I had lost myself in Charlotte's gaze. Reddening with embarrassment, I looked down. Mary had confessed her love to me while we were in Purgatory with Zoroaster. She was a close friend and it wasn't fair to throw my connection with

Charlotte in her face. Mary was over two thousand years old but, where most humans' emotions grew weary with age, hers had only become stronger with time. Her deep red hair and emerald eyes made her look like a goddess of passion. In a sense she was.

"It won't work again," I answered slowly. "I was reborn into my own body, not one manufactured after the fact. Asmodeus is the only one who has been able to replant his soul into a new vessel and he is fractured. His mind is not stable."

"But it's possible," Clytemnestra pushed. She placed the piece of meat she was holding into her mouth and started chewing.

"With time," I confirmed, "with help."

Clytemnestra raised a dark eyebrow, but before she could ask the question, Smithy interjected.

"We have another issue we haven't discussed yet." The pilot was still standing. He moved across the table and leant over to take a pot of tea in his hands. As he poured the steaming liquid into a cup, he looked to Mary.

"Mary, there is the question of how we get to Heaven from Earth once we manage a resurrection. We can't just take my helicopter, that's for certain."

Mary laughed at his joke, her hearty amusement easing the tension in the room.

"I know what you're thinking, Smithy," she said. "And the answer is I'm not completely sure, but I do have some theories. I believe there may be a way. I'd like to do some more research first."

"If you believe with conviction, it will become truth," seven voices chorused from across the table.

I looked over to the Pure Seven. They had been sitting perfectly still until now, eerie to behold. They were like seven gothic statues, each a single color of the rainbow. Each color represented the sin that they had chosen to become completely. Lust was blue, Wrath red, Pride violet, Avarice yellow, Envy green and Sloth indigo. Even though they were individuals, they always spoke as one. They were all perfectly formed angels, with claws similar to mine. None of the angels ate, except for the orange, Gluttony. Now that it was animated, it took food from the platter in front of it and constantly shoved it into its mouth. It swallowed without chewing, gorging itself upon everything at hand without spilling a morsel. Once, the Pure Seven had been followers of Zoroaster, pledged to discover real truth in the universe. Now that Zoroaster was in the other realm, they deferred to Mary. It was curious that Asmodeus had not already driven Zoroaster out of Heaven, but the old prophet had said that unless he directly opposed him, Asmodeus could not cast him out without losing the support of the good souls there. I only hoped that he was still with our cause, gathering an under swell of support for us. I couldn't rely on that however.

"I think the world has had enough blind faith," I said to the Pure Seven. "We need objective proof. I want to seek the truth as much as you, but we need to know, not just believe," I turned back to their new master. "Mary, what do you need?"

"To go back to my map room and consult a bible."

"That book contains nothing but lies!" Marax rumbled from his seat.

"You would be surprised at the amount of truth in there if you care to look," Mary said curtly.

"Do what you need to do, Mary," I said to her. "Does anyone else have anything to add?"

Clytemnestra nodded gravely.

"You're already aware there is unrest brewing in the streets, Lord Michael. We must do something to stop it; otherwise there will be a riot. It doesn't take much for demons to resort to murder and looting."

I bowed my head. Did they not understand that we were doing all we could? The masses weren't stupid, but they could be ungrateful. It was also a reminder that perhaps some of the souls in Hell did deserve to be trapped here, but I had to believe they could change. I wrestled back my anger. If I was to lead these people I had to make them trust me. If I kept them in the dark we would never see the light together.

"Very well. You and Marax take the Pure Seven and spread word that I will give an address on the Great Lawn at week's end. First, I need to try to make a friend see reason and come to our side."

"Who?" Charlotte asked, sitting up straighter.

I drew in a long breath and stood.

"The Perceptionist."

For more, head to:

TimHawken.Com/Hellbound-Trilogy

Lightning Source UK Ltd.
Milton Keynes UK
UKHW040707220221
379180UK00001B/12

9 780648 255833